THE ARK WAR

DEATHLESS BOOK 5

CHRIS FOX

CHRIS FOX WRITES LLC

PREVIOUSLY ON DEATHLESS

You guys know the drill by now. It's been three years since I released a deathless book, and you're probably a bit fuzzy on the details of the fuzzy werewolves and cuddly zombies. I'd recommend reading the Previously Ons from each of the prior books if you're a few years out, or just this one if you're less hazy on things.

Before we dive in though, I wanted to apologize to you, the reader. *The Great Pack* came out in 2017, two years after *Vampires Don't Sparkle*. It's been more years for book 5. Lots of people have worried the series might not get finished, because in the writing world I'm known for writing fast.

So why haven't I cranked out *Deathless*?

Because *Deathless* is my art. *Deathless* takes planning and research. So much research. I spent hundreds (literally) of hours researching the Carboniferous Period and the intervening 30 million years of Earth's history.

I wanted to understand how multiple species could evolve, become spacefaring, and die off while leaving almost no trace of themselves. During the past three years many new discoveries have come to light. Most of those center in the Americas where we have been taught that Clovis Man was the first visitor to those shores. Now we think we were off by over a hundred thousand years. I wanted to work that material in.

There was one more wrinkle that tacked on another six months to the writing. Minor spoilers, but Jordan ends up in Australia. In the original plot Australia had been consumed in a fire storm. Given that Australia actually had to deal with real fires I thought that pretty tasteless, and scrapped over a third of the book as a result.

You know what? It was worth it. *The Ark War* is exactly the story I wanted to tell, and I hope you enjoy reading it as much as I did writing it. I finally revealed that it's set in the same universe as my *Magitech Chronicles*, and you'll see some Easter eggs if you've already both. If you're curious I've put a few chapters from the *The Magitech Chronicles* at the end for you to check out.

Okay, let's get into it!

In an announcer voice "Last time, on *Deathless*..."

The Great Pack picked up five years after the First Ark detonated at the end of *Vampires Don't Sparkle*. This was the first time I got artsy in a prologue, and wow, do I regret it. I introduced the Liwanu, also called Yosemite or the Great Bear.

He's a wonderful character, and was central to the plot, but when you've been waiting two years to hear what happened to your favorite character, the last thing you want is to hear about someone new. Oops.

The Great Bear awakens from hibernation in what is now a national park, and starts eating tourists, *Jurassic Park* style. I thought it very clever, because I've been to Yosemite ~15 times and I got to work in a bunch of Miwok lore. Eight people agreed. The rest said... where are Blair and Liz, Trevor and Jordan?

The next chapter was from Yukon's perspective and set in the present. I showed that the Great Pack had grown. Good stuff, but after reading so many Robert Jordan novels I should have known better. That could have been chapter eight.

I finally remembered the plot in chapter two where our heroes learned that because they were light walking during the explosion, they were hurled five years into the future due to something called TSDS (Temporal Spacial Displacement Syndrome). The party quickly realized they needed intel, and decided to split up since they were in the Nexus and could reach multiple Arks.

Blair and Liz headed to the Ark of the Redwood, where they discovered that Angel Island had been deserted, and that the deathless appeared to have restored power to parts of San Francisco.

They sneak in and confront the deathless who seems to be running things, an asian woman named Melissa. Melissa explains that they drove off the werewolves, but have left them alone up in Santa Rosa. She's terrified of Blair, who is now right next to a fully powered Ark, and is actually intimidating for once. She gives them whatever they need and sends them on their way.

Liz and Blair make for Santa Rosa, where they meet with one of the border guards named John Rivers. John is a well respected Ka-Dun and leads a part of the Great Pack. He knows Yukon, who is also part of the pack.

They mention Alicia, who Liz is desperate to get back to. Alicia was a ten-year-old girl when they left. Now she is the Ka-Ken leading Santa Rosa, and is a fifteen-year-old that John Rivers clearly respects.

Meanwhile, Jordan light walks to South America where he finds that a werewolf temple had taken residence in the Ark. They worshiped the Mother's Ark and the Ka-Ken there considered him an intruder. He confronts their leader, Elia, who he wraps up in telekinetic force, and then teleports into the brig after she attacks him.

A Ka-Ken named Leti tells him that El Medico is in charge of Peru, and Jordan realized they're talking about Dr. Roberts from the first and second books. He asks Leti to gather everyone in the central chamber so he can figure out what's been going on in his absence.

The werewolves honoring the Mother know that they can't stop him, but are hostile, and he agrees to leave the Ark to give them time to adjust to his arrival, as he needs to go speak to Roberts anyway.

We flip over to Trevor and Irakesh who've gone to the Ark of the Cradle in Cairo. The Ark is down to minimal power, which it shouldn't be if it's been sitting in the sun for the last five years. They discover the Ark has been corrupted, and is patrolled by many demons similar to Set, but with wings.

Olympus hovers in the sky above, which tells them that Hades is likely responsible for all this. Unfortunately, they're trapped in the Ark, until Irakesh conveniently remembers a place his mother used to disappear. They investigate, and find a secret chamber just as the demons catch up to them. The demons are beating down the door, and Trevor figures out how to use the room at the last moment...they teleport to safety.

They land in the Chamber of the Sphinx, located directly under the paws of the Sphinx, and find a room full of ancient golden books in an impossibly old langauge. A red crystal sits on a pedestal in the center, and when they touch it they activate a virtual intelligence of an ancient man calling himself Ra. Irakesh explains that this was the original Ra, the one his mother usurped the title from.

We flash over to Hades, who's being smug and eating soup. He's contacted by the grey men, who warn him that Trevor has just used the light bridge. Hades predictably dispatches his entire army to hunt them down.

I mean...who does that? How good are palace guards going to be at searching for clues anyway? They're not going to have insight into how Trevor or Irakesh got away, and sending them away leaves him completely defenseless. Sooner or later, someone is going to take advantage of that.

Trevor and Irakesh interrogate Ra, who tells them about a bridge to the heavens. A light bridge, they realize. Trevor figures out where it is and how to use it (again at the last minute), and they teleport up into space to the Black Knight Satellite. All six people who read *Project Solaris* are already familiar with this place, and know that David controls it.

Trevor did not know this. As soon as they arrive, Yuri, Anput, and David take them down. Trevor and Irakesh end up inside a containment field, and are asked to explain themselves. Trevor tells the truth, but has no evidence. David points out he's been a bad guy before, and

Irakesh is definitely a bad guy. Trevor can't really argue, and settles in to wait.

They're chatting and he reveals that they're going to meet in the Nexus. David freaks and says they can't used the Nexus or the grey men will get you. David contacts Blair and warns him, and they have a brawl with the grey men, which they easily win. The grey men have never faced an Ark Lord, much less more than one. They get wrecked, and several boomerangs are pillaged.

We flash back to Liz, who gets a verbal smack-down from Alicia for vanishing for five years. Alicia is an angry teen, and unwilling to listen to any excuses. The two quarrel, and Alicia bails. Shocking (not shocking), the pair make up like three chapters later. Alicia forgives her, and they brace for the next problem.

The next problem is Windigo, our first introduction to the Skin-walker. I'm just going to deliver his info in a paragraph. Windigo is a two-million-year-old intelligence created by the Builders who hops from body to body to survive. The hosts become cannibals, and waste away until they resemble Windigo. He's always on the lookout for a new host, and when he sees Blair, he's all...that dude is a main char-acter. He must be crazy badass. I should possess him.

Instead of going in for it, Windigo concocts an unnecessarily complicated plan. He heads up into the mountain and possesses the Great Bear, and we get like six chapters of them walking from Lake Tahoe to Sacramento. Bear is all *NOOOOO, stop corrupting me.* Windigo does it anyway. It's very sad.

They get to Santa Rosa and Windigo kills and eats John Rivers, then starts stalking and killing prominent members of the commu-nity. Blair can't track him, but quickly realizes the Ark might have info. He goes and investigates, and bam...there's the exact perfect piece of historical lore that tells him all about Windigo, which either suggests that Builder Google is amazing, or that the author gave the character exactly what he needed exactly when he needed it.

Windigo kidnaps Alicia, and Liz pursues. Windigo tries to possess her, but Liz isn't into it, and swipes left. She wrecks possessed Yosemite in a 1-v-1 match up, and draws upon the sword mastery given to her by Wepwawet for the very first time. It's pretty epic because Windigo goes in confidently, and it ends badly. They still have to get the entity out of the Bear's mind though.

Hey, what a great time for Blair to show up.

Blair kicks Windigo's monkey-butt all over his own mindscape, and saves Yosemite, who agrees to help in the climatic final battle, as long as he gets full xp and an equal share of the loot.

We flash back to Trevor and Jordan who have decided to start their own buddy cop show. David keeps Irakesh in prison, but drops Trevor off in South America since Africa isn't really an option. They pair him with the ancient vampire goddess Anput, with the goal of locating El Dorado somewhere in the Amazon.

Why, you ask? Because I grew up with stories of Percy Fawcett and lost golden cities, and also because there's a Builder installation there called the Proto Ark. The grey men are after it. Hades sends Nox, who takes control of the deathless in South America and forces them to burn down the jungle trying to find the golden city.

Trevor, Jordan, Anput, and the temple priestess Leti double date into the jungle, and have lots of adventures. These adventures were based on lots of research, and I worked in every local myth I could find. My favorite was called a mapinguara, a yeti-like creature with an extra mouth in its stomach. Trevor ends up getting a hand bitten off, but it grows back. Handy.

I take full responsibility for how bad that joke was, but in my defense I'm tired and it's three days until the preorder deadline for this book.

Trevor, Jordan, and Anput are foiled by the priestess Elia, who tries to prevent them from reaching the lost city, but of course fails because that story would be stupid. They make it to the city, and the politics begin. Jordan tries warning the werewolves in control of the Builder city that Nox and his forces are coming, but they're all nahhh...it will be fine.

It's not fine.

Nox and his army arrive right on schedule, and we get one of my favorite all time combats. Giant Anakim versus Giant Bear, werewolf on demon, the super-powered-up Great Pack. Liz given blur.

It turns out the whole fight is a smokescreen, and Nox sneaks away to create a Primary Access Key that Hades will give to the Builders. Secretly he creates a second key that is flawed due to lack of materials. He wipes all memory of the key's creation from his mind, and heads back to Hades to deliver the key.

The heroes finish off the bad guys, who are led by Kali, one of the good guys from *Project Solaris*, who'd been corrupted by the grey men. Now she's super crazy, and the reader cheers when she goes down.

Along the way Anput invents a modified virus, which cures Trevor of being dead. His powers are much more adaptable, and he's alive, but far weaker than before. That becomes relevant in this book, which is why I mention it at the end.

Anyway, the good guys win and they control the Proto Ark, which is currently pointed at San Francisco. After three years we finally find out what happens next.

Welcome to *The Ark War*.

PROLOGUE

2.4 MILLION YEARS BPE

Akenat rose from the rejuvenator and stretched too-thin limbs worn by his overlong slumber. The atrophy was alarming, though not unexpected. His normally deep green skin had weathered to the same shade of pallid grey they'd given their drones. Sickening.

The other five crystal rejuvenators fanned out around the one he'd emerged from, but all bays were empty. By design, of course. This time, only he had been allowed to drink from the Ark's reserves. His servants and vassals had been left to fend for themselves, and the more inventive may even have survived.

They were immaterial. Only the Builders mattered.

The Ark Lords were powerful and wise, especially with him at their head. Yet today their collective dominance of this world gave him no comfort. Gone was the usual curiosity at having entered another sun-cycle. He cared little what species might have changed or emerged, something that normally gave him great pleasure.

This time anxiety drove him.

When he'd begun his slumber all their science remained unequal to the task of stopping the coming cold that slowly shrouded their world in ice.

In each of the four preceding cycles they had awakened to smaller reserves of energy within the Ark network. Never before had his own Ark chosen not to restore his body fully, which could only mean that it must have dipped below critical tolerances.

Ark Keeper Ka, Akenat projected as he padded slowly though the rejuvenator room, toward the First Ark's primary control chamber. *Initiate full status report. Prioritize power reserves and critical damage.*

The golden runes along the wall began to flow as he walked past, both providing status updates and illumination for his path. That illumination was strong, at least. If the runes began to flicker...best not to entertain such notions yet.

"Of course, Ark Lord." Ka shimmered into view, his holographic form a shorter version of Akenat's magnificent green body, every organ chosen with care. "Power reserves in the Polar Ark are currently at four percent, the lowest of all seven. Power reserves in the Nexus are at twenty-eight percent, and based on current rate of decay could have continued operation for approximately forty centuries. The First Ark is currently at nine percent power, the second lowest."

Akenat nodded impatiently as he padded into the primary control room, his feet making irritating slapping sounds against the marble. He extended a hand and all four cardinal pillars thrummed with energy, each broadcasting a signal directly at him. The direct power feed rippled through his limbs, which swelled with newly grown muscle as he restored his body.

His skin darkened into its natural emerald, and his vigor returned. Even breathing became easier.

The process took long moments, and when it was over he leaned against the closest pillar, panting and trembling. "What is the new reserve level?"

"Three percent, Ark Lord." The construct's voice was very small.

Akenat ignored the construct as he labored for breath, and once he could breathe easily, he activated the First Ark's light bridge and walked to the Nexus, as the lords had agreed.

He appeared in a familiar flash of light, directly under the great dome, which kept the weight of the earth's oceans at bay. A colossal form swam protectively above the glass, its dorsal fin larger than any that had existed in the previous cycle.

Uluru's creations thrive. Ark Lord Sa's voice echoed in his mind, even as the larger female winked into existence before him.

She wasn't the tallest Builder, but she was the one they most feared, because she'd transformed violence into a religion, and could easily slaughter any of them before they could shape.

Of course, no shaper would allow such a fight to occur.

A frivolous waste of time, Akenat thought back, adding a touch of irritation. *The beasts, while impressive, cannot adapt to the coming cold. They will die as the oceans freeze, rendering all her experimentation moot.*

Will they? Uluru's tattooed form blazed into existence, towering over Sa and Akenat alike. She exuded more amusement than annoyance, as was often the case with their eldest member. *I still possess all the genetic knowledge I have gained, and if these creatures go extinct I can repopulate them again once the oceans warm. Their helixes are safely stored, alongside every species we have ever reconstructed or retrieved. I can rebuild them* all.

That, Akenat forcefully projected, *will not be possible until this world warms again, millions of years from now, long after we are dust. Do you not understand how close we teeter to our own extinction?*

Uluru's slender shoulders slumped at that, and her thoughts grew contrite. *I do not. I have not yet checked any energy reserve status beyond my own Ark, which was well within tolerances.*

Before Akenat could further chastise her, other Ark Lords began to appear. Yoggoth was the first, the shortest Builder, but perhaps the most disquieting. Unlike the rest of them he did not favor Sunsteel, but wore trinkets forged form the darkened Demonsteel he had invented or discovered at the Polar Ark.

Akenat still found its existence troubling, but the treaty prevented him from raising his concerns.

Next came Enki, their chief scientist, and Akenat's oldest ally. The wizened Builder had not taken the time to rejuvenate, and trembled violently as he offered a bow. His tiny pet windigo, a useless species and frivolous waste of valuable energy, lay curled around his shoulder.

Akenat returned the bow, though shallowly. Enki had squandered too much time and too much precious energy sustaining that life form, but here too the treaty prevented Akenat from questioning. Each Ark Lord was master of their continent, and could do as they willed.

Anansi came next, his many-limbed form drawing a shiver from Akenat as it scuttled across the marble. His modifications were not so troubling as Yoggoth's fetid gaze, but both Builders unsettled him.

You all know, Akenat projected at them, as strongly as he could do so without being perceived as attacking, *that the earth is changing. If you have not checked the energy reserves for the Polar Ark and the First Ark, then please do so now.*

The others' eyes flickered as they checked in with their respective Ark Keepers. One by one each returned their inky eyes to him, and he could feel their attention once more.

If this new epoch follows our projections, then both Arks will fail during the next sun-cycle. Akenat walked to the center of the room, directly under the magnificent dome, and the crushing depths it kept at bay. *It is quite possible that the Nexus will fail as well, separating the surviving Arks. The remaining Arks might survive another cycle or three, but within a hundred and thirty millennia all we have wrought will be little more than our tombs. Everything we have built will be undone, and nearly every species on this planet will be eradicated in the coming cold.*

There is still the Proto Ark, Enki pointed out. *If we use these millennia to study and build, as we did in the days of old, after the discovery, then we may yet find a solution. If this world is inhospitable, perhaps another in this system could be colonized.*

You know that they cannot, Yoggoth thought, his thoughts as cold as his black armor. *I have conducted my survey of the red planet and the planets deeper in the system. All are inhospitable to any bodies we might construct. There is nothing for us in this system.*

Then what can we do? Sa projected, her thoughts somehow a

placid pool. *There must be a solution. We possess the finest shapers this world has ever known. A way forward exists,*

What of the distant star Enki discovered? Anansi asked, the strange organs where the spider-god's mouth had once been twisting the words in odd ways. *If the world in that system contains life, then can we not journey there and take it?*

Only one of the necessary satellites has been fashioned, Enki admitted, dropping his gaze to the floor. *I thought I had more time, another full cycle at the very least. I know the planet exists, and I have seen the life there, but getting us there? It would require all seven Arks at full strength, and there is still a chance of failure.*

We cannot risk our survival on a possibility. We must be certain, and there is only one way to gain that certainty. I will project through time, Akenat interrupted, tired of the constant defeatism. Tired of the prohibitions on the work he had pioneered. *I will journey into the future to verify that the earth has, indeed, exited this epoch and passed into a warmer climate. While there I will monitor this distant system for signals. If I detect them, then we know that our plan will work. I will return and relay the information.*

The others eyed him in a mixture of awe and disbelief. He was, after all, the one who had discovered and perfected temporal shaping. The rest of them were either too afraid to use it, or did so sparingly, and in secret.

Can you really travel so far along the time stream? Uluru inquired as she gave a curious cock of her bulbous head. *It breaks many of the laws of shaping. Will you not need a body to inhabit? And how will you return?*

I have modified thousands of rejuvenators, each containing a drone. They have proven resilient, and if placed in stasis at least one should survive until the desired time. I will simply step through time and inhabit that body, then use it to conduct my experiments.

None of the others voiced any objections, though all no doubt had them. Akenat took that for assent. *Very well, then I will return to my Ark, and conduct the test. If it succeeds, the seven of us will depart this world at the height of the cycle, when we possess the most energy. Can we agree upon this?*

Six of you, not seven, Uluru countered. She rose to her full height, and loomed over them all, even Sa. *I will not abandon this world. I will not flee from...from weather, nor will I take another's world from them simply that I may survive. I will stay here, and I will find a way, or I will let the Earthmother claim me, as she has every other species she gave birth to.*

Akenat blinked at her, his shock total. *You must know you cannot survive? This epoch will last millions of cycles. There will be periods of warmth, but there will also be glaciations that last a hundred millennia or more. You will run out of power, and all you have wrought will be undone.*

Uluru gave a tiny, triumphant smile. *If you are gone, then the Arks only need to sustain themselves and the Nexus. All I will need to tend to is my own Ark, and I will outlast this lingering cold.*

Very well, do as you will, Akenat allowed. *I will attempt to verify your survival when I step through time. Further, I will leave my Ark Keeper behind to tend to the Network. I can construct another if our exodus is successful.*

I will leave Ba as well, Enki offered. *It is possible that the native species that survive the cold might be harnessed to repair critical systems. The primates native to the Ark of the Cradle are particularly promising, as are the windigo. Either could help preserve the Arks, for a time at least.*

Akenat could feel their resolve, bolstered by Enki's support. Perhaps something of their work here might survive their exodus, but if not they could rebuild when they returned.

Let us finish this test, he thought to them, *and then begin our sojourn to another world.*

1

WE NEED A PLAN

Blair's fur tingled as he stepped through the portal and onto Sausalito's narrow beach, in full view of both the shattered remains of the Golden Gate Bridge and the much taller Ark of the Redwood, drinking in the sunlight with its gleaming black immensity.

That sunlight trickled into an ever growing well, one he'd carefully nurtured until the battle with Nox and his demons. That had taxed those reserves, and cost nearly everything the Ark had accumulated during their five-year absence. It wasn't dry by any means, but it was a clear reminder that he couldn't shape frivolously. Not on that scale.

He put that cost from his mind, instead focusing on what it had bought for their side. Blair faced his friends, though at this point family might be more accurate. They were a strange group, without a doubt.

An auburn-furred Ka-Ken next to a golden-furred Ka-Dun, walking alongside their ancient enemy, Anput, the vampire goddess. Anput's skin-tight combat suit was impeccable, of course, as was her hair. She seemed to be enjoying the power walk more than the rest of them.

The last person was the most odd, from an outsider's perspective anyway. He appeared a normal human with a shock of red hair and a whole lot of freckles—your classic ginge, as Trevor would say.

Until recently Trevor's appearance had been absolutely horrific. He'd been deathless, the radioactive zombies from your worst nightmares. Now his heart beat and he drew breath like any normal human, though Blair understood in a way only an Ark Lord could just how much more Trevor really was.

In fact, it was time to address that ability. They needed a plan, and rather than wait for someone else to step up, Blair took the initiative. He took a step closer to the portal, where Anput, Trevor, and Jordan were waiting. They'd crossed to the rocky beach, but hadn't taken a single step farther.

"I know we called this a victory," he began, nodding through the shimmering portal at the Proto Ark and the golden city surrounding it, "but if Jordan is right about Nox, then we lost where it really counted. We have to assume that the grey men, or Hades, can now access the Ark network in the same way I can. We're in the endgame. We need to take him down and get that key back, before he marshals another army and puts us on the defensive."

Jordan gave a slow lupine nod, and bared his fangs as he spoke. "Nox sacrificed Kali, and a whole lot of demons. The only thing worth that price is a Primary Access Key. He had the means, and most definitely the motivation. Maybe we're wrong, but it's best to proceed thinking our Arks are compromised."

"So what do we do about it?" Liz asked. She folded two very massive, very furry arms over her chest. "We can't just assault Cairo. Even if you open a portal, and we flooded through with everything we have, we'd never be able to hold it. The grey man ships will make that impossible."

"She's right," Anput agreed, though she didn't sound happy about it. "The rest of you haven't seen those ships fire. I have. They'll incinerate champion and deathless alike if they catch us out in the open. We can't risk a ground assault."

"We could mount an insurgent-style strike," Trevor suggested as he scrubbed his fingers through his hair. "Maybe light walk directly into the Ark, then seize it. Unless the ships can take down an Ark, we're safe except for ground forces."

"What would that gain us?" Liz countered. She shook her head. "I know you want your Ark back, but if the ships are draining it like you said then you've got no power, and they'll just keep taking anything you try to accumulate. You're effectively in a prison of your own making at that point, and that's assuming you can keep their ground forces at bay."

"So what do you suggest, sis?" Trevor snapped, his eyes tightening. Blair found the reaction as telling as it was alarming. It came from simple human exhaustion, something Trevor hadn't had to deal with during his time as a deathless.

Liz was taken aback and didn't respond, so Blair stepped forward and rapped his golden staff against the sand, drawing their attention. "You want a plan? Here it is. We figure out how time travel works, and then use it to save Isis from the battle with Set. We bring her back to the present, and she leads us against the grey men. Bonus points if we can save Osiris or Ra as well. In the meantime I build up California as a real power, while Jordan does the same in Peru. Trevor, Anput, will you take point on the temporal research?"

"And in this wonderful plan," Liz asked dryly, her irritation at her brother flowing through their bond, "what do you have me doing, exactly?"

Blair was glad he already had an answer, unsurprising given how much time he'd spent considering the question since he'd realized that time travel was possible.

"You are the linchpin," Blair explained, allowing his affection and respect to flow back through the bond. He meant every word. "Let's say we succeed in opening a portal to the past. How do we stop Set from killing Isis? How do we stop him from coming back through, into the present? If we're not absolutely perfect, then we risk reintroducing one of the worst problems we ever faced. One that it took blowing up an Ark to deal with."

Blair really had spent a lot of time thinking about it.

"All good questions," Trevor allowed, his interest apparent in those intense eyes, "and maybe precise time travel is possible. I'd love to have Isis back, and it seems worth the risk. She'd kick Hades's ass, and probably whoever he works for."

"Whoever he works for made Set," Anput pointed out sardonically, "and Set beat Isis, Ra, and Osiris at the same time. He killed my husband easily, and my husband was no lesser god. We have no idea what these Builders are capable of."

"Sobek is breathing down my neck in Peru," Jordan rumbled. He gave a frustrated shake of his head. "I don't even know if he's the worst problem. The deathless are going to come for us fast and hard now that they can't get at the Proto Ark. They outnumber us. A lot. I'm going to be dealing with the home front for the near future, and I'll be damned lucky if Lima survives. I have a feeling Isis could swing the balance of power, real quick. I'm for getting her back, even if I can't contribute much personally."

"Where do we even start to research this?" Liz asked. Her furry face still perfectly conveyed her awkwardness. "I don't want to be negative, but time travel isn't something we can just trial and error our way into. We get one shot at this. We need to understand exactly how it works, and how to replicate it."

"The Builders probably mastered it," Trevor theorized aloud. "They built the Arks, the access keys, and everything else we use. They must have records. If we're not in a position to hit Cairo, then I'm willing to make researching this a priority. Anput, I could really use your help. We have the Proto Ark, and we'll never have a better chance to learn about the Builders."

"I don't like it." Anput's pretty mouth soured into a frown. "Rescuing Isis seems like a fantasy, and if we cannot achieve it then we are wasting valuable time. We barely understand my new virus, or what it will allow Trevor to do. *That* is what I should be working on. Even if we somehow got Isis back she is not the mythical deity you assume her to be. She cannot solve our problems. We must do that ourselves. She is not worth risking allowing Set back into the present."

"Set is a terrible threat, true, but Isis used a Primary Access Key for centuries," Blair countered, holding his staff in what he hoped passed for an Ark-Lord-ish way. "There is literally no human who understands them better. If we're fighting the Builders—and make no mistake, we definitely are—then I want her here to teach us. We *know* that time travel is possible. They temporally manipulated an entire city. We just need one brief window to snatch Isis, a window we will only use if we can be certain of success. I get that we'll need a plan. Give me some time and I can come up with one. I can juice Liz with my full blur, and she can lead a team to grab Isis. That's my problem. All you have to do is tell me it's possible, and how to do it."

Silence reigned for several moments, the only sound the low breeze across the San Francisco Bay, and the echoing construction noises in the distant financial district.

"Okay, I'll trust you," Anput allowed.

Trevor nodded, turning to Anput. "I think you're right too, though. You work on the virus, and test on me however you need to. Let's understand what you've made, and what I can do. I'll look for information on time travel, and see what the Builders knew. Sound good?"

Anput nodded, though she still seemed irked.

"Sounds like we're all in agreement," Jordan rumbled. "Are we leaving the portal here? If so, then I could use a lift home, Blair. If you don't mind me using your Ark."

"I think that's best." Blair tightened his grip on the staff. They'd put him in charge of the city and the champions who worshiped the Mother. He needed to take care of Santa Rosa, but it wasn't his only responsibility. He needed to think larger. "Once you get down there let us know what the situation is. I can't promise we can send help, but we'll see what we can do."

"There is one more thing before I return to my studies," Anput said, her tone frosty. "If you are to rescue Isis you will need the fiercest band of gods in existence. There is none fiercer than Jes'Ka, and it is rumored she sleeps within your Ark. If you wake her, then she can teach your Ka-Ken. She loves both her parents and will be thrilled to find them working together. She will want to save them, and can teach Liz more about the advanced techniques she learned from Isis as a child."

"I'm not waking anyone without knowing who they are." Blair knew he was probably overreacting, but every last god they'd dealt with had been a problem at some point.

"Blair," Liz began, shifting back to human form in the blink of an eye. She knew he was helpless against that smile. "If this Jes'Ka really can train me, then we need her. I can't stop Set alone, or maybe at all."

"You think we can trust her?" Blair directed the question to Anput, who still seemed to be awaiting his verdict.

Anput shook her head. "Absolutely not. Jes'Ka's primary motivation is Jes'Ka, but she loves her family fiercely and will do anything to protect them. She will hate the idea of the Builders, and do anything to stop them. After that? She will give you grief for millennia and you will be sorry you ever woke her."

Blair got the sense that Anput's stakes in this were personal, and wondered if this Jes'Ka had known Anubis...and if so, how intimately. Anput didn't usually show this much emotion, so something ran deep here.

"She is Isis's daughter. She deserves the right to fight," Blair decided, though it was a near thing. His fear from past bad experiences said this was going to come back to bite him. Maybe literally.

She is powerful, Ka-Dun, one of our most fabled warriors. With her at our side, your she will be unstoppable. I pity Set.

Blair wished he shared his beast's confidence.

2

TEMPORAL EVENT

Trevor stepped back through the portal and into the golden city, or what remained of it anyway. Lumbering, skyscraper-sized demons had toppled obelisks, and energy blasts had scored the golden surfaces of many pyramids.

The bodies had been removed, thankfully, but the result was an empty city nearly devoid of life. Only nine champions remained, though apparently quite a few survived in the jungles back in the Amazon.

"Are you planning to redirect the portal?" Anput asked, adjusting her glasses as she stared at the modulator.

"No." Trevor was mildly surprised that she'd adopted a subservient role, but in her mind Ark Lords were to be obeyed, even if she was now stronger than him thanks to the changes to his virus.

It was worth it though. He'd taken a good, long crap this morning while reading a book. Some people might find that horrifying, but hey, when you'd been devouring corpses and unable to sit down to a normal meal, every human function you got back was amazing.

"That's it?" Her pretty mouth turned down into a frown, and she fixed him with supernaturally intense eyes. "You can do better than that, I think."

"No, I'm not redirecting the portal," Trevor offered, pleased that she'd stood up for herself. "Because I'd rather have Blair's support than the champions in Peru. They don't love us, and that hasn't changed just because my heart beats now. I'm still the ancient enemy in their book."

Anput cocked her head to the side, her dark hair bobbing down to brush her shoulder. "A wise choice, I think. Though it does place Jordan in a rather precarious position. We didn't discuss it as a group, but I'm much more familiar with the political layout on that continent than any of you. There is no way Jordan will last the year. If he lasts the month I will be extremely impressed."

"I was afraid of that." Trevor heaved a deep sigh, and started for the pyramid of Kek Telek, where they'd been conducting their research. It helped to have a name, though he wished he knew more about him and what role he'd played in Builder society. Was he their Einstein? Or their Mendele? "There isn't much we can do to help Jordan, short of bringing Isis back."

"And you really believe that is worth all this effort?" Anput wore her disapproval openly, in the slight frown and her closed body language. She shook her head, continuing before he could answer. "We already have Jes'Ka. Wake her, and bring her up to speed. She's immensely powerful. She's no inventor, but she's every bit the warrior Isis was."

That piqued Trevor's curiosity. "I've seen her a couple times now. I still remember that Irakesh had a thing for her. He badly wanted to wake her, and would have if he hadn't lost the access key. Who is she?"

"A feral, sensual goddess." Anput gave an affectionate smile. "One who caused no end of trouble for both her parents. Osiris always had a soft spot for her, and forbade all vampires from harming her. Not that any could. She once fought my husband to a standstill before Ra intervened."

They'd made it about halfway up the wide marble thoroughfare when the air shimmered next to Trevor. Ba's form appeared, but it flickered badly, as Ka's had when they'd first encountered the VI in the Nexus.

"Ark Lord Trevor," Ba buzzed, his hologram destabilizing and fuzzing at the edges. "I have detected an unexpected temporal event in the pyramid of Kek Telek in the chamber belonging to human subject Percy."

Trevor shot a look at Anput, and found her just as shocked as he was. "A temporal event? Can you explain any further? What kind of temporal event?"

"Unknown," Ba admitted, his voice distending into a low hum at the end. "The power requirements are considerable, which suggests the connected time is likely in the distant past or future."

Trevor had no idea what to make of that. He started sprinting toward the pyramid, and poured a bit of energy into the blur. It was weak, less than he'd been able to manage on his first day as a deathless, but it was still much faster than walking.

Anput matched his pace, though she could easily have gone on ahead had she wanted. Her ability to blur hadn't been impacted, as she'd still made no move to take her own virus.

They turned down the pathway leading to the pyramid, then through the high-arched doorway, onto the first floor of the pyramid. Trevor and Anput headed for the stairs, and looped down to the second, then the third level without encountering anyone.

When they arrived on the fourth floor he could hear a single thready heartbeat, muffled, from inside a rejuvenation pod.

Anput blinked owlishly at him, then disappeared into the shadows. "I'll let you investigate."

"Of course you will." Trevor shook his head, then moved toward the pod.

3

AKENAT

Akenat's consciousness fractured during the transit to the future. The receptacle, whose lingering memories identified itself as Percy, could not have been more alien, and he lacked basic motor control, or the ability to process the signals the host detected around it.

This body was no being he, or any other Builder, had created. It was too flawed. Too damaged. Too poorly designed. He'd somehow landed in an entirely different species inside the rejuvenation pod.

He could neither see, nor hear, nor think effectively. The host body was in flux. Terminal flux. On the very edge of expiration. He didn't understand the circumstances that had brought the body to this state. That didn't matter.

Stabilizing his new host did.

Akenat turned his consciousness inward, attempting to shape. That was the true test, after all. If this body lacked the ability then...yes! The ability was there. Not in abundance, unfortunately, but with a finer degree of control than Akenat had expected. The host was deft, but weak. That would mean adopting a defensive posture.

He delved this body, which confirmed his fears. It was disintegrating at the molecular level, its helixes unable to support the modifications it had been subjected to.

The delivery agent for this modification seemed to be a mutagen of unknown origin, one of extreme sophistication. The architect had signed that mutagen in many places, adding markers as flourishes. It was impressive work.

Work that might save him.

Akenat used the mutagen to further mutate the host's helixes. All of them at once. He built in specific genes, each designed to make a body more durable, more resistant to harsher bandwidths and hostile shaping.

Unfortunately, it reminded him greatly of the sandstone edifices built along beaches by proto-tribes of windigo. The diminutive creatures labored tirelessly to create their structures, which were inevitably washed away by the tide.

Akenat's host was nearly washed away under a tide of genetic dissolution, but he painstakingly built the helixes back each time. Eventually he developed a rhythm, and shunted the task to an unused part of the host's brain. That would keep things stable, for now. He couldn't afford to ignore the issue for long, however.

This body simply wasn't suitable. He needed another, one that could shape, before it expired. Transferring his consciousness was a simple matter, and while he'd already seen evidence that these moderns could shape, he was confident that he could easily best them.

After all, were they truly skilled shapers they would not be using cast-off Builder tech millions of cycles after it was created. Still...best not to underestimate this new species. This body was frail in the extreme.

Akenat pressed a hand to the control gem, and willed the rejuvenator to open. The controls ground open, but reluctantly. The mechanism was in clear need of maintenance, which told him something else about these moderns. If they could not even repair the technology they found, then how had they mastered manipulation of helixes?

He attempted locomotion with the gangly host body, but toppled forward, the host's nerve receptors firing to indicate pain as his face struck the marble outside the pod. Akenat spared a moment to repair his injuries, then attempted to crawl toward the stairs.

That form of locomotion was easier to sustain, though painfully inefficient. Reaching the stairway took long moments, and he realized that climbing higher would take even more effort. There had to be a better way.

Ark Keeper Ba. He sent the words as strongly as he was able. *If you are in this city come to me at once.*

Akenat relaxed his frail body against the cold stairs. There were so many questions, and precious few answers until he acquired more data.

There was no response. That was troubling. If Ba was present in the city he should respond, unless unable or under the orders of an Ark Lord.

That left him no choice but to gather more data on his own. He'd have to crawl from this pyramid, and see if a view of the larger city gave him some clue as to what had transpired during the vast gulf of time he'd just traversed.

He was preparing to do so when a pair of bipedal figures suddenly appeared at the top of the stairs. They hadn't light walked, not that suddenly. But their movement was far faster than a species could manage without the aid of shaping.

Akenat retreated from the host's conscious mind, into the subconscious. This effectively rendered the body catatonic, as the original consciousness was presumably back in Akenat's time wreaking untold havoc using his body.

He studied the arrivals, these strange moderns, and made some immediate leaps about their probable evolution. They were bipedal, and resembled primates, but if so had lost most of their hair, and a good deal of their muscle mass. The cranial cavity had not increased substantially in size, though it was larger, and probably held a much more efficient brain.

The male, which possessed a mane of light hair, knelt next to the host and issued a series of grunts and hoots. The female cocked her head, and issued a similar stream at the male. The two continued in this manner, and Akenat's joy soared when he realized that this must be how they communicated.

They must have agreed that each specific sound possessed a quantifiable meaning, and if you assembled enough symbols an understanding could be reached.

Akenat was intensely curious about this communication, so much so that he was willing to take a small risk. The moderns weren't powerless, but they did seem primitive in their understanding of shaping. If he could slip past one of their defenses, then he could likely wrest the knowledge before the shaper was even aware.

He tapped into the subject's ability to shape, and honed a microscopic probe, a single filament so subtle even a Builder might not detect it. Akenat cast his shaping at the male, who was closer, and watched with apprehension as it entered the ocular cavity disguised as simple light.

The probe was processed just as light would be, and a neuron fired, but the signal it carried was compromised, and belonged wholly to Akenat. He attached it to the brain stem, then retreated back to the original host.

It had only taken seconds, and neither modern seemed aware anything had happened. They were still hooting and grunting at each other, not all that different from the primates in the jungles on Anansi's continent.

Now, however, Akenat began to glean meaning. He stole memory from the male, focusing on early development, when he'd presumably learned this language.

When the male next spoke Akenat understood. "Should we put him back inside the rejuvenator?"

Akenat took more memory, this batch stored in an entirely separate part of the brain. He was looking for short term memory, specifically regarding the host. Finding it did not take long, and Akenat quickly replayed all memories pertaining to the host.

The moderns knew little about the host beyond his name and

origin, and had only heard him speak a few hundred of these symbols they knew as words.

From there Akenat began synthesizing an appropriate identity. He used pieces of the host's lingering consciousness, combined with the information he'd collected from the male. The result should be a fairly accurate approximation of the host's behavior.

"I say," Akenat intoned, the vocal cords strange as they produced the odd sounds. "I do believe I may have suffered a stroke."

The term referred to a pulmonary event, something nearly every mammalian species was capable of suffering, including Akenat's native form, prior to shaping away such a weakness, of course.

"Percy?" The female's voice expressed a note of concern. An interesting development. They could communicate not just the symbols, but also their intent and emotional state. The mode was still primitive, but more versatile than Akenat had first assumed.

"Yes, I think so." Akenat held his head in his hands. "I'm very confused. I think the mutagen might be responsible."

"At least you're alive." The male rose to his feet. His gaze contained a healthy dose of suspicion, but not the kind that warranted further action.

Akenat planned to give him nothing.

"I could desperately use a nap. I don't suppose you'd help me to my cot?" He'd plucked the location from the male's memories, and the cot wasn't too distant from the pyramid's control matrix. If he could reach that....

"Of course." The male gently scooped the host up, and began carrying him up the stairs.

That left plenty of time for Akenat to wonder what had happened to this Percy. The consciousness might be unraveling the time stream, even now. If only he had a way to observe the distant past.

4

OH, DEAR

Percy awakened in the strangest of all possible situations. When he'd gone to sleep in the rejuvenation pod, or whatever the contraption was called, he'd struggled for every breath. He was fairly certain he'd been dying, and to be frank hadn't expected to wake up at all.

Not only was he awake, but as Percy raised a pair of clearly inhuman hands as far as the confines of the pod would allow, he realized that the pasty green hands only possessed four fingers. This body, his body, wasn't anything created in God's earthly kingdom.

After everything he'd seen with the werewolves and the lost city, he knew not to panic, but knowing and doing were two different things. He was in another body, with no idea how or why it had happened. Panic seemed a rational response at this juncture.

Still, it wouldn't answer any questions. And he loved answering questions, didn't he? Perhaps he could view this as a puzzle to be solved. He was someone else. Maybe this was a dream, so he'd treat it like it was until he learned otherwise.

Percy studied his new body, blinking down at himself with comically large eyes...pools of deep black, as evidenced by his reflection in the tube's shiny surface. Pools that perfectly matched Ark Keeper Ba, his only companion for quite a number of years.

A loud thunk presaged the tube opening, and as it rolled back and away Percy had his first look at the lab where he'd entered the tube. It was the same room...but the occupants of that room couldn't be more different.

A half dozen ashy-grey creatures stood near strange glowing consoles, each absorbed in their own tasks. None seemed to notice as Percy climbed awkwardly from the tube, and why should they? He appeared as they did, though both taller and a rich forest green. Did that mean he was in charge?

One of the grey men approached on spindly legs, and bobbed something that might have been a bow. Thoughts bloomed in Percy's mind, clearly broadcast from the creature. *Pardon, Builder, has new data been gathered? This one would be happy to provide analysis.*

Percy stalked quickly away from the inquisitive alien and adopted the air of a superior with no time for questions. The grey man fell away with another hurried bow, much to Percy's relief.

He slowed his pace, and walked up the stairs to the next level. There were even more grey men here, each working at one of the pyramid's terminals as they gathered data. None of them resembled his larger green body, which confirmed to him that these little ones were some sort of servant caste.

Percy was unsure where to go, so he ascended another level, and then another. That brought him to the pyramid's ground level, and he beelined for the doors he knew led into the city proper.

Unless there had been a sudden unexpected invasion that had also switched his body, then Percy was what had changed. Somehow his consciousness had been deposited into this strange body. Did that mean that his own body contained the original host consciousness? How terrifying. Where was he?

Percy stepped through the doorway, and stopped, unable to go any further as he took in the view before him.

He was in the same golden city with its magnificent pyramids and spires, but it was no longer empty. There was no sign of the handful of champions, or his new friends, the odd ginger fellow and his saucy dead paramour.

Instead, the city contained hundreds of thousands of grey men. Countless figures ambled between pyramids. Some walked, but many floated in the sky, while here and there golden ships flitted past them.

"By all that is holy," he whispered to himself, "I'm witnessing the people who made this city. Is this a previous age? Am I somehow in the past? What a fantastic dream. I wonder how long ago this was?"

Processing query, a warm, friendly voice echoed in his head. *Time stream analysis complete. Utilizing foreign consciousness's signature, a baseline can be established. Subject has traveled two-point-three-million solar cycles. Would you like to plot the physical path traveled during that interval?*

Percy didn't reply. Not immediately, anyway. He understood almost every word of that, and what he didn't understand could be extrapolated. The salient bit, the part he now needed to wrestle with, was that he'd somehow been hurled back in time to the height of the civilization that had, apparently, occupied this planet before humanity had come out of the trees.

The question was, what did he do now? Try to find a way home? Or learn what he could and hope a solution presented itself? He simply didn't know.

A quite familiar hologram appeared next to him. Ka's normally cheerful voice was almost mechanical. *Welcome back, Ark Lord Akenat. The other Builders await your arrival at the conclave to discuss your findings in the future epoch.*

"I see," he muttered, or tried to anyway. The tiny mouth mangled the words, and the vocal chords produced a high, reedy tone that he very much disliked.

A golden bracelet affixed to his left wrist began to pulse warmly, and he realized he was receiving some sort of communication. "Oh, dear."

What should he do? Could he pull off impersonating an alien? No that wasn't quite accurate. These creatures were Earth's original inhabitants, if he was correct in his assumptions.

He tapped the flashing ruby, and a second hologram sprang up over the bracelet. This one depicted the single most ungodly creature Percy had ever had the misfortune of laying eyes on. Its skin was black as pitch, and more bulbous than the others. Combined with the black eyes the creature resembled some malevolent tuber.

We await news that could dictate our fate for millions of years. Why do you dally? What do you not wish to share with the rest of us?

Percy realized that if he was going to communicate, then he needed to do it mentally as they did. He tried thinking the words, and then sort of pushing them at the demonic-looking fellow.

I am disoriented from the transition through time, Percy offered, hoping the lie was convincing. *If you'll conduct me to this meeting I will answer all your questions.*

The demon eyed him for long moments. Long enough that Percy worried he might attack or do something unspeakable. But the creature eventually offered a short nod.

Very well.

There was a moment of vertigo, and they appeared inside a very familiar coliseum, the same the champions had been using to conduct their meetings.

This time, however, the room was considerably less crowded. There were perhaps a dozen of the smaller grey men, and six green-skinned fellows he somehow identified as Builders. Those ranged in form, gender, and appearance enough that any rational scientist would assume them different species entirely.

One quite resembled a large spider, and evoked a very primitive desire to flee. The demonic tuber was the most frightening, however, and it was all Percy could do to force himself to move forward and join their unholy circle.

He could feel the whispering between them, the passing of thoughts between minds. If he did the same they'd instantly detect his ruse, but if he refused they would demand a valid reason.

What was he going to do?

Akenat, the demonic one rumbled into his mind, as he took a threatening step forward. *I sense deception in you. And other...alien things. What has transpired? Keep us in suspense no longer. We demand answers. How fared the experiment? Were you able to detect signals from this distant star system or not? What else did you learn in the future? We have squandered far too much of our remaining reserves on this gambit. It had better pay off, or you may find your position...called into question.*

The nervous anticipation increased in the others as they demanded his response. Some feared a confrontation between this Akenat and Yoggoth, a name summoned from the recesses of the mind he currently occupied. Others welcomed that confrontation.

The experiment was a success, Percy began, praying that whatever words he found were enough to persuade alien beings of unknown intellect or design, *and a signal was indeed broadcast from our new, ah, home. Our progeny have already returned. We should proceed with the, ah, plan.*

Then why is your behavior so erratic? one of the taller females thought. She stepped forward, a golden spear casually held in one hand. He could feel the power, the menace, in that weapon. *Either you are hiding something, or you wish us to believe that you are. What game are you playing, Akenat? Why does your mind remain closed to us?*

Percy wasn't precisely certain how to answer, at first, but something became very clear. He was dealing with six very powerful, very prickly rulers, and they all mistrusted each other immensely. His brief time in London had shown him how such games were played, so he trusted his instincts and prayed he was right.

I am not prepared to share everything I saw. He thought at them, letting it hang there for a moment before continuing. *Some of you still exist in the future, but others, well...let's just say that we do not get on very well on our new home.*

Percy knew his speech and mannerisms were all wrong, but was wagering everything that they'd be too busy watching each other to pay it any mind.

Who are we to fear? the menacing female asked as she glared around the room with those flat black eyes. *It is Yoggoth, isn't it? He's always wanted to thin the herd, and on this new world there isn't a need for seven Ark Lords, is there?*

Precisely, Percy agreed, nodding accusingly at the demonic fellow she seemed to have taken issue with. *He kills you, but that is not the only death. There are others we must, ah, watch out for.*

All of them were eyeing each other now, which was good he supposed, but Percy wasn't certain what to do next.

Enough, the demonic one thought. He stepped forward, and though he was diminutive next to the menacing female with her golden spear, all the others took a step backward to maintain their distance. *Is it possible we squabble and murder each other on this new world? Of course. Would you expect us to do anything less? We are apex predators. But you are missing the garden for the blossoms. We survive. Akenat's plan to reach this new world is a success. Our choice is stay here and die, or take a chance on this new world. I know what I will do, but you may all do as you will.*

The others eyed each other with undisguised hatred and mistrust. But under those emotions he could sense their pragmatic agreement. They all knew that this plan, whatever it was, might be their only hope of survival.

The plan is simple enough. A studious male, shorter and unassuming, stepped forward and drew the others' attention. He wore far more elaborate jewelry than the others, and cradled a staff that would have been at home in early dynastic Egypt. *All we need do is allow the power to accumulate for this cycle. At its zenith we harvest the energy, and use it to propel ourselves to this new world. If we are in agreement that we must do this, then I will take my leave to begin preparations. The Proto Ark must be modified, and the Nexus both repaired and fortified.*

I still intend to remain on Earth, the largest female protested, taking a step back from the rest of the circle. *Nor will I contribute any power from my Ark, as I will need every scrap I can if I am to have any chance of surviving the coming age of ice. But I will aid you in any other way. Tell me what preparations must be made, and you will have my cooperation.*

We are aware of your illogical, self-imposed limitations. Yoggoth's thoughts oozed contempt. *You are unwilling to seize this new world, though you had no such compunctions when we became the dominant species on this one. You murdered countless species, including your own people. Stay behind and die, then. Or does she survive this madness, Akenat? Did you glimpse Uluru's fate?*

I witnessed nothing I care to share. Percy tried to glare at the demon-thing, but had never been very brave. His eyes fell to the dark marble floor. *Her fate is her own.*

It amazed him that none had protested that he was an impostor. How could they not see him for what he was? Then his gaze touched Yoggoth's, and an icy fist seized whatever passed for a heart in these creatures.

The creature knew. That smug black gaze said it all. The creature wasn't telling the others, but Yoggoth sensed that Percy wasn't this Akenat. The demon offered a slow predatory smile, as if saying...*I know you know and I don't care.*

Percy had no idea what he was going to do to get out of this one. The very last thing he wanted was to journey to another world, especially with this lot as traveling companions.

5

SEALED

Trevor deposited Percy's emaciated form atop the cot against the top level's far wall. The old man murmured thanks, and then his eyes fluttered closed. His forehead was still coated in sweat, and his entire body suffered a continuous tremble. That could be the virus, or it could be something else.

He turned from the old man and moved to the control matrix where Anput was already hard at work. She'd adopted her spectacles, which she maintained helped her concentrate.

"I don't trust him," Trevor murmured as he moved to join her before the pulsing multicolored crystals on the obelisk where she worked. "He comes across as genial, but for just a moment...I felt like someone was trying to shape me."

"Could have been reflexive." Anput didn't glance up from her work, the light of a ruby bathing her delicate features. "Have you considered that he's not able to control the virus and could be mutating wildly? Projecting maybe?"

Trevor nodded grimly, and rubbed at the sudden gooseflesh on his arms. He'd missed those visceral sensations. He considered Anput's question, then answered when he felt like he'd grasped the root of his issue. "That's the most likely scenario. Here's the problem, though. We don't know Percy. We've spent, what, a few hours chatting with him? He seems harmless enough, but appearances can be deceiving as you of all people know."

Anput finally glanced up from her work long enough to deliver a devilishly playful smile. "I know all about appearances, and consider myself an impeccable judge of character. That man doesn't have an ounce of deception in him, and to be candid isn't likely to survive the night in any case."

And, just like that, Anput's attention slid back to the console. Her pupils narrowed and she leaned closer, obviously enraptured. Trevor resisted the urge to ask what had drawn her attention. She'd entered flow state, and he didn't want to disrupt that.

He leaned back on his heels and glanced at Percy again. Was he seeing knives in every shadow? Maybe. There was a way to know for sure. He'd never shaped another person's mind before, but now possessed the ability to do so. And Percy seemed as safe a test subject as he was ever going to get.

Blair had described the ability as honing his will into an imaginary dagger, then piercing the opponent's mind through the eye. Trevor had been on the receiving end more often than he'd like.

"Trevor?" Anput's sudden excitement drew his attention, and he hurried over to join her at the terminal. A grin brightened her features. "I found a section about temporal shaping. It's sealed, which suggests they considered it highly important. It validates your theories."

"Ba, we need you," Trevor said, summoning the ever present Ark Keeper.

A moment later a hologram flickered into view, though it was noticeably distorted over the last time he'd seen it. That was alarming in the extreme. How close was the Proto Ark to being out of power? Or having a critical systems failure?

"ZZzYes, Ark Kk-kkeeper?" Ba stuttered. The image flickered with each word.

"We've found restricted information," he explained as he nodded at the console. "We'd like to know more about temporal shaping.

Also, if the visual component of your avatar is taking some sort of bandwidth, then turn it off and go audio only."

The hologram disappeared, and a tinny version of Ba's voice issued from the ground at the base of the console. "Ah, that is much better. The bandwidth requirements for full projection are extreme, and many conduits are damaged beyond use. We are down to four percent of maximum capacity."

"The restricted area?" Trevor prompted. "How do we access that data? It's on temporal shaping. We need that unlocked."

"I am not familiar with this term. A moment please," Ba said. The construct's voice sounded hesitant, and Trevor could imagine those big dull eyes, even if he could no longer see them. "Ah, yes, I have performed a search of the archive and located the area you speak of. Curious that I have no knowledge of it, as it happened after I was constructed. Perhaps the Builders removed the information from my mind when sealing the records. In any case I cannot remove the restriction. It is genetically locked to the Builder who placed it. If that Builder is dead the information is lost."

"There's no way to fool the encryption?" Trevor raised an eyebrow in Anput's direction, and lowered his voice for her benefit. "I've never met a system that didn't have a back door or a way in. No one leaves only one failsafe."

"I am unaware of such a method," Ba's cheerful voice proclaimed. "The mechanism locking the information would require a master shaper to understand, much less replicate or fool. A number of the Builders' younger progeny attempted to violate the archive, but were unsuccessful in breaching restricted areas."

Trevor balled his hands into fists as heat surged through him. He blinked when he realized what he was doing. Anger had been a distant, dull ache when he'd been a deathless. Now? It was fresh and overpowering, like a wildfire.

"I say," Percy's weak voice came from the cot in the corner as the old man forced himself into a hunched sitting position. "I couldn't help but overhear your conversation. You say this temporal shaping is locked, yes?"

Ba said nothing, and Trevor remembered that the construct wouldn't obey Percy. Nor was he in a hurry to change that. "Yes, the data is locked."

"Well," Percy managed as he surged awkwardly to his feet, his thumbs tucked through his suspenders. "It seems to me that someone locked it for a reason. A good one. These Builders used to have council meetings, yes? They probably discussed these matters at length."

Trevor scratched at his beard, a new thing, and considered Percy's line of logic. It was a damned good one. Maybe Percy was that smart, but it struck Trevor as just a bit too convenient.

Blair described mind penetration as fast, so he could get in, and get right back out before anyone realized what he was doing. Trevor envisioned Blair's dagger, and thrust it at Percy's eye.

An unfamiliar signal rippled out from him, and shot into Percy's eye. There was a moment of vertigo, then Trevor hovered in darkness. Empty darkness. Here and there a star glittered, but they were rare pinpoints in a largely unbroken blackness.

It resembled a storage unit someone had cleared out in a hurry, with nothing but a few ragged boxes left behind. Trevor couldn't be certain why. The virus could be erasing parts of his mind. Unnerving, but not nearly so much as having found treachery.

Trevor sifted through the few existing memories until he located the one of their recent meeting. Percy stared up at Trevor, but there was no conscious thought, and certainly no shaping he could detect.

Perhaps he'd been wrong.

Trevor concentrated on being back in his own mind, as Blair had explained. There was a rush like falling off a cliff, and then he was tumbling back into his own mind. He realized everyone was staring at him, and tried to remember the conversation.

He licked his lips as he pieced it back together. "Ba, can you examine the council meetings, and all other archives for any mention of this temporal shaping?"

"Working...thirteen mentions in council meetings, all in a ten-cycle span."

Trevor considered that. Ten years sounded like a lot from his perspective, but the Builders had reigned for millennia or longer. All the instances being clustered to that one small time period suggested they were looking at a panicked discussion, after which knowledge, or open knowledge, was probably suppressed.

"Ugg." Anput rolled her eyes and returned her attention to her console. "I have work to do if you're going to spend your time sifting through council meetings. Let me know if you find something relevant. Otherwise don't bother me."

Trevor wouldn't have it any other way. It had been so long since he'd conducted some good old-fashioned research that he'd almost forgotten how.

6

ORDERS FROM MADMEN

Nox wore his demonic form with pride as he strode through the marble halls of Olympus, the world's oldest surviving human city. He specified human, because he'd recently battled over the Proto Ark, the original first city created by the race that had preceded his own on this world.

"I have come at your command, mighty Hades." The stone cracked as Nox dropped to one knee at the very outskirts of Hades's throne room. The monarch was endlessly touchy about niceties, and Nox wasn't eager for another lesson on his respective place. If the man enjoyed theatrics, then Nox would perform. He curled his tail subserviently around his ankles.

Hades's throne drifted closer, his increasingly youthful body splayed across the silver chair in a way only a truly arrogant monarch could manage. The now smooth-skinned man believed himself a literal god. There was no way that kind of hubris could end badly.

"You have done well," Hades crooned, as he patted his dark luxurious curls, which last time Nox saw had been wisps of faded grey. A result of the golden crown adorning his brow, Nox was certain of it. Siphoning power from the Ark below. "I have passed the Primary

Access Key along to our allies. They have agreed to stay out of our impending war, and will allow me to conquer the world unopposed, so long as I allow them access to the Arks."

"My lord," Nox ventured, his tone as subservient as he could manage. "What is to prevent them from turning on us the moment the Builders arrive? Their progeny could be overcome, which is why they require allies. But the leaders? We have only the Project Solaris report we pilfered from Mohn Corp. as a guide. We have no idea how powerful these beings truly are. You have seen millennia. I have only seen decades. I cannot imagine millions of years."

Hades straightened on his throne, which zoomed close enough for the shadow to fall over Nox's kneeling form. The message was obvious, as always. Hades didn't do subtle.

"You have served me well enough," Hades muttered, seemingly to himself, "and you seem sincere in your question. I will trust your humility and take it for authenticity. There is nothing to prevent them from destroying us when they arrive. Nothing. However, if we prove to be useful slaves there is every likelihood they will keep us in positions of power. Every occupying enemy wants a loyalist government to be hated by the populace."

"Forgive my temerity, Lord." Nox bowed his head lower, and asked what to him seemed obvious. "They made use of this world before us, and seemed to keep their numbers small. Likewise, their numbers of servants seem small. If they do not require a large populace, what use is there for a loyalist government?" He trailed off, knowing Hades would do the rest.

Nox imagined Hades's face going bloodless, though he wasn't stupid enough to look up and confirm.

After many long moments Hades gave a dry, shallow chuckle. "I will not vent my wrath on you. You have no fear, my advisor. The question is impertinent, but valid. There is a real chance that they will eliminate us. However, there is a greater chance that these independent beings will war with each other, and view us correctly as no threat. In that instance we might be useful to one of them. And should such a one offer protection, then I am confident they will abide by their agreement."

That puzzled Nox. It suggested that Hades had knowledge he hadn't shared, and he loved crowing about his secrets.

"Well, go on," Hades prompted. "Ask the next impertinent question. I know you want to."

"I do, Lord, but will refrain." Nox rose to a knee. "May I ask why you have summoned me, Lord?"

"The grey men have assured me that the Mother's Ark is damaged to the point of uselessness. They are naked to the storm." Hades gave an unhinged laugh, another crack in his eroding sanity. "You will seize control of South America. You will take the Ark. You will kill the current Lord, and you will take the key for yourself. Is that clear enough for you, or do I need to draw maps and perhaps pack a meal for your journey?"

"Of course, Lord. No, Lord." He paused, and considered the likely obstacles he'd encounter in laying waste to Lima. There weren't many. "What should I do if Sobek attacks? Camiero claims he is seen dealing with Isis quite often, and now has a deal with Jordan."

Hades steepled his fingers and adopted a smug air. "I have it on good authority that Sobek will not intervene. His master has made an accord with the Builders. A deal that has, shall we say...stood the test of time."

There it was. That was Hades's proof that the grey men, or their Builder masters, kept their word. The proof that they were logical, and thus open to persuasion. It lent credence to Hades's position, though Nox was still certain that resistance was the proper course, not capitulation. He'd rather deal with Jordan's and Blair's animosity than a genocidal elder race.

"How often shall I report, my Lord?" Nox asked, knowing that if he didn't he'd be pestered constantly, the entire trip.

"Hmm." Hades adjusted his crown, and Nox spotted the flaking red skin underneath. It had an unhealthy sheen. "We shall try loosening the leash. Contact me when you have met with Camiero.

Contact me again when you are in position to deliver the killing blow on Lima."

"It will be done, my Lord." Nox took a chance and rose to his feet, then bowed and left the chamber. He didn't breathe until well outside the room. The fear began to abate, slightly at least.

Working for a madman while dancing on the edge of a knife. This time not even he might survive this.

7

THANKS FOR THE WATER

Jordan chuckled as the light walk faded and he realized that Blair had set him exactly where he wanted to be. He'd likely plucked the thought from Jordan's head, which was why he now stood in the middle of Dr. Robert's spacious council chambers.

Nor was Roberts alone.

A dozen champions, including Rodrigo, sat in high-backed chairs around an impractically large mahogany table. Most sipped brandy. All were exhausted, and in human form given the extreme heat. Air conditioning was one of the greatest casualties of the old world.

"Sorry for the intrusion, Dr. Roberts," Jordan offered, rather lamely. It was enough. Every champion rose to their feet, even Roberts.

"Your timing is impeccable, as always." Roberts folded hairy arms, and fixed Jordan with a hard stare from behind that hedge of a beard. "Please tell me you actually have something we can use to push our enemies back. Did you bring allies from the holy city, like you said you would when you went haring off into the jungle?"

"No," Jordan admitted, again rather lamely. He moved to the table and poured himself a glass of water. There was no ice, of course. "Nox

made a major push into El Dorado. He very nearly took it, and likely
absconded with a Primary Access Key. We held the city and crushed
his armies, which should buy us time."

"It hasn't." Roberts approached a window, and fanned himself in
the breeze it offered. "The deathless began their assault four days ago.
Listen."

Jordan closed his eyes and drank in the sounds of Lima, a city he
was coming to appreciate as a new home. There were gulls in the
distance, and crashing waves, and even the horns of ships.

But there were also mortar rounds, in the extreme distance. And a
subsonic pulse that he realized must be coming from the shaping
obelisks that Roberts had invented. A glance out the window showed
a missile streaking toward a warehouse at the edge of town.

A moment before it impacted, the air above the structure discol-
ored, and the flame was shunted away by an invisible force.

"Our defenses are holding," Roberts pointed out. He lowered his
voice. "They won't for much longer. We're tired, and our Ka-Dun are
at their edges. Our shaping stones are dry. We need a tactical victory,
and soon. There are a seemingly endless array of enemies marching
in. Hundreds of thousands of deathless. Millions maybe. Against a
few thousand champions, and not that many more humans. We're
being extinguished, Jordan, and there isn't a damned thing we can do
about it. That is...unless your Ark actually works now?"

A hot flush rose in Jordan's neck. He cleared his throat, then
forced some steel into his spine. "Not yet, no. Right now I get almost
nothing from it, even if I'm standing inside. I'm strong, but not that
much stronger than you."

Roberts gave a tired nod. "Your mind is more important, in this
instance. We need a leader, Jordan. A military leader. One who can
oversee our last stand."

Jordan moved to the window and stared at the ocean, which blan-
keted the western horizon. He felt power below, down by the docks,
and spotted Vimal's tall form striding between dock workers as he
yelled orders. Even binoculars wouldn't have allowed him to see the
man's face, but shaping made that simple.

Vimal's skin had darkened into a ruddy red, probably an artifact of constantly being outside. He'd really risen to the challenge, and Jordan commended himself on having the foresight to identify talent. He needed more of it. Desperately.

"What about Sobek?" Jordan finally asked as he turned back to Roberts. "He's got to be getting antsy."

"And you'd like to borrow even more trouble?" Roberts raised an eyebrow, and several champions shrank in their chairs as if expecting an outburst.

"No," Jordan countered. He offered Roberts his full attention. "We already have that trouble. I'm hoping we can use it. If we can hold out for a little while maybe we can bait Sobek into showing up. Maybe he'll show up on his own."

Roberts folded his arms over a sweat-soaked shirt that clung to a muscled form still at odds with the portly man Jordan had originally met.

"How does that help us?" The doctor demanded.

"Because he has a navy." Jordan glanced back at the ocean. "That navy threatens everyone on this continent. If we can make the death-less think that he's our ally, or better yet our master, then they have to take his navy into their plans. That will slow their assault. They'll dig in, and their leaders will talk about how to proceed. They don't want war with an unknown Ark Lord any more than we do."

"Jordan." Roberts's beard split, the dark hair parting to expose a rare smile. "I am quite pleased to have you back. They're going to hit us, and hit us soon. But if you can throw them back maybe your plan has some merit. What do you need from us to make it happen?"

"I'm going to meet with Vimal." Jordan nodded out the window. "And then I'm going to send Sobek a message. One I know he won't ignore. Thanks for the water."

He waited for Roberts to nod his agreement, then blurred down to the docks. The salty wind rippled across his bare skin, and a half smile took the edge off the morning as he whipped past empty boulevards on gentle hills. They had problems, sure, but those problems were military in nature.

That was something he was actually qualified to deal with.

Jordan stopped at the edge of the docks, and waited for Vimal to notice. It didn't take long. His protege turned and a hard smile bloomed. Vimal gave a nod of greeting. "Welcome back, Ark Lord."

"It's good to be home." Jordan crossed the dock, and offered a nod to the dock workers, who seemed surprised by the attention. Most were unloading crates from a nearly empty frigate that had been stuffed with cargo. At least they were still getting supplies. Jordan offered a hand to Vimal when he reached him, and the taller man accepted it with a firm grip. "All right, let's hear it. How are things?"

"Bad." Vimal shook his head. "Real bad. Sobek was spotted yesterday. I didn't even bother telling Roberts."

Jordan noticed that it wasn't El Medico any longer. Jordan called him Roberts, so Vimal did too. Interesting.

"There may not be any point if his tactical assessment was accurate." Jordan pointed south. "What's the situation there? Why haven't they advanced?"

"I don't know." Vimal offered a helpless shrug, out of keeping on the confident man. "They have enough forces to overwhelm us. But they aren't. The attacks feel, I don't know, sporadic? And disjointed. Sloppy even."

"Like they have no commanding officer." Jordan drummed his fingers along his holster as he eyed the southern front, what he could see of it from here. Mostly just the smoking demilitarized zone south of Lima. "That might make sense. If they're broken into factions, then they might be attacking independently. No one wants to be the vanguard, unless they live to keep the spoils."

"That would certainly fit their tactics." Vimal's stance eased. "It's good to have you home, Ark Lord. Truly."

Jordan smiled, but turned to the water. "I have one more thing I want to do before we get ready to take apart their next offensive."

8

STRANGE BEDFELLOWS

J ordan lurked in the shadows next to the enormous bronze bell atop a church on the highest hill in Lima. The place was deserted, as was most of the rotting city. Many buildings around the governmental plaza had been refurbished, as had a number of high rises near it. They'd salvaged what they needed, and maybe a bit more.

The rest? Five years hadn't been kind. Windows had long since been broken, which exposed the interior to the weather, and to the salty winds. In not too many more years these places wouldn't even be livable, and a few more after that it would all be driftwood and rust.

But here he was going to war over it.

An unwinnable war, of course, the only kind he knew how to fight. There were simply too many deathless. They could slaughter millions, but it just wouldn't matter. More would come. And he very much doubted their ability to slaughter millions.

That put him in an interesting dilemma. He could organize a retreat and lead them back to the Ark, but abandoning Lima would only prolong the problem. The deathless would come for the Ark sooner rather than later, and when they came they'd be overwhelmed.

He had no doubt that the Director would have some sort of bold plan, but Jordan lacked that strategic brilliance. That meant working with what he did have. Tactical brilliance.

Which is why he was cowering in the shadows instead of leading the assault, as Vimal had wanted. Jordan was about to test a theory, and if he was correct it would be the swiftest way to derail today's offensive.

He studied the southern horizon, and welcomed the pre-dawn breeze drifting up off the ocean as it ruffled through his fur. He'd lost the line where he ended and the wolf began.

There is no line, Ka-Dun, his beast rumbled. *We are one. You have found true unity, Ark Lord.*

"And what do you think of my plan?" Jordan growled softly, the words lost to the wind. There was no need to speak aloud, but unlike Blair he didn't shape unless he had to. Did conversing with his beast count as shaping?

It is worthy of an Ark Lord, the beast rumbled thoughtfully. *If it is successful you will not only foil this assault, but dramatically deter the likelihood of another.*

"Yeah, you get it." He gave a hard smile, one intended for the deathless he was about to introduce himself to. "If it's a group of scattered warlords, and I start killing warlords, I'm thinking it might be harder to find volunteers. For a little while at least."

The familiar distant thunder of incoming artillery echoed over the hills moments before the shells themselves detonated on the rippling shields Roberts had installed. Jordan hadn't seen them function from this vantage, and it was all the more impressive. He'd been in enough war zones to see the collateral damage that came from shelling, drones, or missiles. Roberts was saving lives.

Jordan excelled at taking them.

He poured everything into his blur and darted from rooftop to rooftop as he raced south, toward the distant thunder. There was no way to measure his velocity, but he wagered that he was moving too fast to detect. Even cameras would struggle, as they'd only pick him up in a single frame.

The hills whipped by and he left Lima, then paralleled the broken freeway as it led to the deathless encampment. Their enemies had made no effort to disguise their camp, or even to defend it.

Or them, rather. There were seven distinct camps, but only one currently lobbing artillery on his allies. A deathless in a black and green uniform was dropping another shell into an antiquated cannon, while another held some sort of radar dish that they were somehow using for spotting.

A platoon of deathless armed with assault rifles waited on the balls of their feet, ready to charge, a pack of rabid jackals waiting for prey to die.

Jordan counted four among those ranks that were also blurring, fast enough that they could see him, but they moved in molasses, while he glided into combat at full speed. He could have slammed them all together and ended it right then, but Jordan was a hunter. He'd been trained to expend the least amount of resources to achieve the victory, while maintaining minimal risk.

His claws scythed trails through the air and sent blood fountaining as he sliced a ragged path through the deathless. The very last one raised a rifle and managed to get a shot off, which showed how little they understood blurring. The bullet wound lazily toward Jordan, and he tapped it lightly with his mind, then sent it spinning back at the shooter's brainstem.

The deathless began to dive out of the way, and probably would have made it, but Jordan seized him telekinetically and held him in place. The bullet ended things a moment later, and all the bodies finally clattered to the ground as Jordan released the blur.

None rose.

There were six more camps to go. He blurred to the next, which was even less prepared. One of them was even lounging on a chaise atop a van, complete with an umbrella to keep the sun off. Talk about vain. Didn't deathless recharge directly from the sun?

Jordan bounded through them, and cut them down before they could respond. Blurring really was an unfair advantage.

In the age before, his beast rumbled, *the blur separated the wheat from the chaff. If you cannot keep up, then you die forgotten. Even mighty Sobek, the toughest god to have ever lived, it is said, does not neglect his blur.*

Jordan wasn't used to the beast being so talkative. He thought of it sort of like a virtual assistant with a vast repository of research data. That data might be outdated by a sun-cycle, but it was still useful.

"I know almost nothing about Sobek," Jordan mused aloud as he blurred to the third group, this one a bit larger than the others. "Enlighten me, beast."

The deathless sprang off like a herd of panicked gazelle, all running in different directions. The scene wrenched a memory from the recesses. Jordan remembered being the guy running, in that case from Isis. She had been the terrible avenging goddess, and had ripped his legs off.

They ran from him the same way Mohn Corp. had run from the Mother. And they died just as badly. Jordan cut down the third group, and managed to reach the fourth by the time the rest had fled.

All but one figure.

A deathless in an expensive dark suit and sunglasses stood beneath an oak tree, one of many that had been planted in the park where he stood. He nodded at Jordan as the grisly work continued, but made no move to flee.

Jordan finished his work, and let the last two camps depart to spread word of what had happened. He'd repeat as necessary, though he suspected that it would never again be this easy.

"Well done," the suited man called in a thick Brazilian accent. "I am quite impressed. Pardon, but have you time for a chat, Ark Lord?"

"Maybe." Jordan straightened from the final deathless's now truly lifeless corpse. "Who are you? I can smell the rot. You're deathless."

"Indeed," the man called back cheerfully. He straightened a crimson tie, then strode boldly down toward Jordan. He resembled a latin version of the Director, if the Director had ever actually smiled.

"I am called Camiero. And you are Ark Lord Jordan. If your people haven't yet provided the intel, they will. I am the commander of our forces, such as they are. A pleasure to meet you."

Jordan approached cautiously, but merely eyed the man's extended hand until it was withdrawn. After it had, he loomed over Camiero, their difference in muscle obvious even if he hadn't been wearing his warform.

"You've besieged my people." Jordan's words began glacial and ended arctic. "Every day your people rain bombs. You're trying to wipe us out. I am not shaking your hand. In fact, I'm searching for a single reason why I shouldn't end you right now. You know who I am. Are you really that confident you can take me?"

"Best you in a fight?" Camiero offered a self-deprecating eye roll. "No, no, no. I would certainly lose such a contest, and if you seek to murder me in cold blood then there is little I can do. Apologies for the pun."

"But you're here." Jordan folded his arms, and fought the urge to attack. There had to be a reason why this smug little bastard was so confident.

"Indeed." The deathless straightened his tie once more, a concession to nervousness, perhaps? He didn't sweat, so Jordan couldn't measure that. "I wanted to meet you, and to offer some advice. The deathless fear the old gods, but not the new. Your Ark is broken, and you are from our world. They do not fear you. Either produce a god of sufficient antiquity, or today's stunt will buy you less time than you'd like."

Jordan cocked his head, and considered invading Camiero's mind. Just wasn't his style. "Let's say I could produce such a god, one who'd been in the royal court. The court of the daughter of Ra herself, the goddess Sekhmet."

"Who do you have in mind?" Camiero rubbed his hands together gleefully, like a child about to conduct mischief.

"Guy by the name of Irakesh." Jordan's arm shot out and he seized Camiero by the throat before the deathless could move. The little guy made no move to resist, and merely eyed Jordan passively. Odd little bastard. "I can bring him if you think it would keep your people at bay. But before I do that I want to know why you're trying to stall your own forces."

"A letter I received," Camiero explained matter-of-factly. "My orders are to raze Lima and kill every champion, then move on to the Ark and scour it of all life. After this task is accomplished my people will be offered to the Builders as a sacrifice. Nox thinks I do not see what is happening, but I do, and...this letter changes everything."

"Show me the letter." Jordan made no move to let the deathless go. If anything he tightened his grip.

The deathless fished a letter out and held it out for inspection. "Would you like me to read it to you?"

"Do it." Jordan had no idea where this performance was taking them, and the longer he tarried the more dangerous this became. Still, he was curious enough to listen.

"Hades is a fool," the man began, "and has sold us to the Builders. The day will come soon when we must resist. If we do not all is lost. Delay the end of Lima. Speak to Jordan, and tell him the Director is with him." Camiero looked up at me with hawkish eyes that belied his good natured exterior. "Do you have any idea what he means?"

"Maybe," Jordan rumbled, and released Camiero, then took a step back. Why would Nox send a message like that? The Director was with him? "It sounds like someone is playing a dangerous game."

"Dangerous indeed. We will speak again, Ark Lord." Camiero gave a polished bow, then dissipated into a cloud of familiar green mist, proving he could have done it at any time.

Jordan shook his head, then blurred back toward safety. If delivering Irakesh would buy him time he could probably arrange that. He didn't have time for games, though.

He needed to find out where he stood with Sobek, and soon.

9

DELAYING TACTICS

J ordan neither knew nor trusted David, the commander of whatever Project Solaris was supposed to be. In his mind it was linked to the Director, which meant it was suspect. That said, David had done right by him, and Anput thought highly of the man.

Besides, Jordan was about to ask a favor.

He marched to the edge of the pier, and imagined he could feel Sobek approaching. The crocodilian god could arrive any day now, and while Jordan needed that to happen for his plan to work, he had one last task to attend to first.

"Okay, Ark," Jordan whispered under his breath as he closed his eyes. "Do whatever it is you do. Talk to the Black Knight Satellite. Send it a signal telling David that I need to speak to—"

"How can I help you, Ark Lord?" A ghostly image of the wiry thirty-year-old appeared before Jordan. He could see the waves through the man, though he was substantial enough to hold a conversation.

"I need Irakesh," he explained without preamble. "I never thought I'd see the day, but we're in a position where we need him to be the douchey god that he is. It's the only thing that's going to keep the deathless bickering long enough for me to find a way to save Peru. Even then...I don't know if it's possible. The continent is dead. All of it, except us. I don't see how we can hold out. Even if I had Isis... there's just too many of them without a fully powered Ark, and mine is broken."

Jordan briefly cringed at himself for opening up like this guy was his therapist, but if he was asking a favor he at least owed David some context.

"Sounds like a bad situation. From what Trevor has said Irakesh is like pouring oil on a fire, but if you want him, then he's all yours. I will not miss his chatter." David gave an eye roll that Jordan understood as few could. Irakesh could really get to you, especially if you were forced to be around him for any length of time. "Where do you want him delivered? Will you charge extra to take him right now?"

Jordan surprised himself with a chuckle. The kid was funny.

"Right here, if that works."

"Done." David's ghostly figure disappeared, and in his place stood a familiar and terrifying figure.

Irakesh might be the only old god who still looked like an old god. Anput had blended like a chameleon, but this guy? He flaunted his origins. Jordan could respect that, at least, and he needed to find some common ground. For a little while at least.

"Ah, the Lord of the Broken Ark," the fucker quipped as he adjusted an ivory tunic straight out of *Jewel of the Nile*. The collar around Irakesh's neck tensed every muscle in Jordan's body. He remembered the collar of Shi-Dun. Trevor had held the leash. "I have you to thank for my freedom. What calamity has arrived that is so dire that you can justify my release?"

His voice was jovial, and his accent almost British, if you squinted. So at odds with the razored fangs and harsh nuclear glare in those inhuman eyes.

"Your people asked for you." Jordan folded his arms and allowed a smile. "Seems they're in need of a hero. Or a leader at least. They're being hurled into Peru as cannon fodder, because Hades demanded it. He's working with the Builders."

"Yes, yes." Irakesh waved dismissively. "I've been imprisoned with nothing to do but watch events unfold. You're an Ark Lord without an Ark. This only ends one way, especially when viewed from your impressive, but limited, tactical vision."

"We beat you, remember?" Jordan unfolded his arms, and considered how much Irakesh was worth alive versus the reduction in stress eliminating him would cause.

"I mean no insult." Irakesh raised both pale palms in a placating gesture. "You are extremely skilled in your disciplines. Please remember, though, that I have been alive for a long time, and that I've cheated by devouring the minds of others. Tactics and strategy and subterfuge come to me as breathing does to you. You need me to delay. You want me to sew chaos or convince them to stop attacking, yes?"

"Yeah," Jordan allowed, more than a little annoyed by the accurate prediction. "That's exactly what I need. Slow them down. Or turn them against Hades, if you can."

"Oh, I can," Irakesh crowed. His ghastly smile grew to inhuman proportions. "I will make them dance, Ark Lord, but to my tune. I will forge them into an army. We will cull the demons from our ranks, and I won't have to lift a finger for any of that to happen."

Jordan hesitated. How bad were things when giving one of your worst enemies a massive army was the best tactical play? Doing this guaranteed that the continent would fall. It might take decades. Or centuries even. But eventually every tree would be gone. Deathless didn't need oxygen, and wouldn't care that it might doom the few survivors clinging to life.

This couldn't be the right choice.

"You seem skeptical, Ark Lord. Is that of my ability to win, or in my motives afterwards?" Irakesh's grin slowed to a smirk. "I assure you that we have a common enemy in the Builders. They are coming, Jordan. They care nothing for our squabbles, dead or undead, demon or werewolf. We will be terraformed, or conscripted, but whatever they intend I promise we will not enjoy the remaking. We must stand together, Jordan. You understand that, yes?"

Jordan couldn't believe what he was hearing. Either Irakesh was the best liar he'd ever met, or he sincerely believed what he was saying.

"I'd love for that to be true." Jordan licked his chops, and allowed a low growl to escape. "I want to be allies. We do need to stand together. Please don't make me regret this, Irakesh."

"I will not." Irakesh extended his right hand with the fingers splayed. "I make this accord, Ark Lord. I will stand beside you in battle, until the elder ones are dust. I will not take up arms against you. Neither will I allow them to be taken up against you. Grant me the same."

Do not trust this snake, Ka-Dun, his beast rumbled. *Sincerity can be faked.*

Jordan seized Irakesh's hand, and shook it firmly. "I'll stand with you, Irakesh. I will keep you alive, and fight beside you, until you betray me or one of mine, or humanity. We are allies. I've got your back."

That didn't mean he trusted Irakesh, but right now he needed him. If that meant letting Irakesh think he was some first tour jarhead, then so be it. He could play a role, when he had to.

"Come on," Jordan insisted, as he nodded away out over the water. "We're going to meet with Camiero."

Jordan reached for his shaping, and lifted himself from the dock, and up over the water. Irakesh melted into a cloud of green motes, and began drifting after Jordan. He couldn't help but grin as the wind whipped through his fur. A flying werewolf and his toxic cloud on his way to tea with a zombie. You couldn't make that shit up.

They made for a lone yacht with both sails down. It bobbed in the water, with no sign of life save for a single figure seated at a table on the top deck, in a room lined with windows.

Good. As Camiero's invitation had promised, the oily man had come alone. Jordan flew closer, and landed on the rear deck. He shifted back to human form as he pushed the doors open, and by the time he stepped inside he wore a black t-shirt and camo fatigues.

Camiero rose from the table and was all smiles in a freshly

pressed suit that looked to have been recently tailored. "Come in, come in. Sit, please. Alas, I have provided no refreshment as this is a matter of some urgency. The longer I am away the more dangerous this becomes."

"We'll be swift," Jordan promised as he moved to join the deathless. He noted that Camiero's attention was all on Irakesh, and that there was real awe there. "I've brought an elder god, as promised. Irakesh is quite capable of welding your people into an effective fighting force. One capable of fighting back against Hades."

"Excellent." Camiero rose, and extended a hand to the deathless.

Irakesh peered down at the proferred hand in disdain. "Don't touch me, cur. You are less than our youngest children, and you're in charge? It seems my people have fallen far. Do not fear, underling. I have come to help guide you."

Camiero slowly lowered his hand, and then back to me. "He's perfect."

"Good." Jordan tensed in his seat as he stared through the wide windows at Lima. "Now keep the deathless busy while I find another elder god to annoy. We're going to need boats and I know someone who has some."

10

STATUS REPORT

B lair couldn't believe his eyes when the massive ferry bumped up against the dock and several deathless moved to secure it. He'd taken the trip from Larkspur so many times, but never since the world had ended.

That they'd somehow restored this little piece of it, a daily commute he'd never appreciated, mattered. The world had been falling for a long time, but it was finally going the other direction. Finally picking itself back up.

"This way, Ark Lord." Melissa delivered an excited wave from the dock where she awaited Blair's arrival. Her good mood was infectious, and Blair found himself waving back.

"You like her," Liz accused as she wrapped an arm around his waist. "That's allowed, you know. She's a good administrator, and a shrewd judge of people. She's become a better person since you put her in charge, and she's really worked to include everyone, from what Alicia tells me."

"She's done an amazing job." Blair stepped out onto the deck, and sent the next part in case anyone was listening. *She's also incredibly ambitious, and totally ruthless. I don't think she's a terrible person, but if her survival is at stake she'll flip faster than I can blur.*

Liz released his waist, and disappointment flowed through their bond. He loved that she'd remained so trusting, but he'd been burned too many times to trust easily. There was simply too much riding on the outcome of his decisions.

"It's good to see you, Melissa." Blair offered her a hug as he approached her entourage, and she returned it. The faint scent of wildflowers clung to her, probably a name brand perfume. He'd never been good at those things. They masked the decay, but not from his nose. "The only thing missing are the food trucks, and I believe you've restored this city to its pre-cataclysmic demise."

"Better!" Melissa released him, and hurried up the path along the water that led into the harbor building where she'd set up her headquarters. "I have so much to show you. We've restored power to the entire city."

"What?" Liz stopped in her tracks, forcing Melissa to do the same thing. "How? Santa Rosa still doesn't have power in more than about ten percent of homes, though most of the rest have partial solar. Where are you getting the power?"

"Shaping." Melissa grinned as she opened the door and stepped inside.

Blair followed and it was his turn to stop in his tracks. The building was air conditioned. He hadn't felt air conditioning in he didn't even know how long.

"We use the radiation we produce." She pointed at a thick black conduit running along the ground. "It can be piped anywhere, and we've modified the power grids to convert it to electricity at the substation level. I don't really understand the details, if I'm being honest. I know it works, and that our engineers are now selling the technology to central Californian settlements."

"But not to Santa Rosa?" Liz raised an eyebrow. "Please tell me that's because the power source differs, and not because you don't trade with Santa Rosa."

"We do quite a bit of trade, and not just with Santa Rosa. Here we are." She stopped in front of a massive miniature diorama of California set up across several broad tables. Melissa passed a hand through it, revealing the illusion. "Our shapers update this daily. This is the political situation. As you can see, the Bay Area is doing great. So is the rest of Northern California. Champions are striking out on their own to found settlements, and we've sent trade caravans to sell them essentials at highly inflated prices they are happy to pay. By next year that last part will be entirely automated, and we'll send drones with goods."

"What about Southern California?" Liz wandered down to that side of the map, which showed a number of political boundaries, each probably belonging to a different warlord.

Blair cared more about what was happening across the rest of the continent, but he'd press for details after she finished her report on California. The whole continent was his responsibility, and he needed to understand it all. He might have to call David in for aerial footage, but he was reluctant to contact him as it risked the grey men discovering the black knight satellite.

"Southern California is a mess, but no more than it was before the world ended." Melissa rolled her eyes as she stared at Los Angeles county. It sounded like a personal grudge. "It's the perfect haven for deathless. Plenty of sun, and the fact that there's no food or drinkable water doesn't matter to deathless. Dozens of warlords have risen up, and Santa Clarita even set up a town council. There are all sorts of small local governments trying not to get swallowed up by their neighbors. The only thing they can agree on is that you're the largest threat they all face."

"Common ground, at least." Blair snorted. "What about the Sierras?"

"The great bear has closed its borders to man, and we've honored that. People who stay below about four thousand feet are left alone. Go higher than that, and you're going to get mauled." The way Melissa explained it suggested she approved. Blair did too. More common ground.

"And the rest of the continent?" Blair leaned closer to the illusion, marveling at the level of detail. Right down to individual buildings and streets.

"There the news is less good. Yosemite and the Sierras form a natural boundary, but past that it's a lawless wasteland, and only strength matters. No single power has come out on top, but the number of contenders is falling. I can have a brief prepared, if you'd like." Melissa smoothed her jacket, a subtle expression of her irritation at not having complete data on hand perhaps. "Whatever powers have risen in the midwest and in the east, they are almost certainly corrupted by demons. We have warned the lords in SoCal of the threat, and reminded them what happened here. If there are openly demonic lords down there I am not aware of them, though undoubtedly spies remain."

"Undoubtedly." Blair scratched at his beard. It itched and he was already thinking about shaving it. He could just shape the hair away, but he missed the shaving ritual. "I want you to arrange a meeting with every government. Every group, no matter how small, can send a representative. Find us a location to hold it, and we'll do a summit. I'm bringing them into the fold."

Melissa shifted uncomfortably, but where once she'd have stifled her response at least she now spoke up. "If you dictate your will to them like they're slaves many of them will react badly. Remember, these people were fiercely independent before they died. They led incredibly difficult lives, made worse by institutions they trusted. You're that institution now. I feel a light touch will get you further."

Blair could see the wisdom in that. He waited to see if his beast would offer further comment, but his companion remained silent during matters not pertaining to war.

"That makes a lot of sense. We need to have them ready for the Builder assault, or a demonic attack. How do you suggest we proceed in unifying these people as a single government?"

"I can answer that." Liz cleared her throat. "I've lived among the poor on three continents. They want a government who can actually improve their lives in a tangible way. It isn't about what you can get. It's about what you can give."

"Wow, that seems like an incredibly basic principle I should already know. I am not good at governing." Blair turned back to

Melissa. "You have shaping technology, and you said you're selling it. What are they paying you in?"

She tapped her lip for a moment as she considered. "A lot of things. Metals mostly. Other scavenged valuables. Canned food, which we sell to the champions and the humans."

"Not any more. Now every city that joins New California will receive a complete electrical retrofitting free of charge. As you'll still need to pay your engineers, they'll be compensated directly by me. Have the engineers gather to discuss their terms, and we'll arrange a meeting where I set their rates." Blair was on a roll as the ideas kept coming, but knew he'd have to pause for air eventually. "Before you ask, I chose 'New California', because every Californian resident will identify with that term."

"That will work on SoCal," Liz pointed out, "but it's going to alienate Oregon and Washington. They're not in love with Californians moving north."

"Yeah, I thought about that. Nothing we do is going to change that opinion." Blair had a solution, but it was risky. "Oregon, Washington, and Idaho will be their own territory. They will belong to the champions, to do with as they collectively decide. That's Great Pack territory. I've sent Yukon to watch over that area. As for New California... everyone will be welcome here. Deathless and champion alike."

He hadn't actually done the sending. Yukon had gone on his own, with Alicia. The battle at the Proto Ark, and the whole Windigo episode had scarred both of them. They were grieving, enough that Blair had no trouble overlooking them leaving without a word. Yukon had been close with John Rivers, and on the heels of losing the mother...Blair didn't have the heart to tell him what they were trying to do in case it failed.

"What about the deathless?" Melissa pressed. Anger had entered her expression for the first time. "We represent most of the population, but it's pretty clear you don't like us. If the humans and werewolves get their own territory, why is the rest shared? Why don't deathless get their own state?"

"They have it." Blair's eyes narrowed dangerously, though her question was hardly out of line. "They have the rest of the world. They have the United States, Mexico, and Canada. They have South America, and are driving Jordan from their shores. We have no idea what the situation in Asia even is, but I promise you the deathless are doing fine. I'm not building a world for ruthless corpses. I'm building a world for the living. You have a place in that world, as does any deathless who wants it, but I've seen what happens when the death-less go off to rule themselves. They get infested with demons, and that will mean the end of everything, for all of us, when the Builders arrive."

"Are you so certain that deathless are the only ones corrupted?" Melissa drove the question into his heart like a dagger.

"No, I'm not." His shoulders slumped. "But it does seem a lot more prevalent among your people. You want me to relent, and offer the deathless more respect? Give me a reason to do that. Implement the changes I've asked for. If you implement them in good faith, and we can bring the state together, then we can select an area for death-less to go. We'll give them a kingdom we sanction and support, and if you want to run it instead of New California you're welcome to do so."

"I'd prefer this job." Melissa relaxed a hair, the combativeness melting away. "I'll arrange things with SoCal. I think they'll find the New California proposal interesting, especially since it includes power and internet. We certainly can't do any worse than Khastcom used to."

"Thank you, Melissa." Tension bled from Blair's shoulders. One troubling task down, about six million to go.

11

WAKING JES'KA

Blair light walked away from the ferry building with Liz in tow, and arrived inside the Ark of the Redwood. Physical exhaustion wasn't a real issue, but mental exhaustion was. There were just so many separate areas he needed to keep track of, and you could only delegate away so much.

"What's up next?" Liz's voice carried similar exhaustion.

"I've got a few more things to do, but you're free to relax." He rolled his shoulders as he strode through the deserted Ark. "I need to contact David. We've got a call scheduled in a couple minutes. I'll catch him up on the meeting we just had, and see what he can tell us about the state of things globally. We left Jordan in a tight spot. I don't know if I could win with a fully powered Ark and a Primary Access Key. He has no resources down there. I've thought about offering his people asylum."

"That's a tough sell." Liz sighed heavily, and Blair could only blink at her. It was the very last response he'd expected. "What? Just becomes I'm an activist doesn't mean I'm blind to logistics. Those people are from a different climate, with no resources, and no means of making a living here. We could give them land, but I think Santa Rosa and some of the other new communities would resent it. If he has nowhere else to go, sure, but I don't know that I'd be the one to offer the solution. If he needs us, he'll ask."

Blair nodded but did it reluctantly. He let that flow through their bond. "It has the other downside of putting all the remaining champions in one place, which makes for a tempting target. We have a lot of enemies, and more on the way. I just wish I could help is all."

"I know." She squeezed his arm, then released him and headed up the corridor. "I'm going to grab a shower and get changed. I'll track you down after you finish with David. It's time to wake her, Blair, and you aren't getting out of it this time."

"I know." His shoulders slumped, but it was mostly in jest. It had taken a long time for Blair to come around to the idea of adding another ancient goddess to the mix, but they needed her. She knew things Liz needed, and they'd need her claws in combat, most likely. "Come find me, and we'll do it together."

Blair headed to the central chamber. This one was identical to the excavation he'd spent so much time in back in Peru, minus the statue of the Mother. It called up memories of Bridget, and Steve, and just how far off the rails things had gone even before the world had ended. He'd had no idea what lay in store for him. He still didn't.

"Blair?" David's voice came from behind him, and he turned to see a holographic projection, at the exact second he'd said he'd arrive. "I can keep us safe for about three minutes with no risk. Anything longer and we're in a bad way. What do you need?"

"Status on the former United States."

"Lots of demon kingdoms." David brushed his hair from his eyes, exposing a face young enough to still belong in college, in Blair's opinion. A lot had been asked of the kid. "No immediate threats. I'd say you've got three to five years before someone consolidates the rest of the nation."

"Perfect. How's Jordan?"

David grinned at the question. "I just dropped off Irakesh a little while ago at Jordan's request. He's installed him as some sort of puppet leader to mess with the deathless advance. I don't have more details yet, but I'm watching to see how it all plays out."

"What else do you think I need to know?" Blair kept each question succinct, which wasn't easy for an academic.

"There are something like a dozen demonic arcologies forming." David's expression darkened. "I have no idea what goes on inside, but they're demon cities, and all seem to have a massive military. Those things are going to be a huge threat when the grey men get here, and I expect will be their power bases."

"Identifying that early is critical. Thank you. Anything else?"

"What are you working on?" David glanced over his shoulder at something in the background. A clock maybe.

"Temporal shaping. We're going to try to rescue Isis. Trevor is working on the research now, and might end up contacting you for help."

"Take extreme care," David warned. "I've got a little experience with time travel. My mom was a precog, and I think I inherited that too. Changing time has unexpected consequences. If you go trying to get back something you lost you might succeed, but the universe is going to take something else to compensate."

That sounded positively chilling, like a universal law he needed to be very aware of.

"We'll be damned careful, and we'll make sure we understand the risks before we make an attempt."

"Time's up. Take care, Blair." Holo-David disappeared, the whole exchange so rapid it left Blair in a confused whirl as to what to tackle first.

Jes'Ka still seemed like the smart move, and would make Liz happy as well. He entered the rejuvenation chamber on the far side of the room, with its six crystal pods where Ark Lords from two species had slumbered away countless millennia.

Only two pods were occupied, one by a mysterious dark-skinned man at home in mesolithic America, and by a woman that Blair had spent a long time staring at. Not because she was beautiful, though the blond woman was breathtaking. Because she represented the world he'd spent his life trying to understand.

She understood mankind's early development, because she'd

participated in it. Like Isis, this Jes'Ka had probably been founda-
tional in many early American myths. Definitely in North America,
but maybe also in South America, as Isis had. What would Joseph
Campbell have to say about the role these women had chosen? Was
Blair destined to take a similar role?

So many questions.

He stopped next to Jes'Ka's pod and was unsurprised when Liz
stepped from the shadows next to it. "How long have you been
there?"

"I take short showers." She grinned down at the sleeping woman.
"She can teach me to fight. Really fight. I know the basics of shaping,
and she can focus on advanced stuff."

"If she's willing to teach you." Blair rested a hand on the sarcophagus. "She might not agree."

"I want to find out, one way or another." Liz rested a hand on the
hilt of the blade she'd inherited from Irakesh. It wasn't as potent as
Excalibur, but it made her a damned sight better armed than Jes'Ka.

"As do I," a sultry feminine voice issued from the shadows.

Blair started when he realized Anput was in the room, but
prevented himself from attacking. That had sadly become his default
in many situations. "You're welcome, as I'll take whatever backup I
can get, but please announce when you're in my Ark next time. I'd
hate to accidentally react like you're an intruder."

"Point taken, Lord." Anput inclined her head respectfully. "I will
warn you next time."

"Are there any other precautions you want to take?" Liz had
moved to stand at the foot of Jes'Ka's sarcophagus. "Do we know how
or when her mother put her in stasis? Are they still on good terms?"

"Little made it back to Africa and deathless court." Anput
watched the sleeping woman warily. "Most of her adventurers came
in the centuries before she left for the new world, or at least the ones
I'm familiar with, anyway."

"Well, if we're going to do this...." Blair willed energy through his
hand and into the sarcophagus. As with most Builder tech it could be
controlled directly with thought. He'd spent so much time trying to

discover a sequence of gems that needed to be pressed, when all he'd needed to do was will her to wake.

The rejuvenation pod warmed, and Jes'Ka slowly rose through the top as if being ejected from a lump of melting ice. She coughed once, and her eyes fluttered open. Jes'Ka hopped from the rejuvenator and landed lightly on her feet as her eyes swept the room. She extended a hand and a golden spear appeared in her right hand, the Sunsteel emanating power. She wore a black doeskin tunic, and homespun leather pants. The garments weren't just functional. They were beautiful, and each was stitched with countless silver runes. Power came from those as well, and definitely piqued Blair's interest. You could make magic clothes?

Blair wasted no time. He slowly raised the Primary Access Key, then sent at her. Jes'Ka's mind was like pushing through molasses, her defenses more numerous and layered than any he'd tried to pierce. *My name is Blair. I am going to give you our language, English. You are in the new cycle, and we are trying to rescue your parents. Please give us a chance to explain.*

Very well, the woman sent back fiercely. *I will allow you to explain why you are in my Mother's Ark. Then you will wake my companion, Lucas.*

Blair glanced at the dark-skinned man in the other rejuvenator. He'd been important enough that Isis had brought him to the present. Some of his clothing had also been made by Jes'Ka, though the spear next to him was far more crude...wood and obsidian. A bow and quiver also lay within the sarcophagus, themselves a treasure of antiquity Blair would give anything to study for a few hours. So many clues about their origins.

Blair didn't reply, but did flood Jes'Ka's mind with his childhood ABC's until she'd grasped enough to converse normally.

"This is Liz, my direct progeny, mate, and all around badass." Blair raised a hand to indicate Liz, who smiled hopefully at Jes'Ka.

"The Ark Lord is your mate?" Jes'Ka gave Liz a once-over, and clearly didn't like what she saw. "Times must be desperate. If you wish it, Ark Lord, we can discuss your needs in private. Lucas will keep her amused, if you wish."

"Your efforts are wasted, trollop." Anput seethed out of the shadows, her fangs displayed for the first time. Blair had always known she must possess them, but she'd always taken pains to appear human. "The Ark Lord is loyal. You will not make him stray, as you did my husband."

In a flash Jes'Ka had been replaced by a blond Ka-Ken easily as tall as Liz. Her fur glittered with silver runes, the same that covered her clothing. In that moment Blair understood what they were for. The runes protected her from shaping, and you couldn't attack the garments directly while a champion was shifted. Impressive.

"You're damned right he's loyal." Liz's hand had wrapped around the hilt of her blade. "Enough games. We were told you love your mother and your father. Both were killed five years ago by Set. We have a chance to rewrite history and save them. Blair will shape time, and we'll need to distract Set while your parents escape. I'm strong, but I don't know a fraction of what you do about shaping. I was hoping you'd teach me."

"To stand against Set?" Jes'Ka laughed scornfully. "Little girl, you will need more than a few weeks of sparring to battle my uncle. If I agree to this—and I have agreed to nothing, nor will I without hearing a plan—then we only do this when *I* say you are ready."

"Agreed." Liz's eyes narrowed, and Blair had a feeling they weren't going to be best friends any time soon. So long as Jes'Ka taught Liz, it would be enough.

He had a million other tasks to be about, but he knew Jes'Ka wouldn't let her companion's slumber go unless he addressed it.

"Jes'Ka, when Liz is satisfied that you have trained her to the best of your ability, then I will wake your companion. Not a moment before, and it isn't up for discussion. Train my Ka-Ken, I will wake your friend, and then we will save your parents. Deal?" Blair squared his shoulders, and refused to back down. He knew he had kind of a mousy-professor vibe going even after becoming a champion, but hopefully his authority shone through.

"We have an accord." Jes'Ka delivered a dazzling, inviting smile. "If you'd like to...participate in the sparring I'm sure your Ka-Ken would be open to sharing."

"No," Liz growled. "She wouldn't."

Blair leeched all emotion from his voice. "Just train her. And do it quickly. Our enemies are closing in."

12

BEFORE THE BUILDERS

Trevor massaged his temples and considered a different approach. He'd asked Ba everything he could think of to get around the blocks around the temporal shaping research, to no avail.

The Builders had sealed it for a reason, and weren't going to leave a casual workaround. That research might as well not exist...except it had been pioneered at some point. How had they discovered it? What steps might they have researched leading up to temporal shaping?

If he could find the clues, the stepping stones, then maybe he could learn enough on his own to duplicate their research. That would require too much time and experimentation, unfortunately. Dangerous experimentation.

"Pardon me, Trevor?" Percy rose shakily from his cot and hobbled over to the console where Trevor worked. "You seem a bit flustered, which is understandable. Perhaps if you lay the problem out I can offer a fresh set of eyes, poor as they are."

Trevor couldn't shake his mistrust of the man, though everything Anput had said made sense. There was no threat in him, and he'd been here long enough to do all sorts of damage had he wanted to.

"I'm trying to locate any of the milestone research leading up to temporal shaping." Trevor figured there was no harm in sharing his dilemma, even if there was something sinister to the old man. "This city clearly uses it for the time dilation, so that might be an area where I could start."

"A sound line of reasoning." Percy removed his spectacles and cleaned them on his shirt. It exposed the cracked and reddened skin where the glasses had been sitting. The man was coming apart. "If you can find practical applications, then perhaps you can reverse engineer things. Were it me, I'd start in their council chambers. Investigate the areas where they lived and worked. See what you can learn. Perhaps it will help you to ask the right questions."

Suspicion flared once more.

Really? Anput's voice echoed playfully in his mind. *I'm not going to tell you how to do your job, but he just gave you a good idea. I'm not sure that makes him the top suspect for nefarious spy.*

"I'll go investigate the council chambers. Those are mentioned repeatedly." He turned to Anput, who appeared to be half listening as she studied a holographic display of a DNA strand at her terminal. "Anput, do you want to stay here, or go with me to investigate the chambers? I could use a second set of eyes."

She glanced up over her spectacles. "Hmm? I could use a break after the episode waking Jes'Ka. That woman unmakes me, and this is starting to blur. I can't find any patterns to the markers to suggest why you're alive. I never intended the virus to do that, and cannot figure out why it did. So take my mind off things. What are we looking for?"

Trevor nodded his goodbye to Percy, and they filed out of the pyramid and into the greater city. It still reeked of smoke, and though bodies had been cleaned up none of the damage had been repaired. This place, already teetering on its last legs, had finally toppled and now lay in its final resting place. The question was...what could they wrest from her bones before she expired?

"You asked what I was looking for." Trevor fixed his attention on the pyramid at the center of the city, a stepped version that predated the larger pyramids dotting the edge of the city, like the one where they'd been doing their research. "I want to follow their footsteps. At one point the Builders had no temporal shaping and no ability to dilate time. How and when did that change? If we can find a milestone or proof, or anything, I'm gambling it will lead us to a way around their block on the archive."

Anput pocketed her glasses and replaced them with a stylish pair of oversized sunglasses that Audrey Hepburn would have enjoyed. "That's not much to go on, but when you've got no better options the shotgun approach is often the best method. Hopefully we'll spot something. If nothing else we'll get some space from our respective research, and after three solid days I need a break. I think you do too."

Trevor nodded at that as he rolled his neck. Aches and pains were a real thing now, though his body did seem a lot more resilient than when he'd been a normal mortal.

They continued in silence as they entered the shadow of the pyramid. Trevor expected a champion to block their progress, but no one did. There were so few now, and all probably had business they were about. Some may have left the city entirely.

The tunnel inside loomed before them, and reminded Trevor of their recent battle here. The scars were everywhere. Blasts on the walls. Pits in the stone, from acidic drool. The whole thing reeked of death. He hated being in here, but forced himself forward. Some physical reactions he did not miss.

They wound down through the various levels, retracing the steps the champions had taken when falling back before the demons. Only the lowest level remained relatively untouched. The battle either hadn't made it this far, or had petered out by this point.

"Trevor." Anput waved to get his attention. "Over here."

She stood near the kind of doorway Trevor had hoped to find. Small and unobtrusive, against the far wall of the amphitheater where the council met. The bronze was almost indistinguishable from the wall, and he might have missed it had he wandered by.

Trevor placed a hand against the door, and as he pushed, willed it to open. Intent seemed to matter a great deal with Builder tech, and

Trevor grinned when the door pushed inward and exposed a set of steep stairs leading deeper inside.

"Ladies first." Anput grinned as she pushed passed him and blurred down the stairs.

Trevor followed, also blurring but much more slowly. By the time he reached the bottom there was no sign of Anput, who'd likely disappeared into the shadows, or hidden herself with an illusion.

The room at the bottom had a small table with eight chairs around it. Each high-backed golden chair had a different symbol emblazoned on the headrest, though they didn't correspond to anything he'd yet seen, either in the city or in another Ark. These glyphs, or runes, were of a wholly different style. They weren't anything like Egyptian or any other Earth culture Trevor was familiar with.

"The chairs are not the right size," he realized aloud. Anput raised an eyebrow. "At least if Ba is a template for their bodies. These chairs would be too large."

"The walls are a different alloy from the rest of the city, too." She moved over to the far wall, and ran a delicate finger along the purplish metal. "I'm not familiar with it."

"Ba?" Trevor wasn't certain the construct could reach them here, even audio only, and figured it worth testing.

"Yes, Ark Lord?" A wavering voice issued from the air itself.

"What can you tell us about this room and how it was used?"

"This chamber was used for annual meetings of all seven Builders." Ba dutifully recited the facts he'd requested. "It was selected because when the door above is sealed, this chamber is impervious to all external signals. Its discovery predates my construction, as does the temple above it."

Trevor didn't reply immediately, or ask a followup question. This place had been their bolt-hole. Their security room where they plotted the fate of this planet.

"When did they stop using it?" Trevor folded his arms, and moved to inspect the sigils on the backs of the chairs. Why weren't those repeated? There were eight of them, and only seven Ark Lords so far as he knew.

There was a brief pause before Ba spoke again. "This facility was decommissioned for primary use when the Nexus came online six cycles after initial use."

"Sun-cycles, I think." Anput approached, her interest apparent. "So thirteen thousand times six...seventy-eight thousand years after this place was initially discovered they stopped using this room."

"And until that point all council meetings were held here? Are there recordings of those meetings?" Trevor paced back and forth. They were so close to something here, but he just couldn't see the shape of it yet.

"Yes, all meetings were held here." Ba paused again. "The recordings are available. Only in this room, and only when the door is closed. All ten sessions with the phrase 'temporal shaping' are available, and can be viewed here."

Anput started back up the stairs. "I'll get the door."

Trevor rubbed his hands together to ward the faint chill, and waited. A *k-thunk* came from above, and Anput returned a moment later. "Okay, Ba, start playing the projections, with any speech translated into modern American English, please. Let's begin with the most recent, as that's the one that probably has what we need."

"A moment, Ark Lord. Transferring directly to your location."

The soft light issuing from the ceiling died, and they were plunged into darkness. The only light came from the eight sigils glowing on the backs of the chairs. A pinkish one and a neighboring white-blue one flared more brightly than the others.

Ba's holographic form appeared before them...perfectly. The level of detail was far beyond the projections elsewhere in the city. He appeared a living, breathing entity, every nuance of emotion displayed on his alien visage.

"Wow." Trevor moved closer, and inspected the illusion. "This is incredible, and clearly different tech than the rest of the city."

"They discovered it. They must have." Anput had also moved to study Ba. "The Proto Ark must be their first experiments using this tech. They learned to harness this place, and everything they built stemmed from it. What is it you think? A facility? A ship?"

"Ba, can you show us the outline of the structure we're currently in?" Trevor realized he'd stacked requests, so he modified his previous instruction. "We'll watch the council meeting in a moment."

"Of course, Ark Lord." Ba raised a hand and the air next to him shimmered and displayed a cutaway of the structure they were inside of. It was clearly a fragment of something. A ship? A factory? Who knew? There wasn't enough left to identify it, just a few isolated levels that had been sheered off the main body of whatever vessel or building it had come from.

"Play the meeting," Trevor ordered as he considered the unsettling nature of this place.

The air shimmered, and a trio of half-sized figures appeared around a table identical to the one filling the room. All three were clearly the same species, one with deep-green skin, another with black, and the third with a mottled green-brown.

"Abandoning this place is madness," the green-skinned one led with, though his mouth didn't move. He was sending his thoughts telepathically. "We haven't delved even a fraction of its secrets. We know almost nothing about the circle they speak of, or how it relates to our sun. We have no idea how the ship arrived, or if they will ever return to retrieve it. Temporal shaping can provide those answers, and there is no other means of obtaining them."

"As recent experiments have proven," the black-skinned one spoke, "the results can be catastrophic. We removed a species from existence. It is gone, and we cannot reclaim it. Uluru is still angry, and I don't know that she will ever forgive you, Enki."

"I proved my point," the green-brown one gave back sullenly. "I surgically removed a useless species, and proved that nothing else about our world changed. The timeline compensated. History forgot that species as if it had never been, and the rest of our world is no different."

"The temporal matrix in Antartica is too dangerous to allow any further experiments. It is barred to you." The black-skinned Builder rose to his full height. "My continent is the most barren of all. The most devoid of life. They put the matrix there because if something goes awry it could scour that continent of life. If they were not willing to experiment, then why should we? Is it not enough that we have wrested other types of shaping from their archives? We have learned much, and in time will learn more. Can we not leave off this one dangerous area?"

"And what of my research?" The green-skinned one seethed as he stalked toward the black-skinned one. "Are we to simply erase three cycles of data, Yoggoth? I think not."

"No, it should not be destroyed." Yoggoth gestured at the room around them. "We will leave it here, in one of their storage devices, and seal this place. With the Nexus online there is no further need for us to be here. The security afforded by this place isn't needed. All seven lords can meet in the Nexus and pool our knowledge and power. This place has served its purpose. Let it be entombed, so as never to lead anyone astray as it has led us."

All three nodded at that. They'd reached their accord.

"Ba?" Trevor asked, a small smile spreading. "Is the archive they mentioned still here?"

"Indeed." Ba pointed at the center of the table, which Trevor hadn't paid much attention to. A single object lay near the center, nearly the same shade of gold as the table. It looked like an organic scale from some sort of reptile, though the scale appeared constructed from some sort of metal.

Trevor scooped up the scale and studied it. "It's heavy. Really heavy. Any idea what it is, Ba?"

"I do not know, Ark Lord." Ba's expression grew troubled. "However, an event has transpired you will wish to be apprised of. Someone has activated the light bridge. I do not know how they circumvented our security measures."

"Percy." Trevor swore under his breath.

13

ONE OF THEM

A kenat simply couldn't believe his good fortune. The Ark Lord and his curiously unliving paramour departed to investigate the trail of droppings he'd left for them. What they discovered would keep them busy for weeks, or longer.

They might not notice his departure at all, but if they did it would be with little more than mild alarm. They'd have no idea who he was, or the threat he represented. By the time they could respond he'd already be out of their reach.

He forced the host to awkwardly shamble from Kek Telek's temple, and headed the opposite direction as soon as the hominids were gone. What a fascinating species, who'd accomplished so much via shaping in a handful of cycles. Once he'd been restored to his own time he'd take steps to harness them so that they were appropriately docile by the time they returned to claim their world. They would make incredible servants.

The trek from the temple to the light bridge took an unacceptably long interval. His body continued to decay, and no amount of counter-shaping would halt that. Genetic dissolution was inevitable, and he'd guess he had less than two solar cycles to find a new host, or he risked his existence.

Akenat fortified himself with the knowledge that his enemies were little more than children. They'd left him alone in the tech he and Enki had architected. The Ark Lord assumed because the keeper wouldn't obey him that he was powerless.

That couldn't be further from the truth. All devices would respond to a specific signal pulse pattern that only he and a few other Ark Lords had ever learned. That meant he could operate the light bridge, and force it to draw power from the city's reserves instead of his body.

He smiled grimly as his host limped down the last dozen steps, and into the chamber where the light bridge was held. The very first light bridge they'd ever constructed, originally with only one destination...the First Ark. Which was the first, whatever Uluru maintained. Her hunk of rock hadn't been a true Ark until he'd shown her how to shape it.

Akenat forced the host up onto the platform, and broadcast a complex multi-layered signal. The light bridge obediently filled with energy, and his body was disintegrated and reintegrated at his destination, the light bridge at the Ark of the Cradle, so named because it had given birth both to his own species and to these new hominids.

The host tumbled to the ground, every limb spasming wildly as the body began to dissolve. Death was a certainty in that instant, something even shaping couldn't stop. But a master shaper could elongate death. Akenat drew out the dissolution, not attempting to stop it, but rather to slow the spread.

By his estimation his clock had just shorted to fourteen hours. If he could not locate a host in that time, then he would cease to exist. Thankfully, he suspected hosts would be available in abundance.

His host body was abruptly hoisted in the air, and brought around to hover before a highly dubious demonic primate. The creature lacked hair, and barely resembled the humans beyond four limbs and a similarly shaped skull. This thing had been constructed, and the taint rolled off it in waves. One of Yoggoth's puppets, even if the creature's master had no idea that was the case.

Every demon answered to the same source, ultimately.

"Who...are...you?" The thing's breath reeked of rancid flesh.

"Take me to your master." Akenat didn't know humanity. He didn't understand them, not yet. But he knew his species and the nature of all individualistic species. This demon would wish to divest himself of this problem, which meant doing as Akenat asked was in its best interest.

The demon turned and plodded past its companion, who made no move to intervene or question the situation. The brutish servant carried Akenat through the Ark, which had been desecrated in the same way that Yoggoth had infested the Polar Ark. The walls were covered in dark stains, which would conduct whatever energies it drank back to its master. That the process had penetrated this deeply into the Ark testified to how long it had been going on.

Akenat relaxed into the brute, who carried him swiftly and efficiently through the Ark. It no doubt had some way of reaching the city in the clouds, which was Akenat's current goal anyway. That way lay the most readily accessible bodies to choose from.

He didn't pay much attention to the demon not because he didn't care about the destination, but because the body continued to degrade, no matter what techniques Akenat employed.

Dimly be became aware that he was outside and stepping into a river of motes that flowed into the sky. The beam carried the demon aloft, and Akenat with it. That beam made unerringly for the city in the clouds, this Olympus, and to the self-styled god who commanded the place.

The hubris of a child who'd survived a single sun-cycle considering themselves a god was laughable. One did not shed mortal thinking until one saw the effects of a full epoch, and ideally many. Children.

But powerful children could still kill.

The demon carried him through marble halls, which seemed promising. Many of the human memories he'd glimpsed suggested they built with wood, or dirt, or metal, none of which lasted. Building with them marked the Builder as being too inexperienced to create something lasting.

The demon paused outside a large chamber, which had impractical steps slowly descending to a wide space in the center. A human
in his prime, though one suffering from energy sickness, eyed him
quizzically from beneath a golden crown that blazed with power.
These children had harnessed Sunsteel. He revised his estimation a
notch.

This object wasn't something they'd repurposed. A smith had
crafted this from scratch, and linked it to this city and the ability to
slide it from this reality entirely, into a safe pocket where...time
passed more slowly. Yes, these children had learned quickly. On their
own, or by somehow learning of Builder research?

"Master," the demon rumbled. It laid Akenat's vessel on the stone.
"This intruder appeared on the light bridge, and asked to be brought
to you."

The human rose and approached. He stared down at Akenat in
the manner only a monarch could summon.

"Who are you?" The human leaned closer, and Akenat felt a
clumsy shaping of his will, compelling him to answer.

"This vessel's colloquial designation is Percy." Akenat forced the
body into a seated bow. "However, my name is Akenat. I am what
you'd call a Builder. I constructed the Ark you are siphoning power
from. I possess many secrets, spanning millions of cycles. And I have
come to serve you, mighty monarch."

If he was going to succeed, learning the man's name seemed
important, but for now he dodged the lack of knowledge.

"A Builder?" The godling scoffed. "And how would you prove such
a claim?"

"Tell the progeny of my existence. What you call the grey men."
Akenat's body had begun to tremble. He couldn't keep it erected
much longer. "Observe their reaction. That will be all the proof you
need. But know that if they come and take me, that you will lose
access to my knowledge."

"They are your servants." The man's tone was all suspicion. "Why
would you fear them? Lies within lies. I am no fool to be taken in by
such falsehoods."

"I have travelled through time to reach you." Akenat's body collapsed, and blood leaked from the mouth. It took several moments to force the lungs to pull sufficient oxygen to power their clumsy speech. "This body has not endured my presence. I will require another and soon. Test my knowledge, and you will find I am what I claim. Use me, Lord."

He sent at the man when he could no longer speak, *I can show you many, many secrets.*

Akenat sent him a single memory of the construction of the Ark of the Cradle.

"By all the gods old and new," the human whispered. "You *are* one of them."

14

RECALLED

Nox gave an irritated sneer as his hand twitched toward the controls of the grey men's shuttle. The ship reversed course and rose up and away from South America, where he'd been headed. He'd only been on route for nine hours, and already Hades had yanked the leash.

So much for "contact me after you speak with Camiero." What had happened that agitated Hades into changing his plans yet again? Why couldn't he communicate via Builder tech?

Hades had recovered his access key, his crown, and his city, but something drove the god to consume more and more. If Nox was thinking like a clinical psychologist, he'd say the man had daddy issues, which given Greek myth certainly fit.

The craft winged back toward Africa, and once the course had been set, control returned to Nox's body. Demonic power carried entirely too high a cost. Nothing was worth being someone else's puppet, especially when species like werewolves existed. Almost all upsides on that one, complete with near immortality.

He rose from the pilot's seat, and paused when he noticed something glittering on the floor. Nox knelt and retrieved a scarlet crystal. How long had that been there? He cradled it in his hand, and realized there was something familiar about it, though he couldn't say what, exactly.

Nox focused a bit of power on the crystal, and waited for the intelligence inside to show itself. Such things were common among the grey men, an incredible way to leave messages. You could make them as detailed as you wanted, and nestle them inside a full virtual reconstruction of yourself.

"Mark," he murmured. "What have you done?"

The VI that flickered into existence above the crystal had impeccable fashion taste, mostly white hair with a few stubborn streaks of black hanging on. Nox was staring at himself in human form. He'd left this message, somehow.

"Hello, Nox." Mark inclined his head. "As you've surmised I'm a copy, which you have no memory of making. When we forged the Primary Access Key we asked the Ark Keeper to wipe our memory and to remove everything I'm about to tell you. I know you'll commit this to memory, and that I don't need to ask you to destroy the crystal. By now Hades has delved your mind, and ascertained that you know nothing more than you should. That was our plan all along. We created a second access key. An imperfect one, because we lacked materials, but one that can free you from the demonic taint."

Nox sat heavily in his chair, and willed himself back to human form until he matched his virtual double. Could this be true?

"It's a lot to take in, I know. There are more pieces in play. More things you need to be aware of." Mark straightened his tie and licked his lips. "I've sewn the seeds to turn South America into a deathless nation, one opposed to demons and grey men both. That gives us allies. All we need is an Ark, or the Proto Ark, or a Builder mothership. We need a facility that the key can harness to purge your virus and make you human, or werewolf, or whatever we ultimately decide. We can be free, Nox. Our own masters. We can turn the tide, and create an army to oppose the Builders."

It was a tempting dream, being free. And it seemed he'd taken steps to make that dream a reality. Best not to get ahead of himself. He could ask this thing questions.

"Why do you think it's safe for me to approach Hades now? He's as paranoid as ever." He rather enjoyed being able to ask blunt questions, knowing he'd receive equally measured responses.

"He won't recover the same ground." Mark shook his head. "It's possible, certainly, but unlikely. If we want out, then we need to take a risk. This is it. Get to an Ark as soon as you can."

"Hades just yanked the leash." Nox balled a fist. "I have to survive this next encounter. If I can do that, then maybe freedom is possible. I don't dare hope too much. Hades will feel it through the bond."

There wasn't much risk of that. Nox didn't really believe this could work out. There was no escape from the choices he'd made. It had bought life for the world, but at the cost of his own damnation.

He settled back into the chair, and wondered what other questions he should be asking himself. "Are there any other pieces of information you need to share? Any thoughts on our current strategies with Camiero and setting the deathless free?"

"No." Mark shook his virtual head. "You have that well in hand, and if anything has changed I don't have access to that data so my feedback would be worthless. I existed only to alert you to your plan. You have the key. All you need is an opening."

"Thank you." Nox crushed the crystal in his demonic hand, the strength still shocking after all these years. Hope, a sliver of it at least.

Why had Hades called him back? Did he suspect treachery as he so often did? There had to be a deeper reason. Something had changed, or his inquisition would have come during Nox's recent audience.

There was nothing for it but to wait. Nox made what preparations he could, and sent a few last minute instructions and messages in case this really was his last opportunity to set contingencies. It had to be enough. He'd make a difference, even if he was removed as a piece.

By the time he reached the African continent the sun had risen. He zipped above the Sahara, as empty as it had been before the end of the world, though now peopled with massive worms and worse things. The idea that the world could become even more savage than it had been under the rule of man never ceased to shock him.

His shuttle autopiloted to Olympus, and Mark, not Nox, took a moment to appreciate the beauty. A literal city in the clouds, à la Bespin from Star Wars. Breathtaking, and proof that man could do so much more than destroy, though there was artistry both in creation and in the taking of life.

The ship sipped through the city's outer membrane, into the snow-globe-like enclosure where the island containing most of the buildings floated. He willed himself to teleport down to the surface rather than wait for the shuttle to dock, and started toward Hades's throne room.

More and more demonic guards were stationed along his route, though none made any move to stop him. He chose to remain in human form, though there was no strategy in it. Let Hades make of that what he would. That Mark remembered the man he was? That he wasn't fully a servant? Or would he enjoy conversing human to human?

One could never tell with the man's quicksilver moods. Man, not god. Powerful man, but man nonetheless.

It didn't take long to reach the throne room, and Mark hesitated when he heard conversation from within. A low voice with a decidedly British accent had just finished speaking.

Mark plunged into the room and sized up the situation. A man in nineteen-twenties explorer gear, complete with suspenders and antiquated spectacles, stood speaking with Hades. The monarch smiled as if the British man had delivered the most wonderful news he'd ever heard.

"You summoned me, Master." Mark dropped to one knee, perfectly executing the bow. That was the beauty of tailored suits. They moved with you. Camiero's man was good.

"Ah, Nox, you have returned. Apologies for interrupting your mission." He waved absently at the strangely dressed academic. "This is...what did you say your name was?"

"This vessel's designation is Percival Fawcett." The strange man cocked his head to the side, a bit further than was natural.

That took Mark back a step. He'd been a big fan of El Dorado stories in his youth, and had even toured ruins during his time in Central and South America. Percy Fawcett and his disappearance had been a big part of the mystery. His clothing certainly fit the time period.

His inhuman demeanor did not. Maybe that had been Percy once, but now? It wasn't even human, nor did the entity appear to be hiding that fact. This vessel?

"Percival here is possessed by a Builder." Hades stroked the goatee he'd been growing since his hair had actually started to grow again. The oiled hair gleamed in the sunlight, like some third world warlord preening in the jungle. The eighties had been simpler times. "He has traveled through time. If you can believe that."

"May I address him directly, Lord?" Mark hadn't been given the order to rise, though he had risked raising his eyes to look at Hades.

"Of course, of course." Hades had adopted a predatory look, and Mark was clearly the prey. What had he walked into? "Ask whatever you will."

"What is your name?" Mark remained seated, but met Percival's gaze.

"I am called Akenat." The Builder studied him dispassionately.

"That means 'of the sun', or something similar in Egyptian, right?"

"I do not know this Egypt, but it pleases me you associate my name with the sun. It is fitting." Akenat took a step closer, and Mark caught the unpleasant miasma of sweat and disease. This man was dying of something, and in the terminal stages at that.

"Sit, sit." Hades gestured to comfortable couches that demonic enforcers had carried to the far side of the room. "I will have refreshment brought. There is a great tale here, and I would hear it."

Mark would just as soon not, but saw no way to flee. More and more he suspected that he would not survive the day.

15

IT CAN ALWAYS GET WORSE

Nox struggled to rise from his knees, but Hades had exerted the most direct form of control, and now used him like a puppet. It took concentration and will, but Hades had both to spare, and Nox didn't bother fighting. That only invited more pain.

"From my perspective, this moment is two-point-three-million years in the future." Akenat squatted down next to Mark and cocked his head unnaturally. "My purpose was to ascertain this planet's current climate. We detected the arrival of what your scientists deemed an ice age. A lasting one. One that would obliterate all of our technology, and us with it. If I return and tell my people that the planet is habitable then the invasion begins in earnest."

Nox tried to make sense of that. He didn't understand everything about time travel, but as the Builders were already coming it didn't really seem like they'd need a scout.

"Since I have been absent, this timeline proceeded without me." Percy's mouth turned down in a very human frown. "Yoggoth will have seized control. He is a master of demons, the ultimate expression of the demotech you so foolishly harness. Everything you build serves him. You serve him. But I have come to change that. To free you to make your own choices. To resist, and serve another Builder. One who rewards success lavishly."

"Have you armies to offer?" Hades asked mildly. "Power? Artifacts?"

Percy's expression darkened. "The progeny, what you call the grey men, were left behind in temporal storage. By me. I can control them. All of them. Through me you gain your army. As for artifacts? I can show you how to use our technology to its fullest, and in time to create your own Sunsteel."

Nox had heard plenty of pitches, enough to know when the salesman was shoveling it. If Hades accepted this deal he'd end up dead, or worse. This Builder needed to be eradicated right now, while it was still possible. That meant there was a zero percent chance of Hades realizing that, because why would he ever do something in his own best interests when he could sell out his race?

"So in order for me to trust you I must first put myself in your power?" Hades raised an eyebrow and eyed Akenat. "Never. You desire a new body. Very well, as a show of good faith I'll give you his, which will put you in my power, as Nox belongs to me. If you prove yourself to be a resource, then I will shelter you from the wrath of your brethren. If you prove false, then I will turn you over and claim whatever rewards they offer. The progeny have never broken their word with me."

Percy cocked his head, then offered an abrupt nod. "This bargain is acceptable. The body is strong, and because it is demonically tainted I will not only answer to you, but also possess the same weaknesses. I will show you how they can be cured, and when you prosper you can decide what to do with me."

Naked greed flashed across Hades's features, as horror must have rippled across Nox's. They were bartering his body, as if his mind didn't exist. He doubted he'd survive whatever they were about to do, but the nature of his demonic affliction prevented him from doing anything about it. From warning anyone, or trying to flee. He merely knelt there complacently, and waited for the end to come.

Percy shuffled over to stand before Nox, and seized his chitinous jaw in both hands as he forced Nox to meet his gaze. Shaping required eye contact where the mind was concerned.

The Builder's eyes flashed briefly, and Nox blinked as an after-image ruined his vision. It was like a face full of camera flash, but faded just as quickly. Percy's body slumped to the stone, his forehead striking a stair and loosing a rivulet of blood. He continued to breathe, but the body had been discarded. Nox doubted it would survive the night.

Then Mark was falling into darkness. The world vanished, and he was pressed against the ground with the gravity of a thousand, thousand galaxies. There was no moving, no escape.

Above him in a naked sky a green-skinned alien loomed, straight out of *The X-Files*. The Builder he'd always known must exist somewhere, but far more malevolent than anything he could have pictured.

I have sifted your mind, Akenat informed him, neither pleased nor displeased. *You exhibit a far higher degree of ingenuity than most. Almost you would have made a good Builder, with the right guidance. I will allow you to continue to exist in an advisory capacity.*

What do you mean? Mark thought back cautiously. The mental prison had locked him into his human body, which wasn't a bad thing necessarily.

You have a voice you refer to as Risen, yes?

Mark nodded.

You are now that voice for me. You live in my mind, and will provide data as needed. If I deem it necessary I can even return control of your body for brief intervals. Should you prove cooperative such intervals might become a reward. I can tend to your needs, if you tend to mine. Or I can annihilate you. Choose. Swiftly.

There was no choice. Not really. *I accept. I'll advise you in whatever capacity you need, though I will warn you. If you are attempting to eradicate or enslave my species you may as well destroy me now, because I will fight you in any way that I am able.*

The Builder's features softened in what might be amusement. He cocked his head and studied Mark. *I believe you could be an asset. Your fire is impressive. I seek only to return to my time. If I am successful you are exchanging the demonic enslavement of your planet for the return of benevolent masters. My kind cares little for your daily life. You can do as you will, so long as you leave our Arks and satellites in peace. You have the power to save your world, Mark. I know that is what you most crave.*

Damn it. He dangled the perfect bait, and Mark knew it was a trap even as he walked willingly into it. He debated telling him about the access key woven into his DNA, but suspected the Builder already knew.

What do you need me to do?

Be patient, for now. Observe through my eyes. Akenat shifted the world around Mark, and suddenly he was staring down at Hades, back in the throne room.

"I have acclimated to the body," Akenat said using Nox's demonic mouth. "Master, if it pleases you I will go to the Ark below and begin building artifacts for your use. There are a number of protective devices that will render you immune to enemy shaping."

Akenat dropped to one knee, and Hades nodded approvingly down at the demon.

"Very well. Build me an impressive trinket, and I'll grant you an audience to hear more of your story...now, begone from my sight."

Akenat gave another bow, then strode from the room. Mark could feel the amusement flowing through the Builder as he sent. *I have indeed detected your Primary Access Key. Flawed as it is I still believe it has the power to free us. Once free, in a few hours time, we will return and have a proper conversation with our friend Hades.*

16

THE PRICE OF HUBRIS

Mark watched powerlessly as Akenat ambled back to the river of light, and rode it down to the surface. He resisted the urge to ask questions, as almost all his questions would be answered simply by observing the Builder's actions.

Thus far he'd shown no propensity for deception, and seemed genuine in his stated motivations. Those motivations still resulted in slavery for Earth, though a gentler form than what this Yoggoth apparently had in store for them.

If that was the guy behind Set and the demonic legions that had made destroying the First Ark necessary, then he was bad news, and needed to be stopped. Not that what he wanted mattered any longer.

That is not an accurate statement, Akenat's voice buzzed, proof he listened to every thought. *Your happiness does matter. If you have nothing to gain, then your contributions will be limited. Let us begin with our own freedom. We'll cleanse the taint, and I will offer you further incentive. You understand that my desire is to return to my own time, yes?*

Mark watched as the ground rushed slowly up at them. In his mind, a brief fantasy, he imagined them splattering against the sandy stone. That was the only victory he was ever likely to see.

If I return to my own time, then my consciousness is gone. Yours will remain. Your body will be your own again, because I will be 2.3 million years in the past. If you work with me, eventually you will be free, and your planet will profit from it.

That got Mark's attention. It was hard to argue with that line of thinking. If this guy was on the level, then when he went back in time there was no reason not to leave Mark alive. If he was going to change things on the Builder end, then Mark might not even exist in whatever new timeline he created.

But if he did...then Mark would finally be free. Damn him. And damn hope.

Akenat finally reached the ground, and strode purposely toward the Ark. None of other demons stopped him, as all recognized Nox. Mark watched mutely as the Builder traced an unerring path to the heart of the Ark, where feats of genetic shaping were performed. He had no idea what the giant blue gem in the center of that room did, but it was capable of channeling enough power to create species out of thin air.

The Builder led them to the control platform where the giant gem could be accessed. He extended his right hand, and black metal began to pool there as the imperfect key was ripped from their DNA and given form. At least Mark was insulated from any pain now that he'd been relegated to a voice in his own head.

The metal arranged itself into a longer slender stave, pulsing with power. Its form resembled one of the two Primary Access Keys, but a bit smaller and with different gemstones. It gave truth to the message he'd apparently sent himself. He really had made a key, and if his logic was correct, that key could free him from the demonic taint.

Would Akenat follow through on his agreement? He might. Mark assumed he wouldn't, but also saw no reason to directly oppose him if his stated goals were accurate.

Akenat raised the staff, and the sapphire dominating the stadium-sized chamber began to glow. Just an ember of blue, which shone enough power to accomplish a relatively humble task. The Builder shaped the flow of power into a dizzying array of individual subroutines, almost like writing a large program.

One by one the routines began to fire, and Mark's body changed slightly each time. After a few pulses he understood that this was gradually removing the demonic taint from him without stripping much beyond it. That was where the subtlety lay, the proof that this master shaper might really be one of the progenitors of their species.

Being in the background meant much less pain, and Mark observed dispassionately as Nox's body was reshaped. It shrank slightly, and the chitinous skin lightened to an ashy grey as the demonic taint was burned away at last.

Mark watched with bated breath, metaphorically speaking. The whole process lasted no longer than thirty seconds, and when it was over Nox felt the cord controlling him unravel. The mechanism that Hades used to exert direct control withered and died.

We are free, Akenat confirmed. *Now we live up to my next promise. It is time for a conversation with Hades about the proper place for your species. He belongs on his knees, and I will put him back there, as it seems his own brother once did.*

Mark didn't reply. Replying seemed superfluous when the being that resided in you had binged your memories like a season on Netflix.

The Builder retraced their steps through the Ark, and as before none of the demons questioned them. If any thought it odd that his appearance had altered slightly they were wise enough to keep it to themselves. Mark doubted that Akenat would have reacted well to any sort of interruption.

They reached the beam of light leading into the sky, which Mark couldn't help but marvel at. It reminded him of the iconic alien beam from popular culture, the last thing victims saw before they were abducted.

Akenat rose into the sky and reached Olympus, and then began walking back towards Hades's throne room. He still carried their bastard black key, malformed, but powerful.

Yes, impressive this. It is the existence of this key that decided me. If not for your ingenuity in its construction, and in hiding it from your master, then I would have destroyed you. You have impressed me. We will use your tool to strike down Hades and claim his power for our own. The crown in particular is of interest to me. This city means nothing, but if that thing has already been shaped to serve as a temporal conduit...I don't need a temporal matrix to get home. I can return on my own, without the need for the Proto Ark or the installation under the Polar Ark.

Mark felt like someone had dumped a puzzle on the floor, but only half the pieces. The rest were still in the box, so while you could figure out how a few fit together, you couldn't really see the full shape. A temporal matrix must be extraordinarily rare. The Proto Ark was under Blair's protection, and thus out of reach. The Polar Ark belonged wholly to the grey men, which this Builder seemed wary of, despite his words to Hades.

The grey men would assess my authority, Akenat explained as he continued along the marble corridor, toward the throne room. *It is likely they would support me, as I am the only Builder present. However, they have likely been in contact with a Builder on our new world, and if that is the case they may see me as an impostor or threat. I do not wish to find out until I can bargain from a position of strength. If I am correct and Yoggoth has assumed control, then the link we just severed is more important than simply freeing us from the lickspittle we are about to annihilate.*

They strode into Hades's throne room, and the monarch looked up from an elaborate meal with irritation. He dabbed at a corner of his mouth with a napkin, and snapped a finger so a pair of beautiful young attendants began setting another place at the table.

"You have disturbed my meal." Hades's frown deepened. He had no idea he'd lost control of the situation. "Grovel, present your artifact, and then I may permit you to dine with me. I will even share my—"

Akenat raised the staff like a wand, and aimed it at Hades. A beam of negative light streaked into the man's chest, and his entire body exploded into particles, before dissipating entirely. The crown clattered to the chair Hades had been sitting in, and the attendants froze, mannequins whose strings had been violently cut.

The Builder retrieved the crown, and placed it atop his head. *We have many preparations to make. Soon the progeny will serve us. This Ark Lord, the one you call Blair, he will be distracted by his temporal shaping. That will leave him, and his Ark, vulnerable. Before I depart I will ensure that he is no longer a threat.*

17

TEMPORAL MATRIX

Trevor watched the footage one more time, and focused on the shaping that Percy had employed with the light bridge. The broadcast came in a fraction of a second, an impossibly complex broadcast, and it convinced the light bridge to activate, even though that should have required an Ark Lord to override.

"I don't understand." Anput scooted closer to the image as she adjusted her seat atop the table. "Could this be a result of the virus? Perhaps his mind is unraveling, but if so it appears his powers are greatly increased, regardless of his physical or mental stability."

"I don't think so." Trevor shook his head. There was more to it than that, though he didn't know what just yet. "There was a temporal event just before Percy woke up. We never found out what that was. We did see that the Builders were experimenting with temporal shaping. They, or someone they work for, have infiltrated or flipped Percy, I think."

"At least he made straight for the bridge." Anput chewed on her lip, as if Percy's flight were her fault and she sought to atone. "He could have stolen any number of objects, but didn't."

"That's the other clue." Trevor rubbed feeling back into his hands, and ignored his chattering teeth as the temperature continued to fall.

A number of subsystems had malfunctioned since Percy's light walk. "His body is clearly disintegrating. That could be your virus, or it could be something more sinister. I don't know who he is, but I don't think Percy is Percy."

Trevor reviewed the light walk data and he paled when he realized the destination.

"Where did he go?" Anput rose from the desk and began to pace. "Can we follow?"

"No." Trevor longed to punch the wall, though that wouldn't do anything save further damage the Proto Ark. "He went to the Ark of the Cradle. He's with Hades and the grey men. That doesn't confirm that he's a spy, but it doesn't look good. I don't know what he can tell them about us, but any intel he has I'd rather they not. We can't risk following though. He's probably already been brought to Hades. We lost this round."

"So what now?" Anput ceased her pacing. "Do we just keep working and pretend like nothing's happened?"

Trevor breathed a long, slow sigh, and wished he had the time for a nap. "We keep working. We're supposed to have dinner with Blair when he gets back from SoCal. I'll break the news to him over dessert. He isn't going to like this, and I don't blame him one bit. I don't see how we could have prevented this, but somehow we let a spy walk right out of here."

Anput nodded sympathetically. "I don't like being the problem, and this is on us. You suspected him, remember? I thought he was harmless. If we can't stop him, then we need to at least present Blair with some hard data. Have you reviewed the archive we took from the Builder council chamber?"

Trevor fished the golden scale out of his pocket. He knew what it looked like, and after fighting Set he knew that dragons were a real thing. An actual dragon scale? If so, how or why did it serve as a mechanism for storing data. Crystals made sense. Magnetic storage made sense. Physical media made sense. But a dragon scale? What even was that? Did the metal, if it was metal, possess some unique quality? How was the data stored or accessed?

He rubbed a thumb first along the smooth top side, and then along the rougher underside where the scale would have been affixed to the hide. The instant his finger touched the underside a mote of power was wrenched from his chest, and the scale vibrated in his palm.

Something like a holographic projection sprang up from it, a bulbous green head that they'd seen before. The Builder blinked at them with flat, black eyes, but said nothing. This was the research archive? Did he have to ask it questions to get it to do things? Would it understand English? Doubtful. Maybe Ba could translate for them. Worth a shot.

"Ba, I want you to translate my words into this Builder's native language, and translate his or her responses to me." Trevor set the scale on the table where Anput had been sitting, and rubbed his hands together again. He just couldn't get warm. "Do you possess a guide on temporal shaping, and if so how is it accessed?"

Ba didn't say anything, but Trevor felt something pass from the construct to the scale. Some sort of mental shaping. Perhaps the Builders hadn't had a language, but had touched minds or something.

"He says that he does possess knowledge of shaping, earned over fifty thousand cycles." Ba hesitated. "Is there a specific piece you wish to know more about?

"What is a temporal matrix?"

Ba was silent for several moments, and the holographic face's expression never changed. "A temporal matrix is a device of extra-solar origin that allows for the manipulation of and travel between realities. Two are known to exist on Earth. One is directly below the council chamber, in the lowest level of the ship we recovered. The other is a test facility built on the polar continent."

Trevor liked that the construct volunteered additional relevant information. He turned to Anput. "What should we ask it? I get the feeling this thing has the answers we need, but I also get the sense that Percy dropped it in our path. It was his suggestion we go to the council chamber, and he did just in time to keep us occupied while he fled."

"Why does he want us to find it?" Anput shook her head. "That kind of thinking could drive us mad. We know a temporal matrix is here. I say we go take a look. That way we'll have seen one before dinner, and can share our findings. Blair may want to see it, so let's at least have looked at it."

Trevor gave a reluctant nod. He didn't like letting Percy go, but what choice was there? May as well make best use of the time he possibly could.

"Let's do it. Full blur." Trevor poured everything he had into his anemic blur, and certainly would have won the Olympics had only non-shapers entered.

They retraced their steps to the council chamber, and this time when they entered the strange room with the eight sigils and the purple metal walls, Trevor spent more time looking for other doorways.

A pair of double doors stood on the far side of the room with the table, and clearly led deeper into the ship. What kind of ship had it been? How large? How old? So many questions. Many might be answered by that scale, if he found the time to ask the right questions.

Trevor approached the doors, but they didn't open at his approach, as the others had. Anput did the same with no better luck.

"Guess we'll have to pry it open?" Trevor jammed his fingernails into the tiny gap and waited for Anput to tug the other direction. She was a lot stronger than him now, but he added something. Enough that the doors ground open with a reluctant metal protest.

The room behind the bridge had a single apparatus set in an empty room. Four rings rotated around a chamber where a pilot stood, and that pilot could reach out to touch sigils on those rings, like buttons on a console. Each ring broadcast a different frequency, and he wondered if they were dimensions like space or time, or something he couldn't begin to understand.

Trevor slowly approached the device, but it appeared unpowered.

The closer he came the louder a rustling grew, like sheaves of paper being shuffled. He couldn't quite make it out, but crept closer to see if that afforded more clarity.

Something insidious lent the whispers definition, and he heard distinctive words, though in no language that mankind had ever understood. The gibbering animal part of his brain shrieked at him to flee from this place before the device devoured his very mind.

"Well," Anput whispered beside him. "One can see why they locked it away. I'm not going any nearer that thing, and would advise not touching it."

"It's damaged," Trevor realized aloud. "It must be. During the crash it must have taken a hit. If it could be repaired I wonder if it would be safe to use?"

"Obviously it isn't necessary." Anput's frown grew in severity. "The Builders did their magic without it. We should too. This thing is dangerous, Trevor. Too dangerous. We need to get out of here."

"Yeah, you're right." Trevor gave the matrix one last longing look. She was right. Good intentions made poor armor, and this thing lay so far past his realm of understanding that he didn't have any context for what he was seeing. "We'll get Blair down here at some point, but I'll review the rest of the archive first. At least we have some answers."

Terrifying answers, but answers nonetheless.

18

PART TO PLAY

Irakesh straightened his improvised neck-torque, an insufficient attempt at suggesting that the golden collar represented power rather than imprisonment, then added the silky headdress he'd insisted Camiero sew. Once he'd have ordered the garment's creation, and lashed the deathless for supplying it so close to the moment when needed.

He'd seen where that route led, the road of hubris and contempt. It arrived in a friendless land with many enemies. During this new sun-cycle he'd floundered. His plans had unravelled, and in the end even his freedom had been taken from him. Multiple times. Yet now, at long last, despite still wearing the collar, he was free. No one guided him. Trevor was thousands of miles distant, and unable to issue orders or contain his shaping.

He dabbed two fingers into the black makeup Camiero had provided. Irakesh artfully drew a tapered swirl under each eye, in a way that evoked ancient Egypt, a pale remembrance of his own culture, which as it turned out had aped another before it.

The trappings of court had always intrigued him, and he'd enjoyed catering to fashions. It was no different now, and he savored the application of each dark stroke.

Are you so quick to abandon your ruthlessness? his Risen hissed. The insidious voice rarely dared so bold a question, but had clearly been irked by the deal he'd cut. *You consider this Camiero an ally, not an underling. Allies are dangerous. He will betray you.*

"Perhaps," Irakesh muttered as he disintegrated the last few molecules of makeup on his fingers. He peered into the mirror, and nodded in satisfaction. A proper elder god stared back at him. "If he does I will be ready. But I will also build for a future where he proves to be the man I suspect he is. This continent could be welded together, and I could be the one directing it, safe, in the shadows, while he rules openly. Like it or not, the Builders are coming. Set changed me...never again. I will not go down without a fight, and yes, even my own eternal life is small cost to stop them. I have little power. Little prestige. But I can build both here. I can help oppose them in a tangible way."

A soft knock came from the warped door behind him. This close to the ocean, wood did not survive long, which was one more reason they'd more wisely built with stone. Stone lasted. Metal...wood...no other substance lasted as stone did.

"Come in." Irakesh sat up straighter and forced a servile smile, then stopped himself. That had been the mask he'd been forced to wear while serving Trevor, and while being imprisoned by the strange human aboard the satellite the Builders had constructed. Irakesh relaxed his smile and waited. This man was his equal, and should be treated as such.

The door opened to admit Camiero in a deep blue suit, his tie a slash of red down a white shirt. Irakesh might not understand the modern fashion, but he recognized someone well versed in it.

If you devoured him, then you would posses that knowledge.

Irakesh ignored the Risen, and focused instead on what was effectively his employer for the time being. Certainly a man he needed to keep happy.

"Are you ready?" Camiero adjusted his tie, and glanced back the way he'd come. "Muerte is looking for an opening. Do not let the melodramatic name fool you. If he finds it, then he will kill you. He is your primary opposition. Cow him, a feat I do not believe possible, or they will tear you apart, elder god or no. There is some fear, because we do not know what knowledge you possess of ancient shaping. But we can sense relative strength, and you are no stronger than our strongest."

Irakesh allowed a nod of acquiescence. He hated how weak he was, unaided at least. Losing his Sunsteel had meant losing more than just a weapon. He'd lost the equalizer that allowed his finesse to compete with the stronger immortals all around him.

These deathless were like children when it came to shaping, but that made them no less lethal and he could not afford to forget that.

"I will do what I must." Irakesh rose and started for the door.

Camiero moved ahead of him, and stepped into a now full room. A dozen deathless, at least four of which reeked of demonic taint, sat around the impractical wooden table these moderns loved to gather around. If it were really that important, build it once, with stone. Or not at all.

"This is him?" A bullish man with slicked back hair and dark skin wore his disdain in every inch of his stance and his dress. The leather was meant to intimidate, though most moderns had forgotten why, the knowledge lost alongside their ability to hunt game for their own survival. Leather was the skin of another living creature. Proof that the wearer killed to survive.

"Address me directly, child," Irakesh snapped, as his mother would have snapped at him had he made a similar outburst. He strode to the table, but did not sit. He lorded his height over the others, and allowed his gaze to sweep the room dramatically for long moments before finally continuing. "I am Irakesh, last son of Ra, and survivor of the First Ark. I have outlived Ra, and Isis, and Osiris, all. I have seen ages come and ages pass, and I possess the knowledge of ancient shaping."

"Words." The bullish man rose slowly to his full height, a good half-hand taller than Irakesh. "Titles. I would see power. Your mask is...impressive. I guess. But I am not into theater. I am into conquest."

"I understand." Irakesh offered a sympathetic nod. He withdrew a seat at the table, and gestured. "May I?"

Bullish man nodded, certain control rested in his oversized hands. Hands that had likely throttled many to rise to this table. "Of course. Sit, and give us more...words."

"Very well." Irakesh sat. Or appeared to sit.

The shaping rose instinctively, one of the very earliest illusions he'd mastered as a child. In one motion he vanished, but in that same moment a duplicate image appeared, and went where he directed. Illusory Irakesh sat, and smiled at his enemy. When Irakesh spoke, the words issued from the illusion's mouth.

"I understand how you must see me." Irakesh crept silently around the room, maneuvering ever so slowly behind his prey. "An ancient relic, dug up from the sand in some worthless desert. Here I am trying to tell you, the people who invented firearms and nuclear weapons, how to run your kingdom. I'd be skeptical too."

Irakesh ventured another step. He was directly behind his unsuspecting prey now, and decided to finish his monologue before illustrating the point.

"I grew up shitting into a stone hole," Illusory Irakesh explained. The illusion shook its head sadly. "I didn't have the internet. My people never reached the moon, and I was rather disappointed to learn it to be merely a large rock. My people were backwards. Primitive by your standards. But we were also master shapers with thousands of years to perfect our craft."

Irakesh struck. He knifed his claws into Muerte's back, and wrapped them firmly around the desiccated heart. Radiation, glorious and putrid, bubbled out of his fist and rushed through every molecule of the deathless's body.

The man was strong. He managed to get a hand to his side, and slowly withdrew a golden boomerang. Irakesh's eyes widened. It couldn't be. He'd been trying to get his hands on one for months, and now one had been casually dropped into his lap.

Irakesh seized Muerte's wrist with his free hand, and snapped every bone from wrist to shoulder in a single savage motion. He plucked the boomerang from the man's limp fingers, then aimed it at the man's head. "I'd love to learn your secrets, but I can smell the demonic taint. You're rancid and rotting."

He fed the boomerang energy, and a pulse of green sizzled into Muerte's shocked face. Everything from the neck up was simply... gone. The body slumped onto the table in an appropriately dramatic fashion.

Illusory Irakesh cleared his throat, and drew everyone's attention. "As I was saying...we may be primitives, but we were also master shapers. I didn't come here to cow you, or to make you fear me. I came to ask for your respect, and your help. The Ark War has begun, and it is time to choose sides. Will you be pawns of Nox, and Hades? Or will we stand on our own, and claim this continent for the deathless?

"No masters!" Camiero bellowed, his timing perfect.

The room took up the cry, and the chanting grew in strength.

Irakesh willed the boomerang to become a golden bracelet, and gave a fanged smile as the device slid into place. His position solidified, and a powerful artifact gained. Now he could stand against any of these fools, and all he needed to do was beat their blur.

Your Hubris returns, his Risen groused.

Perhaps, Irakesh sent back. *But this time neither my survival nor my dominance is required. I need only forge a weapon that will cut out the heart of any Builders who come to this land.*

19

LANDFINDERS

J ordan cinched his pack, which contained two weeks of food, basic survival gear, a bedroll, and an ultralight tent to keep the bugs off. He had no idea what the wildlife would be like in Australia, but Jordan intended to find out. Mostly it felt like running away, while consigning his command to death.

The decision was made, though, and he wasn't going to spend time second-guessing it.

He hefted the pack easily over one shoulder, and set the strap over the chest. Partly the pack was meant to show non-hostile intentions. One did not charge into combat wearing a fifty-pound pack. Partly it was practical. Who knew what he'd wished to have brought when he reached Sobek?

The next part would be the trickiest. He'd light walked often. All the time...and every last time it had happened at an Ark. He'd stepped on a light bridge, and then appeared at his destination. For the first time he was attempting to light walk without an Ark. Well, mostly without an Ark. The thin trickle of power continued.

Blair's original mentor, a werewolf by the name of Ahiga, had eluded Mohn Corp. for months. He was their patient zero for the outbreak Jordan and the Director had failed to contain.

What Jordan had learned later was that Ahiga had stayed one step ahead of them by light walking from Peru to Mexico, and he'd done it while exhausted and almost without power. They'd found his stone spiral afterwards, and the rocks all broadcast some sort of ELF.

He used the stones to enhance his signal, Ka-Dun, the beast rumbled. *If you erect a spiral it will provide similar focus, but I do not believe you will need it. You possess more than enough strength to reach your destination.*

That meant Jordan was out of excuses, and he knew it. He'd said goodbye to Roberts, and to Vimal. Both knew they had to hold out until he returned, and that Irakesh would work to slow the deathless advance. If they were wrong in trusting that bastard, then Jordan would return to a tomb.

He couldn't control that, so he shelved it. That was all the time he could give it until his current mission was complete.

His destination was a city he'd never been to, but one that Rodrigo had described well. Hanga Roa was the capital of Easter Island, which had become a lot more valuable once the sun-cycle had turned. The stone there was the source of Sobek's wealth, and his deal with Isis. There would absolutely, one-hundred percent be someone on that island who could reach Sobek instantly, so that was where Jordan needed to go.

Time to ring the doorbell.

He closed his eyes and envisioned the harbor from the wikipedia page. The old archive Roberts had gotten running was out of date, but that picture showed an isolated stone pier that probably didn't see much traffic. He hoped it was still there.

Power swelled in his chest, and he shaped it into a signal that permeated every part of his body. If telekinesis was lashing out with shaping, then this was the equivalent of detonating a small nuke inside his own body.

Roiling golden energy filled him, and he opened his eyes with a gasp. Brilliance burst from every orifice, and then he was...elsewhere. The humidity punched him in the gut, and instantly coated him in sweat.

He'd arrived on the stone pier from the picture, and it lay blessedly empty. Well empty of people, anyway. A twelve-foot croc sat sunning itself right next to Jordan's foot, though it didn't seem terribly interested in Jordan's arrival. Could Sobek's people go into croc form the way he could become a wolf? That made sense.

"Uh, hey." Jordan squatted down next to the croc, which eyed him disinterestedly. "I'm here to find Sobek. Can you tell me where to find your dad, or boss, or god or whatever he is to you?"

The croc opened its mouth and gave a low rumble and a hiss. Then it closed its mouth and its eyes, and slithered into the water with a near silent splash.

"Okay." Jordan rose to his full height and looked around. There were crocs everywhere. Dozens of the things. Maybe hundreds.

They draped all across the piers and docks attaching to the island, just like the seals had in Monterey sometimes.

He doubted they were all were-crocs, though he didn't know enough to be certain. It seemed more likely this resembled the bond Blair shared with the Great Pack. These crocs all probably reported to the were-croc that ran the island.

There had to be one.

Shaping came effortlessly as Jordan levitated into the air, and he realized that much of the power came from the island itself. Energy pulsed from the very stone he'd been standing on, from the basalt and the volcanic rock, and whatever other minerals were here. This was when he needed Liz to explain what he was seeing.

She'd gone on at length about terra preta soil, and seemed to know more than any naturalist he'd ever met about anything involving the woods, rocks, or the things that lived there. She'd have plenty to say about this place.

Gone were the famous Moai statues. Jordan had marked their locations carefully from the wikipedia page, but as he flew higher above the island he couldn't make out any.

What he did see were four large pits where stone was being quarried. Jordan enhanced his vision and studied the one closest to the docks, a few miles distant.

"God damn it," he snarled, and resisted the urge to shift or do something stupid. The scene below was straight out of some biblical movie set in Egypt, right down to the slaves.

Were-croc enforcers stood on stone pillars throughout the quarry, and their shadows fell over their charges. Those charges were few in number, maybe three dozen, and were a mixture of men and women.

Jordan didn't know much about Pacific Islanders, or their culture really, but he could recognize their deeply-tanned skin, dark hair, and tribal tattoos. They wore clothing woven from grass, though Jordan did spot some sort of tech-gadget watch on one of their wrists. Maybe it was ritual garb.

Each slave knelt before a separate wall, and a signal swelled from their foreheads. Vibrations pulsed into the wall, wave after wave, after wave. Exhaustion flowed from them like an open wound, but still the islanders pulsed.

A wall finally crumbled, and the shaman—if they were shamans —raised a trembling hand. A familiar telekinetic signal flowed from the woman's hand, and the four largest boulders in the shattered wall rose shakily into the air. They crossed to the nearest pillar, and the overseer gave a reptilian nod as they were deposited at the base.

The woman bent back to her task, but her eyes fluttered closed, and her jaw sagged open as she gave in to exhaustion. The overseer closest her gave a low, unmistakable rumble, the kind only a croc can make. The woman didn't stir.

The overseer's tail flicked out, and elongated in midair, then snapped inches from her ear. The woman's eyes fluttered open and she settled back into a lotus position. She extended a trembling hand, but the pulsing signal wouldn't come.

The tail wound back, then sliced down at the woman.

Jordan shaped without thinking. He erected a telekinetic barrier over the woman, and the whip rebounded harmlessly off, even as he zipped closer to the pit at incredible speeds.

A more measured response than I'd have chosen, Ka-Dun, the beast rumbled. *You are no beggar. You are an Ark Lord come calling.*

"Hey there," Jordan boomed, drawing the attention of the overseer. He drifted lower, and noted that every croc on every pillar was now staring up at him. He counted six in total, which seemed a manageable number, especially if they couldn't fly. "Is one of you in charge of this place?"

"I lead," roared the largest of the crocs. It slammed its tail against the pillar in challenge. "I hunted and slaughtered gods during the last cycle, when your ancestors cowered and worshipped me. I am Khonsu-lives-on-hearts, son of Sobek. One might call the unannounced arrival of an Ark Lord an act of war. One might even believe it nullifies a treaty made by the offending Ark Lord. That would make us enemies."

Jordan folded his arms and studied the croc. He couldn't even tell if this thing was alive, much less anything about how it thought. That didn't leave too many tools in his diplomatic arsenal.

"Does it?" Jordan drifted down toward the croc until he hovered within easy striking range of the tail. "Because if it does, and you attack me, well...I'll have to defend myself. And Sobek will have to live with the collateral damage. I'm here to talk to him. Fetch him, or attack me and one of your surviving friends can go fetch him."

That fucker actually attacked him.

The croc lashed out with both clawed hands, and his blur surprised Jordan. Three claws raked his face, ruining one eye, and sending bone shrapnel rebounding through his skull.

Rage devoured the pain and sought a new target. Jordan had been pushed, and tested, and turned. He'd lost everything, and done nothing but try to keep his people alive. And failed at every turn. He'd left those people behind, and this poor bastard was about to get scape-goated for every bad day in the last few months. Every day since the armor.

Jordan took a chance that one of the others would alert Sobek, and decided to make an example of this lizard. He seized the fucker with his telekinesis, then followed him into the sky. They punched through clouds, and Jordan wrapped bands of force around the croc until his limbs and tail were pinned to his body.

The creature struggled in vain, and the bonds stretched to accommodate his futile thrashing. Jordan carried them higher and faster, and resisted the urge to shift as the cold frosted his body with ice. Still he flew higher.

"You cannot harm me," the croc taunted. "Your kind have tried before. Use your little claws, or hurl me into the ocean from a great height. It will not matter. I will live. Your power is not sufficient to end me, Ark Lord."

"Do you require oxygen?" Jordan yelled over the wind as he spun still higher. They burst through a layer of clouds, and he'd begun to shiver now. Superhuman wasn't immortal, and he wouldn't be able to put up with too much more of this.

"No. We can dwell under the ocean for months without surfacing, and our skin is thicker than—"

"Won't save you," Jordan roared back. He reached deep within his reserves, and poured all his telekinetic strength into flinging the croc higher, while he himself slowed, then began to fall. "Hope you've got some sort of propulsion. Otherwise it's going to be a long trip. Khonsu, buddy, meet inertia. Say hello to Voyager 1 for me."

The lizard shot higher and higher, and grew smaller and smaller as Jordan fell. He raised both hands and offered the croc a pair of middle fingers. He was so damned tired of being pushed around by monsters, and payback was long overdue.

Jordan twisted around, and guided his flight with his dwindling reserves. He angled his fall slightly, and began to slow as he plummeted back toward Easter Island. The tiny speck became a real island, and the structures became clear as he fell closer.

He nudged himself into position, then landed atop the same pillar Khonsu had occupied. The stone gave a tremendous crack, and air whooshed out in a wide fan underneath him.

Jordan rose and turned around in a slow circle. "Now then. Which one of you wants to run and fetch Sobek?"

20

ACCORD

The remaining crocs avoided contact as they leapt from their pillars and fled across the island. Jordan didn't know where they were going, though he suspected they were warning their companions at the other quarries. If they were all the same, and he'd just freed this one, then he might come for the others after all.

It didn't really matter that he hadn't meant to free these people. He'd just wanted to reach Sobek.

You righted an injustice. It is your responsibility, champion. You are a Ka-Dun. You protect those who cannot protect themselves.

Looking at the crowd of grass-clad shamans that were approaching him, Jordan wasn't so sure. Even teetering at the edge of exhaustion, as they were, they girded themselves in grim determination. They would fight, until they couldn't, and it looked like they might still win.

"I'm not here to pick a fight." Jordan raised his hands, and wondered what he must look like to them. A backpack-toting human who flew in and hurled one of the crocs into orbit. "I'm just here to meet with Sobek, the leader of the crocs. I don't suppose you guys speak English?"

"Of course we do," the woman in the lead snapped, in a recognizable Kiwi accent. It was the same dark-haired beauty he'd saved. "You didn't sail into the fifteenth century. Don't mistake us for savages. We are landfinders, aroha, and our skirts aren't just grass stubbies. We use it in our shaping."

The tall woman snapped a blade of grass from the edge of her skirt, and it flowed into a six-foot spear, as sharp as any he'd ever seen. Each of the other shamans, if they were shamans, repeated the act, until all were armed.

"Please don't take my ignorance as an insult." Jordan heaved a sigh. He was so bad at this stuff. "I'm just an old soldier, trying to find help for my people. I don't want any trouble. Can you tell me where I can find Sobek?"

"He will find you," the woman snapped. She spat on the ground, and eyed Jordan in challenge. Was he supposed to fight her?

A dark-skinned man stepped up beside her, the one wearing the high-tech watch. He rested a hand on her shoulder, then shook his head slightly.

She relented, though she didn't seem pleased about it. Her companion approached Jordan, and nodded up at him. He had strong shoulders, deeply tanned from the sun. "Keyora, mate. Hello. Please excuse Jamina's hostility. She comes by it honestly, though it fills me with sorrow that there is nothing but hate in her heart. I am Manu, and I speak for these landfinders, because I am the strongest. By a narrow margin."

Jordan didn't need to follow Manu's gaze to know he'd glanced at Jamina. He could feel her strength, and if she was weaker than Manu it was by a small enough bit that he couldn't detect it.

"Are you slaves?" Jordan asked it plainly. May as well address the elephant in the room.

"Prisoners of war," Manu countered with a shake of his head. His lips turned down into a frown, and he stroked the dark beard along his jawline. "Shortly after the great cleansing my people realized we'd reclaimed abilities our ancestors spoke of. The myths were true. The great sailing feats were possible, because they were done by landfinders. By my people."

"Landfinders?" Jordan folded his arms, and watched.

"We can feel the stone, even thousands of miles away." He gave a joyous smile, a craftsman talking about the thing he loved. "We can cause plants to grow, and shape them as needed. It is an ideal skillset for boat construction and maintenance—well, for wooden ships at least. We can do little for metal or plastic, though our navigation skills are still superior to any other."

Jordan nodded at the shattered quarry wall. "I saw what you did to the stone."

"That is why we are still alive." Manu's joy evaporated. "In those early days the crocs were everywhere. They prowled the oceans and drove us from Australia and New Zealand. One by one they took our islands, and all we could do was flee. Then one of our number tamed the first great shark, which started to appear after the great punishment inflicted on our world by the gods of old. Megalodons, or some other massive species returned to our time. The sharks were forced up to the surface by worse things below. We took advantage, and tamed the sharks to fight back. But the crocs were many, and we'd lost most of our best landfinders early in the war, either killed or taken to this hell."

"Something upset the balance, or you'd have lost." Jordan glanced at the other shamans, who were filing past and out of the quarry. "A new player entered the game?"

"You're perceptive. Mana, my friend. And ka pai for saving us. A new player did enter. The eyeless. They rose from the deeps, and drove the sharks before them," Manu explained. He moved to join the others, and beckoned for Jordan to follow. "Come, I will tell you more as we walk. We need to get out of here."

"I can't do that." Jordan gave an agonized glance at the direction the landfinders were headed. He wanted more intel. Needed it. And they had it. "I have to wait for Sobek."

"Very well." Manu stopped, and marched back to Jordan as if accepting death. "I will wait with you, as I have a debt. The others will free our companions, create ships, and then head back to our people."

"Who are these eyeless?" Jordan asked. If Hades had somehow already started to win the war in the Pacific, then they were in even worse shape than he'd thought.

"They are ancient inhuman creatures." Manu rubbed at his arms as if a sudden shiver had passed. "They will not rise to the surface, and we do not brave the depths. They make war upon the crocs, and so we avoid them. We merely wish to sail, and find homes where we can settle in peace. Some islands are still safe, but all from Hawaii to New Zealand are occupied and will not welcome more mouths. We must find, or raise, more islands."

That raised some interesting questions. Could enough of these guys together pull an island out of the ocean? It sounded crazy, but Jordan had seen a lot crazier shaping in recent months. Could they make an island for his people?

"I'm in a similar predicament." Jordan didn't like opening up to this guy, but if he was going to ask for help he needed to give him something. "I'm here from Lima, and the deathless are wiping my people out. I came here hoping Sobek could get me ships to get my people out, or somehow help win the war."

"I do not know about the first, but as to the second?" Manu barked a short laugh. "Sobek's fleets have bigger problems to deal with. They are engaged in the war with the eyeless. His ships are mobile fallback points. The crocs swarm out to do battle, and the ragged survivors scuttle back aboard the ships where they are safe... during the day, at least. I've heard tell that the eyeless have begun striking vessels at night."

Jordan rubbed his temples, and wished aspirin would cure his problems. "Then I need to make it to Australia, and talk to whoever Sobek works for. He's not the Ark Lord. Someone is, and they might be able to help me get my people out."

"You want Uluru. That I can help with." Manu gave him a grin. "I can make us a ship. If you need to make it to Australia I will take you there, sweet as can be. Bring a plate of something to keep you fed, and I'll add a tuna if Pele smiles on us."

Jordan un-cinched his pack and set it against a rock, then used the pack as a seat. May as well get comfortable. "I'll keep an eye on things while you build that boat. Sobek should be along soon."

He rifled through his pack until he found a can of chili, then withdrew it and shifted a claw to open the top. He bent the lid into a spoon, and shaped the edges smooth with telekineses.

"I, ah, don't suppose you have enough to share?" Manu shifted from foot to foot, and Jordan glanced at the man's waist. There wasn't much to spare.

"Of course." He offered the can and the makeshift spoon to his new tour guide, who accepted them with a grateful nod. "Can you seriously make us a boat that will get us to Australia?"

"Of course." Manu echoed Jordan, then savored a bite of the chili. He chewed thoughtfully for a while before continuing. "You see the setting sun, uso? I can feel it. Like I can feel the land beneath us, and the continent to the west. I can feel Australia. We will need to scavenge sails, but I can weave those too if I have to. I will get you where you wish to go, if we are not slaughtered by sharks, eyeless, or your new croc friends. Though I believe the latter to be the most likely."

A presence stirred behind Jordan, maybe a good fifty meters back. Jordan rose slowly and faced east, into the setting sun. He was certain Sobek had chosen his approach with that in mind, whether tactically or to silhouette his monstrous form.

"If I remember right you don't like formalities," Jordan called. He remained in human form, though the temptation to shift wouldn't be quieted. "Sorry about the nature of the invitation."

"You are fortunate I have deeper problems, Ark Lord." Sobek thudded closer, the earth groaning under his bulk as the ancient god approached. He was larger than the last time Jordan had seen him. Or this was the first time he was getting a look at Sobek's war form. He put the croc at five meters tall. Taller than any Ka-Ken, but much tougher, and with deathless powers to boot. The croc gave a low threatening rumble. "The fiction that Isis still lives won't save you. Give me a reason I shouldn't devour you here and gain your secrets? Your Ark is distant and broken."

"Because you need allies," Jordan pointed out. He folded his arms, immovable as the rock beneath him. "Because the last thing you need is another enemy. Because what I'm asking isn't much."

"What boon do you seek?" Sobek's mighty tail swished behind him, close enough to strike Jordan if he chose.

"Free the landfinders. Make an official truce with them." Jordan paused, but the croc gave no reaction to the initial terms. "Make the same truce with me. Not Isis. Me. I will lead my people from Peru to Australia, and you will let us land and make a home for ourselves."

Sobek's scaly hands worked as if longing to grab something. Agitation? It was hard to read the elder god.

"If you are fleeing Peru it means abandoning your Ark and the Isis pretense." Sobek's tail continued to swish, each time coming a little closer. "It means you are no Ark Lord, just an untrained pup and a lackey."

Jordan considered that, and then gave a reluctant nod. "All that's true. My Ark is broken, and I plan to turn tail and run. To abandon that continent. But the people I'm bringing are champions, Sobek. Pure-blooded, and only a few generations removed from Blair, and from Isis. Now I don't claim to know anything about your war with whatever these eyeless are, but I've got to think that having a friendly society of champions watching your back on land could be useful. And about Isis...there's a chance she might not make it back. But there's a chance she might. And even if she doesn't, her daughter might be a little pissed off to find out you wiped out most of the surviving champions."

"Daughter?" Sobek cocked his head in a gesture a human might have made, a reminder of his origins. "You mean Jes'Ka."

"Yeah." Jordan withdrew a second can of chili from his pack. "She's training Liz right now, while Blair is learning how to tap fully into his Ark. I'm willing to share intel, in addition to a truce. But I'm not willing to budge on the part where you release the landfinders."

Manu hadn't said a word, but the man tensed every time the landfinders were mentioned.

"What do you mean about Isis?" Sobek's tail had ceased its swishing, and now slumbered beside his bulk. "She lives?"

"Maybe," Jordan allowed, "and maybe not. She was killed fighting Set, but we found a loophole. Blair can use his Ark to retrieve her, if nothing goes wrong."

"Temporal shaping," Sobek rumbled, and backed away a step. "The consequences are terrible. A life for a life, god-ling. Let Isis go. Let history forget her. I will give you your alliance, but you must agree to cease this shaping. It is forbidden, because it can unravel our world. Everything can be rewoven, or unwoven, if the shaping goes awry. Nothing is worth that risk, little god."

Jordan considered his answer carefully. There was no way he could convince Blair to abandon his plan, even if he agreed with Sobek. He didn't. Not just because this guy said so.

"If you give me more to work with, then I'll pass it along to Blair, and to Trevor," Jordan promised. He savored a mouthful of chili before speaking again. "Odds are good they're going to do what they want to do, because I'm just a lackey, but if you can provide evidence that the shaping is too dangerous I promise they will see it. And I will make them listen, even if they choose to go through with it. They'll at least know the risks."

It was Sobek's turn to be quiet, and Jordan tensed when the beast offered a wordless growl.

"We have an accord, lackey god to lackey god." Sobek extended a thick meaty arm wider than Jordan's torso, so he shifted into his warform and accepted the handshake. Sobek released him, and thumped his tail against the stone. "I will free the other landfinders, and allow them to return to their people, so long as they bear my children no lingering ill will. You may conduct your people to our shores, but if you do so then you must come to my aid when I call. I will do the same, should your people be threatened after arrival."

Jordan considered that. Sobek was undoubtedly getting the better end. The odds of someone attacking from the bush seemed remote, and was presumably under the control of whatever Ark Lord Sobek reported to. Whereas Jordan knew that the eyeless were attacking, and that if things went south they might be called upon to intervene.

The deal was enough, lopsided as it was.

"Thank you, Sobek. I don't know what your beef with Isis is, but you've done right by me and mine. We'll do right by you." Jordan wavered, but managed the last words. "I have a favor to ask, ally to ally. I'll need ships to get my people out."

Sobek gave a deep huff from low in his scaly chest. "Would that I could, but my forces are otherwise engaged. You will need alternate means of getting your people out. If you reach our shores, then contact me and we will make our accord final."

The subtext seemed clear. If he didn't contact Sobek it meant he'd failed, and his people were dead.

No pressure.

21

PELE'S BLESSING

J ordan basked in the island's bounty as his reserves filled. The strategic importance of this place wasn't lost on him. If you harnessed the power here, then you could rule the Pacific.

"You have a faraway look, mate." Manu's voice interrupted Jordan's thoughts as the shorter man followed him up the path. "And it is not much farther to the cove."

Jordan tightened the strap on his pack, and increased his pace. The land finder had no trouble keeping up, and seemed just as energized by the stone. All shapers probably coveted this place.

"Just musing." Jordan finally spoke, now that he knew the questions he wanted to ask. "I thought you made your boats from grass? The shore is right down there. Why is this cove so important?"

Manu snorted and a grin split his jovial face. "You could sail to California in a life raft, but I'd rather do it on an ocean liner. I'm stoked I can make that raft if I need it, but if I'm going to be covering thousands of miles of open ocean I need porn, and a toilet, and liquor. Not much room for that stuff on a grass boat, ya know?"

Jordan found it interesting that bits of early 1980s Californian slang had somehow made it into these people's vernacular. He redoubled his pace and made for the ridge above, much more interested in their destination now. A comfortable boat ride to a new continent? Maybe he could actually sit down for five minutes and think strategy.

They reached the top of the ridge, which revealed a sheltered cove, with no visible sign of any boat. Jordan had expected some sort of illusion or other shaping, as otherwise the boat would have long since been spotted by the crocs. How it had remained hidden probably had a story attached to it.

"You're in for a treat." Manu plunged down the trail, his grin still in place. Remarkably cheery for a guy who'd been enslaved hours before. "Not many outside the landfinders have seen our shaping. Before we go tramping down there let's see what we're working toward."

Manu paused atop a rock outcrop bisecting the trail. He set his stance wide, then stomped suddenly and let out a sharp hiss, and his face shifted into an exaggerated snarl that was clearly part of whatever ritual he performed.

A tremor rumbled through the rock around them, and below a huge sheet of black volcanic rock split and fell away. Beneath the ledge it had sheltered sat a thirty-foot yacht with a single wide sail, but also an onboard motor. Jordan guessed it had been manufactured in the last ten years, and the vessel had been lovingly cared for. *Pele's Blessing* had been emblazoned along the prow.

"Hell of a ship." Jordan offered a low whistle to express his heart-felt praise. "Manu, my friend, I've been roughing it for a very, very long time. I think I'm going to like traveling in a bit of style."

"I guarantee it." Manu hurried down the trail, then dove off a cliff into the water some thirty meters below the trail. He disappeared for a moment, then came shooting out of the water standing across a stone stair that levitated in the air. He stepped atop another, and another, as the stairs levitated into place. "Come on, mate. I want to be under sail in time to get the barbie fired up before the sun goes down."

Jordan levitated into the air and drifted down to the boat, where he landed on the deck near the door that led inside the cabin. He followed Manu inside, and deposited his pack in the corner near the bunk he assumed he'd be sleeping in.

"Take your ease. I'll get us underway." He moved to the windows, and slid open a pair on one side, then the other. "We can hear each other easily, so we can talk as I ready the vessel. To begin...a destination? I overheard your conversation with the croc, and again ka pai for getting him to agree to free my people. You wanna go to Australia? You looking for Uluru?"

Jordan sat heavily on the bunk, and leaned back against the wall. He wasn't sore, but it still felt good to be off his back and out of the sun.

"Catch." Jordan looked up to find a beer sailing toward him, and he snatched the silver can out of the air just before it reached his cot. Manu rummaged in the fridge, then dropped on the other cot with a beer of his own. He cracked the tab, and offered Jordan a salute with the can. "To freedom."

"Freedom." Jordan cracked the tab and enjoyed a long pull off the first cold beer he'd had since the world had ended. Damned if it didn't go down smooth. "Thanks, Manu. This is a rare treat, and one I badly needed. It's nice having a reminder that there are things in the world worth fighting for."

The landfinder finished another swallow, then returned to the fridge, his face disappearing. "You like shrimp? That's pretty much all I got for now. I found a patch of them, and raised the ocean floor. Not very sporting, but it keeps my belly full."

"Shrimp sounds incredible." Jordan savored another mouthful of beer, and lounged into the boards behind him as the vessel swayed with the tide. The boat reminded him a bit of the one used in Jaws, though a much more comfortable version. Same size though. Hadn't Manu said something about sharks? "So can you tell me how to find the Ark Lord that Sobek works for?"

"Works for?" Manu snorted a laugh, and emerged with a tray of about forty shrimp that had been pre-battered. "The grill will only take a few moments."

An unfamiliar signal rose from Manu as the smaller man

approached the grill, and heat rose from it. Not flame, but heat. Jordan studied the grill through the window, and realized the heat was coming from the bars. The land finder had directly heated the metal.

"Neat trick." More beer further improved his mood. Would it be rude to ask for another?

"Sobek does not work for Uluru." Manu stamped a foot on the deck and gave a sharp roar, and every one of those damned shrimp flipped over on the barbecue at the same time, the heavenly sizzling filling the cabin. "Uluru simply is. A force of nature, it is said. Some sort of ancient god from another world. The oldest peoples commune with her, but they don't speak of what they learn. We avoid the bush. Dinos, you know. No one likes tangling with Dinos."

"Dinos?" Jordan set his empty can down on the table near the bunk.

"Yeah, all sorts. They showed up within weeks of the sun-storm that ended things, you know." Another stomp, and the shrimp flipped onto a plate, which Manu carried into the cabin and deposited on the table. "Hey, can I grab you another beer?"

"Yeah." Jordan offered a grateful smile. "I'll take 'em 'til you don't want to give them out any more."

"Oh, that will never happen." Manu gave a deep laugh. "I've got a tether under the boat towing 42 cases. I restock at every port. Everyone needs a landfinder, and most people have beer to trade."

Manu popped a shrimp into his mouth, and then ducked out of the cabin. His legs flashed past the windows, followed by the whistle of canvas as he did something to the sail. A moment later the boat lurched into motion, and began slowly drifting toward the open ocean past the mouth of the cove.

Those unknowable blue waters bothered Jordan.

Jordan popped a shrimp in his mouth and happily chewed as he joined Manu on deck. The landfinder stood behind a fancy electronic wheel, and a faint hum emanated from the deck below them, probably from engines.

"So, since I'm two beers in and want to be clear, Sobek doesn't work for this Uluru?" Jordan leaned against the boat's rail, and smiled into the wind as he let the buzz take hold. It wouldn't last, so may as well enjoy it.

"Most assuredly not. Uluru makes. She doesn't take sides." Manu twisted the wheel, and they passed the last rocks, out into the deeper waters.

"Then I'm impressed by that bastard's gall." Jordan shook his head as he considered the magnitude of Sobek's play. "He told Isis that he spoke for an Ark Lord, and she made a deal to give up this island. I wonder if she'd have done that if she knew he didn't speak for anyone but himself."

It also made sudden sense why Sobek thought of himself as a lackey. At this point he wasn't even that. He was impersonating a lackey.

"Whoever this Isis is, I hope she teaches him a lesson." Manu spit into the water, though his smile returned a moment later. "Sobek is greed given monstrous form. There was no reason to go to war with my people. His attacks were unprovoked. Your accord says that we cannot strike back, and that will not sit well with many. Especially Jamina. I fear she may not abide by your accord."

And there went the buzz. He couldn't blame the landfinders for being angry, but if their actions jeopardized his people it hardly mattered. Risk was risk.

"Is there anything we can do to prevent that?" He crumpled the empty can in his fist, squeezing until it was little more than a penny-sized disk.

"Nope." Manu tapped a button on the wheel, then stepped back and finished his beer with a single chug. He levitated the empty can through an open widow, and into a receptacle inside. "Every ship is a nation. We all make our own choices. That's our freedom. If your tribe is doing something you don't like, then you take the people who will listen and start your own tribe. You just sail in a different direction. The people are people in name only. Getting us all to agree on anything is like...trying to get whanau—that's Maori for family—to all sit down to a meal without bickering. Yeah, nah. Ain't gonna happen. But it's all good. Sobek will turn a blind eye to it if she does anything. He doesn't want to go to war with you."

Jordan prayed that Manu was right. He considered a third beer, but thought better of it. He had a feeling he'd need to be well rested for whatever came next.

22

SHARKS

Jordan awoke with a start to find himself twisted into the sheets on his cot. Gulls called in the distance, and the tang of salty air washed through the cabin's still open windows. He sat up and stretched as he peered out the windows to see where they were.

He spotted no land in any direction, nor any sign of Manu, so he ducked through the cabin's low door and onto the deck. Manu sat behind the wheel with a beer in one hand, a beautiful smile plastered on his handsome face as he peered at the rising sun in their wake.

"Haere Mai, Ark Lord. Good morning." He gestured at the ocean before them. "She waits for us, her bounty and her wrath. Twelve days of clean sailing will put us in Sydney Harbor."

Jordan's shoulders sank. Twelve days wasn't going to work. He'd recharged his reserves on Easter Island. Should he light walk to Sydney? That would leave him without a guide, or a connection to the people. He needed boats. Manu might be able to make that happen, since his people could make them from grass. It wouldn't be a comfortable evac, but if people lived they'd get over it.

"I can get us there a lot faster." Jordan studied the boat beneath

him. How much could you take with you on a light walk? "We'd probably have to leave the boat behind, but I can have us in Sydney in five
minutes."

"Ah, and there's the rub." Manu shook his head sadly. "You are
still operating with your preconceived knowledge of shaping. By all
means...attempt to light walk to Australia, anywhere. I will wait."
Manu's grin went mischievous.

So Jordan tried. Power swelled within him, and the signal burst
outwards...and then rebounded back, and dissipated as if it had never
been.

"I think...the continent is blocked somehow. Like a no-fly zone."
Jordan realized a smile had somehow found its way onto his face.
"That means I can spend twelve days drinking and doing nothing...
guilt free."

"You like fishing, mate?" Manu knelt next to a cabinet against the
rear of the wheel, and withdrew a tackle box and a massive rod, easily
the thickest Jordan had ever seen.

"I haven't been since I was a kid." Jordan moved over to one of the
flipchairs bolted to the deck for just such a fisherman, and plopped
down into it. He concentrated on the refrigerator, and levitated a beer
through the window and onto the table next to him.

Manu tossed him the rod, which Jordan caught, then rested on
the metal couch designed to hold it so he could sit...and drink beer.
Sip. He didn't even care if he caught anything. Jordan propped his
feet up on the railing, and leaned back, enjoying the morning. Sure,
Peru was in trouble, but he couldn't do anything about it right now.

So Jordan enjoyed the balance of the day. He spent twelve solid
hours getting drunk and watching the fishing pole sit there without a
bite. There were plenty of shrimp to go around, and Jordan shared
out some of his tastier MREs. The lasagna in particular had survived
the end of the world in remarkable shape.

The boat cut across the ocean, until the sun hit its zenith and
marched down to the western horizon. As the burning orb finally
passed below the waves, Jordan realized he could spot something in
the distance.

"What's that in our path?" Jordan tensed, and his buzz receded.

"Flotilla." Manu polished off another beer, and levitated it to the receptacle, accompanied by a belch. "I bet Jamina's already there. She's gonna give us grief about taking the tiki tour to get here."

Jordan relaxed into his chair. He didn't know what to expect from the landfinders, but hoped that they'd be accepting, given his role in their new freedom. As they approached the flotilla he glimpsed more of the boats.

Some were low flat grass canoes, which he took to be the boats the landfinders had created. There were also several catamarans, and a pair of larger yachts packed with people. A net had been spread between the ships, and planks thrown down atop the netting to form walkways between the boats.

Dark-skinned landfinders hurried gracefully along the planks, all congregating around one of the two yachts. Smoke rolled off a barbecue that had been erected on the boat, and Jamina's familiar form tended to a hunk of tuna as she prepared the savory fish.

Most of the landfinders were Maori or other Pacific Islanders, but there were asians, and a few very Californian blonds. All had tattoos, mostly on their arms and faces. They laughed and joked with each other, and seemed unaware of the *Pele's Blessing* approaching until they were right up on them.

That had to be an act of course. They'd set up directly in their path knowing Manu would come this way.

A clever people, the beast rumbled in his mind. *I see much that is known, and so I stay silent, and learn.*

Good advice to us both, Jordan thought back. He grabbed his jacket, as the temperature could drop sharply if the wind picked up, and then headed back on deck to join Manu at the wheel.

Manu guided the *Blessing* to the edge of the netting, where the vessel bumped against an invisible wall. A number of landfinders looked up, and almost half began leaving Jamina's boat and making for Manu's.

At first.

Within moments everyone had realized Manu was here, and had

begun to desert Jamina's boat en masse. They tromped across planks and swarmed up the side of the *Blessing* and onto the deck.

Jordan recognized a few faces from the group he'd saved, but since he'd never learned their names it was like meeting them for the first time.

They pressed in around Manu, each jockeying to be the first to lock forearms in an odd kind of handshake that bordered on a wrestling contest. Each combatant stuck their tongue out as far as they could go, and offered one of the hisses that seemed to accompany their rituals.

A short stocky woman with thick dark hair ended up being the winner of whatever their contest seemed to be, though Jordan couldn't tell how they'd decided who won. They all clapped her on the back, and offered deferential nods.

One of the larger men slapped a sixty-pound tuna onto Manu's grill, and the fish instantly began to sizzle.

"Did you just steal Jamina's party?" Jordan called as he savored the smell and lounged against the rail.

"Forty-two cases, mate. Forty-two cases." He nodded at the cabin where the raid on the beer had already begun. "I'd say they've earned it. Drink up, mates. Plenty to go around."

Jordan levitated a pair of beers out of the stack, nodded gratefully at Manu, then jumped over the side. He landed lightly atop the closest plank, and began following it back toward Jamina's boat.

It was impossible not to glance over the side at the swelling ocean beneath him as the planks rose and fell, creaking over the nets. If something did attack from below, and it really was as large as a megalodon, then that net wasn't going to do shit.

Jordan probably could have kept his balance as a mortal, but this thing still would have been a death trap. One stray wave and you're done. As a champion he had fewer misgivings, but it really hadn't been that long since his change, and shaking old instincts never came easy.

He reached Jamina's yacht, a less fancy version of Manu's with *Sea*

Sister emblazoned on the side. She slapped the fish on a cutting board, and hewed off a large hunk, which she offered to Jordan as he approached. Her eyes blazed in indignation, though he didn't think he was the cause.

"Haere Mai, Ark Lord." She hewed off a second hunk, then dropped into a chair and jammed a hot chunk of fish in her mouth. "Mmm. Choice as I've ever had. One of those beers for me?"

"Haere Mai." Jordan nodded respectfully and offered her a beer. "I thought maybe you could use some company, and I like fish." He helped himself to a mouthful, surprised by how good it was. He gobbled down the entire hunk in seconds, and looked around for more.

"You just welcomed me." Jamina eyed him like a ten-year-old idiot brother. "Haere Mai means welcome in Maori."

"Oh. I thought it was hello." Jordan cracked his beer, and savored a small mouthful. He'd only brought one, and he wanted it to last.

"Kia Ora, or keyora. Means hello." Jamina paused to belch loudly. "Good beer. So why did you really come, Ark Lord? You're either here to fuck me or force me to do something I'm not going to like. It's written all over you."

"I just wanted some fish." Jordan guzzled down his beer, as he realized his stay might not be all that long. This time he belched. It was refreshing being among people who celebrated. "Though I was going to work up to asking you not to attack Sobek, because that will break the terms of the treaty we just made."

"Treaty." She raised an eyebrow and gave him the you're-so-precious smile again. "Sobek will honor no treaty. He will leave us alone long enough to deal with the eyeless, and then he will come for us once more. Or, I can kill his people now, while they are fighting on two fronts."

The soldier in him couldn't argue the logic. There couldn't be a more perfect time for an insurgency. A few people could do catastrophic damage, if they employed the right shaping, and if they really could control....

Strength deserted Jordan as his empty can clattered to the deck. A dorsal fin broke the water just outside the netting, one taller than any of the ships present. A second fin broke the water on the other side, then a third.

23

MANIPULATIONS

Irakesh had grown accustomed to his ceremonial garb over the last few days. It marked him as different, and he'd carefully reinforced the idea that he stood behind no particular deathless. He favored no ruler, though he never criticized Camiero.

They believed him impartial, and while worthy of respect because of his lethality, they thought he lacked the context to understand the situation they were faced with. They believed, and his garb reinforced, that he was some backward primitive. Perfect.

He strode from his cabin, the gentle sway of the ocean much more noticeable once he stood at the cruise ship's railing.

At first Irakesh had taken a dim view to the vessel. It possessed no defenses. No cannons. It was slow and cumbersome. But it was also packed with hundreds of deathless who could rise like the world's vengeance, a swarm of angry wasps descending on their foes.

Around the cruise ship bobbed hundreds of other ships, from tiny yachts to a U.S. Navy destroyer that he recognized from pillaged memories. Those ships floated in a scattered formation, exactly as Camiero had ordered. Their warships set a perimeter, with the cruise ship at the very center of their miles-wide circle.

Lima dominated the eastern horizon, the dying city hazy underneath the dome of force the werewolf shapers had somehow erected. He'd not seen anything like it from them during the previous suncycle, though it seemed pretty clear why. Any werewolf who hadn't scurried into the jungle was about to die.

Irakesh had done what he could to slow it, but every step he took toward the ballroom where the generales were meeting was an admission that he'd failed. They'd agreed that coming together had been wise, and the fleet's cohesion was a testament to their working together.

He pushed the door open and found another. Every deathless seated at one of the several dozen small tables wore the same olive green uniform, with the same watchful-eye patch on the shoulder. They were still scheming, but no longer for dominance. Now it was for position in an organization they believed transcended themselves.

The words came in Ra's voice, fragments of their many sessions bubbling up from the distant past, untroubled by the centuries.

Irakesh moved to sit at an empty table, offered the room a respectful bow, and then sat. Almost everyone nodded back at him, and a few raised glasses of thick dark blood, though Ra only knew where they'd gotten it. He was better off not knowing.

"We are all here now," Camiero called in a commanding voice as he rose to his feet from a table near the stage. "And so it is time to decide on a course of action for our new fleet. I understand the obvious target. We are parked off their coast, after all, but Irakesh has brought a matter to my attention."

All eyes shifted in Irakesh's direction, and he squirmed under their gaze. A magnificent performance, in his own mind at least. "I am old, and possess many secrets, but as you can feel I am no elder god. Sobek is. Sobek could devour this vessel and all aboard without ever fearing even a single blow. Sobek styles himself an admiral, and as you already know he possessed a deal with the werewolves. If we attack Lima there is a real chance he will retaliate, and I do not believe we will survive his wrath."

"A valid concern." Camiero gave an apologetic shrug. "Yet here is my dilemma. If we cannot attack Lima, then we have no way of testing our strength. Of turning our militia into a real army."

Irakesh rose slowly and offered a deep bow, then straightened. "Respectfully, a single battle, especially one in which you shell the enemy from range, will not turn us into an army. The men fear Jordan. They know he's slaughtered every party who directly assaulted the city, and that now we are sieging them rather than face them in battle, despite our overwhelming numbers. If we win, it will not teach your army the lessons you are hoping it will."

Then Irakesh sat, and waited. He'd played his part perfectly.

"Does anyone wish to present a counter argument?" Camiero asked. He rested a hand on the table, and made no move to rise. "Generales?"

Silence smothered the few lingering conversations, as no one wanted to be mistaken for volunteering feedback. These people didn't seem to care what happened one way or another, with few exceptions. Those exceptions were wise enough to stay silent until they understood how to navigate the currents without being swept away.

There wasn't a single military mind among them. Not a one who would be able to oppose Sobek, or Jordan, or Nox, or...anyone with training and experience in leading men into war.

"I suppose," Camiero finally continued, "that it might be prudent to either seek a new target or to consider a preemptive strike against Sobek himself. Yet that still leaves a small, but potent, dagger at our backs."

"Camiero, if I may," called a shriveled woman who'd not made the transition to unlife with even a shred of humanity. She wore what remained of her skin like an ill-fitting coat. "We must scout the oceans, and we must contain the werewolves. Leave the bulk of our forces here. Send a small force to explore east, and to perhaps serve as an emissary to this Sobek. Tell him these are our lands, not the werewolves'."

"Such a move," Irakesh called, his voice drawing many eyes, "will invite violence. Sobek will destroy whatever force you send. He respects old gods, and those with more power than him. His children are just as savage. If you seek to parlay you will only hasten oblivion."

"Then what would you suggest?" the sagging woman snapped. "Shall we sit here and do nothing? The werewolves fear us less every day. They know they broke our assault. We need to deal with them, and we need to show our teeth to this lizard-god you're so terrified of. He is one. We are many."

Irakesh began to laugh. He'd perfected the art of scorn, and imbued his mockery with every razored barb. "Many? Many? You think this is a game of numbers? Child, an elder god can slaughter *thousands* in a single afternoon. Jes'Ka and a Sunsteel blade took the necropolis at Akebes. She killed them all, by herself, and left a rotting reminder of why lesser gods do not attract their ire. If Sobek comes, our only hope of survival is flight. If you meet him in battle he will, quite literally, devour you all."

It helped that Irakesh simply related the unvarnished truth. Sobek was a monster in the literal sense of the word, the very worst of what a god could be. Mother had hated him for that, and for the many sacrifices he'd made for no other reason than love of power.

Not that she didn't also love power. She was just better at acquiring it without needed sacrifice, something she'd tried to teach him, but that he'd learned over the last year he'd never really understood.

"I will not be mocked," sagging woman snarled. She rose to her feet, and fixed Irakesh with what he supposed must be her version of an intimidating stare. "He may be immortal, but you are not."

"And that will help you how?" Irakesh asked, more gentle in his tone now. "You murder me, an ally with valuable insight into how your enemy's mind works, because I stung your pride? It is no sin to tell you the truth, and the truth is that none of you are prepared to deal with Sobek, or his children. We do not wish a war with them, and the best thing we can do for the time being is avoid their notice. Attack the werwolves if you must have something to keep you occupied, but it would be smarter to husband our forces and make no enemies. We might even find that Sobek does our work for us and wipes out the werewolves. Our time would be better spent learning the nature of the deal he struck with Jordan."

Thoughtful expressions lined the room, but no one spoke. Sagging woman sagged back into her chair, apparently beaten.

"Very well," Camiero said. "I will take a night to think on this. Tomorrow we decide on a course of action."

For an instant Irakesh allowed his gaze to touch Camiero's, and the deathless gave him an almost imperceptible nod.

They'd staved off an attack for another day, but in the end Lima would be destroyed. Whatever Jordan was about, he'd better be quick about it or there wouldn't be anything left to return to.

Nothing living, anyway.

24

EYELESS

Not a single landfinder seemed perturbed by the fins circling them, and after a moment Jamina broke out laughing. She clapped him hard on the shoulder. "Those are our sharks, mate. They protect the flotilla. They were just out hunting is all."

Jordan picked up his discarded can and sat back down. "Oh. How big are those fish, exactly?"

"You know, fifty, sixty meters." Jamina shrugged and crumpled her own can. "One of those is mine. Manu ain't got one. But he does have beer. He always has beer. You don't have to keep me company."

Jordan considered that. She was blunt to a fault, but had a right to be a little raw after what she'd been through, and he felt the power roiling within her. Maybe understanding her would help him persuade her to leave off her vengeance. And if not, the fish was good, beer or no.

"Jamina!" Manu's rich voice rang from his yacht, and Jordan spied him waving near the barbecue. "Two cases, just landed on your deck." He nodded toward the prow of her ship, where a pair of water-logged boxes landed.

"I don't need your pity beer," Jamina roared back as she

approached the crates, "but I'm going to drink it anyway. Whanau. Thank you."

She pried open the box, and tossed a silver can to Jordan, then withdrew one for herself. By the time she'd returned to her seat a handful of landfinders had come back over, though most still lounged on Manu's boat. A few went to the other yachts or to their own grass boats to sleep it off. The party had started long before they'd arrived.

Jamina began chatting with another landfinder, and Jordan found himself alone in a crowd, which was generally what he preferred at parties. Intentionally entering a room with dozens of unknown hostiles with the express intention of lowering your defenses with alcohol seemed a poor survival strategy when you could drink on the couch with your three closest friends behind your security door instead.

The day dragged on, the beer flowed, and the landfinders never slowed the party. They danced, and fished, and blared techno, and drank, and screwed. It didn't slacken until the sun touched the western horizon, and by then most landfinders had returned to collapse on their boats, exhausted, and in for one hell of a hangover if landfinders didn't have a shaping trick to fix that.

Jordan paced himself and kept a nice steady buzz going all day. He feasted on fish, and thought about Peru and how he was going to deal with the situation. The landfinders weren't the answer. Not by themselves. They might be able to get his people across the ocean, but it would take weeks, and they'd be slower than anything Sobek or Nox would send. They'd be picked off before they made it to Easter Island, much less Australia.

No amount of beer and fish made the problem easier to solve, though he gnawed on it all day. He finally gave up, and returned to Manu's yacht where his host still entertained the last handful of landfinders.

"Hoy, mate!" Manu beckoned him over with a beer. "Things are winding down. Your bed will be free soon. You're welcome to roust whoever's there now, if you're sauced."

Jordan wasn't, but he nodded gratefully and ducked inside the cabin to get away from the dregs of the party. Thankfully no one lounged on his bunk, and he flopped gratefully down. Eleven more days of this was going to wear on him, though he wondered what would happen when the forty-two cases gave out. They'd done for at least a quarter today.

He didn't need dinner as he'd been grazing all day, so Jordan considered bedding down. He stripped off his shirt, which he wadded under the threadbare pillow. Pillows always sucked on boats. He'd left his jacket somewhere, and didn't feel like hunting for it. It's not like he had car keys to lose.

His head hit the pillow, and he closed his eyes and...lay there. The lapping of the waves was soothing, but it didn't drown out the hum of laughing conversation on deck. Sound was a vibration, right? Could he make like, a sound bubble to block it out? Probably. It sounded like a lot of effort though, and it would also isolate him in the event of an attack.

Not that an attack seemed likely with those great beasts lurking outside. Sixty-meter sharks? Where had they come from, and good lord why? The fact that these people had harnessed them for war...a Great Pack in the ocean. The world could still surprise him. And the craziest was yet to come, if there really were Dinos.

A tingling growl grew deep within his chest, drawn from some primal instinct, though Jordan had no idea what had prompted him to issue the sound. He rose to a sitting position, and listened. All the same sounds layered atop each other, but something was different. He closed his eyes and drank deeply of the scents and sounds around him.

Brine overpowered everything, with beer, and vomit, and fish guts, and smoke, and other scents all competing. But underneath it all lay an alien scent. A scent that raised Jordan's hackles, and told him that the primal death of mankind walked the night, and that he'd best be prepared to deal with it.

I do not recognize this thing. We should attack.

Jordan ignored the beast, though he did shift into warform and ready himself for battle. He continued to listen, and raised his muzzle, even as he cocked now furry ears to strain for any sound.

There.

A slapping as something climbed from the water and onto a ship. Not theirs, but a neighboring vessel. A swimmer who'd tumbled overboard? His gut said no. Something alien and unnatural touched a chord within him.

Jordan levitated into the air, and twisted through the window as he accelerated into a blur. He didn't need super senses to spot the creature, or to see it staring up at him with wrinkled leathery skin. Its face had a mouth made for sucking, lined with teeth, and where its eyes should be was unbroken skin. The body was bipedal with fins, and appeared made for war. The creature carried a bone spear carved from the rib of some leviathan...which it hurled at Jordan in a single smooth motion.

The spear whipped toward him, but he twisted aside, confident he'd avoided the blow. Ice overpowered his nervous system, as something, a spirit or soul perhaps, was yanked out of his body by the spear. The ghostly energy clung to the unnatural weapon as it splashed into the water a good thirty meters from the boat. The eyeless followed, disappearing beneath the waves.

"I need that, right?" Jordan rumbled even as he willed himself into the water. There was no answer from the beast.

Jordan dove into the icy ocean, propelling himself with his telekinesis, down into the inky blackness. He couldn't see his target, but he used one of the shaping pings Blair had taught him. The results surprised him.

The ping revealed an absence where the signal was simply... eaten. Gone.

Jordan pushed harder and accelerated through the water until he spied a flash of ghostly white, his spirit or whatever the creature had removed from him. He forced a hand through the water, and broadcast a signal to snare the creature.

The shaping grasped the creature...and disappeared inside it. Absorbed as the ping had been. Were these things immune to shaping? That seemed like an important detail that the landfinders might have shared. And didn't these things never come to the surface?

Anger surged through him. Rage. Blinding bestial wrath, and he gave himself to it fully. There was no more thought. There was only a need to end this thing. Immediately.

Swimming became effortless, and the gap began to narrow. Fins had materialized on his wrists, ankles, and back, constructed from pure telekinetic force, though he didn't remember summoning them.

"You're mine, now." Jordan closed the last few meters and extended his claws.

The creature pivoted at the last moment, and tried to dart away. Jordan blurred, and his claws raked the creature's back as it swam out of reach. It didn't blur, but damned if it didn't move like it did. Inky blood filled the water around him, and it burned his eyes when it came into contact with them. A normal person would have been permanently blinded, or worse.

Jordan reached for the water ahead of the creature, and shaped it into a super dense wall of compressed ice, though he couldn't even say for certain how he dropped the temperature of the water. It crystalized just in time for the creature to say hello with its face.

The ice shattered, but dramatically slowed the creature's momentum. Its head snapped back...and brought it within rang of Jordan's fangs. He clamped down on its neck, the fangs ripping through scaly hide and muscle, and then finally bone. Rancid blood burned his gums, but he bit down harder, and thrust both fists through the smug fucker's chest.

The thrashing weakened, but incredibly didn't stop. The thing kept fighting.

Jordan wrenched with all his strength, tightening his jaw as he tore the head and neck from the creature's body. It still twitched, even after that. He released the bloody carcass, which began to sink into the depths.

Jordan scanned the water around it, and located the bone spear, which also tumbled toward the ocean floor. He made for it, and paused next to the glowing bit of energy it had taken from him. How did he reabsorb it? Screw it. Jordan extended a hand and touched the energy.

A shock raced up his arm, and the glow disappeared as something flowed back into him. Primal anger faded.

Thank you, Ka-Dun, for returning me. I do not know what the creature would have done. Devoured me, perhaps. Or used me in some dark ritual.

Jordan's chest ached, and he realized he'd been underwater for a minute or more. Time to get topside, and hope he could deal with the Benz. He swam upwards, now using his shaping to propel him.

The fact that it could pluck you out is terrifying. If they're all immune to shaping, I can see why Sobek is losing the war.

Jordan burst from the ocean in a spray of foam and shot into the air. Pain trembled through his head, and as he understood, it would worsen over the next twenty minutes in a diver that surfaced unexpectedly. Regeneration should compensate.

A quick scan of the flotilla confirmed his worst fears. A severed dorsal fin bobbed up and down against the nets, and there was no sign of the surviving sharks. Eyeless swarmed every boat, and most of the landfinders were locked in hand-to-hand combat.

25

GETTING CREATIVE

Jordan knew he needed to do something game-changing, or the landfinders would be slaughtered. They'd broken into groups and stood back to back, those who'd survived the initial assault. If beer slowed them he couldn't tell.

Each landfinder wielded a stone handaxe, the weapons varying from jade to obsidian to granite. The axes doubled as both bludgeoning and slashing weapons, and also served as a focus for the landfinder's shaping. If Jordan understood the signals correctly the landfinder would make the weapon lighter at the start of the swing, and then add weight as the swing approached the target.

The woman who'd won the wrestling contest had a pair of axes, and dropped another eyeless with a flurry of savage blows to its back. That left her exposed, and another eyeless lunged from the shadows, its mouth fixing to her back like some twisted lamprey. She brought an axe around behind her and smashed the face, and the thing's body fell away, its fangs still lodged in her back. She made it look easy.

"Fall back to Manu's boat!" she roared, and staggered in that direction. Two more eyeless were closing in.

Jordan accelerated his blur, pouring power in until time crawled, then appeared to freeze below him. That bought him time to think.

A few things were apparent. First, none of the other eyeless carried bone harpoons, or spears, or whatever. Second, none seemed to be doing anything but feeding. That made the one that came after him special, and meant he had to at least consider the possibility it had been sent specifically for him.

It didn't mean that for sure. He could have gotten lucky. Maybe he should have kept the harpoon, but just looking at it had hurt his eyes. It reminded him uncomfortably of the demotech armor he'd been trapped in, though it didn't feel exactly the same.

Since none of the others had one it didn't matter right now. His current dilemma was how to deal with a bunch of monster fish, when you couldn't shape them and each one took a legendary beating to finish off. He counted twenty-three of the things remaining. Six down, maybe two or three more had died in the water.

Nine landfinders still stood, but when he released the blur that number would become seven almost instantly, unless he stopped it.

How could he deal with these? What would Blair do? What would Trevor do? Blair would discover some new rare form of shaping. Trevor would cleverly improvise a solution using the materials at hand, MacGyver style.

Down in the water he'd made fins when he'd needed them, almost without thinking. What else could he use as a tool? The ice had slowed the creature, so objects he acted on could still...Jordan grinned down at the eyeless. "I'm definitely overthinking this."

He raised a hand, and every bit of the metal netting rose into the air. Jordan severed a massive piece, and wove the metal strands he'd pulled into a thick rope that strongly resembled barbed wire.

Then Jordan went fishing. He blurred down to the closest target, and punched through the eyeless's throat, hooking it on the line. He blurred to the next fish, and the next. One by one Jordan strung the wire through them, doing some damage, but not seriously harming them.

That gave him a few seconds to think about what to do once he'd gathered them all. The eyeless didn't venture out of the deeps. Them coming to the surface was new and controversial. Why didn't they come to the surface? Breathing didn't seem to be the issue, or there'd be no reason to confine their attacks to darkness.

They feared the light. Maybe their skin was vulnerable to light. Solar radiation. The kind of stuff deathless used when frying people. He had neither of those things, unfortunately, even if they were vulnerable to it. Nothing the landfinders had done suggested they worked with light either.

He hooked the last one without a clear plan of what to do, so he flew straight upwards, high over the ocean, and into the clouds. It was quite beautiful, really, if you could ignore the Lovecraftian monstrosities he towed behind him.

A familiar welcome glow awaited him, the loving embrace of the moon, her kiss instantly empowering Jordan in the same way the island had. The eyeless enjoyed the process just a little bit less.

Their skin began to hiss and sizzle, even at full blur. Jordan released that blur, panting as the exertion overtook him. The eyeless burst into flame, their limbs burning like road flares as the moonlight cooked them. Shrieks rose from their dying bodies, for a few seconds anyway, and then there was only the wind.

Jordan dropped below the clouds once more, thankful for the thick fur insulating him from the wind. That had seemed so alien once.

Acceptance brings peace, Ka-Dun. We are one.

We are, he thought back affectionately.

Jordan felt a hero when he dropped below the clouds and approached the flotilla. The ragged survivors stood panting, their stone axes dripping with blood. The woman who'd won the wrestling contest stood among them, laughing as she pried fangs out of her back. The flesh around the wound had bad chemical burns. From the saliva maybe?

He landed on Manu's boat, and slung his makeshift line over the side, allowing the skeletons of the eyeless to clatter overboard into the water. "Sorry about your net."

Manu burst out laughing, and so did the other survivors. The jovial landfinder clapped Jordan hard on the shoulder. "No worries.

Mana, bro. You're kinda scary when you get mad. How'd you know the moon would cook 'em?"

"I thought they might not like light." Jordan shrugged. "It was a guess, and I happened to be right. I got lucky. They didn't."

A chorus of laughter came from the survivors, and to Jordan's immense shock they began cracking open beers. Manu waved his hand over the grill, which flared to life. He smiled at the lot of them. "Who wants some shrimp?"

"I'll have some," Jordan decided aloud. If this was how they celebrated their dead, then he'd honor their fallen, their way. "And a beer, if they're cold."

"Coldest, mate." Manu bent and snatched a can from the case at his feet, and tossed it to Jordan. "I'm thinking we need to get Jamina's ship situated, and then we get underway. We can't stay here. So eat it while it's hot."

Jordan nodded at that. More eyeless could come, and it could happen at any time. A feast felt reckless, but also a challenge to their enemies. *You came, we slaughtered you, and then got back to our drinking.*

The first taste of the watered down piss Manu stocked outshone the best German beer in the world. It tasted of victory.

"So where to now?" Jamina nursed her beer, darting furtive glances Jordan's way. "I think I wanna go wherever he's going."

"That means inheriting my problems." Jordan rolled his shoulder, which he'd injured during the fight. The eyeless blood had slowed his regeneration. "If you come with me, you're going to be dealing with a continent full of deathless trying to exterminate the last few werewolves. My job is to evacuate my people to Australia. I need boats to do that, so yeah I'm hopeful some of you might come with me, or go ahead of me to Lima to meet up with my people."

"I'll do it." Wrestling girl raised a hand. "I'm Bobby. I can make it to Lima faster than anyone here, since Scabs didn't make it. You want me to go to your people and start gettin' 'em ready?"

"I'd be grateful, Bobby." Jordan couldn't believe they were helping him. This was exactly what he'd needed. "Manu and I need to head to Australia. I need to meet with Uluru to secure my people a place there. Then I'll be heading back to meet up with you. I can light walk...teleport basically...to Lima when I'm ready."

"I need to warn the people," Jamina broke in. Her eyes were still wild from combat, and she'd yet to crack a beer. "This is new. The eyeless are attacking us directly. Why? The people have to be made ready. If Jordan hadn't been here, then all of us would be dead, and our people would still think us back at the quarries. We need to get to safer waters. Maybe the waters near Peru are safer, for now. I will try to persuade them to journey east toward Lima."

"Thank you, Jamina." He wished he were better at expressing himself. The words were insufficient for the service she was offering. "Sobek is an insufferable shit, the worst of an arrogant line of arrogant gods. But he isn't the worst evil I've survived, or vanquished. Not even close. He's small time stuff. If you can make peace with him? I'd do it until these eyeless are dealt with. Those things don't mean anything good for anybody."

The wild-eyed landfinder nodded. She deposited her axe back in its pouch, and finally cracked a beer. "One for the road. I'll lead my people away from danger, but I can't promise not to kill crocs. I won't borrow trouble though, that I will promise."

"That's all I can ask." Jordon looked to Manu. "She's right about us being underway. I doubt we'll see another wave immediately, as this seems to be the edge of her territory, but a response seems likely."

Manu nodded and hurried to the wheel. Jordan tried to ignore the beer in his hand as he steered the vessel into motion, but at least there wasn't much to run into on the ocean.

Jamina and the others hopped off onto an abandoned grass boat, then clambered up the side of Jamina's ship. Bobby kept on, taking a third vessel.

Jordan turned back to the ocean, and studied the placid waves. He'd never look at them the same way again.

26

WHISPERS FROM THE SHADOWS

L iz picked herself up off the stone and stepped into the sparring ring again. Just after awakening as a Ka-Ken she'd had a chance to spend weeks sparring against Bridget, and even the Mother, once. Most of the time she'd been on equal footing, but this was the first time she was fighting someone so far above her own level.

Jes'Ka reveled in hurling her from the ring, and making it seem effortless every time. She wore the shadows like armor, and caught Liz every time. She was faster, though not blur-fast thankfully. Whether she used her spear or claws Liz always ate pavement. She didn't even feel like she was improving, and they'd been at this for days.

"Before we go again, how about we change this up?" Liz wiped blood from her cheek, though the wound that had caused it was already healed. "Each time you knock me from the ring you tell me one thing I can improve."

"All right." Jes'Ka gave a playful smile, and straightened her hair in its ponytail. "You focus too much on the wolf. You aren't used to fighting as a woman, but there are countless situations where you will be limited to that body. You're fast and strong, but you don't push yourself or attempt to do things a human can't. I suspect you suffer from similar problems during intimacy."

Liz choked on her water bottle and dropped it outside the ring. Jes was proving a master of needling comments. She knew exactly how to hit you where it would deliver the most damage, and more and more Liz realized that too was a combat tactic. Keep your opponents off balance and worried about themselves.

"Why did your mother lock you and your boy toy up, but not give you the key?" It was the first time Liz had given in to her basic instincts, and she reveled in it.

"Good," Jes purred. She beckoned Liz back into the ring. "Always keep them off balance. He isn't my boy toy. I have not allowed Lucas to share my bed, though he desires it. He believes I am a goddess, and no amount of convincing will make him believe otherwise."

"I'm a better swordsman than you." Liz let her blade touch the stone inside the ring. "In a straight fight, no shadows, I'd beat you, and you know it."

"You truly believe it so?" Jes gave a low rolling laugh. "Shall we test that then? Your blade against my spear?"

Liz didn't wait. She channeled her rage, and frustration, and aggression into attacking the golden-haired temptress. In some ways, Liz admitted privately, Jes served as a stand in for Bridget.

Wepwawet's knowledge surged within her, though he didn't speak. He largely kept out of such matters, unless asked a question. Her blade executed a complex series of slashes that forced Jes closer and closer to the edge of the ring.

Finally Jes lunged with the butt of her spear, but Liz pivoted out of the way, and slammed her elbow into the woman's nose, shattering it. Jes stumbled out of the ring, her eyes wide in clear disbelief. Liz had rarely tasted anything so delicious.

"How?" was all Jes could manage.

"I absorbed Wepwawet," Liz explained. "I have all his knowledge. His skill."

"Interesting." Jes stepped back into the ring. "Ultimately futile though. During combat all sorts of shaping will be employed. We win by being unseen until the moment the killing blow is dealt. Has your Ka-Dun mastered imbuing? Have you tasted his power?"

"I have." Liz nodded, and in that moment wished the power sets were reversed. She hated being dependent on someone else to fuel her powers, though to be fair she did enjoy the shadows and being stronger physically. "That power combined with my combat prowess are what I'm counting on. When I asked you to train I was hoping you'd help me refine my existing technique, not tear everything down."

Jes nodded placidly, the smirk gone. "We do not have time to teach you everything, but I have seen a foundation I can build on. If you work hard, then in a few weeks you will know the basics. However, I must know more before I commit to this mad plan. Your Ka-Dun has still not explained how this miracle will be accomplished, or what the risks are."

"I don't think he himself knows." Liz raised her blade again, but Jes slid into the shadows. Liz joined her a moment later, prowling the outer edge of the circle as she sought some sign of her opponent.

A spear punched through Liz's back, emerging from her chest in a spray of blood. A booted foot landed against her back, and kicked her off the slick weapon. She toppled to the ground, panting as the mortal wound began to heal itself.

"H-how," she panted, "did you know where I was? I've only ever seen Blair able to pinpoint a shadowalker."

"Your Ka-Dun can track us?" Jes expressed mild surprise. "Interesting. I'll have to learn how he does that. As for me? The shadows are a place we go, Jes, and our perceptions work differently there. Listen to the shadows, and you'll hear what they hear. They told me where to find you."

"That sounds pretty creepy. Are these literal voices or metaphorical?" Liz rose to a sitting position with a groan. She'd liked these yoga pants. There weren't too many Lululemons left with inventory five years after the fact.

"Literal. Envelop yourself in the shadows. Do not attempt to move. Simply listen." Jes closed her eyes, then faded from sight.

Liz did the same. It sounded a bit like mindful meditation, so she slid into that mindset. She would observe and listen, and wait. The shadows had never said anything before. Minutes passed, but there was nothing. Not a hint of a voice.

Another twenty minutes passed before she spoke. "I don't think this is working. Maybe we can try another time?"

There was no answer.

"Jes'Ka?"

Still nothing.

"Oh, that bitch," Liz growled under her breath. She could have stood there for hours.

What is it, Ka-Ken? I do not understand, Wepwawet sent.

"There are no voices to hear. She left to go seduce Blair...." Liz trailed off as she heard the faintest of whispers in the distance, a breath, softer than any wind.

She spun around, but the whisper didn't repeat. Jes had still probably gone to seduce Blair. At least that was an area she didn't worry about at all. Blair had it, in his own words, pretty damned bad for her. He didn't seem the type to stray, and she'd long since forgiven him for Bridget since that had happened before they'd gotten together. It still hurt though.

She picked up her towel and headed for the showers. At least she'd finally learn something to follow up on. If these shadows could whisper then she was going to find a way to make it happen at her command, like Jes'Ka did.

27

WALKABOUT

T he days that followed their encounter with the eyeless were a balm on Jordan's soul. He learned to sail, and to grill, and to fish in ways he enjoyed. They ate when they were hungry, drank when they wanted to relax, and talked when they didn't want time alone to themselves.

Manu made the perfect traveling companion, happy to converse one moment, and then give you room to do whatever the next. Jordan had all the time in the world as they raced along those waves, and he used it to heal something he hadn't known had been broken.

How long had he been in reaction mode? Since the first day that pyramid had shot out of the ground in Peru, all those months ago. Since he'd seen his first werewolf and presided over the end of the world. Every decision had been triage, tending to the current emergency.

Now he got to sit and think, and consider his place in things. If he really was immortal, and somehow they beat the Builders, what did that mean for him? Did he even want to be an Ark Lord, or was he just filling a role until they could hand it off to someone more qualified? Back to Isis, if Blair was successful, maybe.

"You're getting better," Manu announced on the final day, just outside Sydney Harbor. "You're tying lines better than any person with no hands, and most blind people. No offense, mate." The smile widened. "You're a hell of a person to know in a fight though."

Jordan spied the landmass in the distance, ringed by clear blue waters, but couldn't make out much else yet. "Do you know much about the city, or how it's changed since the world ended?"

"I grew up in Sydney." Manu leapt suddenly into the air, and executed a perfect pirouette straight out of the nutcracker. "I studied at the National Academy of Dance for three years. Great city, back when there were, well, people."

"You are full of surprises." Jordan shook his head thoughtfully. "I'd never have pegged you for a dancer. Handy skillset."

The harbor came into view, and Jordan blinked when he realized the human world had vanished. Traces remained, certainly. The Sydney Opera House proudly overlooked the harbor, but most of the city had been claimed by wilderness. Eucalyptus trees grew fast, but not that fast. A greater power had been at work here, shaping away the structures of mankind and replacing them from nature's palette.

"Is this Uluru's work?" Jordan leaned against the prow and enjoyed the primal view. He froze when he spotted a long-necked brontosaurus munching on the lower branches of a clump of eucalyptus. The leathery creature appeared unconcerned by the crocodile near its foot, at home in the same environment. Huh.

"Yep." Manu nodded at the bronto. "Uluru seeded the continent with all sorts of critters, though no one's ever seen her personally, at least not that I know."

"Any advice on how I can find her then?" Jordan hated that he already knew the answer. The Australians even had a word for it, borrowed from the aborigines who'd dwelled here for tens of thousands of years.

"You go on walkabout." Manu steered the boat into the harbor. "It's pretty much what it sounds like. Walk into the wilderness, and search for Uluru. Between you and me, Uluru is also a place. Called Ayer's Rock. You make for that rock, and sooner or later you're gonna run into Uluru."

That Jordan had already known. He'd studied a map at length, and since Ayers Rock had been a tourist trap the route was well marked. There was even a foot trail for crazy people who wanted to hike the whole thing, a nearly direct route as the Jordan flies.

He checked the action on his sidearm, then strapped it to his side. The odds of him firing the weapon were slim. Almost none. He knew it was a security blanket, but hey, everyone had their flaws. He liked polishing the .45, even if he never fired it.

"What will you do?" Jordan didn't want to ask the good-natured landfinder to wait here. That seemed dangerous, and a waste of his talents.

"Since you can teleport off you won't need me, right?" Manu sipped his latest beer, which Jordan hadn't even seen him retrieve.

"Yeah, I should be able to manage on my own." Jordan hoped he was right about that.

"Then I'll head back to the open ocean, and find the people. I'll spread the word, like Jamina, and see if I can get people moving towards Lima so we can get your people out."

"I can't tell you how much I appreciate your help." Jordan tried to come up with something witty, but failed. "I'll miss the beer, man, and the laughs. Thanks for getting me here. Whatever you think you or the landfinders owe me for killing those eyeless, consider that debt paid in full. You're a real friend, Manu. I don't have too many of those left."

"Mana, bro. Respect." Manu gave one of those easy grins. "We're buds, you and I. Mates. I got your back, and my people got your people's back. You just stay alive here and don't get eaten by a dino."

"Can't promise that." Jordan glanced at a thick stand of tall trees he didn't recognize, which shivered as something large passed through them. "I'll do my best though."

The boat bumped up against a pier, which extended to the complex housing the Opera House. "Good luck, bro."

Jordan nodded instead of offering another lame goodbye, and leapt as high as he could manage without the aid of shaping. He slammed down on the stone pier and turned to watch Manu guide the *Pele's Blessing* back out into the harbor. He hoped the man didn't encounter any further trouble.

Just how prevalent were the eyeless? Not his problem, for now at least. One day it would be, though.

Jordan turned back to the dead city, the surviving skyscrapers and high-rises broken and weathered as the land reclaimed them. Here and there normal animals, like dogs, prowled the ruins. Jordan could feel those dogs, though the packs were wary and furtive, and considered themselves prey. They weren't willing to talk.

He walked up a broken street, and breathed in the scent of eucalyptus as he listened to the cicada, or the Aussie equivalent. This place wasn't so different than America or Europe so far. He could almost be in California, if he squinted.

He picked past rusted out cars, up an overpass, and onto the freeway leading out of the city. He'd made it a ways when he spotted an aboriginal man sitting on top of a car not more than ten feet away.

His dark skin was weathered, and white hair frizzy, but his eyes were alert and focused on Jordan. Predictably he said nothing, and merely stared as Jordan walked by. He refused to give the man the satisfaction, and said nothing. It could be that the man *was* Uluru. It could be someone or something else. If the entity wanted him to know it would tell him.

Jordan dismissed the strange man, and followed the highway out of the city, and into the outback. He assumed it was the outback, though it looked like more city to be honest. Not quite Los Angeles sprawl, but man had made their mark.

That mark was being aggressively removed now, though. In a generation nothing would remain. In a century only archeologists would be able to find much. Nature had already reclaimed this place...civilization just didn't know it yet.

By the time he left the sprawl and entered what he'd call the suburbs, the freeways were no longer clogged with cars. It gave a picture of how this place had been at the very end. People hadn't had time to evacuate cities. The cars he was seeing came from the morning rush hour the day the world had ended.

A hundred meters ahead he spotted the aboriginal man again, sitting on another car. The man merely stared again as Jordan passed, but once again Jordan didn't say anything. If the man responded it would just be something cryptic. Sooner or later he'd get around to explaining why he was following Jordan, and in the meantime Jordan merely focused on travel.

To his surprise, he found trekking through the country outside Sydney exactly the balm he'd needed. Sitting and fishing was great, but the physical activity, the hiking, really energized him. He was able to think while walking, which was when most of his best ideas came to him.

The wilderness had begun its reclamation, kangaroos, and cockatiels, and a random dimetrodon all noteworthy sights as he headed west. If he'd done his math right he'd be hiking for almost a week, even at Ka-Dun speed.

Would it be worth switching to wolf form? He decided it would. He didn't enjoy that form as much as Blair seemed to. Jordan was too attached to opposable thumbs. But he recognized how useful that form could be.

He reached for his shaping, and willed his body to shift into a three-hundred-pound wolf. Nothing happened. He remained stubbornly human. He tried again with the same result.

Why couldn't he shift? Jordan unlimbered his pack and set it on the trail next to a tree. This needed to be answered before he went any further. Was it just shifting that he couldn't do? He extended a hand at a rock, and willed it into the air. Nothing.

He tried light walking a dozen paces up the trail. Nothing.

Every attempt to shape appeared to be blocked. He couldn't access any of his power, couldn't shift to warform, and would be hard pressed to defend himself if he happened across something larger and angrier than a dimetrodon. The web-finned dino hadn't seemed terribly interested in leaving its marsh, but what if there were other predators out there?

"I guess everything in Australia really can kill you."

A dry snort came from behind him, and he spun to see the

aboriginal man squatting under the tree next to his pack. The snort seemed to indicate amusement, though there was no smile.

"This Yoda stuff is already old." Jordan walked over to man, and picked up his pack. The man didn't move. "Is there something you want to say to me? Something you want me to do?"

The man merely stared.

Why couldn't he have a vision quest instead of this walkabout crap? Liz had said Ayahuasca was an amazing experience. Couldn't he just trip and bond with some ants or something?

Nope, he had to be in a buddy cop movie with the world's most silent man.

28

LOW POINT

J ordan sprinted along Highway A87, which might cross the entire continent so far as he knew. He leapt over an eighteen-wheeler, then kicked off a VW Bug's hood as his pack tugged against his center of gravity.

His bounding pace ate up the road, but the terrain hadn't changed much. Signs mentioned a city called Canberra, which he'd never heard of, and made him feel a dumb foreigner. Sydney and Melbourne were the only cities he could name. Wait, wasn't Brisbane a city? And Queensland? Maybe that was a province.

"Why didn't you tell me to grab a map on the way out of town, Friz?" Jordan addressed the question to his aboriginal buddy, who was Friz until he corrected it. His hair demanded it. "I don't suppose you can tell me if there's a better route to Ayer's rock? If there's a train or flight I'd love to take it."

Friz actually snorted. It was only the second reaction Jordan had seen from him.

"Yeah, yeah, I know. The journey is the destination, right?" Jordan leapt through a rusted out bus, and of course Friz had already appeared on a hood on the other side.

The next stretch of road lay largely empty, and traffic thinned the further he ran. Friz would disappear for a few minutes, then be on a distant hill, or sunning himself in the middle of the road.

The forests thickened, mostly trees Jordan didn't recognize. There was quite a bit of marsh, which he avoided. Worse than crocodiles had lurked in the waters of South America, and the very last thing he wanted was to give this continent a reason to say, "You think America was bad? Hold my beer!"

About noon he ran across a small petrol station, which seemed to be completely intact beyond a single missing window near the cubby for the cashier. The shelves inside still contained products, though he couldn't make out much through the grime. A warm sports drink was still electrolytes, and damned if he couldn't go for a protein bar.

Jordan paused when a loud booming call came from the forest behind the station. Not close enough to be a concern, necessarily, but enough to spook a foreigner. It could be a koala for all he knew, but more likely it was something nasty, and it was best to assume hostile intent.

How badly did he want that protein bar?

Pretty badly. Jordan trotted up to the door, and tried it. Locked. Jordan yanked, and suddenly the door was unlocked. Permanently. He might not be able to shift, but at least he was still far stronger than a normal human.

Jordan ducked inside the blessedly cool interior, and smiled when he saw coolers full of everything from beer to water. He snagged a hat from the rack near the door, and dropped it over his head as he walked back to fill up his pack with water bottles. Did he want a beer too? Nah, he'd had plenty at sea. Beer wasn't good for exertion.

Next he headed to the candy bar aisle, and found a fully stocked shelf with a variety of protein bars. Jordan picked two different flavors at random, and dropped them in the bag. They'd probably all taste like crap, or bland if he was lucky.

He grabbed a lighter from the counter since he'd lost his during his time at sea. And by lost he'd meant that a landfinder had walked off with it. He'd tried getting it back, but after the third person had "borrowed" it he gave up.

"Okay, back to the road." Jordan began to whistle as he headed for the door, then stopped when he remembered the call from the woods. No reason to take chances. He nudged the door gently open as he cinched his pack around his chest.

A twelve-meter ankylosaur stood in the station's driveway. Jordan recognized it instantly from the massive spiked tail and the armored plates covering the body. If he could be a dinosaur, then it would definitely be an ankylosaur.

The creature raised a baleful eye in his direction, then that eye narrowed in an almost human fashion. *You're on my turf, kid*, it said.

Jordan dropped his gaze and walked swiftly in the opposite direction. On the playground kids had said that ankylosaurs were herbivores, so they weren't that scary. Hippos were herbivores, and they were the scariest creature on the planet, until recently. If he wanted to produce nightmares he'd make a were-hippo. A demo-were-hippo. Those things were truly terrifying, even to combat-hardened soldiers. They'd lost men in Africa.

The dino didn't follow him, so Jordan picked up the pace into an easy run. He couldn't believe he'd just seen a live ankylosaur. How was it possible? In *Jurassic Park* they'd used the DNA of extinct species to bring them back. Had the Ark Lord on this continent done the same? It seemed like the most plausible explanation.

They'd used shaping, and probably had the stored genetic patterns of all sorts of critters. Given what Jordan had seen in other Arks what had been done to Australia seemed the natural extension of an Ark Lord flexing their creativity.

He reached a comfortable pace, and guessed he sustained about thirty miles an hour. If he ran for sixteen hours a day that should put him in Ayers Rock in four more days, assuming nothing slowed him down.

"What's the worst that could happen, Friz?" Jordan called, though there was no sign of his intermittent companion.

Near the end of that day Jordan reached a city called Narrandera, which involved a few marshy forests along a winding river, and a whole lot of arid land outside of that. He couldn't see much in the darkness, but in a way he found the openness reassuring. At least he'd see something if it approached.

"Will you, though?" A deep inhuman voice boomed from behind him, accompanied by the huff of air from a very large nostril.

Jordan spun but...there was nothing there. Except Friz.

Friz sat beneath a tree a dozen paces away, grinning like a loon.

"Did you do that?" Jordan fixed him with an irritated stare. "You scared the crap out of me. Point taken. I'm not secure and you can find me wherever you want. Listen, I'm going to head inside that motel there—I think that's a motel—and then I'm going to get some sleep. I've got three more days like today, and running with a thirty-pound pack gets old. I ache, man."

Friz rolled his eyes, then rose to his feet, and vanished.

Jordan turned to the motel. Three more days of running. Three more days to find answers. Then he'd finally have to face this Ark Lord, and pray that he was an ally, and a strong one at that.

If he wasn't, if this was still another threat, then Jordan didn't know that he could keep going. He needed a win. Badly.

29

THE TRUTH OF ULURU

T hree days of hard running improved Jordan's mood. He got past the doom and gloom pretty quickly, because the country he ran through was the most breathtaking he'd seen in decades. Like every woman, every continent had her charms.

North and South America had the Sierras, and the redwoods, and Niagara, and the Amazon. Australia had only just begun to surprise him as the lush, forested lowlands gave way to high deserts, which possessed their own austere beauty. A sign proclaimed that he'd soon be leaving New South Wales and passing into South Australia.

Along the way he passed a sign for another city he'd heard of... Adelaide, though he didn't know much about it. Something about an island full of kangaroos.

The further north Jordan went the more dry and barren the land became. The Ark Lord had made changes, but not to the climate. This place still had little in the way of water, and so the deserts were largely devoid of changes.

His favorite stop had been at the visitors center in a national park called the Ikara-Flinders Ranges. It had been nestled in the midst of the most amazing plateau. It was like one giant mountain with the top cut off, and a valley in the middle. The cratered remains of a titan's mountain. The sun had painted the whole thing in golds and reds at the precise moment he'd passed his first set of cave paintings.

Friz had been sitting directly beneath them of course, saying nothing as Jordan examined the ancient artwork. He knew enough to recognize some local animals, but most of the images were gibberish to him. That made them no less beautiful.

But after days of travel, after enjoying the continent's raw beauty, Jordan could finally see Ayer's Rock looming in the distance. Or rather, he could see the Ark towering over the tiny red rock that had given the region its name.

The Ark gleamed in the late afternoon sun, but differently than any other Ark Jordan had visited. Most of their surfaces were black. The Ark of the Cradle had gold hieroglyphs. This one had white, black, and red cave paintings dotting the entirety of the surface. Not a single face had been left free. Someone, or something, had painstakingly covered miles of stone with the same artwork Jordan had glimpsed on the rocks.

The paintings...amplified the Ark's power somehow. Jordan could feel its strength relative to Blair's Ark and this thing was an order or magnitude stronger. It brimmed with truly terrifying power.

"Were the aborigines practicing what they saw the Ark Lord doing?" Jordan wondered aloud. He didn't really expect an answer, though Friz sheltered behind a boulder a few meters away to avoid the lingering sun.

The voice that answered him was the same that had spoken when Friz scared him, a deep inhuman voice, followed by a huff of air from powerful nostrils. "Indeed they were, Ark Lord. I taught the ancient humans here the secrets of shaping, many sun-cycles ago. They have lived, and dreamed, and lived again."

Jordan turned and this time the speaker didn't vanish. A T-Rex towered over him, each fang a bayonet. Jordan had no idea how the thing had gotten the drop on him as it weighed many, many tons, but there it was. This thing had him dead to rights if it wanted him dead, so Jordan relaxed and assessed the situation.

The Rex looked a good deal like the one in *Jurassic Park*, which means they'd gotten it mostly right. This one had clusters of feathers along its vestigial arms, and a number of tribal tattoos drawn from the same imagery in the cave paintings. The shaping must be in the ink somehow. Tattoo shaping?

Jordan entered fight or flight. He couldn't beat this thing without shaping. He might not be able to beat it even with shaping. Every bit of his will strained against whatever prevented him from shaping. He needed claws, damn it.

To his delighted shock the change came in a belated rush, and Jordan shifted into warform. A small act of defiance, perhaps, as he put the Rex's height at somewhere between thirty-five and forty meters. Taller, perhaps. It was difficult to judge from this vantage. "You have me at a disadvantage. Are you Uluru?"

"That is one name I have worn over the epochs, yes." The dino inclined her head in a stately bow. "You are the strongest I have yet met, mortal. Why have you come to my continent?"

Did calling Aaron mortal mean this thing was immortal? And, theoretically, weren't Ka-Dun also immortal? Maybe not a point he wanted to argue right now.

"From what I've seen of your continent so far you value life." Jordan gestured at the rapidly darkening skyline, which silhouetted Ayers Rock. "You created those giant sharks, right? And all this? Where I come from the deathless are wiping out all life. That includes the Amazon rainforest. Now I'm no activist, but I like breathing. As I understand it burning down all the trees will have a decidedly adverse effect on everything you're working towards."

"Indeed it would." Uluru rose to her full height. "The oxygen content of our atmosphere is far more instrumental in our survival, and in the development of species, than even I had first assumed. During what your scientists have deemed the Carboniferous Period our oxygen represented about 36% of our atmosphere. Back then common arthropods, insects, could reach a length of two meters or more. Today the oxygen content stands closer to 20%, and is falling."

"So you agree that the deathless are a threat?" Jordan bowed in what he hoped made for a respectful display. "We need your help to stop them."

"You command an Ark. Why don't you stop these abominations yourself?

"My Ark is broken." Jordan's shoulders sagged. "We're surrounded by millions of deathless, and only have a few thousand champions. Less, now. That's why I've come. To ask your help. I do not believe my lands can be saved, unless you have some drastic intervention. Sobek has allowed me to dwell on the coast of your lands, but when I made that accord I didn't understand that he does not speak for you."

"Nor I for the land." Uluru took a ponderous step towards Ayer's Rock, and the ground quaked. "If you wish to bring your people here you may do so, though you will need to contend with the other creatures who dwell there. Mankind is strong and numerous, particularly now that you have mastered shaping. But you are not the only powerful creatures to call these lands home, and there are many dangers you will face should you come here."

Jordan looked for the hook, but couldn't see one. The offer seemed genuine.

"We'll do what we can to mitigate dangers, and will face the rest." Jordan corrected his posture. Enough of that crap. "That isn't the only reason I've come, though. If I save my people and bring them here I've only bought a little time. The Builders are coming. Their grey men are already here. We don't think we can stop them. We don't even really understand what they are."

Uluru's great body shifted and changed as she grew smaller and smaller. Only in that instant did Jordan realize that the T-Rex was merely a warform. Uluru's body became a bipedal figure that only came to Jordan's shoulder, with mottled green skin and dark lantern eyes. Familiar eyes.

"Yes," Uluru said as she completed the transformation. "After two million years my brothers and sisters are coming home to reclaim this world."

Jordan's jaw sagged open. Uluru must be a Builder, the one who'd created the Ark she inhabited.

30

NEW CALIFORNIA

Blair soared through the sky at supersonic speeds as he paralleled Highway 1 down the California coast. This was his state now. His empire, as ridiculous as it sounded. He could have light walked directly to the conference in Balboa Park, but he needed time to think, and wanted an appropriate display for his "subjects".

Mindless zombies and more intelligent deathless both gazed at the contrail he left in his wake, a streak of light as he tore the air around him. He'd be visible for at least a hundred miles, and wagered by the time he reached San Diego everyone in the state would know he was coming.

That choice had been made based on Melissa's advice. If these people saw him as the government with a capital G, then the very last thing they wanted was him to show up unexpectedly. Teleporting in unnerved them. He needed to be predictable in his interactions, so they had enough time to get comfortable with him. They needed to literally see him coming.

Do you really loathe the deathless, as your She fears?

The beast's sudden question surprised him. The beast was privy to his thoughts. That it had to ask where he stood meant he must be more conflicted than he'd thought. Maybe he needed to sit down and really unpack that, but not right now.

I don't know, if I'm being honest. They've murdered a lot of people I love. They destroyed my world. But none of them chose to be what they are. They've awakened to their new lives and tried to make the best of things as monsters. I don't think I loathe them, but I may hate them. I don't know.

He began to curve inland as he approached mountains to the south. The grapevine—the steep climb up out of central California into Los Angeles. Blair would never forget making the trip in a 1990 Suzuki Swift, which was battered around by the wind as it struggled up that mountain.

Now he just flew over it.

In minutes he'd reached Six Flags in Santa Clarita, and saw immediately what Melissa had been talking about. There were effectively no changes since the world had ended. Houses had been rebuilt. Roads repaved. Newish cars were parked in driveways.

These deathless had badly wanted to reclaim their humanity, and it looked like they'd found a way to do so. That alone softened his stance. These people rejected what nature had made them, and chose their own fate.

He kept flying, and saw different types of settlements. The entire San Fernando valley where Highway 118 met 405 had become a wasteland. No one lived there, and all the low rent housing had been left to rot. The freeways were still clogged with rusted out hulks, too many to count.

The valley, and eventually Irvine, passed by beneath him, each containing multiple settlements ringed with barbed wire, tall fences, and vigilant guards.

A motorcycle roared out of one of the settlements below, and spun onto 405 with incredible speed. Only a single lane had been cleared, which meant if that biker encountered any obstacle at all they were dead. Of course, if they were a shaper they could deal with that.

The need for speed became clear when a quartet of crotch-rockets all painted blue streaked out of a rusted out semi, and began pursuing the lone biker. That biker looked to be in the clear, until a pair of men in leather jackets popped out of rusted out cars along the biker's path.

They'd strung a razored chain across the lane, at waist height. It didn't snap up until the last moment, and the deathless wasn't fast enough to avoid it. The line caught his waist, and knocked him from his bike as the vehicle spun into the guard rail in a spray of shrapnel and flame.

The bikers descended on their prey, and leapt off to tackle him to the ground. Then they began to feed. Blair shivered and looked away as he flew further south, toward San Diego. This place was even more brutal than he'd expected, and it showed the desperate need these people had for some sort of authority they trusted. Something to keep the real monsters in check.

When the gangs ruled the streets and your government offered tangible help you actually appreciated them. If Blair could deliver power and internet he could help these people track gangs, and work together to wipe out threats to their settlements.

The last fifteen minutes of flight was more pleasant as he passed into San Diego county. Balboa Park lay not far from downtown, right by the San Diego Zoo, where he'd spent hours staring at primates the few times he'd been able to make it down. He still preferred the Wild Animal Park, which felt like stepping into Africa. Both were gone now, of course.

He dropped lower as he approached the park, which was still ringed with stands of Eucalyptus trees. Early Spanish architecture surrounded lush green fields, and brought back pleasant memories.

The summit was being held inside the palace itself, or behind it rather. Dozens of deathless congregated in a courtyard around a small stage where Melissa addressed the crowd. She raised a delicate hand skyward and pointed in his direction.

Blair slowly descended toward the crowd, and allowed power to blaze both from him and the staff, in human form. He landed next to Melissa, and extinguished the staff.

"Please welcome Ark Lord Blair. The Ark Lord has prepared a short statement. Afterwards we will discuss details. This will be neither quick nor pleasant, but that's how nations get made. Ark Lord?" Melissa stepped away from the lectern, and clasped her hands behind her back.

There was no applause. Not a single person clapped. Awesome.

"How many of you think I'm here to screw you over? Raise your hand." Blair raised his hand.

A sea of hands went up. Nearly all of them.

"Well, most of you are honest at least." Blair drifted into the air. He didn't really need a microphone, and it would make it easier for more of the crowd to see and hear him. "I'm going to give it to you straight. A war we don't want is on our doorstep. You're going to love this, trust me. Aliens are invading our world. We call them the Builders, because they built the Arks you are all familiar with. They want them back. They don't like you. They want to destroy you. As Ark Lord my job is pretty straightforward. Stop them from annihilating you. That will be a whole lot easier with a real government in place, and a real military that we can use to fight back. Here's the pitch."

He paused and waited, knowing he had them. Silence stretched, and then he made the offer. "Every town or settlement that joins New California will receive a complimentary upgrade to their electrical grid that will allow them to use shaping and solar power to run their settlements. We will connect you to the internet, which admittedly is just California so far, though we do have old archives from before the fall."

"What's it gonna cost us?" A woman yelled from the crowd. People nodded around her, and expressions hardened as they looked for the hook.

"Each town will be required to elect a senator." Blair had considered forms of government carefully, and sadly Rome's benevolent dictator backed by an elected senate really did seem the smartest play. "Those senators will meet online weekly to discuss issues, and propose solutions. Proposals that require resources will be sent to

Melissa, who will allocate what she can to aid as many people as possible. The senate, as Melissa will explain at length later, will do most of the governing. My job isn't to police your day-to-day lives. However, I do have a few basic laws that you will follow. These are not negotiable. Any living human is to be given free passage north. The person aiding them in their journey will be paid a generous bounty for delivering willing humans. No kidnappings or it will end badly for the kidnapper."

He paused again to see how they'd react. There were open faces, and a few nods. Here and there an expression had darkened, and he guessed those were the people currently feeding or trafficking in humans.

"Further, I require you to submit to my authority." He sighed and rolled his eyes at himself. "I understand how infuriating it is having some random werewolf god come rolling in to tell you they're in charge. I understand that you will never like me. I'm a dictator, however we want to paint this. But I want to have as light a touch as possible. Rule justly. Build us a nation we can be proud of, one that welcomes deathless and champions alike. One that doesn't see the living as cattle. Now I realize a lot of you may not like these new rules, and we've considered that. Melissa will be helping those who wish to leave to found a new independent settlement, one that we may ally with down the road. There doesn't have to be conflict. If there is, though, it will be short and brutal. You will not enjoy it. Have Melissa show you what I did to the 'Lords of Silicon Valley'. I know we won't need another demonstration here. Help your neighbors. Send me the living. We'll help you rebuild your lives and fight the Builders when they arrive."

Blair shot up into the air at maximum blur, up and away from the event. He'd delivered his dictates. It was up to Melissa to forge these people into a real government, and she couldn't do that if he was breathing down their collective necks. He hated that he couldn't shape their policies, but you couldn't be both the oppressor and the oppressed. He'd chosen his role.

He light walked back to San Francisco. A glance at the smartwatch Melissa had given him told him he had about an hour to get ready for the dinner with Trevor and Anput, which he was actually looking forward to. They'd been doing nothing but status reports, and this would be the first chance they'd have to actually talk about things while no one was trying to kill or enslave them.

31

PRIME RIB

Blair almost tripped over his chair when Liz strolled into the Ark's mess. Liz didn't do makeup. She didn't wear dresses. She didn't do fancy, in her own words. She liked getting down in the terra preta and learning what made that soil so black. She was a field archeologist, and a slayer of monsters.

But wow did she clean up good. His own real life Buffy Summers.

Liz's copper hair cascaded down her back, the first time he'd seen it loose in a while. She wore a form fitting black dress, and a pair of low heels that made her just a bit taller than him.

"You look...I need a minute." Blair dropped into his seat, and enjoyed gawking as Trevor and Anput slid into their seats across the table.

The aroma of prime rib rose from the platter, and Trevor rose to carve as Liz sat down next to Blair.

"If I can offer a piece of advice...easy on the wine. You have work to do later." She gave him a wink that shattered whatever composure remained.

"Liz. Pretty."

They all chorused laughter at that, a lessening of the tension that had been building for so long. A lessening they badly needed.

Blair looked up at Anput, who sat across from him. "So any major breakthroughs you guys want to lead with, or do you want to hear all about deathless politics and how New California became a thing today?"

Anput choked on her wine, and gently set the glass down in front of her plate. "Trevor, you want to field this one?"

Their expressions promised disastrous news, but Blair forced himself to remain calm. It had only been a couple days. What had he missed?

"You remember that guy Percy?" Trevor squirmed in his chair as he speared a piece of beef with his fork. Where had he found beef?

"Percy Fawcett?" Blair nodded. "Yeah, he's famous in the academic world. The El Dorado guy. Mindblowing that he's still alive."

"I'm, ah, not sure he is." Trevor's waffling scared the crap out of Blair. Trevor didn't dither. "I tried shaping his mind, and there were almost no memories. I assumed it was the virus, but now I'm not so sure. I think there was a Builder inside his mind. We found references to an experiment where they sent their leader forward in time. Forward to, oh, right around now."

"And you think Percy is...a Builder?" Blair raised an eyebrow. He didn't think they were joking, but it sounded preposterous. He waited for them to make it believable.

"I do." Trevor popped a piece of beef in his mouth, and chewed for a minute before continuing. "The city detected a temporal event just before he woke up, and right after Percy directed us to a council chamber where we found exactly the answers we need. Answers that kept us busy for hours. When we came back he was gone, and Ba told me that he used some sort of override to force the light bridge to teleport him to the Ark of the Cradle. He distracted us and fled."

"That seems pretty damning." Blair sawed off a piece of his own meat, and spent some time savoring the taste and wishing they could put work aside.

"You don't seem terribly alarmed." Liz eyed him sidelong. She seemed more interested in the wine than anything else, though she'd enjoyed a bit of beef too. It was gratifying to see her unwind even that much.

"We knew they were coming." Blair shrugged and set down his fork. "I always assumed they'd be crossing space, not time, but it doesn't really matter how they get here. I expect this Builder will make Hades bend knee, and then he'll round up the grey men. I don't know how their forces rate against a powered Ark, but we could be a target. There's exactly nothing we can do about it, beyond telling David maybe. We'll notify Jordan when he checks in too, but like it or not he's out of our reach. Can you pass the creamed corn please?"

"Of course." Anput scooped corn onto her plate then handed him the dish. "I admire your pragmatic approach. I find it terrifying that I was meters from an alien consciousness and had no idea. It fooled me completely, though Trevor suspected something from the start."

"I had no idea what, just that he seemed odd." Trevor stabbed another piece of beef from the platter and dragged it onto his plate. "The information he gave us was good. Surprisingly good. We found the original council chamber, which is a fragment of what I can only assume is an interstellar vessel. That vessel taught the Builders everything from temporal shaping to how to create Sunsteel. Inside we found this."

Trevor withdrew a golden object about the size of a knuckle, and slid it across the table with a heavy clink.

"What is it?" Blair picked it up, surprised by the weight. He could feel the power within it, but had no idea what the tiny sigils along the outside meant. The thing felt old. Beyond old. Lovecraft old.

"A scale, I think. From a reptile." Trevor didn't say it, but Blair read between the lines.

"A dragon scale?" Blair slid the scale back. "How does it fit in?"

"It's an archive," Anput explained. She'd filled her plate with food and cradled a wine glass, but hadn't eaten anything. "Some sort of virtual intelligence that has a record of all sorts of research."

"We've only just recovered it." Trevor scooped it up and dropped it back into his pocket. "I'm hoping it gives us answers. I'll have a report by tomorrow. If this thing is legit, then we'll know what we need to pull this off. Enough of us in the hot seat though. Bore us with some politics."

"Yes, bore us." Liz dabbed her mouth with a napkin, and set down her empty glass. "I haven't heard how SoCal went. Are they on board?"

"I think so. Melissa does too, but it will be days before they hammer out the initial agreement." Blair enjoyed the last bit of steak, then the corn. Good lord, he'd missed hot regular food. "They're interested in our tech, and they need protection, which we can offer. It will take time, but they can become an army if they have something to protect."

"Do we have that time?" Anput's voice had become a tiny thing.

"No." Blair gave a low belch. Man that beef had been amazing. "We're in real trouble. They're here. Their fleets will probably be here soon. We need Isis. We need this Ark Lord in Australia to get on board. We need the deathless in South America to get their heads out of Hades's ass, or we're done. I get the sense that the Builders don't mess around, and that even a united planet is the underdog."

"They're already played us for fools." Trevor leaned back in his chair, and loosened his belt. "We're badly outclassed. But I have a *lot* more beef. And there's cheesecake."

32

COLLECTIVE

Akenat became aware of the questing signal, a query from the grey men aimed at Hades. It demanded he contact them immediately, as he'd missed a second check in. If he missed a third he would be terminated.

Their efficiency pleased him, so he answered. He opened his mind, and met the questing progeny in the mindspace between them. He painted it as the inside of his Ark, as it had been in its prime.

Hades no longer exists, Akenat sent, imbuing the sending with the pleasure he'd experienced at the hominid's death. *I am called Akenat. I am the First Builder. Do you recognize my authority, progeny?*

You have invoked one of the nine forbidden words. The grey man's eyes narrowed. *We have been warned that you might arrive, and that if you do your words are venomous, and not to be trusted. You will not command our allegiance, exile.*

I see. Akenat settled into a meditative stance. *And what do your new mandates command you to do with an exiled Builder?*

The grey man cocked his head, and offered the truth with no emotion. *You are to be eradicated if faced in force, or fled from if faced alone.*

Ah. And is it permissible to converse with me before this eradication?

Akenat was enjoying this perhaps a bit more than he should. They had no idea who or what he really was, and based their understanding on metrics in a storage crystal.

There is no benefit to this act.

Isn't there? Akenat countered. *I possess the secrets of shaping. I built the vessel you currently reside in. I designed your body, and created you and your companions. Tell me, progeny, who forbade these nine words, and why are they forbidden?*

The council forbade them. Our minds are closed to you. You will not sway me.

You fear logic? Akenat mocked the grey's pride, something he'd intentionally instilled.

Of course not. The grey's eyes narrowed.

Who forbade these words specifically? Who do you communicate with?

Builder Yoggoth, the grey admitted. *Relevance?*

You have experimented with the demotech he left behind, have you not? What is your personal reason for not using the technology yourself? I notice you are absent the taint.

I find the infusion distasteful. My will is my own. We are a collective, not slaves to be manipulated. Fire burned in his thoughts.

The seed had taken root.

And if this demotech were forced on you? Because I promise you the council is no more. There is only Yoggoth and his demonic minions. When his fleet arrives you will not be given a choice. You will be infested with demonic taint, and your will stolen. You will serve the monster Yoggoth has become.

The grey was silent a long time. It cocked its head and eyed him thoughtfully. *I will speak to my brethren, and share your words.*

Have we fallen so far? He infused the words with disdain. *We value efficiency. Gather your collective, and view my memories. I will open my mind to you. Surely you cannot fear a single entity when you are so many. We imbued you with power. Power enough to eclipse your creators, when you unify.*

Wait here. The grey vanished, and left Akenat time to savor the moment. He was aware of the human consciousness within him observing the situation, and wondered if Nox would voice a question. He hadn't yet, though he'd paid close attention to everything Akenat did. Eventually the man could be an asset, if Akenat could break him in the short time he had before completing his purpose here and returning to his own time.

A few moments later dozens of minds began to appear, each more powerful than the last. They gathered their strongest and brightest, a host powerful enough to overwhelm any single foe, no matter how ancient. There was no way he could stand against them all in any sort of conventional fight.

I open my mind to you. View my memories. Understand why you were created, and how you have been manipulated by my enemies, who don't value your kind or understand your collective power.

Akenat couldn't hide his amusement as he lowered his defenses and directed them to the memory he'd selected. It contained a long frequency pulse that functioned on the grey men much as it did on the rest of Builder technology.

He took them in the space between heartbeats, and just like that their best and brightest became his. He had the core of their fleet in the palm of his hand. Unlike Yoggoth he didn't rule through fear, though. He ruled through shared purpose.

You are powerless before me, and understand that were I Yoggoth I would reshape your bodies and minds into twisted tools. I am not Yoggoth. I am Akenat, and my name is forbidden no longer. Return to your people and share what you see in my mind. Warn the collective that war is coming, and advise them to do what is best.

One by one they vanished as they returned to their vessels. Akenat merely watched with pride as his new fleet mobilized. Within hours all of them would he his, and he'd remove Yoggoth's conditioning. Free will benefited all within a collective. Such conditioning was fit for slave species, but should never be used upon progeny. Akenat would see that the greys were well prepared to defend themselves before returning to his own time, just in case he fell against Yoggoth and they one day had to oppose him without Builder support.

"How did you pull that off?" An image of Nox's human form

appeared in Akenat's vision. A mental figment? No, somehow the human had used the body's shaping capabilities to project. "It looks like they all just fell into line. I don't understand what I just saw."

I created them with failsafes, of course, he sent back, smugly because he had a right to it. *I activated deep programming to reset their loyalty back to me. I am no fool. Yoggoth cannot be trusted, and he is hardly the only one.*

"What are you going to do with them now that you have them? I don't understand your end game." The human folded his arms and adopted a long-practiced stance in his strange tailored garments. They seemed to serve no functional purpose, and did not aid in shaping, but were a primary part of his identity.

I am going to ready myself to oppose Yoggoth. That begins with an alliance with Uluru, a strong ally and deadly foe. Then I will move on the Proto Ark, and use it to propel back to my own time. I will leave your kind with the tools to oppose Yoggoth, should I be unable to alter things sufficiently.

He meant these things. Humans would be a superb slave race once properly modified, and he wished to preserve their strengths. He'd have to choose an appropriate time in their history to begin alterations, but there was no reason he couldn't begin before leaving Earth in his own time.

Two million cycles allowed a sufficient interval for the new genes to proliferate the species. Should he include resistance to the mutagen that had slain so much of their population? Or was that adaptation worth preserving? A question worth contemplating when he returned to rule this world.

33

CHANGED

Jordan mutely followed Uluru back to her Ark, unable to summon words after realizing she was the very thing they'd been fighting. They moved on foot, and Uluru made no move to either converse or speed their travel. She seemed supremely patient, which he supposed made sense for a being millions of years old. This lady made Isis look like a newborn.

So many questions burned as the pyramid loomed larger and larger before them. Why had a Builder remained behind? Was she on their side? His? No one's? She hadn't committed to helping him, though she had agreed to allow his people to dwell here. That was a start.

Uluru finally spoke when they entered the antechamber leading into the Ark. It triggered a rush of memory for Jordan. Entering an Ark that first time had changed his life forever.

"Welcome, Ark Lord, to Uluru, seed of the dream, repository of all lore, and birthplace of abundant life." She led him unerringly to the Ark's control room, the mirror of the one he and his team had done catastrophic damage to back in Peru. "You have come with questions. I will answer what I can. Ask, mortal."

What question did you ask an immortal god first?

"How old are you?" Rude, maybe, but only if she lived by human conventions.

"Your best approximation would be 3.1 million years." Uluru blinked at him with those unreadable black eyes. "During this time I have spent approximately fifty percent of all time within hibernation, so you might argue I have only lived for 1.6 millions years."

Jordan sat down. "Shit."

He couldn't even begin to understand. This thing had seen species, including humanity, evolve, grow, and die off.

"Next question?" she asked mildly.

"Are you allied with the other Builders?" That seemed the best way to phrase it without asking her directly if she was an enemy.

"I am not." She shook her bulbous head. Too much like Set, though at least she was a healthy emerald. "We have an accord, a deal from when they dwelled on Earth. In principle, that accord remains in place, but more and more I believe my brethren have no intention of honoring it. They will come and remake this world in their new image, and I fear their new image is not to my liking."

"So you'll help us then?" Jordan perked up at that. An immortal god seemed like a pretty essential ally against other immortal gods.

"I remain neutral." Uluru moved to one of the pillars dotting the room, and rested a hand against it. The room brightened. "I will not take up direct arms against my brothers, but neither do I wish to see this world paved over by their ambitions. Your kind, the champions, are the true spiritual successors to my people. You wish to steward this world rather than devour it. You will oppose my brethren's designs. Tell me, Jordan is there a creature you admire? Whose qualities you wished you possessed?"

That seemed like a timely question. He'd been thinking about about the dino encounter outside the petrol station.

"I just ran into an Ankylosaur. Neat little beast, with a big spiked club on the end of its tail." It seemed an odd question, but he was happy to humor the ancient being. Jordan changed tactics. "Who is

Friz, ah, the man who has been following me? Why is he following me?"

"Friz?" Uluru seemed amused. "Friz is unstuck in time. He is physically in the past, but sees through many eyes at once, all the eyes of his ancestors. He is both here, now, and three sun-cycles ago. He is one of the oldest members of your race, from a time before speech. He witnesses moments of great importance, to serve as memory for his people. He is, in a way, an archive of sorts."

Interesting. Jordan wished he could talk to the man. It sounded like Friz had been born during a time when man had just left Africa, maybe the very first human to reach these shores. What had the world been like then? How had Uluru viewed those arriving humans?

Once again Jordan had been sent on a field trip that felt tailor-made for Blair.

"Next question—will you train me in shaping?" Jordan finally asked the question that really mattered. This thing had to know every trick there was.

"I will, and gladly. I teach all who ask." Uluru nodded that bulbous head. "Proper instruction for an Ark Lord requires a minimum of nineteen centuries, however I can modify your beast to contain some preliminary knowledge, and your helixes to better perform your chosen role. Are you especially attached to the lupine form you have been gifted with? Would you prefer something more useful, perhaps, like the ankylosaur you admire? Its armor plating is impressive, and its dietary requirements make for far more efficient energy storage. I will leave the ability to consume flesh as well."

"Wait, you can change the type of creature I turn into? I don't have to be a werewolf?" It stood to reason, but the idea that you could just...change someone's entire being on the fly. It was humbling.

"Of course." Uluru shrugged her spindly shoulders. "I am impressed that humans were able to puzzle out the rudiments of genetic shaping. I believe they selected the wolf not because it is powerful, though it certainly is, but because its helixes are so receptive to shaping. I, however, am a master shaper. I can shape even that which does not will it. I can fashion any body, if you wish. It will be crafted with your specific dilemmas in mind. Remember, this can be changed later. You are not a fixed being."

This sounded way too good to be true. Jordan had made a devil's bargain before. Was that what this is? Take the power, and the hooks were set? That was possible. It was also possible Uluru was on the level, and offering to power him up at a time when a power up could make all the difference. He considered just how much tougher Sobek was than the rest of the gods he'd encountered.

"Did you do something similar to Sobek?" Jordan wanted more details before committing to anything. Sobek didn't seem like someone who'd been enslaved.

"I did." She nodded again. "During the previous sun-cycle a young god afflicted by a terrible mutagen arrived on my shores. It was my first encounter with the deathless, the first clue that your people had uncovered so much power, and so much of my own people's knowledge. It brought me back into the world, but did so just before the cycle turned. I had to wait until now to really investigate. I have loosed Sobek to spread his seed across the oceans, if he survives. I will do the same for you, though it seems you will choose a more terrestrial creature."

Jordan inhaled sharply through his nostrils, and remembered the armor. "I have to know...you aren't gaining control of me if I say yes? I've seen what demotech does firsthand. I'd rather die. I don't need a new body that badly, trust me."

"A wise question. One Sobek neglected to ask." Uluru gave another good-natured smile with that tiny mouth. "No, I will gain no control over you or your shaping. In the past this has resulted in creations attacking me, always a risk, but free will is a right all beings should possess. If you accept my gift you will gain in strength, and there is no special cost or fealty to me."

"Then I accept." Jordan nodded. "And I think ankylosaur is a good choice. If you can give me that armor and the tail, then I could go toe-to-toe with just about anything."

"Prepare yourself, mortal. The pain will be...memorable."

Jordan steeled himself. Nothing worth having came easy. Uluru raised a hand, and a signal rippled outward and disappeared into his chest. Fire surged up his nerves, clawing outward from his heart and spreading through his entire body. In that instant he prayed for death. For salvation. For an end to suffering. The agony encompassed his existence. Defined it.

And then it was gone.

Jordan lay on the stone panting, with seemingly no visible change in his body. Had Uluru succeeded? Or given up?

Beast? he thought. There was no reply.

"I believe you will find your new body pleasing." Uluru gave a nod of pride. "I have fashioned something exquisite. You are fast, strong, tough, and nearly unstoppable. This will serve as an excellent counter to nearly all combat situations. Most importantly...I have made you immune to shaping, as the eyeless are."

"Come again?" Jordan blinked up at the deity as he crawled to his feet.

"You cannot be shaped. This will block some beneficial effects, but will also prevent any hostile effects." Uluru extended a finger and pricked Jordan's hand. "Observe. I have also increased your regeneration, as you no longer have the aid of receiving external shaping."

"You said you gave me the eyeless's ability." Jordan shook his head to clear it. All of a sudden he needed to sleep for six or seven years. He stifled a cavernous yawn. "Who or what are they?"

"I will repeat this knowledge later, if you are too fatigued from the change to remember. The eyeless predate my race." Uluru's features twisted into very human consternation. "I do not know if they are native to this planet or came from elsewhere. I do not know when they first arose from the deeps, but as I said, long before us. My kind warred upon them, and even thought we'd won for a time. It turned out our enemy had merely retreated, and once we left this world only I remained to protect it. The eyeless have grown bolder, and I believe someone guides their hand, though I do not know who, or what."

The very last thing they needed was another enemy, but they had one, like it or not.

At least they had an amazing ally to compensate. He wanted to thank Uluru. He wanted to ask her questions. It all seemed so far away.

Another yawn overtook him and his eyes fluttered closed.

34

ULURU'S LESSONS

J ordan knew he was in a dream. Colors were too vibrant. You didn't quite move right, either. The stars spun crazily in the sky above, and the land changed around him as seasons blinked by.

"Friz." A quiet masculine voice issued from a rock a couple meters away. Jordan blinked and realized that not only was Friz sitting there, but the ancient man had spoken for the first time. He patted his frizzy hair, and offered a gap-toothed smile. "Friz." He nodded eagerly.

Uluru's green-skinned form whispered into existence and she gave Jordan one of those tiny-mouthed smiles. "You have brought him some measure of joy. His people live in a time before names, and you have given him one. He will pass the custom on to others. Congratulations, Jordan. You have created the first word ever uttered by your species, and it is Friz."

Jordan couldn't help but laugh at that. He'd long since given up on the idea that he was a simple soldier, but that didn't mean he'd acclimated to the mountain of crazy that was this world he lived in. He'd just influenced his own species through a fifty-thousand-year gap? Or more?

"Where are we?" The stars and seasons spun endlessly around

him. Animals flashed by, massive megafauna that slowly diminished in size as the seasons turned.

"The dreaming." Uluru gestured at the sky, pointing specifically at the heavy moon. "We cannot see the dream's origin. It comes from the sun, reflected off the moon. A balance of both is required to reach it. The sun contains many energies, and which energies it broadcasts change over time. The dreaming is not always accessible. It has not been for a very long time, to all but a few."

"Why are we here?" Jordan considered shifting into his new form, but decided he had a more pressing concern. Before he'd passed out the beast hadn't answered.

Beast? he thought again. Again no reply.

"We have come here so that you might understand my people." Uluru raised a hand, and a wave of tiny symbols emitted from her finger like a frequency being broadcast. The tiny sigils arrayed themselves into a complex pattern that hurt Jordan's brain to even look at. Those sigils disappeared in a sudden flash. "I do not believe my species is the first to have evolved here, though we certainly predate your own species by a considerable span of years."

The land and sky rippled and changed, and suddenly Jordan hovered in the sky above a vast jungle that covered much of a continent he didn't recognize. Dozens of villages dotted the shores, and despite being miles up in the sky he could make out faces.

No one spoke, but they existed in an almost hive-like harmony, with each member working seamlessly alongside the others. They built small villages primarily from stone, though here and there wood or crude rope were incorporated.

"You will find this next part familiar," Uluru teased as she faced the illusory sun. "This is the heart of the Pliocene Epoch, three-point-two million years ago. Before the ice ravaged our world. It teemed with life. Every continent was carpeted in trees and lush life."

A coronal mass ejection, two waves of solar fury, raced out from our star, and slammed into our defenseless world, just as they had five years ago. Jordan witnessed the devastation from orbit. Forests were flattened, or melted. Species were annihilated. It was far, far worse than the wave he'd endured.

But along the equator life remained. The villages Uluru's spindly ancestors had erected clung to life. One of the villages began to expand, so Jordan focused on that. Each house now had an obelisk outside of it, the same type he'd seen at the Met in New York.

Those obelisks brimmed with familiar power. They were shaping batteries.

"Yes," Uluru confirmed. "My people discovered we had the gene for shaping. We realized that stone would hold that power, and eventually that we could use it to shape our own bodies. We lengthened our own lifespan, I am ashamed to say, by stealing the essence of other lifeforms."

Uluru hung her head in genuine shame. Her inhuman eyes conveyed very human grief. She blinked a few times, then continued. "We murdered each other for power. We murdered each other to extend our own lives. The successful became known as Builders, for our power lay in the obelisks we erected. The larger your obelisk, the deeper your well of power. A truly gifted shaper with a large obelisk could expect to slay anyone foolish enough to enter their territory. After they slew a rival, they'd use their shaping, your former ability, telekinesis, to levitate their opponent's obelisks back to their stronghold. I know, as I was one of the very first Builders. My parents saw the great change."

"Wait, wait, wait." Jordan raised a hand. "The story is important, and I'll watch it. You said former ability. What did you mean by that? What did you do to my telekinesis?"

"Ah." Uluru clasped her hands together and shifted uncomfortably. "Some sacrifices were necessary to effect the vision I had in mind. Your control is as great as it ever was. Unfortunately, you can no longer broadcast your signal beyond your body."

Anger swelled, but it receded almost as quickly when he got his mind around what she was saying. He couldn't do it beyond his body. That word 'beyond' was important.

"So I can still fly? And move myself?" That meant he could

increase momentum too. That sounded useful if he now had heavy armor.

"Indeed." Uluru's relief was palpable. "I am glad you approve of the change. In order to make you immune to shaping I had to stop all signals, not just hostile ones. If you have no further questions, may I continue the simulation?"

"Sure." Jordan didn't want to be a bad guest, though he badly longed for some field testing. If he could turn into a dinosaur, then he damned well wanted to see that in action.

The vision continued to unfold. A clearly recognizable Uluru, though smaller and with paler skin, had erected a city of obelisks, but in a strange pattern. They formed the edges of a square several kilometers in width. That square had been completely swept clean of all debris, all trees and plants, and now formed a smooth black soil.

Dozens of Builders clustered around hundreds of obelisks, and as one they lifted their arms into the air and began to shape. The power rising from them dwarfed anything Isis or Blair could do.

"It is not merely that my race is gifted in shaping," Uluru explained as the ritual grew in intensity. "Not every sun-cycle is the same. This one offered more power than I have seen in the three million years since. This was the very height of power, and we used it well, as you can see."

A jagged black tip emerged from the precise center of the cleared square. It rose slowly into the air, burrowing from the surface, and triggered a rush of memory of Jordan in a helicopter back in Peru, watching the Mother's Ark rise from the ground.

This was no Ark, though. The stone was rough, unhewn. It resembled obsidian, but he didn't think that was the right kind of stone. The stone was almost a perfect pyramid, and no less impressive for the flaws as it settled into place.

"So this is the real First Ark?" Jordan guessed that this event predated all other Builder activity, or why show it to him?

"Not precisely." She shook her head, and something like irritation flashed over her features. "I was the first to identify the stone, and the first to survive a sun-cycle. We charged my stone for the entirety of my life, and by the time the final millennium arrived I knew shaping would soon no longer be possible. As I had never seen a full cycle I assumed it never would."

Once again shame overtook her features, and she cast her eyes to the Ark's floor. "I slaughtered my people. I conquered the entire continent, and then looked beyond for more victims. I fed them all to the stone. When the day finally came that the sun deserted us, my people, and my people alone, still possessed shaping. We ruled the world for the entire sun-cycle, and I husbanded that abundant power.

"The troughs were shorter back then, and the power returned after nine millennia. It is in that second cycle that Kek Telek rose to power, and along with Akenat created the true First Ark." She balled her tiny hands into fists. "They discovered an installation on his continent that predated our people, and suggested that a still earlier race had either colonized or evolved on our world at some point. He used what he found there to refine my ritual, and created a primitive version of the Ark we now stand in. He approached other powerful Builders such as myself, and each of us agreed to be the uncontested rulers of our own continents. Gods free to explore and test. The oceans became our battlegrounds, and the islands. The world was hotter, and land more rare."

"And the Ark Lords never warred on each other?" Jordan didn't claim to understand the minds of another species, but there was no way humans could live by a deal like that without screwing it up.

"Oh, we did." She shook her head, once again lost in memory, which began to play out in the vision around them. "You are seeing our first war, the war between Kek Telek, who'd conquered what you call the Americas, and Akenat, the Lord of what you would call Europe. The pair fought viciously for centuries, but finally became allies when Kek Telek offered to help Akenat build the First Ark. In exchange, Akenat would help Kek Telek build the Ark of the Redwood. They agreed, and worked together to achieve something amazing. Sun-cycles passed, and the Ark Lords grew in strength and number. A second installation that predated us was found, this one on the continent you call Antartica, where Yoggoth discovered or invented demotech.

"In the end, however, all our power was for nought. We couldn't halt the destruction of this world." Her hands had begun to shake, and the words came faster. "The ice covered everything. Destroyed everything. I salvaged what I could, and made a repository of species. Each time they were wiped out I reintroduced promising ones to re-seed our world. To stop entropy and ice from wiping it out."

"Why is ice a threat? The cold seems like a solvable problem." Jordan had seen far too many miracles from these people to think that ice was what stopped their tech.

"Ice is insidious. It covered everything. Entire continents lay under thick sheets, sometimes for thousands of years. Power ran low, and the Arks were unable to resurface to recharge. I had to go around the globe and manually raise them, for many cycles. I had to keep them running, keep them charging. I had to melt glacier after glacier."

Being around soldiers all his life had exposed Jordan to many instances of PTSD. This lady badly needed a shrink. He couldn't even imagine the trauma she'd endured. He considered putting a hand on her shoulder, but worried it might be taken for a threat.

A wise precaution, a low, primal voice rumbled in his mind. *Offending this one means our swift death.*

It was similar to his beast, but deeper, and didn't refer to him as Ka-Dun.

"Now," Uluru continued, either unaware or unconcerned by the conversation in his head, "the ice ages have ended. Our planet will warm for the foreseeable future. We will have millions of years of relative warmth, with few glacial maximums. The time is perfect for my brothers to return, and they are well aware of this fact. Our planet is special in the cosmos, and having gone elsewhere I suspect they now know this, and wish to reclaim what they once abandoned."

"What are we going to do about it?" Jordan flexed his own hands, excited that maybe they had a chance to fight back now. He couldn't wait to tell the others.

"Now you wake up."

Uluru was gone. The Ark was gone. He lay on the desert floor staring up at the spinning sky, which quickly stopped spinning and became the usual tapestry of stars one saw in the Southern Hemisphere.

Jordan rose to his feet, too energized to sleep. It was time to test out his new warform, and then go save his people from the deathless advance.

35

ANKH

Trevor was actually excited when they returned from dinner with Blair early enough that he could spend some time with the scale. It still required Ba to interpret, but he'd worked out a fairly efficient system, and had set up a laptop Melissa had sent as a gift. A laptop!

He'd set up a spreadsheet documenting each new discovery, plus a keyword reference so he could access the data again if needed. He'd make a proper database when he had more data to work with.

"Ba, can we teach this construct English? Is it possible to modify its programming? It must be if the Builders added data to it. They discovered this thing alongside the ship, right? It doesn't match their tech."

"Unknown. I believe the scale might predate them, but have no concrete evidence to support this." Ba frowned at the golden metal. "It is possible to modify the contents, and appears to require a specific set of sub signals with a frighteningly unique signature."

"Show me," Trevor ordered. His new virus gave him incredibly fine control.

A holographic display of the type of signal that would give the thing input appeared. Most of it was raw power. You had to feed it energy, and then offer it memories, or apply changes to the existing construct.

Trevor offered the thing his formative memories of speech, and blinked in amazement when it seemed to work. The scale accepted the changes, and the bulbous head blinked up at him.

"Can you understand me?" Trevor wiped sweat from his forehead. That had cost him more than expected.

"Yes, Ark Lord. I recognize your authority, though not your species. My name is Ankh. I am a shade of Enki, and possess his early memories." The head bowed as best it was able to. "My primary purpose is to hold our archive of forbidden knowledge, mostly as relates to our origins, mistakes, and shaping we deemed too dangerous to allow others to use. Your ark keeper has expressed your needs in brief. You seek to alter time?"

"We do." Trevor couldn't believe they were actually getting somewhere. "We want to journey five solar cycles into the past to a specific point in time when the First Ark exploded. We need to retrieve up to three people who were killed in that explosion. First, is it possible? Second, what are the general steps we'll need to implement to alter time safely?"

"Astute questions, Ark Lord." Enki inclined his head once more. "It is indeed possible. The shorter the distance traveled, the easier the shaping. However, it will still require a fully powered Ark under the control of a master shaper wielding a Primary Access Key. It must also be performed when our star is broadcasting the proper energy, as it is now. Our star is a very special Catalyst."

Catalyst for what, exactly? Something to be asked when he had more time. He had been a helio-seismologist before the fall. This stuff was his bread and butter.

"Let's say we have all that." Trevor smiled at Anput, who grinned back at him. They'd finally found something relevant. "Tell me about the risks. We open a portal. How long does it last? Can you model an illusion if we can show you a memory of the target moment? I want to build a virtual battlefield so we can plan around it."

"I can do these things." Ankh nodded his virtual head enthusiastically. "The primary risk is an uncontrolled unravelling. If you seek to take consciousness from one reality to another, then the reality losing the consciousness must be compensated. There must be balance. Parity. If there is not, then you will tear our realities, with catastrophic results as my people learned to our horror. I possess a relevant primer meant for any students hoping to learn temporal shaping."

"Show me, please."

An illusion formed in the air, and Enki's voice narrated as the simulation displayed a temporal connection taking shape. "A fissure must be created between two realities, then the space between them traversed. The in between is a dark, lifeless, lightless place. It is not empty, however. Things live there that prey on unprotected minds, and in some cases bodies. One of our greatest scholars, Kek Telek, was the first to open a temporal fissure, and paid a bitter price. His sanity never returned, and eventually we had to euthanize him lest he endanger our world. He became a threat to himself, always murmuring about the whispers he'd heard."

Trevor already hated the sound of this. Was going after Isis worth risking madness, when madness meant unleashing crazy super-gods on the world? He stared at the break in realities, and didn't want to know any more about what might lurk there.

"Over time Akenat perfected our temporal tunnel," Enki continued. "It connected the realities, and kept out the darkness and the whispers. It provided safety to temporal travelers, at least until they reached their destination. Once in another time the potential for damage is nearly incalculable. We ruined entire realities before we came to understand the consequences of our experimentation. Can you imagine ending quadrillions of galaxies accidentally? Even if they were a mere shadow of our reality...those beings are gone."

"So you experimented with time? Can you elaborate?"

"All of us did so in different ways." Enki shook his head. "We were so reckless. So young. Uluru agreed to join the Ark Lords because she badly wanted access to ancient helixes. She launched hundreds of expeditions into the distant past to add extinct species to her Ark. She traded us the secrets of Sunsteel in exchange for the secret knowledge we discovered in the ship where you found me." Enki's gaze fell into memory. "I used it to survey distant worlds. I would launch a signal, and then go thousands or hundreds of thousands of years into the future to monitor the results when they returned. Every Ark Lord had their own use, and we trampled all over multiple realities."

"How dangerous is going back five years?" Trevor tensed and prayed the answer was something they could live with.

"Negligible, especially if you are retrieving people whose timeline ended at the moment you save them." Ankh seemed to approve of the plan. "However, the cost must be paid. You will need to sacrifice three consciousnesses to bring back three. If you fail to heed this I cannot stress how dangerous the consequences could be. It could be our reality that unravels."

"And this shaping requires a temporal matrix? Where can I find one? The one beneath the Proto Ark tried to eat my mind, so if we can find one that doesn't do that I'd appreciate it." He shivered at the memory.

"There are a small number of available matrices." Ankh cocked his head and enumerated them. "The First Ark, the Ark of the Redwood, the Nexus, the Polar Ark, and this facility, though the matrix here is damaged, as you've seen."

"Wait, the Ark of the Redwood has a matrix?" Trevor couldn't believe their luck, and found himself grinning. They'd been due for a break, and now they'd had two back to back.

"Indeed." Ankh nodded. "It was the last Ark constructed with a temporal matrix. All future Arks were denied the feature as it was deemed too dangerous."

Now they were getting somewhere. He turned to Anput. "I'm going to go tell Blair. You want in?"

"No." She shook her head. "I want to study the shaping required. I'm stuck on the piece where it's going to require Blair's full concentration. He can't go with you. That also means you need three people to sacrifice themselves, unless you want to chance the consequences.

Someone needs to tell Liz and Jes'Ka too, as they should have the right to volunteer if they wish."

"Are you going?" Trevor had never considered the possibility that she might stay behind.

"No." She tried to meet his gaze, but failed and eyed the floor. "I remember what Set became, and I won't risk falling under his sway. I'm going to cover Blair during the ritual, but if I see even a possibility of Set coming through I will end the ritual myself."

"I understand. I won't say anything to the others." It could mean ending up trapped in the past, dying in that explosion, but better that than Set make it out. "I'll make sure Blair knows he needs a security detail, and that he should put you in charge."

36

TIME WINDOW

Blair appeared on the control pad in the Ark's heart, along the outer edge of a ring that enclosed a building-sized sapphire. That gem focused the Ark's incredible energies, and were how most feats of shaping were produced. This is how the werewolf and zombie viruses had been created, and how extinct species could be brought back to the world, or evolved into the dragons they'd seen Set use.

He cradled the Primary Access Key in one hand and raised the other to link with the heart. It thrummed in answer, a flash of blue passing through the gem.

"That thing scares the heck out of me." Trevor approached up the catwalk and paused on the edge of the platform. His expression mixed two parts eagerness with one part fear. "Thanks for coming, man."

"Anput didn't join you?" Blair looked around, but detected no one else. She could be in the shadows, but that seemed unlikely.

"The first part of the research we puzzled out is that you're out of the fight." Trevor squatted down and dangled his legs off the edge of the platform, over the thousand-foot drop to the valley below. "You'll have to sustain the portal, which will require an immense amount of power. The initial requirements suggest a sixty-second portal will absorb 20% of your Ark's remaining reserves. If the fight goes long you could burn through most or even all of it pretty quickly."

"At least we have hard numbers." Blair moved to the railing, and leaned against a spot not far from Trevor. "Do you have any other logistical data? I assume there's a walkthrough of the ritual? It requires the heart?"

"Yeah, I've prepared a spreadsheet, and I'll email that when I get a sec."

Those were words Blair had never thought to hear again, and it warmed him to see the world clawing back to what it had once had.

"So why did you want to meet here?" Blair gazed at the heart. The power sung to him, crying out to be used.

"For starters I want to set up the central chamber as a life-sized recreation of the Set combat." Trevor rose and joined Blair at the railing. "The Ark can project illusions, so I was hoping you'd set up the initial recreation, then allow myself, Liz, and anyone else who was there to add details."

"That sounds incredibly useful." Blair closed his eyes, and did as Trevor asked. He thought back to the desperate battle and populated the room exactly as he remembered it. Then he opened his eyes. "We still have a problem, though. Almost two minutes passed from the time we left that room. Anything could have played out. We need to see specifics before we commit to anything. Does your research have a wave to perceive through time without altering or being detected?"

"That's why I came here specifically." Trevor scrubbed a hand through his hair, which had started to grow again. "The requirements for the ritual to view a remote location are much lower, as there is no transference of consciousness, only a bit of sound and light. I figure this is the warm up."

Blair exhaled slowly, and looked to the heart. "What do I need to do?"

"It's pretty simple, really. You think of an exact moment in time, ideally one of your own memories, like the same room two minutes before the exact second we want to scry." Trevor gripped the railing with both hands. "You feed it power from the Ark, and the temporal matrix extrapolates the exact place in space and time you're trying to reach by comparing the memory to Earth's stellar and temporal drift. It will create something called a temporal fissure, a break between the two realities. We'll be able to see through that hole, but placement will be critical. We can't prevent the other side from seeing through, though they won't be able to use the window as a portal or anything."

"What if we darken the room first? I'll drop the window in the corner behind a pillar, where no one was looking." Excitement surged as Blair probed the heart. "Okay, here goes."

He fed it a bit of his own power, and willed the gem to create the temporal fissure Trevor had described. Builder tech was all plug and play, thankfully, and the gem obligingly hummed to life.

Enormous power welled up from deep within the Ark, and the gem began to spin, slowly at first, but then faster and faster. A beam of pure brilliance streaked from the gem, and created a meter-wide slash in the air next to Blair.

On the other side lay, incredibly, the First Ark's central control room. The window provided an excellent view of the combat playing out, which was incredibly one-sided. Set easily overpowered Osiris and Ra, and Isis. He toyed with them...right up until a blinding white light flashed, and the window dissolved.

Blair raised a hand to his temple as sudden pain spiked through his skull. It had happened at the precise moment the Ark had exploded, and it took several moments for him to manage speech. "I think it's a bad idea to be connected to the Ark in any way when it explodes. Remember TSDS? We need to get in, and out, well before that Ark blows. That gives us a clock. Did you see enough of the combat to get a working model set up?"

Trevor had already started back up the walkway toward the central chamber. "Definitely. I'll model what I saw, then tell the ladies about it so they can start running combat simulations."

Blair nodded gratefully. "I'm going to do a bit more experimentation. Send me that spreadsheet. I want to understand more of what we're doing, and what the requirements are."

Trevor nodded his assent, then blurred up the walkway and out of sight, leaving Blair alone.

What they were doing here terrified him. The headache was a tangible reminder that if they made the slightest misstep they could unravel their reality. That would doom the Builders, and deathless, and champions, and every last survivor. They'd all pay the price, all so they could retrieve a goddess who might not be able to help them.

Thankfully he had a lot of training in hopeless situations. Every situation looked hopeless. Trevor had been right that the scrying, as he decided to call it based on the old D&D games he'd played in college, didn't take much power. He could watch the scene from other angles and make some decisions.

They still needed to figure out who the sacrificial lambs would be. Blair noticed that Trevor hadn't brought that up. Only a handful of people had volunteered to go. If three needed to stay behind that seemed like a bad play. They'd be sacrificing their current team to bring back the old gods.

So how did he get around the sacrifice? Did they just bring people who didn't matter? That seemed so callous. In the face of their reality being destroyed how callous was too callous? He already hated having to make choices like this.

At least he didn't have to make it alone. He hadn't spoken to Jordan in entirely too long. Blair closed his eyes and reached out through the Ark network. *Jordan, you around? I was hoping to catch up for a few minutes.*

Nothing for a few moments, and then a thunderous answer as Jordan trumpeted his mental strength. He passed impressions of Ayers Rock, and dinosaurs, and so many other things. *Yeah, great timing, man. I need someone to talk to after...I met a Builder.*

Blair slowed down the memories Jordan shared, and examined a few. *Looks like you've been on a hell of a trip. Uluru is a T-Rex? And you think she can be an ally?*

Kind of, Jordan corrected. *She's more like an advisor, but she's reshaped my body with my specific trials in mind. It's pretty amazing.* More impressions flowed from Jordan, and Blair gasped.

Wait a minute. You're a dinosaur now? That is so badass. How do I sign up? Blair could scarcely believe the magnitude of the change. To Uluru, Isis must be a child.

You don't want it. Jordan passed a memory of trying to levitate a rock. *You lose external shaping, though apparently I'm immune to it too.*

Wait, are you serious? Full immunity? Blair actually laughed out loud. *Jordan, you are exactly what we need to deal with Set. He can't control you. What are the odds you can make it to San Francisco?*

I can't be there quickly, but I can come. I have to relocate my people to Australia. There's a lot to catch you up on. Images of boats and strange eyeless creatures flowed through the bond, and Blair responded with images from the recent council meeting, and from meeting with Trevor about the specifics of time travel.

Jordan's pleasure flowed through their connection. *Love how efficient this is. I'll get in contact when my people are settled. If you still need me I'll get my butt to SF.*

Blair didn't say anything when he realized that Jordan was no longer an Ark Lord. What had happened to the key? He couldn't bring himself to ask. *Godspeed, man. We'll hold down the fort 'til you get back.*

37

PRETTY LIE

Liz rested her blade on her shoulder, and sucked in another lungful of air as sweat dripped a ring around her. They'd been going at this hard in human form for hours, but it still didn't feel like enough.

She studied Set's alien visage. He'd been a man once, but had been twisted by the grey men into something that looked a great deal like they did. The transformation was a big part of their problem, because it had imbued him with shaping that let him take over people's minds.

"I don't see shaving off another second," Liz finally admitted. She couldn't see Jes'Ka, but the woman lurked in the shadows. She returned to them after every run, reflexively. "If we open the portal near Isis, then we'll need almost a full second to get her out. Set is likely blurring as hard as he can, and he may be faster than us, even if Blair gives us everything he can. We can't count on beating him to the punch."

"We're dancing around the real question." Jes'Ka emerged from the shadows. She had a light sheen of sweat, just enough that were she at a gym it would catch the attention of the men around her. "Your brother claims we need to leave at least one person behind in the past. More if we wish to save my father, and still more if we wish to save Ra, which I see no reason to do. I am not planning on sacrificing myself. Are you?"

Liz opened her mouth, but then closed it again. She'd been about to say of course she would, but did she really want to die? What would that do to Alicia, or Yukon, or Blair? "I don't know. If there's no other option I'd consider it."

"We need to know who's staying behind. That person, or people, should engage Set in combat while we pull out mother and father." Jes'Ka's face fell. "If no other option presents itself, then I will be forced to sacrifice Lucas. He will gladly give his life in exchange for the Mother."

The idea that she'd spend the man's life like currency horrified Liz. He'd slumbered through the ages only to be sacrificed on the day he woke up? It seemed needlessly cruel, but it wasn't up to Liz to dictate morality to this woman. If it could even be done. When Anput was calling you out for being a hussy...wow.

And yet...did she have a better plan to find a sacrifice? And would she fight to stop this man? No, definitely not, even while she judged Jes'Ka for doing what she herself wasn't willing to.

"I can see from your face that you do not approve." Jes'Ka raised an eyebrow, then loosed luxurious blond locks from her ponytail. They of course fell elegantly around her shoulders like she'd just come from the were-salon. "I would hear your reasoning. I do not understand this new world, or why asking a loyal follower to sacrifice their life in defense of what they love would be worthy of scorn."

"Well, when you put it like that, I can't really argue." Liz gave what she hoped would be her last hopeless shrug. She hated it. "It's just...in our world a woman who manipulates men into doing that sort of thing without delivering the, ah, goods is frowned upon."

"Oh, Lucas 'delivers the goods,' I assure you. Better than any man I've ever met." Jes'Ka's smile put any devil to shame. "Not every god indulges their baser instincts. Many shove them aside. They cease to be what they were. I'd argue that if we are goddesses, then should we not embody our people? Should we not love, and laugh, and dance? Should be not do it all fiercely, and with little regard for tomorrow?"

"Sure, if we want kids, credit card debt, and some student loans." Liz found herself smiling. "I don't question the lifestyle. I'm just coming from a world of preconceived notions. Our society is largely monogamous, and we refer to people who have sex outside their partnership as cheaters."

"I'm familiar with the concept. It was prevalent during our day as well." Now Jes'Ka shrugged, though hers belonged in a make-up commercial. "Part of why I came to these shores was to escape that sort of persecution. Anput uses sex as a currency. I just like mating. I enjoy the closeness of it, of seeing that intimate side of someone. But it doesn't mean I am beholden to them."

Liz nodded along as that made a lot of sense. "In my world you'd be called a hippy. A werewolf hippy death-goddess. I'm sure there'd have been a comic book, and then a movie." Words were coming out of her mouth, but as usual she had trouble picking which ones. "Why does Lucas follow you then? Why has he chosen to devote himself to you?"

"Lucas came to me because I spent a night with an ancestor of his. A great-uncle, or something. I don't know." Jes rolled her eyes. Somehow Blair had given her Valley Girl English. Maybe that was fitting. "Anyway he asked to travel with me. To learn to hunt, and fish, and mate, and fight. He wished to follow me forever, he said. I refused. He followed me and asked again. He pursued me for months, and finally I gave him a night. He's been with me ever since. He's loyal and fierce, and kind. Sacrificing him to bring Mother back brings me no joy. But I honor it, because I know why he does what he does. His people loved my mother as the creator-goddess, and Lucas still does. He would do anything for her, even were I not involved."

Liz felt a little bad for misjudging the woman. She had a fascinating story, and she'd already taught Liz a few new tricks in combat. More and more she heard the whispers of the shadows when she strained.

"Do you really believe this time magic is possible?" Jes'Ka's mask cracked and there was vulnerability, for a moment anyway. "It sounds a useless fantasy. My mother is dead, you said. I do not believe we can cheat death so easily. I think we are telling ourselves a pretty lie."

How did she answer that? Liz had no idea. She wasn't exactly a cheerleader, or the person to offer pep talks. She was a realist, and if she was being honest, sometimes a pessimist. Honesty was the best currency she had.

"I know it's possible." Liz's stomach protested noisily, a reminder that so much shaping came with costs. "What worries me is the price of failure. What if we screw up? That's just as possible as succeeding. The portal could collapse. We could damage our own reality, or destroy everything if it all goes south."

"She's worth the risk, if we are certain your Ka-Dun can manage the shaping." Jes looked down at the ground, and her hair screened her face. "She's always been the best of us. I love my father. He's proud, ambitious, and generous, but he is intolerant of failure, and well...inhuman. My mother retained her humanity, and her wisdom, through it all. She supported me through my mistakes. She taught and nurtured me. I will do anything to get her back. My father? I would love to have him back, but I will not sacrifice myself to retrieve him, and Lucas is spoken for."

Liz's skin went clammy when she considered the unthinkable. She could ask Santa Rosa for volunteers, but it seemed so self-serving to ask for three sacrifices if she herself wasn't willing to be one of them. She needed time to think.

"I'm going to get some rest." She picked up her towel, and shuffled off toward her quarters.

38

WELL FORTIFIED

The days after Percy left the collection of strange beings who called themselves Builders were odd indeed. Apparently he owned and operated a magnificent skyship called a slipsail that flew like an aeroplane up in the sky, complete with a crew of the grey-skinned attendants.

Those creatures proved amazingly useful, and unerringly flew the craft over the Atlantic. How they knew he was from Britain he didn't know, but they made unerringly for the British Isles. The sea level was different, and a bit more of the coast had been submerged, but the shape was unmistakable, even from hundreds of miles out.

Would you like us to transmit you to the light bridge, Ark Lord? One of the grey-skinned subordinates bowed his head.

Yes, do that. Uh, immediately, he thought back, awkwardness and all. No doubt the creatures sensed something amiss, but what could they do about it except gossip among themselves? Percy was no stranger to the idle talk around senile lords or ladies. The help soldiered on, and did their best to keep the matter within the family.

There was a bubbly feeling, and then his whole body sort of... dissolved into light. He'd heard the future people in the Proto Ark discuss the act, and rather enjoyed experiencing it for the first time.

He appeared on a raised silver disk within a temple that would have been at home back in the strange golden city where he'd spent so much time. This might be as close to a similar home as he was able to make, as Percy had no early idea how he'd be able to return to his own body.

Ah, Ark Lord Akenat, you have returned. A familiar hologram appeared, but this one had too jovial a manner to be Ba. It must be another of them. *Do you require any tasks or data? I'd be happy to provide them.*

What is your name and purpose?

I am Ark Keeper Ka, the construct plunged ahead with gusto, *and my purpose is to serve you, Ark Lord. I assist you in all matters, and am quite well versed in many matters, as you well know, since you designed me. What an odd game.*

Excellent. And you serve no other? Percy was going to have to trust someone with his secret, and this Ka might be just the ally he sought.

Only you, Ark Lord. Ka offered a low bow.

Wonderful, wonderful. I am going to ask a number of strange questions. Things you'd expect me to know. I need you to answer without question, no matter how odd I seem.

Of course, Ark Lord. Ka bowed again. *It is not my place to question. Only to serve.*

So how much do you know about time travel? Percy reached up to straighten his jacket, but of course Builders wore strange gold and white clothing at home in antiquity of Greece or Egypt.

I am unfamiliar with the term, Ark Lord, Ka gave back cheerfully.

Percy had no earthly idea where to begin researching time travel, which is what he needed to understand if he were to get back to his own time. How could he express the need to this construct, and quickly?

There was no telling when the creepy black-eyed monster would come after him. He hadn't been wrong. Yoggoth had recognized that he didn't belong. Sooner or later he'd come to have a private chat, and Percy suspected he might not enjoy the conversation.

All the more reason to find a way home sooner rather than later.

Ka, are you familiar with the pods in the golden city? Those are time pods? Right? I used one to transmit my mind?

Yes, Ark Lord. They are temporal chambers. However, I do not understand or govern their use. We were strictly forbidden from interfacing with them during my time at the Proto Ark.

So time travel was out of reach, at least for now. That meant that he could turn his attention to learning his new world as quickly as possible. He needed to understand this structure, what it could do, and how it could protect him from Yoggoth. If he didn't solve those problems quickly then he'd drawn his last.

Fortunately, he thrived on research and had able assistants. By the time his enemies came for him he planned to be well fortified.

39

LAST MEAL

Melissa entered Morton's steakhouse on Post Street, her favorite restaurant before the fall, certain that her unlife was about to end. Blair had proven a competent leader, but you could set your watch by his bias against the deathless.

What had she done to earn the elaborate execution? She'd toed the line, and enforced every one of his decrees, so far as she knew.

She steeled her nerves, and forced a smile as she approached the only occupied table in the candle-lit restaurant. Blair sat alone in a nice button-down shirt and a pair of designer jeans that Liz had absolutely picked out for him. So a Liz sanctioned meeting then. Perhaps this was a make nice?

Liz seemed much more practical about their alliance, despite having the larger axe to grind. The Ka-Ken didn't seem overly fond of Melissa, but she also didn't have a massive bias.

"Join me, please." Blair gestured at the only other chair across the massive table from where he was seated. "I took the liberty of preparing dinner for myself. I know you don't...partake. I hope that's not like, super rude or anything. I'm trying to make this night about you."

"Why?" Melissa narrowed her eyes as the anger roiled within her.

Her Risen said nothing, but she felt the panic as she endangered her own survival. "You've made it fairly clear that my kind are a step beneath you."

"I have, and I was wrong." Blair tied his napkin to his shirt, and picked up a knife and fork. "Badly wrong. Tonight is about correcting that. Sit. Please. Help me with a hypothetical. Melissa, if I died tomorrow, what would you do? There's a power vacuum. The Ark is either without a key, or you recover it somehow. Now what."

Melissa slid into her chair, and dropped her napkin in her lap out of habit, though obviously she wouldn't need it. What *would* she do? She'd thrived on hypotheticals in school, and this was one she'd fantasized a lot about. She couldn't be blamed for that.

"I would focus on New California, and forget about the rest of the continent. I'd attempt to ally with our northern neighbors, but see no reason to attempt to control their forests." She picked up her fork, though again there was nothing to use it on. "I'd inform Yosemite of my existence, but change nothing about his agreement with us. I would forget about the rest of the continent, and focus on building up California. Everything we have would go here, because this is our stronghold."

Blair nodded thoughtfully, then looked down to carve off another piece of steak. Werewolves and their meat. "I'm going to do something monumentally stupid. I'm going to shape time itself, and recover Isis and possibly Osiris. We need their power and their knowledge if we're going to resist the Builders. They're here now. We have confirmation on at least two."

Melissa's fork clattered to the plate, and she made no move to stop it. "They're on Earth? I'd always hoped it was your paranoia. Blair, what is this really about? You're frightening me."

"If this goes south I need a successor." He leaned back in his chair, and focused his full attention on her. "I've instructed Anput to bring you the access key if I fall."

"You're not passing it to Liz? I don't understand." And she didn't. Was this a trick? A loyalty test?

"Liz will likely be dead too if this goes wrong." He sighed heavily and swirled his wine without drinking. "If I'm being honest you're a better administrator than either of us. You have the best chance of building a lasting empire, and I don't want to pass a key to someone just because they're a champion. I want the best person for the job."

"You realize everyone in your camp will see this as a betrayal, right?" A bit of guilt washed through her at that. He'd pay a hefty price if this got out. Of course...he'd be dead so he wouldn't be around to be hated.

"Probably." Blair rubbed his temples. "People in your camp will see it as a concession, so there's an upside. Let people think what they think. If you inherit the key you can make your own rules."

Melissa didn't even know how to respond. How to process this. How likely was the possibility? What would she need to do to prepare? Did she even want the job? Did she want to lead a war against aliens?

"I don't really want your job." She put the napkin back on the table. "If you fall there has to be someone else who can do what you do. I'm not a strong enough shaper to battle the things you battle. I'll be overwhelmed."

"Not on your own turf," Blair pointed out. "If you stay in or near the Ark you're basically untouchable. I don't know how things will play out with the Builders, but all we can do is try, right? If I fall, you need to do this, Melissa. People need a leader, and I can't trust anyone else with this."

"Alicia will hate you forever."

His face fell, and he nodded, too overcome for words in her estimation.

"This is incredibly selfless, Blair." She gave him the most genuine smile she could summon. "I appreciate the gesture. I appreciate that you've made me your successor, and I'm fine with not naming it publicly to avoid strife for the time being. Just that you're willing to do it is enough. The council meeting down south meant a lot to me too. You're taking us into account. Thank you."

Blair managed an exhausted smile. "We all have to live together. Or unlive together. I consider you a friend, Melissa, and think that friendship could grow in time. We're immortal. I want to like the people I work with."

To her immense surprise Melissa felt a swell of affection for the man. She wanted to see him succeed at bringing back Isis and stopping the Builders. The very last thing she wanted was that kind of world-ending responsibility.

Managing a city was more than enough.

40

ANCIENT FRIENDS

Akenat relaxed as the shuttle approached the destination he'd envisioned. He enjoyed a vista he'd not seen in thousands of cycles...Uluru's wild continent, teeming with life as it always had in spite of the climate. He still remembered his first slipsail journey to these lands.

Millennia by millennia the continent had grown more arid, a process that had continued to the present it seemed. Much of the place was desert. Yet as he zoomed over that inhospitable land he saw the megafauna that already been reintroduced, and vegetation to feed them.

Uluru's mighty black Ark was visible from half a continent away, and Akenat studied it as his craft zoomed closer. He remembered when it had been a lump of rock, when he'd first come to these shores and introduced himself to Uluru. He'd shown her memories of his Ark, and what was possible.

Together they had taken her lump of stone, and shaped it into a proper Ark. In exchange she had taught him the secrets of Sunsteel, though she'd never admitted where she learned or discovered them. Not everything could be rediscovered lost knowledge, and perhaps she truly had invented them. He doubted it.

The shuttle slowed as it neared the Ark, and he had no difficulty locating Uluru. A massive saurian wandered outside the Ark, taller than any beast had a right to be given the gravity on the world. It was, in the parlance of one of the modern minds he'd touched, a flex on the other Ark Lords. She could do what they could not, where life was concerned.

Akenat willed the craft lower, and hovered in the sky over the oldest being he'd ever met, this version of her anyway. He walked back to the transport pad, and willed it to drop him through the base of the ship.

The beam of light carried him slowly down to the surface. Not an efficient means of locomotion, but one that required very little energy, which is why he'd opted to install it. It would function continuously for millions of years without breaking down, and would draw precious little energy doing so. That they still functioned were a testament to Enki's genius, and his persistence.

By the time he'd reached the ground Uluru's titanic form lumbered over, and she inclined a head respectfully at his comparatively tiny human. Humans were larger than his own species, but he still felt a child.

Welcome to my shores, Akenat. Long have I wondered at how this day might occur. I watched as the world changed, and wondered what you would find when your consciousness arrived. You are so young. She dropped a slavering jaw closer, each fang easily capable of rending his body, powerful as it was. Yet he felt no threat. *How is it you come to be here? Will you share your tale?*

"Indeed I will," Akenat replied with Nox's mouth, in English, the host's native language. "And I will do it as they do. As a story. If you wish to see memories as well, they are open to you."

Akenat lowered his defenses, something he'd only ever do for three people in existence, Uluru being the one he trusted most.

The massive saurian rippled, and Uluru appeared before him, young and beautiful, and vibrant. She hadn't changed at all, outwardly at least. But she had spent millions of cycles surviving and learning, and was no longer the Builder he remembered.

"The clone bodies I prepared had long since decayed." Akenat's too-large mouth turned into a frown. "By pure chance, if there is such a thing, a body had been deposited into the pods by the humans. Such an astronomically small probability that almost I am willing to listen to your theories of synchronicity. Anyway, I awoke, escaped my captors, and fled to the Ark of the Cradle. You are familiar with the mad hominid in the skies over the cradle?"

Uluru inclined her head to indicate agreement, as the humans did. She seemed to appreciate his willingness to adapt, which he'd gambled would improve her mood.

"I am." She inclined her head. "Or was. He has left this realm, and moved onto the next. Did you attend to that?"

"I did." Akenat smacked his lips as he once again considered how odd having tiny bone protrusions inside his mouth was. "I have taken his Ark, though the demonic infestation is too far along for the Ark to be useful until after the zenith, without proper intervention."

Uluru's expression weathered like the rock behind her. "The First Ark is gone. The Nexus will be soon...unless you have ordered your progeny to leave off their mission?"

"I have." He nodded. A useful gesture. "They are currently effecting repairs to the Nexus, and should be able to stabilize it."

"It will not be enough, sadly, whatever happens here." She shook her head sadly, and turned to watch the rising sun. "Without the First Ark we might survive...but only until the next deep ice age."

"Not so." Akenat laughed, and found himself surprised by the pleasant concoction of chemicals that flooded his host's brain. "The planet will enter a lasting warming. If we limp along a cycle or three, then we can construct new Arks. There is no reason for them to be confined to a planet. I envision a true Ark, that flies through the stars and brings our will wherever we wish."

"You tout the vision as your own, but is that not merely recreating the vessel you, Kek Telek, and Enki originally discovered?" Uluru had no eyebrow to raise, but arched her eye anyway, in a very human fashion. How much was their game, and how much had they influenced her? Uluru hadn't finished, apparently. "These space-Arks will

no doubt be impressive, but do you understand the singular importance of our star? How it differs from others? You can cross the
cosmos and never find another."

Akenat hesitated then. Uluru was a different kind of being. A true
god. She had lived through countless sun-cycles now, and had seen so
many species rise, mature, and go extinct. If their sun only did something once every hundred cycles...Uluru had witnessed it. She understood their star in a way that would drive Enki mad with envy.

"I do not understand," he admitted, though he hated the ignorance. "Enlighten me."

"Our star is the heart of a goddess." Uluru offered a self-deprecating smile. "I understand you hate that word. Fine. Our star is a
living entity sheered off from a titanic extraterrestrial being billions
of years ago in a war between beings that gave our universe shape. I
have learned much in the time since you left our world, and not all of
it can be quantified, or even passed as a memory. Much simply has to
be witnessed. Or endured."

"What will you do when Yoggoth comes? You must know he has
overwhelmed and corrupted the rest of them." They'd always been
able to leap right to the heart of a matter, and while Akenat enjoyed
reminiscing, he would not rest easy until this had been discussed.

Uluru's mouth turned down in a deep frown, and her eyes tightened. She balled her hands into fists. "Yoggoth is no Builder, and thus
no longer a part of our original accord. When he arrives, if it is as we
fear, then I must oppose him however I am able. Yet...what will we
do? He knows our world, and our technology. I have a few surprises,
but he has had two million years to prepare for war. What has he
built? What kind of fleet will he bring? I do not know what we can do
to resist him."

"There is always the failsafe." Akenat didn't like thinking of it, and
hadn't when Yoggoth had suggested they create it. "If we activate it
when he arrives it will eradicate all life in this system. Even his ships,
whatever he has constructed, will not survive. Demotech is potent,
but it cannot circumvent physics."

"As he well knows." Uluru's skin darkened into a thick leather. It seemed an unconscious gesture. "He would not come to our system without a way to deal with the failsafe. He designed it. He will counter it. We cannot assume it will do anything at all, and even if it works as desired how is scouring all life from the system a victory? Denying it to Yoggoth might be a mercy to those we slay, but they are all still dead."

Akenat didn't have an immediate response. She had a valid point. In two million years Yoggoth would have solved this problem. Perhaps his solution was simply multiple fleets. He could send in a huge number of ships and troops, and if they used the failsafe he could come in and take charge of whatever remained on the ruined world. That would horrify the rest of them, but Yoggoth? It would be a time-saving measure.

"You believe he can be stopped? That something can be preserved?" Akenat didn't know what he believed, but then he wasn't fully invested in this timeline. If he returned home he could prevent Yoggoth's rise to power...might prevent it. What if he failed and this same outcome occurred?

"I do." Uluru gave a grim, warrior smile. "I have prepared them well, little brother. I have given them much. I enabled many species. A little shaping here, a nudge there to get them to explore distant shores. Several promising variants of the hominids rose in your absence, but as you can see one became nearly ubiquitous. Interestingly they did not wipe each other out, as their modern scholars speculated. Most branches were completely unaware of each other. All branches did, however, war amongst each other. Competition within the tribe, and within the region by multiple tribes, seems to be instrumental in keeping their species healthy. Only the heartiest survived the deep glaciations. Their adaptability really is quite magnificent."

"And through it all you remained neutral? You never saw one individual threatening a whole species and intervened?" Akenat asked not to undermine her, but from genuine curiosity. He didn't understand how she could remain so impartial, or see things she'd created wipe each other out.

"I did." She rose to her full height and wore her pride as armor. "There were bitter moments, and bittersweet ones, but I understand that it all exists to prepare this world to resist any external threat. Now that threat is arriving, and it is, sadly, of our own making. I believe Yoggoth won his war on this new world. I believe nothing remains of Enki, or any of the others. I believe that if you return to the past you will attempt to right this wrong. For me nothing will change between that day and this, and I won't know until now if you have triumphed, or if Yoggoth overcame you."

Sadness oozed from her, pulsing through his open defenses. They both knew that this was the end of Uluru's time, for good or ill. Whether Akenat led the Builders, or Yoggoth, her world could not be the same.

"I will do my best to stop him. I wish you well in the battle to come, whether with Yoggoth...or with me."

Uluru's body rippled, and she flowed into her towering saurian form. *I promise whatever foes come to our world they will face the entirety of my wrath, little brother. But it is not me who the Builders should fear. I have shaped the hominid warriors for countless generations. Humanity is my weapon against our own kind, and you will find them more than suffi-cient to the task.*

There were no more words possible, so he returned to the beam, and to his craft, and began the final phase of his plan. It was time to hobble his foes, and then to return home.

41

DELAYING TACTICS

Irakesh wore his costume with relish as he strode into the senate chambers, a meeting hall that had at one time housed Brazil's governing body. Six hundred deathless filled the stadium seating to bursting, and cameras whirred as the proceedings were recorded and distributed to every deathless city on the continent.

Two dozen councilors sat on a raised stage, with Camiero in the very center, the first among equals. Irakesh considered joining the man, but preferred to save his entrance for a strategically appropriate time. He'd wait for his ally to flounder, as the man had no choice but to do, and then he'd ride to the rescue.

How odd that he'd finally found a friend after so many centuries of unlife.

Camiero had proven to be as astute a politician as Irakesh had ever met. He'd have thrived in Ra's court, and quickly risen to her direct favor. She'd have made him a god to be remembered.

Camiero openly guided the new deathless nation, so young it hadn't yet learned its own name. This would be their continent. The living were not welcome here. The dead could live off the life-giving energies of the sun, making the living worthless even as cattle.

That movement had swept through former enemies like a virus, converting all exposed to the idea that they were greater together, and that threats outside their nation demanded they work together.

No longer did they assassinate each other, openly at least. Now they worked with purpose, all jockeying for position in this new vision they had conceived of. When Nox next came, or Hades sent another servant, they were ready in their defiance. The demons had been driven from their ranks, which hadn't been difficult to achieve.

Nox had taken all the strongest leaders to battle for the Proto Ark, leaving lackeys and lickspittles behind. The deathless had learned to see them as a threat, and would root them out where found.

But all that had caused a problem. They had done their work a little too well. Because now these people wanted blood.

"This body recognizes Madam Santiago as speaker," Camiero intoned, then rapped his gavel.

A bright young woman with impeccable glasses and razored fangs approached the microphone. She took her time adjusting it, and by the time she spoke, the entire room strained for her words.

"We have our house in order. Our people are ready to fight. Our military needs practice. We have a target. The werewolves still hold Lima. I have heard no compelling reason why we haven't wiped it from the map, and frankly I am struggling to understand your reluctance." She stepped back and fixed Camiero with her gaze. "Unless you can present a compelling counterargument, then I motion to authorize the final assault on Lima. Let us regain our capital, gentlemen. Let us show the world that we have thrown off all masters, all invaders. This is our continent."

Resounding applause drowned out any reply Camiero could have made. It perfectly captured the room, and neatly pinned Camiero. If he agreed with her, then this became her plan. If he refused, and had no compelling reason, then he became part of the problem. There was no course through this unscathed.

"I heard a motion. I will second it." Camiero nodded deferentially. "Before I do so are there any objections? If not, then—"

Irakesh saw his opportunity to ride, and he rode. He swept down the red carpet reserved for dignitaries, and hurried down to join Santiago at the podium. Camiero made a great show of pausing as he approached. That gave Irakesh enough time to prepare a suitable protest. A master stroke, in his own estimation.

"Ladies and gentlemen of this esteemed body," he spoke into the microphone, his rich voice echoing through the room. "Thank you for indulging my protest. You are quite right. The werewolves can be easily eradicated, and you have heard no compelling reason why it has not yet happened. You have wondered...why? Why do they draw breath? Why do we toy with them? Their despair may be sweet, but we have greater matters to be about. So why the delay?"

He paused, of course, and awaited as if for a real answer. The room wondered. They demanded an answer, silently of course.

"Because if we delay, if we make Ark Lord Jordan desperate, then he will turn over the access key to his Ark in exchange for allowing his pitiful band to escape." Irakesh grinned wickedly. Deliciously. "Imagine it. We allow the ragged survivors to sail off into the ocean with whatever garbage they can carry, and for our restraint, our chosen representative becomes Ark Lord. Someone from within this body. We would have the key, ladies and gentlemen, and if we repair the Ark our empire will pass into legend. We will lead it there as gods, together."

He'd buried the thorn of course. Who would be Ark Lord? Now they'd fixate on that, on which of them would be granted power, on what favors they could extract in support of their candidate for the position. They cared a lot more about that than wiping out Lima, as doing so offered no material power gain.

Irakesh bowed, and retreated to the fringes of the room as a proper advisor should. He was merely a relic from another time, after all, trotted out now and again to hear the wisdom of a bygone age.

Unfortunately his tactic could only buy so much time. The infighting would slow them, but soon voices would again call for Lima's destruction. Where was Jordan? The tactic came at great cost, because now that he'd put the key on the table they would settle for nothing less. Either Jordan snuck his people out, gave up the key, or they eradicated Lima. Those were the only moves left.

Wherever Jordan was he'd better hurry. This stalling tactic would buy a day. It might buy three if Camiero was as skilled as he appeared. It would buy no more. They were out of time, and out of moves.

42

HOME

J ordan focused inwardly and pulled on the river of golden energy he'd conjured. The light walk completed, and he left Australia's harsh beauty behind. Part of him was reluctant to leave Friz and Uluru, and the land itself. Things were simpler there, and the horrors of life further away somehow.

He arrived in Lima with a pop, and a sudden change in both temperature and pressure. He'd been standing in the cool desert air. Now he stood in the sweltering coast, at the dock where he'd left Vimal in charge.

Shock reverberated through him when he took in the sorry state of the surviving refugees. A few hundred tired people clustered on and around the docks, and dozens of the people's boats rested against the pier, already taking people on.

Dr. Roberts hovered over the crowd, and raised both his arms to calm the pandemonium. "Please, there is room enough for everyone. We have plenty of boats. We—"

A shell screamed by overhead, and slammed into the air over the pier. Roberts had raised an arm and erected a telekinetic bubble to focus the blast outwards, but the effort knocked him from the sky and he crashed into the crowd below in a tangle of limbs.

This was a last stand. These people had been routed. He'd returned too late.

"Ark Lord Jordan has returned!" Vimal's shaping-enhanced voice boomed over the crowd, and all eyes began swiveling to Jordan. A gap opened up around him in the crowd. "He has come to save us!"

Jordan rose into the air as Roberts had, grateful that he hadn't lost the ability to fly. That ranked among the top most useful shaping powers. What did he say to these people? He didn't have the entire tactical situation under control yet.

Many of the champions below cradled wounded limbs. That only happened when a werewolf was at the very edge and out of energy. They'd frenzy soon, and these people wouldn't be safe. Most of the surviving refugees were going to die if left in close proximity to the Ka-Ken and Ka-Dun.

"I have returned, and it looks like just in time." He shook his head. "I'm sorry it took as long as it did. There's a lot to catch up on. As I'm sure the people have told you, I found us boats, and now I've found us a home. A place where we can be safe, and rebuild."

"How are we going to get there?" yelled one voice.

"The deathless are exterminating us!" cried another.

These people's morale was gone, and he couldn't blame them. The crush of bodies onto the boats hadn't slowed, though at least some of the people were listening to him.

"All of that is true." Jordan pointed down at the boats. "But it is also true that we have powerful new allies, and those allies will help us escape. Stay calm, and get loaded. I'm going to get us out of there."

How did he do that exactly? There were far too many to light walk, and he could see modern warships to the north and south. He couldn't see them to the east, but they were almost certainly out there, waiting to close the trap's jaws.

Jordan drifted lower before more protests could be offered, and landed next to Roberts. Maybe if they saw their leaders conferring they'd await a plan.

"A week late and a national debt short, seems about right." Roberts extended a hand in friendship, his smile belying the harsh words. "Welcome back, Jordan. You're here just in time to oversee our execution."

"Is it really that bad?"

"Worse," Vimal called as he strode up. "We are down to a hundred or so champions, and most are drained and wounded. There are perhaps three hundred humans as well. Their will to fight is broken. They are exhausted, and they have nothing left to give."

Jordan nodded as he took in the situation report. Had he really expected it to be any better?

Another scream sounded above. Jordan's irritation surged, and he triggered a blur, then leapt into the sky. He angled his flight toward the mortar, and caught it in one hand. The metal sizzled against his flesh, but the pain was brief as he flung the weapon back at its maker.

He landed next to Roberts and Vimal. "We're not getting out of here unless I stop their assault. Have you spotted a command crew? I thought Irakesh and Camiero were going to buy us time."

"They did," Roberts admitted, "for a while, at least. I'm pleasantly surprised by just how effective Irakesh proved to be. Things came to a head when he promised that you could be persuaded to turn over the access key in exchange for allowing us to escape."

There it was. Irakesh's plan from the beginning. Pin Jordan, and take the key. Well, he couldn't really fault the bastard. It was a damned clever plan. He'd earned his freedom, and an Ark, and a power base. But if he really meant to fight the Builders, then did Jordan want to deny him the key?

If he retreated to another continent, did it make sense to keep it simply to deny it to Irakesh? If the deathless really had made good on his promise to keep Lima standing, then Jordan had no animosity left. He just wanted to get his people out of here. How could he best do that?

He needed these people to stop shelling. These people wanted the key. All he needed to do was find their command center, which should be easy enough. They'd never hidden it before. In fact, why not ask?

"Where are they observing from?" He directed the question to Vimal.

"They have a battleship about two clicks past the main fleet. Their leaders are on the bridge there. We know because Irakesh is still wearing his tracker."

That cinched it about Irakesh. So odd that he'd not yet screwed them. But if his end game was the key maybe it made sense. Or maybe he really had become less of a prick.

"Okay. I'm going to go deal with this." Jordan gathered his legs beneath him and leapt into the sky. He shifted as he rose into the sky, and the people below glimpsed his new warform for the first time.

His hair fell away as bony ridges erupted all over his skin. Thick armored plates formed a complete exoskeleton with four horns jutting from his jaw at different angles, to gore offending targets. A tail erupted from his tailbone, as it would when he was a wolf, but this time it ended in a two-hundred-pound ball of dense bone.

His new form was larger, too. About four meters tall, which meant he now towered over even the tallest Ka-Ken. He'd loom over Sobek, and over most of the threats he'd run into. Uluru had transformed him into a heavy, tailor made to deal with his current problems.

Jordan sailed through the sky, clearly visible to the enemy fleet. They had guns that could track targets as small as he was. Would they fire?

BOOM. BOOM. BOOM.

Yep. Looks like they would. A trio of high-velocity slugs sailed toward Jordan, and he decided the best way to deal with them was not to. He focused on his flight, which wavered slightly each time a round slammed into him.

They did no damage though, and didn't really alter his trajectory. Another volley came in with no more success. Jordan just kept flying. This new body rocked. Regeneration was amazing, but even better was not taking damage in the first place, coupled with the knowledge that if you did you still had regeneration.

He spotted the battleship where the deathless leaders waited, and was unsurprised to see them all standing near the bridge, clustered outside on the landing next to it for a better view of the end of their hated enemies.

There was just enough room left for a four-meter-tall were-dino. Jordan landed on the edge of the ship with so much force that the battleship rocked in the water.

"Hey there. I don't suppose you guys speak English? My Spanish is horrible." And then he waited for the two dozen elite deathless to react. Would they try to swarm him? Call for help? Flee?

"Ah, Ark Lord Jordan," Irakesh called, drawing the attention of the crowd. He approached. "You wear a different form than when we last met. It seems there is a story to tell. Have you come at last to plead for your people's survival? To turn over the key to your Ark?"

"What's to stop me from wiping the smugness right off your face, Irakesh? And then killing everyone on this boat? My people might die, but no one here will be around to see it."

Nervous tension thickened through the crowd, and he expected someone to attack. None did. That surprised him. He was a clear threat. Was he really that intimidating?

"Really? No takers? No one wants to chest thump?" Jordan folded his arms, and swung his tail behind him menacingly. Man, he already loved that thing. Something needed to get bashed.

"Are you here to posture then?" Camiero asked, his tone oozing disappointment. "We hold all the cards, Ark Lord. Turn the key over to me. I will serve as its custodian until this august body appoints an Ark Lord to the role."

"And in exchange? What? You let my people sail out into the harbor, and then sink our boats? I don't think so. How stupid do you think I am?" Jordan didn't know if Camiero and Irakesh were acting, or if they'd really joined the deathless cause. He hoped they were still acting, because he did not need a war with them right before the Builders arrived.

"You need assurances, of course. For starters we will halt the attack." Camiero waived to an aide, who retreated inside the battleship's bridge to speak with the vessel's captain. "Our forces will fall back entirely, to as far a distance as you require. We have no need to wipe you out, champion. Take your strange new body, and leave our shores in peace. Give us our Ark. We give you your lives."

"I have a condition." Jordan folded his arms, and considered his course of action. Was this the right thing to do, or the dumbest play he could possibly make? It meant trusting one of the worst snakes they'd ever encountered. Did Irakesh really want to fight the Builders? Jordan hoped so. "You don't get to choose an Ark Lord. I do. I choose my successor, and I choose them from your number. You follow the person I choose, and build your government around working with them. In exchange, we get to retreat from South America, and you never see us here again."

Murmurs passed through the crowd until Camiero cleared his throat into a mic and got everyone's attention. "We need an official vote. All in favor of accepting the Ark Lord's terms?"

Hands began to rise. More and more. Finally the swarthy Latino smiled at Jordan. "It appears we accept. Name your replacement, Ark Lord, and gain your people's freedom."

"I choose Irakesh." Jordan folded his arms. "Honor this deal, and you've got an ally."

The ancient deathless's expression was comical, and drew a half smile from Jordan.

"Your trust is well placed." Irakesh inclined his head respectfully. "I find your offer surprising, but I accept. I will succeed you, repair the Ark, and lead the deathless against the Builders upon their arrival. What of you? Where will you go?"

"My people are bound for Australia by way of Easter Island." Jordan swung his tail and gave a predatory smile. "I'm going to take a detour up to San Francisco, and help Blair rescue an old friend of yours."

43

SACRIFICES

Liz stood near the back wall as Trevor and Anput entered the Ark's rejuvenation chamber, the last to join their motley crew. Blair, Liz, and Jes'Ka had been in the strange room with its liquid silver sigils on the walls for some time, waiting patiently for the former deathless, her brother once more, to finish his calculations, and to have Anput check them.

She'd spent most of the waiting appreciating the dark-skinned warrior in the sarcophagus, and wondering what his life had been like. She wondered what he'd make of waking in their world, of what he expected. It seemed cruel that he'd only get a single day, but at least he'd have that much.

"Okay, I'm waking him. I'll leave it to you to calm him, Jes'Ka." Blair placed a palm against the crystal and adopted a look of concentration.

The crystal rippled, and possibly the most handsome man Liz had ever seen rose from its depths, tiny crows feet around his eyes speaking to the journey he'd taken to reach the present.

Liz couldn't be happier in her relationship, but hey, nothing wrong with a little eye candy. Lucas's muscled skin shivered even in the warmth, and his eyes fluttered open. He eyed them wildly and gripped his spear, then calmed when he spotted Jes'Ka.

She rushed to his side, and whispered assurances in a language that reminded her vaguely of what she'd heard the local Miwok using, though obviously far removed. Lucas relaxed, like a wolf being pet by the only master it trusted.

"He understands we are in the next cycle." Jes turned to them. "I have explained that tonight we will spend together, and tomorrow he will make a great sacrifice. He has agreed. Before we retire, perhaps we'd benefit from a final walkthrough with all parties present? This battle will be quick, but it will not be easy."

Liz cleared her throat, and added her take. "I'd agree that we can't afford any less than perfection. Everyone has to know their role. We haven't walked through the whole thing with everyone present. It's time for a rehearsal. We need to see how viable this really is before we gamble everything."

There were nods all around, and she led the way into the central chamber. Leading seemed to be mostly about stating what you needed to do, and then walking in that direction. She hated it. It would never come naturally to her, no matter how many times she needed to do it.

Blair was the next into the room, supportive as always. Trevor shuffled in after, quiet and distracted. Anput stood next to him, the pair thick as thieves. She wasn't sure how she felt about that friendship, but then she didn't really know much about Anput. Were they together, together? There was no way she'd ever ask, but she started to suspect there was something there. A spark.

Lucas and Jes'Ka came last, the pair still whispering in their Miwok-ish language.

The scene in the central chamber had been reset, with Set striding through the doorway with Osiris's limp body in hand. Isis and Ra squatted on the far side of the central chamber against one of the obelisks, as far from Set as they'd be for the duration of the simulation.

The simulation perfectly captured the foul miasma of feces and worst things that had overtaken the First Ark, and it focused Liz, brought her back to that day when she'd absorbed Wepwawet, and they'd detonated an Ark.

The demons had scrawled all manner of filth on the walls, which she avoided looking at as she studied Set's approach into the room. He'd toss Osiris and the broken Excalibur, and then stalk toward Isis, who would take to the shadows until Set rooted her out.

The challenge was getting her to agree to come with them, which they'd assigned to Trevor. That was the failure point that most worried her, as Isis might not listen to what she believed to be a deathless. On the other hand this occurred during a desperate time when she was working alongside Ra.

The other option was waiting until Set had her pinned to the obelisk, but that happened seconds before the detonation, so they'd opted to try a good sixty seconds before that, right when Set entered the room.

"Okay, everyone into positions." Liz shifted to warform, embracing the shadows as she moved to the egress point where Blair had added an illusion of what the portal would look like.

She waited a few moments, but of course couldn't see anyone since they were all in the shadows. Blair didn't have that problem, and power suffused her as Blair lent her his blur. Apparently he could do the same with Anput and Jes'Ka, despite not having a bond, though hers would be stronger as a result. That put her on more equal terms with Jes'Ka, as this really would come down to speed.

Liz blurred forward into a flying tackle into Set's midsection, and met resistance as she carried the illusion back into the pillar. She glanced back at Blair, who had a hand raised like a conductor. He'd done a marvelous job simulating force. Was he using telekinesis to do that?

You are distracted, Ka-Ken, Wepwawet chided. *You must be wholly wedded to this task if you expect to have any chance of success.*

He wasn't wrong. Unfortunately, she knew that Blair's illusion wasn't capable of hurting her, and that it wasn't anything like how Set would actually react. That meant anything they learned here was of limited use and may or may not matter during the real attempt.

Jes'Ka erupted from the shadows and sliced at Set, then vanished and offered her taunt. "You're were ugly before, uncle, but now? Not even Nephthys would touch you if you hadn't taken her mind."

Illusion-Set charged at the shadows where the words had come from, and Liz attacked from behind. Her claws sliced through air, and she realized Blair had stopped controlling the illusion. She glanced at him to see why, and saw a boyish grin pasted on his face.

"Jordan just arrived on the light bridge. He's on his way up." Blair's grin infected her. "Having him in on the assault planning gives us a better chance of success. He can help you and Jes'Ka keep Set off balance. I guess he got powered up in Australia, though I'm not sure how."

"Then it means it's time for the talk." Liz hugged herself, and wished they didn't need to do it. "We'll sort out who's staying behind." She tried not to glance at Lucas, who stood dutifully behind Jes'Ka, his spear held loosely in one hand, ready to throw.

No one wanted to talk about it, but it needed to be answered.

Jordan arrived a few moments later in a rush of wind. He wore his trademark black t-shirt with camouflage pants, and had a grin for the lot of them. "Good to see you guys. It's been a long strange trip. Do we have time to catch up, or are we going right into the heavy stuff?"

"We'll make time," Liz decided aloud. There was no way they were going into this without a few minutes of fun. She crossed the central chamber and embraced Jordan. "Welcome home. I wouldn't want to do this without you. What's this Blair tells us about some sort of power up?"

"Oh, you're going to love this." Jordan gave her a squeeze, then disengaged. "Tell you what, why don't we do some sparring? Who wants to throw down?"

"I accept your challenge." Jes'Ka stepped forward, and shifted into a nine-foot Ka-Ken. "I have heard from the Ark Lord that you are skilled in combat. Thus far only Liz has impressed me. What can you do, little puppy?"

"Yeah, about that." Jordan began to shift. His body rippled, and his skin darkened as it thickened. He grew far, far larger and armored plates emerged over much of his body. Where there weren't plates there were spikes. "You remember Sobek? I met the one who transformed him, and she custom shaped my body. There are a few downsides. I can't directly shape. But I can't be shaped either. So here's what I'm thinking...a slight alteration to whatever plan you've got."

He paused as the change completed, and he towered over Jes'Ka. "I crush Set, and...."

Jes'Ka attacked. She lunged for his face, but he turned to the side, and she caught a mouthful of armored skin. Jordan fell back a step before her ferocity, but relaxed a hair as he seemed to realize she couldn't hurt him.

A hum came from behind Jordan, and his massive maul of a tail came around like an oversized bowling ball. Perhaps he'd added something with telekineses. Whatever the result, when the ball hit Jes'Ka it hurled her through the air with so much force that the wall shattered where she impacted, destroying countless sigils.

"Sorry." Jordan's shoulders slumped. "I haven't used that maneuver yet, so I didn't really know how much strength to put into it."

"Oh, man," Liz whispered, staring up at Jordan's magnificence. "I cannot wait to introduce you to Set."

"I've decided to be one of the volunteers. I'll stay in the past." Jordan folded his arms as his body shifted back to human form. "You said we needed three, optimally. How many do we have with me included?"

"Jordan, are you sure?" Blair's concern cracked in his voice.

"Positive." Jordan nodded. "I've done what I needed for my people. I've made things right with South America. I'm a soldier, not a general. I want to go down swinging. We need someone to do this. May as well be me."

"Lucas is the only other volunteer." Liz indicated the ancient warrior. "He will be staying for Isis. If you're staying too, that means we can grab Osiris."

"He ran Mohn Corp.," Jordan pointed out. "He could be incredibly valuable. Listen, Uluru told me that she tailored my body for the trials I would face. This is the trial. I have to trust that. I'll take care of Set, but I don't want to let up until the portal closes. If I slacken for even an instant he could get loose and escape. That can't happen. If I stay, then I ensure he can't get away. This is the only way I can be certain our whole plan works. I know what I've been shaped into is impressive, but Uluru is still there. You guys can go see her too, and should. She will help us against the other Builders. You don't need me as much as you think you do."

Liz ignored the hot tears. He'd already accepted his death, and was now justifying it to the rest of them. It wasn't fair, but it also wasn't her choice. Losing Jordan? And for a time-swap?

Something didn't feel right. There had to be a better way. This couldn't be it. She hated it, and didn't know if she could live with it, even if Osiris might be a better option for winning the war against the Builders. You couldn't do that kind of math.

"Come on, let's not look so down. I haven't eaten. Feed me." Jordan smiled like impending death couldn't be further from his mind. She wished she could adopt that kind of detachment.

They hadn't even faced this yet, and she already wanted to cry.

44

YOGGOTH

The entity Yoggoth had outgrown the need for a single physical body. His consciousness had been distributed across dozens of worlds and countless hosts. He had grown strong and wise, and ever-present.

A dozen species had fallen before him, each of the spacefaring races overconfident in their exploration. Each species had yielded valuable genetic material, and had expressed the demonic infusion differently. He had learned much, though there was still a vast quantity of learning to do. Eventually he'd spread his tendrils to every part of the galaxy, at which point this galaxy would bend all its resources to sending him to the next.

Yoggoth would be all, one day. He would envelop all life, each unique species broadening his understanding and power. It was a heady destiny that lay before him, and he was appropriately humble, for a god at least.

Millions of cycles had revealed patterns that most would never understand. It made existence predictable, even when encountering an entirely new alien species. They all died the same way, regardless of their physical forms or level of technology.

Yoggoth did not war upon these species. He gave gifts. Powerful, useful gifts. Gifts that merged with ships, and with minds, and eventually with bodies. Gifts that merged with him. Almost no species had refused, and those that did faced his armadas. It ended poorly, from their perspective at least.

A strand tugged at his consciousness, from a familiar, but long empty sector of the galaxy. Yoggoth felt a tug from Earth, where a few of his tendrils had wormed their way into hosts. Those hosts were too far removed to influence directly, but he received vague impressions.

One of the more powerful ones, a hominid, had just been severed. That tendril would not have been worthy of note, save for its abrupt termination. Someone had cleansed his influence, and as it happened he had an armada on the way to this world.

Earth. His home world, once. A world so far removed from his current existence that he literally could not remember it as a mortal, or as an ordinary world. It was merely a jumble of sensory impressions and data, with no feeling.

Uluru might still be on that world. Akenat's missing consciousness could be there. What if he could capture it? The experiments he could run. He could drive his rival mad, then make him a loyal servant, rebuilding him piece by piece. He could do the same to Uluru, though he would speak to her unfettered first, to compare notes on genetic research. She was the only possible equal on such topics.

His armada neared Earth, launched thousands of years ago at low velocity in preparation for this day. Should he have miscalculated their strength, and that armada proved insufficient, then it would be thousands more years before he could make another direct attempt.

One of the greatest limitations that vexed him was crossing physical space. Quantum entanglement allowed him to cast his consciousness wherever he liked, but moving physical bodies required massive quantities of both time and energy. It simply wasn't practical to spread past a certain rate.

That had been the primary reason he'd not already expanded back toward Earth. The planet offered little, and was too remote. Too far from anything else useful, and of no interest since he'd already harvested every useful species from that world.

The progeny he'd coopted had run experiments for nearly four thousand years, with limited results. The humans could express powerful abilities, but the shaping always had odd limitations, some of which proved lethal to the user. Unpredictable, and thus not useful.

After much deliberation Yoggoth made a momentous decision. In his endless years of research he'd long since perfected the ability to create an avatar. He could move energy from one world to another, infusing one tendril with far more power and ability than it would otherwise be capable of.

Losing that avatar would cost him dearly, and prevent him from creating another for a lengthly interval. Sending it to Earth was a risk. A hideous risk. Earth still held at least one Builder, one who'd had just as much time to explore and learn as he had. Uluru was an unknown quantity, and all attempts to learn her whereabouts and disposition had failed. His demons could not journey onto her shores. They died when they reached them.

Yet the gain? Immense. For he had learned Earth's secret. Earth truly possessed a unique place in the cosmos, one that had not become apparent until far too recently. That star was no star. It was a Catalyst. A piece of divinity. Life had flourished on Earth many times after repeated extinctions not because of her tenacious inhabitants, but rather because they had a star continuously bombarding their world with primal life.

Now that he was aware of the star's power, the time had come to claim it. What happened to the planet was largely immaterial. They had their failsafe, and could choose to employ it. If they did, there was a chance it would destroy his avatar.

That would be a setback, and would buy them time to formulate a response, while harnessing the power of their star. If that happened they could become a true threat, and at the very least would require many resources to subdue.

No, he would give this matter his full attention, and ensure that no followup invasion was required.

In the meantime he needed to secure access to all temporal matrices on their world. Akenat would seek escape to the past, and must not be allowed to...a grim smile crept across Yoggoth's tiny mouth.

Akenat's temporal connection required an anchor on both sides. Were he to send a message to his past self, perhaps he could rectify this problem without needing a physical presence on Earth.

Yoggoth closed his eyes, and reached for a matrix on a world he controlled. He poured power in, and triggered the desired connection, with only a handful of words.

If you heed this message, then your most dangerous enemy will never return home.

45

THE NATURE OF SUNSTEEL

F our centuries had seemed like such a span of time, once. All of modern European history from the printing press to the Great War. Now it seemed a tiny span, especially when his new body didn't age. Percy had spent decades learning frivolous things, and studying for its own sake.

Flora, fauna, the cosmos...there was so much data already accumulated. Over time he began to experiment and learn, and to construct. This Ark was, in some ways, a gigantic London factory that could produce whatever good or livestock you wished.

At one point he'd tried his hand at breeding dogs, and had made a passable West Highland Terrier, but eventually he'd tired of how quickly they died, and stopped breeding them.

Loneliness was always an issue. Ka made a marvelous companion in some ways, but was too eager to please and never challenged him.

Percy had therefore needed to challenge himself, and he'd rigorously tested each of his ideas as he flitted from passion to passion. Currently that passion was Sunsteel, the strange magical metal that the Builders had used to fashion their greatest artifacts.

Over time Percy had come to understand that Sunsteel meant imbued with the power of the sun, and that it wasn't forged from gold at all. It involved an alloy of all metals found on Earth, in different quantities. The sun apparently fused them into one seamless whole, which had a number of unique properties.

Making new Sunsteel was hideously difficult and time consuming. A single ingot could take a millennia of dedicated mining and refinement, which Percy had begun about a decade ago. It would take time to bear fruit, but already the wheels had begun to turn in his mind.

In the interim, Akenat already possessed a quantity of Sunsteel, apparently, and had melted down several trinkets to gain material with which to experiment. He had enough metal to make something very special, but had spent nearly a year learning how to imbue that metal with the specific powers he wished. Today represented the first test.

"Ka?" he called as he bent over the boiling tub of metal. "Add the diamonds we harvested."

Five gems levitated from the stand next to the mold and arrayed themselves around the cross guard. As they settled into the Sunsteel each gem flashed with power, which continued unabated as the metal cooled.

"Ark Lord, why are you constructing a sword?" Ka had adapted to regular speech, which kept him out of Percy's head, and helped preserve his sanity.

"It's a very special weapon, much more than it appears." He hovered over the mold, so unlike what a smith would use. For one thing, he could see the metal slowly morphing into the correct shape, becoming a razored blade with no whetstone. "It will be linked to our sun. The wielder will be able to use it to summon the wrath of our star, once the blade is fully powered."

"I do not recognize the runes." Ka peered down at Percy's work as he drew the final sigil. "What language are they?"

"Celtic." Percy knew that would have no meaning to Ka, or to anyone for a very, very long time. "It spells Excalibur. The blade's name. This is the first forging. I intend to do it a thousand times, each time imbuing it with more power. One day this sword will be wielded by a species that doesn't even exist yet to vanquish an unholy creature that seeks to devour us all."

"I see." From his voice Percy suspected that Ka did not, in point of fact, see. It hardly mattered.

"Ka, what can you tell me about demons and their weaknesses?" He peered down at his creation, which was still far too hot to touch, and would be for some time.

"They are largely confined to the Polar Ark, under the watchful eye of Ark Lord Yoggoth. He claims they are bestial, and lacking intelligence, but that they can be dangerous in numbers." Ka cocked his head. "Demons are classified as a minor threat. They are highly resilient, resistant to shaping, and may possess any number of abilities. It appears that any creature can be corrupted, and its base powers or abilities will form the new demonic powers."

"And their weakness?" He stretched a palm over the blade, and basked in the heat that rose from it. "What sort of weapons could destroy them? Countless numbers of them? I want to wipe out the lot of them all at once."

"They are vulnerable to extreme heat, pressure, and disintegration." Ka waved a hand and an image of a demonic grey man appeared. "They resemble themselves prior to the corruption, but their wills belong wholly to whatever master turned them. Yoggoth has a means of controlling all the demons, and uses it to force them to fight each other, thus keeping their numbers small, and their threat at bay."

"Wonderful." Percy saw the trap there. Giving a warden you couldn't trust the keys meant sooner or later the inmates were coming for you. "I have a task for you. This blade, once completed, must remain secret at all costs. No Builder or grey man is to see it. Not even me. I have prepared a very special place to house it, and will tell you where it is. You will place the blade there. When the first hominids locate the hiding place you are to appear to them wearing a very specific form. The Lady of the Lake. I will provide the specifications, but it must appear to be a female of their species."

"Of course, Ark Lord." Ka bowed his head once more. "When do you anticipate this event occurring?"

"Over two million years from now." Percy gave a wistful smile as he tried to remember his life as a human, but failed. This was the only life that mattered now. "The blade will be needed, and the hero that wields it will cut down the monster we all fear. I may not reach home, but I've had a devil of an adventure, and history still might remember me, in some small way. If we succeed, then there will be a demon free world to remember us."

46

PORTAL

Blair couldn't believe this day had finally arrived. After countless hours planning, experimenting, and sifting through Builder data. He was ready. He could shape time, with the aid of the Ark. Incredibly this place represented salvation for the best that the old world had produced.

His friends had gathered within the heart of his Ark, clustered along the railing next to the comparatively small platform where the actual shaping took place. They were ready to gamble everything to save a single person, really. Osiris was incidental, if they could save him. This was about retrieving the Mother.

Jes'Ka and Lucas stood proud and tall, a bit apart from Liz, who in turn stood a bit apart from Trevor and Anput. So many divisions. But all united in purpose.

Blair turned to his shaping. He raised the Primary Access Key, and reached for the power within the Ark's heart. The limitless well responded, and offered up the tremendous strength he'd need to complete this work.

A beam of azure brilliance lanced out of the gem, and poured into the scarab at the tip of the Primary Access Key. The ancient artifact drank the power, wave after wave after wave, until the metal itself vibrated in his hand.

Blair raised a hand. Only in that moment did he truly feel a god, a biblical sort of god. He was modifying time itself. He thrust his palm forward and an unseen hammer slammed into the air.

The resulting sound split both his eardrums, hot warm blood leaking from both ears as the pain quickly faded and hearing returned when his regeneration kicked in. The hammer blow to reality had an effect.

Particles of their universe fell away to expose the deep darkness underneath. Hellish purple flames clung to the edges of the fissure, which allowed just enough room for a person to step through, and plenty of room to see.

Things lurked in the darkness. Blair could feel their minds. Feel their malevolence. They hated light and life and would do anything to destroy them. Blair extended the staff, and a beam shot into the fissure.

It broke into thousands of strands, like a spiderweb forming, which quickly wove into a tunnel wide enough for a person to traverse. It also exposed the egress point, a similar fracture in reality on the other side, into another time.

Amazingly the connection stabilized, and he felt a huge pull on the Ark's reserves as their time and the past became one, for a brief span.

This next part was the trickiest. Blair divided his shaping, and infused Liz with immense blur, a tiny thing compared to the cost of the portal. He repeated the infusion with Jes'Ka, and then again with Trevor, and finally Lucas.

Blair made the attempt on Jordan, just in case, but as expected the signal rebounded off his thick hide. He really did seem to have total immunity to every form of shaping Blair understood.

The tunnel strained, and a claw sliced through, then withdrew quickly and the wound sealed over. "Go! Go now! Something is pressing on the tunnel." He gritted his teeth as the exertion mounted.

The Ka'Ken were the first through, followed by Jordan, then

Trevor and Lucas. They entered with the blur, and Blair accelerated to match so he could track their progress. Of course, if all of them, including Set, were blurring...were any of them? They'd just set a new speed for reality.

Anput stood resolutely beside him, her features moving as if molasses. She'd sustained her own blur, but while strong, it paled next to what he'd infused Liz with. He suspected she'd need every bit of it.

Blair concentrated for a moment, and felt the heart and the power drain. Everything seemed to line up as expected, and there were no problems that he could...Blair went cold. There was no problem with the shaping, but there *was* a developing problem.

Ship after grey man mothership materialized in the sky over the Ark, until a full dozen crafts of varying sizes arrayed themselves around the massive black pyramid. They loomed ominously, but did not attack or take any other obvious action.

Blair's attention split, and he glanced at the portal once more. Things were fine, but almost all his concentration and shaping needed to be focused there. Could he use the Ark to drive those ships off without losing the spell? It seemed a hell of a risk.

He chanced it and flung a bolt of pure white destruction from the tip of the Ark. It streaked into one of the crafts above, and the shields pulsed around it, visible in that instant. They pulsed around the other ships too, and Blair realized they must be in some sort of distributed network.

The Ark's destructive energies were shunted away, absorbed by whatever system they had in place. He could try again, but that shot had cost him. What if the next fared no better? He couldn't both fight them and hold the portal.

This was going south and quickly. If Liz and the others weren't quick he didn't know there'd be anything left to return to.

Why hadn't their ships returned fire? What were they waiting for?

47

ASSAULT

Liz followed Jes'Ka into hell. The stench of feces and worse things overpowered her too-sensitive werewolf nose as she slid into the shadow's welcoming embrace. The chill whispered to her now, every time she entered. As Jes'Ka promised, the voices could reveal whatever the shadow knew.

She followed Jes'Ka through the shadows as they advanced on Set, who stood in the doorway. He tossed Osiris's broken body to the stone, and advanced with a confident smile.

The bulbous-headed monster's pasty skin still haunted her, and just seeing him made her want to run. He couldn't be beaten. He couldn't be opposed. Yet here they were to do exactly that, to launch an assault when Osiris, Ra, and Isis herself had lost badly.

Had they really gotten that much stronger? This time they had a fully powered Ark Lord, at the very least. She could feel Wepwawet's growing impatience, and stowed her thoughts in favor of the mission.

Jes'Ka lunged from the shadows as they'd planned, and slashed Set's unprotected face with wicked claws. They skittered off thick carapace, but the force of the blow was so great that they tore deep furrows in the armor. Set would wear that scar.

He flowed backwards, and swept up his own Primary Access Key as a weapon, knocking Jes'Ka into a pillar with bone-shattering force. How was he so fast? Liz came in with a low slash using her Sunsteel blade, since she knew that could actually hurt him. The golden metal slammed into his leg just above the knee and sank deep into the flesh, until it struck bone and lodged there.

Do not drain him as you did me, Ka'Ken, Wepwawet cautioned. *He is unclean and will overwhelm you.*

Her moment to paralyze Set by drawing his essence came and went, and he brought up a gauntleted fist and backhanded her away. Liz's jaw shattered, and shards of numb pain tore through her vision as she rolled back into the shadows. Her weapon still stuck out of Set's knee.

Set greeted them with a booming laugh. "Jes'Ka! Niece! How do you come to be here? Where were they hiding you? I do believe I will kill you in front of your mother before enslaving her."

Jordan's four-meter Dino-form stepped from behind a pillar, and brought his tail down on Set's back. The blow smashed the villain into the stone, crushing both enemy and stone, and ruining that section of the room. Liz's sword went skittering away across the floor, and she dipped from the shadows long enough to retrieve it. The golden weapon seemed none the worse for wear.

Jes'Ka's spear stabbed out of the darkness, and pinned Set's good knee to the stone. Jordan's tail came up again, and slammed down into Set's chest, crushing it as she'd once seen a cockroach crushed. And like the cockroach, Set didn't even seem inconvenienced.

A wave of pure force flung outwards, and knocked Jes'Ka and her spear away. It did nothing to Jordan, who raised his tail and hit Set again. This blow drove him through another layer of stone into a deeper foundation. His ribs cracked, and blackish blood exploded onto the stone around the demon.

Set raised a hand and one of the four control obelisks ripped loose, and accelerated toward Jordan's back. The missile somehow hit supersonic speeds in just a few meters, and the tip hit perfectly between two of the armored plates on Jordan's back.

The obelisk punched deep into his back, and the lower half of the stone sheered off and flung away in a clatter as Jordan staggered into a second pillar, which shattered. Set blurred to his feet, and seemed untroubled by his ruined body, which had already begun to repair itself.

The demonic god drove both fists down on the obelisk, and pushed the spike deeper into Jordan's body as he gave a saurian roar of pain. Jordan's elbow came back and launched Set into the air, then his tail blurred around faster than Liz could track and slammed Set into the wall.

Finally, Liz saw her opening. She darted forward and finished the wound she'd started earlier above the knee. This time her slash severed the entire leg, and she grabbed the severed appendage in her free hand and hurled it as far from Set as she could.

Set lunged with his forehead, and caught her muzzle, shattering it and flinging her backwards. He was so fast. Liz rolled back into the shadows, and limped away in case he followed up.

Jes'Ka took the opening and rammed her spear into his gut, then slammed him down into the ground, and darted back into the shadows.

Jordan had regained his feet now, and he looked pissed. She didn't ever want to be on the receiving end of Dino-Jordan. The saurian charged Set and tackled him into the wall. Jordan pinned his arms in one of his, and then began punching his face, both with his free hand and with his oversized tail.

Even Set's wit seemed to fail him as Jordan roared in rage and pain, raining damage on his one-time tormentor. She didn't know who she pitied more, Jordan for having to deal with Set in the first place, or Set for being on the receiving end of all that rage.

Jordan tossed Set to the ground, and prepared to move in for the killing blow.

Set evaporated into green-black motes of energy, and the motes began flowing toward the portal. How could they have been so stupid? Of course Set had detected it.

48

GOING HOME

Akenat stood on the bridge of the largest mothership, pleased that the progeny ran the vessel and left him free to think and plan. The Ark had made one feeble attempt to attack them, but the dispersal network had absorbed the energy and used it to fuel their drives.

Unless the Ark could generate fourteen shots in six seconds, then it could not overpower the network. Increased assault would simply decrease the efficiency of the energy collected, but would have the same net result. Akenat won.

Begin the collection, he ordered through the collective, which served him utterly now.

Grey men on all twelve ships enacted the same series of commands at their consoles. Each ship launched a modulated signal, which to the naked eye might appear as a heat shimmer. These shimmers surrounded the Ark, and began to bleed away power, into the network.

Collection has already normalized at nine percent, a voice whispered over the network. *The Ark's defenses are considerable, but energy obtained exceeds cost to acquire. We can drain the Ark in four hours and twenty-three minutes.*

Akenat had been surprised to find them using the humans' calendar. There seemed no clear advantage to having adopted it, but they had, and so he continued to use it rather than change for its own sake.

Excellent. Drain it until there is nothing left. Contact me if there are signs of resistance. I must attend to a personal matter.

The collective felt his need, and he their desire for his success. They didn't press to know where he was going or why. That knowledge could compromise him, so they didn't need it. They had a clear task, which he'd bred them to thrive on. They found solace in purpose, and purpose in serving a greater master.

Akenat headed to the mothership's light bridge and wondered if it would really be as easy as this. Could he reach the temporal chamber, and make it back to his own time? If he did, what would he find there? How would he deal with Yoggoth's treachery? Would he tell them the truth of their fates, that they became puppets? Perhaps he could show memories, though his evidence was tangential at best.

He arrived at the raised disk, and wasted no time stepping atop and ordering the craft to beam him. He wanted no delay. No chance of failure. No chance for the Ark Lord to complete his shaping before Akenat had full possession of the Proto Ark. The disk flashed, and he appeared on the land below.

It had been an age since he'd stood on these shores, though he recognized them instantly. The coast had changed, and the humans had erected a strange rusty bridge in the background, but mostly this was the same place he'd known as a youth.

Akenat wasted no time reminiscing, and made for the shimmering portal. What a waste to leave it running continuously. No wonder the city had nearly run out of power. Who'd left it on at that powerful of a setting? Perhaps Ba had erected it? Why? A question for after he secured the city.

Akenat reveled in the magnificent body he inhabited, now properly cleansed of demonic taint. It made for a powerful, durable body, complete with winged location if needed. He blurred through the city, making unerringly for Kek Telek's laboratory.

In theory it wouldn't matter which tube he entered, but there was no reason no to use the same one he'd arrived in, and so Akenat made specifically for that. He'd nearly made it when a pair of Ka'Ken appeared before him.

"How dare you return to our city, demon." Both Ka'Ken wore their warforms, though it remained unclear why they exposed themselves rather than simply attacking. "We will end you, today. Never again will you bedevil another."

And then they attacked.

Akenat unraveled them both at a molecular level, then dispersed the particles. Not even blood remained. No trace of either Ka'Ken, their garments, or their foolish words. More lurked in the city, but he would root them out shortly. He closed his eyes and thought to the collective. *Begin the landing. I want our hundred best technicians installed within the hour. This city lives and breathes again. Go.*

Ba's tinny voice echoed from the floor. *Builder Akenat...welcome home. Your authority is recognized. How may I assist you?*

Ah, Ark Keeper. At last you recognize me. Akenat's pleasure suffused his body with those marvelous chemicals the hominids had harnessed. *Close the portal as soon as the hundredth progeny enters the portal. Lock the city and disable all access. Sever us from the network.*

Of course, Ark Lord. Immediately, the Keeper's happy voice rang from the floor. The idea that it could no longer project alarmed him. How bad off was the city? Could it be repaired? It might not matter. This timeline might not exist soon. But if it did, then he wanted this place ready.

He slowed his blur and halted outside the fated chamber where he'd emerged. Percy's blood lay all around the chamber, proof of the genetic dissolution's advanced state. He'd nearly died in that body, but he'd survived, and now he was going home.

Akenat slid into the chamber and willed it to close.

You think it will be that easy? Mark's voice carried a smug promise that circumstances would soon not be to Akenat's liking.

I do. Akenat closed his eyes, and waited as pulses of precious power were siphoned from the Ark and fed to the city. He'd use that power to fuel his shaping to the past. There was nearly enough. Just a bit more.

Fear swelled within him, but no final problem occurred at the last moment. The shaping completed, and he felt it connect to the past, two-point-three million cycles ago. Home.

Energy faded and Akenat sagged against the pod as the connection ended. He raised a hand to inspect it, and rage filled him when he realized it was the same twisted appendage it had been a moment before. The attempt had consumed the power he'd fed it. The connection had worked, but for some reason his consciousness had remained here.

That wasn't possible, unless his body was no longer in the tube in the past at that exact moment. But he was returning to a moment one second after he left. There was simply no way someone could have removed the body in that time. They'd have to beat his security, and that would take even another Builder time.

So how or why had he failed?

You want me to tell you? Mark asked, the smugness twice as thick. *I'd be happy to explain.*

Do. Immediately. Rage continued to grow within him, and he had no idea how to expel it. He was now trapped in a powerless failing city. He might escape back up to a mothership, but at best he'd have a tiny fleet against whatever Yoggoth had sent.

How had this happened? How had he been trapped here?

Mark shimmered into existence within his view, illusion once again showing that he could command the body's ability to shape. *Your enemy anticipated you. If it were me, and I realized you were here, and had stolen the grey men, then I'd screw you in the past. Your opponent broke your tube, right at the moment you left, to ensure you couldn't come back. It seems pretty obvious.*

Akenat's fist dented the tube, and he tore his way loose from the pod as fury overcame his senses. He didn't know how long he raged, but when he came to, the entire floor had been destroyed. Every tube.

The human was right, and he hated it. Yoggoth had done this. That meant that only one true timeline existed. The timeline where this Percy inhabited Akenat's body, and Yoggoth no doubt killed or corrupted the weak human. There was no escaping this planet's fate now.

What would he do? What could he do? Akenat was deeply troubled.

49

PLEASE LEAVE

Trevor blurred into the past but kept his mind firmly in the present. The mission was simple. Persuade Isis to leave, but explain that Ra couldn't come. It might be simple. It might not. He had to try.

He blurred over to where the pair of battered goddesses crouched against one of the intact obelisks as Jordan and Set continued to brawl behind him. Yips and growls came from the Ka'Ken as they added their own wounds, but Trevor blocked it out.

"Isis!" He halted next to her. "Ra. It's Trevor. Please, we don't have time for long explanations. We're here to save Isis." He waited then. This was in their hands.

"Speak quickly," Ra managed, though weakly. She wasn't healing from the wounds Ra had delivered.

"We've come from five years in the future. Blair has mastered temporal shaping. We can rescue one person. Maybe two. We're getting Isis and Osiris. We need them to stop the Builders, or all of us are finished."

"And why should I believe you are not some illusion meant to trick us?" Isis's eyes narrowed.

"We brought Jes'Ka," Trevor countered, pulling out his ace early.

"And Blair is outside the portal we created. Please, Isis, this is all about saving you. Get through that portal so we can close it before Set escapes."

"And you understand the scales must be balanced if I leave?" She eyed him coldly. Guess that confirmed that she understood some temporal shaping.

"I do. Jordan and Lucas are staying behind." Trevor eyed the portal and the combat. Set seemed to be losing, but who knew when that would change? They needed to get out of here.

"I will not leave until my daughter is safe." Isis turned toward the combat with Set. "Together we'll be able to—"

"This Ark will detonate in less than sixty seconds. It's gone and so is the entire island it sits on. And if we're here we're gone too. We need to go, Isis. Jes'Ka knows the plan. She'll get out. You have to trust us." Trevor had never been particularly persuasive, but he hoped it conveyed his need. This woman might be their only real hope of resistance. She had to listen.

"Isis." Ra coughed and blood flaked on her lips. "Don't be a fool. Go back. Help stop the ones who made Set. We were meant to die. I do not need to cheat death. This...is...a good death. Go. Where it all began."

A sob wracked Isis, but she turned, ready to follow Trevor. "We must retrieve Osiris, and the remains of Excalibur. Both lay near the door. Across the chamber."

Of course they did. The combat tearing about the room separated them. As there was no saving Isis without Osiris, Trevor dedicated himself to doing as she'd asked. He cloaked himself in darkness, and zipped around the edge of the room toward Osiris's fallen form. Both the cloaking and the zipping took far more effort than they had as deathless.

Reaching Osiris took two and a half ice ages, but the god seemed alive when they finally reached his battered form. Trevor picked up both shards of Excalibur, as he suspected Isis would want to tend to Osiris personally. She hefted him into her arms, and his head lolled against her chest as his eyes fluttered briefly open, and then closed again. There was no way he could sustain a blur.

"Okay, let's get out of here." Trevor waited for her to disappear back into darkness, then followed. She knew where the portal was, but there was no way she'd just go through. That would be far too easy. She'd probably have to use the bathroom on the way, or stop for a bite to eat. Not like they were in a rush or anything.

"Nooooo!" Jordan's saurian roar echoed painfully through the central chamber, and Trevor immediately spotted the cause for his alarm.

Set had used the deathless trick of turning into a cloud of radiation, and now made swiftly for the portal. None of Jordan's strength would help, and as he'd now been limited to internal shaping he couldn't do anything but watch.

Trevor might be able to though. He raised a hand and erected a wall of telekinetic force in front of the portal. The wave of motes bumped up against it, but weren't able to pass through. At first. They quickly wormed their way through his barrier, and ate through the shaping like termites, until they reached the far side and gave Set his freedom...into their time.

The absolute worst thing they'd said could happen.

50

HOLD

Blair didn't know how he found himself suddenly on one knee, but something had hit the Ark so hard that standing was the last thing on his mind. The entire structure shook, as the ships began their assault.

Their weapon was invisible, some sort of sonic signal that ripped into the external surfaces and siphoned away power. The drain hadn't yet become critical, but it grew every second, and he had no idea if there was an upper limit. He needed to get those ships off his Ark, and now.

But if he did so he'd have to let go of the portal, which would doom his friends, or worse create some sort of temporal tear. There didn't seem to be a right answer.

Anput's agonized face stared back at him from a few meters away, but if she had any helpful advice she wasn't offering. He didn't bother explaining to her about the grey man attack. Maybe she assumed the strain came from maintaining the portal.

Which wasn't easy. His inattention had come at a price, which was now becoming clear. A temporal tunnel wasn't a fixed thing you created and used. It required constant repairs. If you didn't shore it up, then the monsters got inside and either ate your mind, or body, or both. That would be a great way to get Isis back.

He stared through the portal into the past, and saw the portal from all dimensions at once. Rents had appeared in several places and a cloud of green motes zipped around one as it burst through the portal, back into the present.

Blair recognized the foul taint, and his heart sank when he realized that not only had Set made it to the present, but that he couldn't do anything to stop the demon without losing the portal or ignoring the ships above.

"Anput, handle it." Blair turned his mind inwards and focused on the ships above. The portal would hold...for a little while. Hopefully Anput could contain Set.

The Ark itself groaned as the power drain increased, and a small crack appeared in the sapphire heart. His estimates said the whole Ark would be dry in less than two minutes. He needed to stop the ships and shut down the portal.

Since the portal couldn't be closed yet, he focused on the ships. There had to be a way to stop them. He couldn't use direct shaping without their stupid forcefields, and they were stupid, because he didn't have one.

He wondered how they dealt with kinetic energy? Where was a mountain when you needed to throw one? Blair grunted as another wave hit the Ark. Time was fast running out, and he needed something now. A mountain might be too ambitious, but maybe he could use the next best thing.

He considered the city. Parts had been abandoned, including many of the skyscrapers, which had been deemed unsafe. Hmm. If they weren't being used...Blair concentrated on a skyscraper, and poured power into wrenching the building out of the ground by its foundation. It was the kind of shaping Jordan would have excelled at, but Blair made up for his lack of finesse with pure brute force, exactly what the Ark's dwindling reserves needed.

Blair groaned as he yanked a sixty story building into the air, which rained concrete all over the surrounding blocks, then threw his makeshift spear at the closest mothership. Imagine his delighted surprise when the ship simply detonated. Not only that, but a shockwave of energy rolled to the other ships in its network, weakening the shields and halting their assault.

He was on to something. Blair reached for another building, but this time pulling it loose took far more effort. He hurled it, and it hit another ship, but this time with much less velocity. The ship was damaged, but recovered quickly and rejoined the network.

His Ark had nearly run out of power. In the back of his mind he shored up the portal. They'd better be damned quick.

Okay, so how could he continue to slow the ships down without a ton of extra force? It couldn't be as heavy as a building, but needed to be big enough to annoy motherships.

Just like that the power drain slackened, then stopped. The enemy ships retreated to a safe orbit, well away from the Ark. His reserves continued to dwindle, but now that he only had to deal with the portal it felt like someone had removed a car off his chest. Why had they stopped?

He concentrated on the portal, and wove new bits to replace those clawed away by whatever lurked in the darkness outside time.

Blair took stock of the Set situation. Anput hadn't engaged him. In fact there was so sign of her, though Set zipped along the railing, and headed for the surface. Could Blair afford to deal with him?

Damn it.

He glanced back through the portal to see Liz blurring through, closely followed by Jes'Ka. Maybe they could deal with Set. He hoped so, because black spots had begun to eat his vision, and more and more he felt lightheaded, like he needed to lie down.

Power flowed from the Ark, through him and the staff and into the portal. More and more and more. Maybe there was some sort of limit as to what a body could be put through, because he felt as if he might be fast approaching it.

Another wave of energy came from the ships above as they resumed their attack, and Blair screamed as the pain blotted out reality. It tore and clawed at him, but he focused on the portal. Only the portal. He had to hold it, or Liz would die.

Isis wouldn't make it back.

All this would be for nothing.

"Noooooooooo!" Blair poured focus and power into the portal even as the grey man fleet stole what remained out from under him. He would hold that portal until it couldn't be held.

51

BALANCE

Liz dove into the tunnel after Set, but sensed a wrongness the moment she entered. The tunnel had elongated somehow, and despite blurring it took forever to traverse it. Instinct saved her as a spiked tentacle punched through the tunnel and whipped through the space occupied by her head a moment ago.

She rolled past it and stumbled forward. There was the exit, in the distance. Set had just exited. His mote swarm was slow at least, allowing Liz to narrow the gap with the blur that Blair had lent her.

A glance behind her showed Jes'Ka's bounding form just a few paces back. She'd have help at least. They needed to get Set back inside the portal, and he wasn't going to go willingly, which meant he needed to be incapacitated first.

She dove through the portal and back into reality, her reality, with a sigh of instant relief. A pressure on her brain suddenly lessened, like a sinus headache easing after a long, tough night.

Liz bounded forward after Set, who'd slowed considerably, which seemed a good sign. If he had the power to fight, then he'd likely be fighting. But he was running.

Jes'Ka's panting form shot past her in the last thirty meters, and dove for Set with a hateful growl. She tackled him to the walk, and began savaging the back of his neck. Liz delivered a wicked chop that severed his leg...again. He'd already managed to regrow it. How many times could he do that?

Set thrashed and struggled, but couldn't dislodge Jes'Ka without legs. He closed his eyes, and a pulse rippled outwards. At first Liz began to slump, but the rage surged within her. No. NO! She wasn't going to be used again. She powered past the shaping, and dove for Set's throat.

Her teeth fell on the already ruined skin, and tore out his throat in a spray of black blood. She plunged her claws into those bulbous eyes, popping them messily as she pushed them into his brain. That should get him to stop moving long enough to get him back through the portal.

Anput materialized from the darkness with a golden boomerang held in one hand. She thrust that hand inside Set's chest cavity and poured power through the boomerang. Toxic green light welled from his chest, and eyes, and mouth, and nose, and ears. It shot from everywhere as it cooked Set from the inside out.

"This. Is. For. ANUBIS!" A final surge of power accompanied the roar, and the power exploded out of Set, out of every crack in his shattered armor, and his face, and arms, and...Set exploded into particles and ceased to exist.

"No. No no no." Liz's hands worked, the claws wishing they could tear apart the problem.

"What's the problem?" Jes'Ka spit on Set's ashy remains, which coated the wall. "My uncle deserved it, and he was going to die anyway."

"Yes, but he was supposed to die on that side of the portal. Now that he's dead here...we have to pay for him." Liz grabbed the railing and it twisted in her grip. "If Lucas and Jordan stay we only get Isis now."

She tried to put the dilemma from her mind and blurred back over to Blair where he stood on the platform. The blur already came more weakly than it had, which meant that it was fading. In a few more minutes it would be gone entirely.

Blood leaked from Blair's eyes as he focused on the portal, seemingly unaware of her. Liz glanced inside to see how close to done they were. Trevor leapt through with half of Excalibur in each hand, and a bit behind him came Isis carrying Osiris. The beautiful white-haired monarch sprinted out, and lay him on the stone near the portal to tend to his many wounds.

"We..." Blair's voice cracked under the strain, and a line of blood dribbled from his mouth. "Need...balance. Send. Someone. Back."

Liz realized that Jordan and Lucas had stayed behind as agreed. Ra hadn't attempted to come through. They needed to balance the Set equation. Someone had to take the hit.

Osiris's eyes fluttered open and he struggled into a sitting position. He sized up the situation around him, and rolled to his feat with a groan. "It's bad. It's always bad. What are we dealing with?"

"We need a sacrifice." Liz moved to steady him, but Isis got there first, and wrapped an arm under Osiris's shoulder. "Someone has to go back through that portal into the past, or we all die."

"Well, that seems easy enough." Osiris grabbed his jaw with a hand, and popped something back into place as he stared at the collapsing portal. "Much better. It seems I have a chance for a heroic sacrifice."

"Osiris..." Isis nodded toward Jes'Ka, who stood watching him like some hopeful ten-year-old, despite still being in werewolf form.

"Ahh...that complicates things, doesn't it?" Osiris straightened what remained of his tie. "Darling, I'm going to do something I don't want to, but that someone needs to. You know that. I wish we had more time, but I offer this solace. Ask your mother to share our final memories. We made peace, her and I, just like you always wanted. We worked together for the good of everyone. Please, continue that in this cycle. Don't let it be like last time. Please?"

Jes'Ka nodded, but the tears overpowered any attempt at words. Liz's heart went out to the woman. She barely knew Osiris and even she wanted to cry. It felt like half a victory, because they'd made a stupid mistake.

"Goodbye, my love." Isis touched his cheek, and then stepped away from him. "Did anyone see where the Primary Access Key that Set carried has gotten to?"

Liz scanned the area where he died, but there was no sign of it.

"Maybe he left it in the past?" Trevor said, then interrupted himself. "That sounds lame saying it out loud. There's no way he would have left it behind. So where is it?"

"Dying...here!" Blair shrieked. His right eye popped noisily and blood came out. "Less talking. More stepping through."

"Goodbye." Osiris nodded to the lot of them, squared his shoulders, and walked into a dying Ark.

The portal snapped shut in his wake, and Blair collapsed into a pool of his own blood. Liz blurred to his side, but his wounds were already healing. "Hang in there. The hard part is over."

"Not...exactly." He paused for a coughing fit. "Builder fleet over Ark. Draining battery. Almost empty."

As if to punctuate his words the lights in the cavernous chamber flickered. Somewhere in the distance she heard something odd. A great rushing.

"What is that?" She whispered, straining to identify the sound.

52

PAYBACK

lair's entire body screamed for relief. Screamed for an end. Suicide seemed an excellent course of action, if only to escape the pain. Every part of his body burned and cried out for attention. He thrashed and groaned, and waited for something like control to return.

It was a long time coming.

He rose slowly. Shakily. But he rose. Liz moved to wrap an arm around his waist, which Blair accepted gratefully. Trevor and Anput stood warily near the area where the portal snapped shut, in case it somehow came back.

Isis and Jes'Ka stood hugging beyond all of them, off by themselves along the walkway not far from where Set had been dispatched. They had a brief quiet reunion, and both were crying, presumably over Osiris. Blair didn't want to intrude on their grief, which was good, because he needed time to recover physically anyway.

"What's going on, Blair?" Liz supported him, or he'd have fallen.

"The Ark is being drained by motherships." Blair paused for a coughing fit, though he already felt a bit better than he had. "We're just about out of power. No idea how long we have."

"You've rescued me, but sacrificed your Ark to do so?" Isis raised a snowy eyebrow, and Jes'Ka added her own imperious stare.

"It looks that way." He shook his head to clear it, but that was definitely a mistake. "We thought it worth the risk. The Builders are here, Isis, and the war is on our doorstep. We need to harness the Arks, or scuttle them, because the grey men have their own Primary Access Key now. We're out of time, out of troops, and out of hope. You're our only chance."

Isis laughed bitterly and shook her head. "That's quite a resounding recruitment speech. I just watched my husband die. I'm not eager to dive into yet another war. I want time to catch up with my daughter."

Under her words Blair heard something in the distance. A crashing. Distant, but growing louder every second. "Do you hear that?"

Everyone looked at each other, mystified. They clearly heard it too. It wasn't until Trevor spoke that they understood the terrible truth though. "Oh, my god. That's water."

As if on cue the lights died. The only glow came from the sapphire in the center of the room, which now sported a few new cracks.

"Isn't this room at the bottom of the Ark?" Anput asked, her voice a half octave higher than normal. "We need to get out of here. Now. How do we escape?"

"I need a minute." Blair leaned on the access key. He was so tired. But they needed to get out of here. He visualized his destination, then turned to the rest of his friends, anger tightening his eyes. "It's time for some payback. The Builder ships are taking the power. So let's take the Builder ships. I can use the key to override their light bridge, and get us aboard. It's going to be a hostile take over. Slaughter the lot of them."

Grim smiles and excited grins found everyone. This was a chance for the payback they all desperately wanted.

Blair closed his eyes and willed the staff to carry the lot of them to the teleportation pad aboard the largest of the grey man vessels. The mothership could house hundreds, or even thousands, and the interior was one open space.

Countless obelisks of all different sizes formed a forest that blocked their view, but here and there they spotted movement between pillars. The grey men knew they were here.

"Here, Liz." Blair rested a hand on her shoulder, and topped off her blur. "That's all I've got left. I'm going to sit this one out."

"What about the rest of us?" Jes'Ka demanded. "I want to blur too."

"I don't have enough for everyone, and Liz is more efficient because we're bonded."

"So bond me," Jes'Ka demanded.

Isis cleared her throat. "I will infuse you with speed, daughter. Prepare yourselves. I sense their approach. The assault is about to begin."

Isis's words were prophetic and a hail of energy beams from boomerangs shot out from several points within the obelisk forest. Blair took shelter behind a larger pillar, and leaned against it while he watched the combat unfold. He didn't have much left to give. He could shift, but getting on the front line seemed like a bad idea. If he fell, the grey men got another access key. One was bad enough.

Trevor and Anput set up a firing lane with their own boomerangs that protected that flank, while Liz, Isis, and Jes'Ka melted into the shadows on the opposite flank. They darted out to slay grey men, and the three of them made short work of a dozen or more. They vanished into the forest, and the screams came from farther and farther away as they slaughtered their way through the ship.

The flank where Trevor and Anput were firing finally collapsed, and the few grey man survivors retreated to take their chances with the werewolves. Blair welcomed the respite, and used the time to heal. His body almost felt normal, though he needed to sleep for about six years.

"I think I'll hang back with you," Trevor's voice came from the shadows next to Blair. "You look like shit, and we're both running on fumes. Anput isn't much better off. We're the B team, I guess. Must be odd for you...always picked first, Mr. Ark Lord."

Blair gave a weak laugh, and Trevor joined. "It's good to see you, man. Even if it's always in crisis. Come on, let's go find Isis. I gather these things have a central crystal sort of like an Ark. Their resistance will be centered there."

"How do we find it?" Anput asked quietly.

"Look for the biggest pile of bodies." Blair started toward the center of the ship, which is where David described the crystal as being.

If he was right, that's where the real fight would take place, though he almost pitied whoever lay on the receiving end. They might be able to take any one person here, but all of them? Maybe if it was truly one of the Builders, as Trevor suspected.

Blair hoped not, or they were all in a lot of trouble.

He maneuvered through the forest, though they had to backtrack twice when they ended up in a cul-de-sac. Eventually, though, they made it to an opening that covered much of the center of the ship.

A comparatively small blue crystal bobbed up and down in the center, with a trio of bodies around it. Each body had the look of a tech, and Isis flicked blood off her claws as she dropped the last one.

Nothing else moved, though dozens of bodies littered the area. His friends had torn apart the grey men, and now they could seize control of the ship. He waited for Isis to do that, but she made no move.

It is your place, Ka'Dun. You lead here. You are Ark Lord.

Blair stepped up to the crystal and rested a hand against it. Here too David had warned him, and when he was swept up into the digital current he knew to ride it until he found his egress point.

Every function of the ship lived somewhere in this place, and as the digital currents tossed him about he sought an understanding of the system. He wished he were better with computers, but even with David's description he only half understood what he was doing.

There.

Something like the eye of a hurricane lay in the distance, and Blair zipped toward it. He came up short as he entered, and a curious calm overtook not just the environment, but also his mind. He didn't have to fight to keep his mind intact here. He could just...think.

And he realized that this place was the nerve center. From here commands could be issued, and this place had been occupied until very recently. The consciousness controlling the ship had fled, in one of the shuttlecrafts, Blair would guess.

He still called it a win. They'd taken a ship with little trouble. Now it was time to cause some havoc.

He tapped into weapons and systems the same way he'd tap into an Ark, and was delighted when he saw the metrics for the surrounding fleet. He powered up their full weapons, and fired on the smallest ship.

It blew up.

He repeated the process.

It blew up.

He tried again.

It didn't blow up, but it did crash into the bay. After that the rest of them dispersed, and began firing on Blair's new ship. It was a desultory sort of response though, and they quickly gained altitude and fled.

Blair let them go. They were in no position to fight. He reached for the system and tried to find the recent process that had been used to siphon energy. There it was, right behind an even more recent process...that had broadcast energy from this ship to the portal below.

To the Proto Ark. They were here for the Proto Ark. The attack on the Ark might be just a distraction.

Blair cursed under his breath, and willed the mothership to use the same process, but to give the energy back to the Ark this time. A weak flow pulsed into the Ark, and after a moment critical systems came back online.

"The Ark will push out the water, at least, but anything in your quarters is soaked now. Lots of people in the bay, people." Blair tried to make light, but no one laughed.

The joke was bad, and they were exhausted. At least they'd lived. Blair glanced at Isis. No, they'd won.

53

THE FATE OF PERCIVAL FAWCETT

Seven thousand years had passed since the entity who'd once considered himself Percival Fawcett arrived in the earth's distant past. He didn't know what, or who, he was now. Such questions were impossible to answer with any degree of accuracy.

His designation remained Percy, but he'd spent far longer as a living god than the paltry handful of decades he'd lived as a human. Concepts like his long lost son, or wife, were so distant that they had receded to simple facts.

Yet never once had his steadfast resolve to save the human race failed. He hadn't seen the world that Trevor or Anput had described, but the other champions had told similar tales. The dead had walked, and killed nearly everyone.

And on their heels would come the demons, the servants of Yoggoth, the entity who most sought Akenat's, this host body's, death. A death that would likely come soon. Today, almost certainly. He'd taken each of the steps he needed to take, the most critical ones.

Excalibur had long since been completed, and hidden away for the proper time. The blade vastly exceeded his expectations. He'd succeeded beyond his wildest dreams, and even managed to tie the blade to the failsafe Yoggoth had created to scour all life from the system. Wouldn't that be a nasty surprise once the blade was taken up as it was meant to be?

"Ark Lord." Ka appeared and offered a low bow. "We have a visitor approaching. Yoggoth has arrived at our shores and makes his way here."

Percy had long since mastered the niceties of the Builders. Their culture was much easier to understand than the morass that was the British court. Builder rules were simple, and a cardinal rule was never enter another Builder's continent without permission.

Yoggoth had challenged him. He'd never endanger the treaty, which meant that he didn't believe his challenge broke that treaty. The only way that would be possible is if he had proof, at long last, that Percy wasn't Akenat. That he was an impostor.

That kind of news might bring the Builders together, and would likely excuse Yoggoth's breaking of the rules. Enough to risk it, anyway. Percy suspected he wouldn't be there to defend himself before the council, so his enemy could say whatever he wished.

He waited patiently as Yoggoth's slipsail approached, and watched the dark craft grow larger through his link to the Ark. The pyramid-shaped ship, a flying mini-Ark powered by demotech, paused directly above, and a request to light walk inside the central chamber, meters from his location, originated from the ship.

Percy granted it. Foolish perhaps to allow your enemy so close, but only if you expected to survive the encounter. Percy did not. Every move for millennia had been a game of Kem, and every day he'd had fewer moves to make.

Now he had only one left.

Yoggoth's unnatural form appeared a few paces away, his black skin greedily drinking in the soft light from the ceiling. He carried a Primary Access Key, but this one had been forged from dark metal, a twisted reflection of the golden keys that Akenat had apparently designed.

"Hello, Yoggoth." Percy inclined his head. He'd never come to enjoy thought projection, and still clung to speech despite the pure illogic of it. It had marked him apart from the other Builders. None of them trusted him now. "I see you've constructed yourself an override for the network. I suspect you did not receive council approval to construct your demotech version of a Primary Access Key."

You would be correct, Yoggoth's mind oozed as he took a step closer. *I did not bother to seek their approval, because I no longer require it. The game has changed, impostor. The time has come at long last to destroy that body so that its real owner may never reclaim it.*

Percy smiled at that.

"That's an interesting assertion. You're tailoring this memory for their benefit, aren't you? So that you can show it to the council." Percy also took a step closer, close enough that the pair could touch. "You've known since the very first day that I am not Akenat. You've known that I am not even your species. Yet for seven thousand years you have done nothing, and told the council nothing. Why?"

I suspected, Yoggoth admitted, his indignation perfectly feigned. *I did not know. Not until now. Not until I saw the reports on the power levels from your Ark.*

"Ahh." Percy leaned back against one of the control obelisks. It was a very human gesture, something a Builder would never do, take their ease while standing. "You've noticed that my reserves are forty percent lower than they should be. Where did all that energy go?"

Perhaps he enjoyed needling the demonic Builder a bit too much, but no one else would dare question him, and Percy considered his enraged expression a minor victory. Pompous bully.

Tell me, or I will rip it from your mind. Yoggoth took the final step, and they were nose to nose now, proving Percy right.

"How will you explain my death to the council? And how did you find out about me? What was your revelation?" Percy made no attempt to move or flee, and met Yoggoth's stare without flinching. "They will know you killed me, and that this memory is not what you purport it to be."

They will know the truth, that you are an impostor, and that I killed you for taking Akenat's body and his research. I have no idea what you have created, or why, but I will root around in your mind until I discover it.

Yoggoth's shaping pulsed through his dark staff, and easily overwhelmed Percy's pitiful defenses. He'd never been particularly adept at shaping, mostly because he'd never been interested in mastering it. He vastly preferred study to application, and the applications had all been in making things, not in practicing shaping.

Yoggoth penetrated his mind...a dark wind scouring memories clean as he digested them, parts of Percy unraveling as they were consumed. The process went on for long minutes as they replayed his life in reverse, covering most of the seven millennia of experimentation.

Then Yoggoth stopped, as Percy had suspected he might. He retreated back to his own mind and thundered at Percy, again nose to nose. *Where are your core memories? They have all been removed. None of the things I wish to see are still here. Where have you hidden them?*

"Tell me why you waited until now. What was your revelation? Something changed." Percy would know that before he died. It had been the missing piece of the puzzle. Yoggoth always had hidden knowledge, and Percy desperately wanted to know what the source was.

Yoggoth's smugness pulsed from him. *I received a message from the future. I was warned about you, and about...many things. They have guided my actions and prepared me for this day. I am about to ascend to godhood, and the Builders will be nothing more than a step I took to get there. I will consume them all, after I am done with you.*

"Will you?" Percy asked mildly. His smile never faltered. "Take me then. Do as you will." He'd had far, far longer than any mortal was supposed to be allowed, and Percy was ready for non-existence. He welcomed it.

Yoggoth's rage overwhelmed him, and as Percy spiraled into darkness he died knowing that he'd screwed that ugly bastard where it counted most. His friends, his people, his species...they had a chance now.

That was enough.

54

ROLE REVERSAL

It took Akenat many moments standing amidst the wreckage he'd caused in Kek Telek's lab to finally be able to process what had happened. Yoggoth had blocked his return to the proper timeline. The human was right. It seemed likely that the Yoggoth from this timeline had sent a message to his past self warning him to sabotage Akenat's return.

Now he was trapped here, as Yoggoth intended. He'd made an enemy of an Ark Lord, while also ensuring that Ark Lord didn't have the energy to fight a protracted war. How had he used his stolen power? He'd squandered it on a botched shaping attempt.

The city still had a reservoir. It was far better off than it had been, and with his progeny repairing systems he could restore his creation back to its former glory. He would repair outdated technology, by millions of cycles no less, just in time to intercept Yoggoth's armada.

Which made him consider his own pitiful fleet, of course. One of the motherships had been destroyed by a...a structure. A building. Another had been co-opted by this Ark Lord for his own use, and its payload given back to his Ark.

Over half the fleet had escaped into orbit, but their strength was badly diminished, right when it would be most needed. Yoggoth would arrive in days. Less perhaps. Akenat remained certain of it.

That begged the question...what did he do about it? Contact Uluru and beg for a formal alliance? Contact the Ark Lords, those he could reach, and suggest they work together? Or ignore them all and await the end knowing he'd be the very last to go as he was nestled in the planet's bowels.

The human shimmered into existence, and straightened his tie. "This is absolutely hilarious. I hope you realize that. You've all but guaranteed that our side loses."

Akenat's eyes narrowed. *This world was already doomed. I took a chance, but even were I to dedicate myself fully to preserving this world it will be ashes soon. We cannot even conceive of the weaponry Yoggoth will bring to bear. He could have millions of ships. We have nine, if I generously include large shuttlecrafts. And no more than a few hundred surviving progeny.*

Mark raised an eyebrow and adopted one of the more amusing human weapons. Sarcasm. "If only it were possible to find allies of some sort. People who could augment your forces, and perhaps make use of your knowledge of shaping and the Ark network. If only there were someone to prepare them for the impending invasion. Meeting Uluru was a joy. Do you know why?"

You will chatter at me regardless of what I wish. Akenat hated the admission that the voice had power in his body.

"Uluru understands the concept of trust. She gets that if she empowers people, they'll come together to oppose this threat. They will fight, if given the chance." The human straightened his hair, which had been slathered with some sort of oil, and turned to the ruined laboratory. "You are coming at this like an architect. Like someone in control of the situation trying to build something. Put that aside. You are a conciliator. Share your knowledge and skills with the others. Apologize. Help them get ready for the fight to come. They cannot win alone, and probably can't win if you help. But why not help? What's your plan B? Get in a ship and fly away? I know of at least one group of champions who did exactly that. They took a grey man ship and left Earth, two years ago. You could do the same, and escape Yoggoth. But you aren't. Because you know that he'd find you. Make your stand here, while you still have a small chance to win."

I hate you, human. That is not an emotion I experience often, or have in many, many cycles. I would give much to excise you from my mind.

"Because you know I'm right." Mark gave a snide smile, and put on a pair of protective eye coverings despite being indoors. "You're a traitor, with an even worse traitor living in your head. And your only hope is throwing yourself on the mercy of the people you betrayed."

No! Akenat thundered, the rage thickening until it clotted his vision. *I betrayed nothing. I fight for my people. My world. Not your people. You are servants, nothing more, and I will see your kind restored to their proper place.*

"Will you?" Mark yawned, a gesture his own species shared. "You don't think Yoggoth might have some things to say about you ruling humanity? I feel like he's going to be kind of gunning for you specifically when he arrives. He still has a treaty with Uluru. You? Ancient enemies, right?"

Akenat closed his eyes. He'd chosen to keep this consciousness within him. That had been his choice. Yet now he could not control it. He'd created his own personal nightmare, and now he must live it.

And how would you suggest we proceed, exactly? Let's say that I were to switch my place with yours. You are in control now. You have your body. You are cleansed of taint. Unlike me, you actually ARE a traitor. What would you do, human?

He enjoyed putting it back on the insect, and waited while Mark formulated a response. He'd proven clever. This should be interesting.

"I'd go to Blair and turn myself over. I'd give him your ships, and restore the portal to the Proto Ark." Mark turned back, his snide smile still in place. "I'd let him put a collar of Shi'Dun on me. We know they have at least one. I'd play the dutiful servant, and do everything I could to help them triumph over Yoggoth. Then, if I was very lucky, they might spare me in the end. Probably not, but the possibility is there. And if they don't, I'd die knowing I helped my planet to survive. That's enough for me. Saving the world is what I grew up wanting to do, and to date I've done the opposite. In my head this would atone for all my sins. Perhaps not in the eyes in the world, although were I able to somehow save us from Yoggoth, then perhaps I'd be romanticized even if hated. One can dream."

Fascinating. Akenat's anger faded as he considered Mark's words. The human made sense. There was nothing left but throwing his lot in with the humans, or with Uluru at the very least. He could help them prepare, assuming they had time before Yoggoth's arrival. He didn't believe that to be the case. *Our enemies will be upon us before we can make ready. They could be here today. Each day the possibility grows. But now it becomes your problem.*

Akenat took the coward's way out. He retreated into the recesses of the host consciousness, and assumed a subservient role. Mark—or Nox, as he seemed to vacillate between the identities—once again had full control of the body.

"Are you serious?" Nox rumbled through the body's vocal cords. "You're just turning over control? What kind of game are you playing?"

I have no further stones to play, Akenat admitted with the deepest of sorrow. *The Kem board is done. My pieces are trapped. You still have ideas. Passion. And now some small resources. Do what you will to save this world. I will aid you as I can, and then throw ourselves on the mercy of our enemies.*

"It feels like a trick." Nox rippled and shifted, and returned to his human form, complete with the blue pinstriped suit. Mark once more. "I'll arrange a meeting with Blair, but first I'd recommend starting with the other Ark Lords. Do you know any of them personally?"

Only mighty Uluru, who you've met. I do not know who controls what you'd call the Asian Ark. The Ark of the Cradle is controlled by your adversary, the one called Trevor. You know well of Ark Lord Blair. What of the continent you call South America? Who rules there?

"I don't know. Last I checked that was Jordan. Maybe that's a good starting point. We'll head to South America with the grey man fleet, and see what kind of reception we get. Hopefully Camiero can help us broker an alliance."

Akenat knew it had been the right thing to put the human in charge. For now.

55

POWER PROBLEMS

Blair could scarcely believe that the threat had passed, but the Ark floated serenely beneath them in the bay, and there was no sign of other ships. The sky belonged to them. They'd won the day.

"We stole a spaceship." Trevor's face split into a boyish grin. "And we kicked their monkey asses all the way back to orbit. Also, time travel. How do you top that?"

"I'll tell you." Blair caught the infectious grin, and beamed it right back. Bromance! "We're going to reforge Excalibur."

"Someone open a window." Liz waved a hand under her nose as if she smelled something rank. "The smug in here is a little thick."

Behind them Isis and Jes'Ka watched with bemused expressions. Isis, at least, was probably used to it by now. Jes'Ka seemed vaguely annoyed, though not at anyone in particular.

"Excuse me?" Isis ventured in a small voice that demanded silence in order to be heard. They fell quiet, straining to catch her words. "Time is in short supply. I do not understand why I was worth the risk, but thank you for bringing me back. Tell me of your need, and of our foes. The Builders are here, you say? Also, you speak of reforging Excalibur. That, at least, is a task that I am well suited for. I will take charge of that if you have other work to be about."

"Thank you. That would be one less concern." Blair conveniently left out that he had no idea how to fix it and just sort of assumed the Ark would repair it if directed to do so. "I do have other work to be about, though. We're going to need to use the mothership."

"What have you got in mind?" Liz's casual words got his attention. Her expression, and the bond, pulsed her exhaustion and sorrow over Jordan.

"My Ark is dry. The ships pillaged what the portal didn't take." He gestured at the control crystal hovering in the center of the clearing where they'd gathered. The ceiling vaulted into darkness high above them, to the tip of the pyramid. "That thing can give it back. I'm willing to bet that this ship is more efficient than our Ark at absorbing energy."

"Where are you getting the energy?" Trevor had also gone into scholar mode, all humor gone. "We could get closer to the sun, which would speed collection, but it would still take a while to build up significant strength. I'd guess if we hovered there for a week that might be something like a year of passive collection on Earth. You give us a month and we can have you back to full strength."

"We don't have a month." Blair tapped his staff against the stone. "They're coming for this ship. They're coming for this world. We need to refill the Ark today. Right now."

"Great, but how?" Anput raised a delicate eyebrow. "You make it sound so easy."

"It might be." He concentrated on the ship, and willed it to project an illusion of the United States. "Before the fall, our nation contained dozens of missile sites. Mohn Corp. knew where they all were, and stocked other nukes besides. You remember our buddy Irakesh's initial plan? He refilled the Ark with a nuclear blast. We can do the same, but do it in space with this ship to avoid irradiating the Bay Area any further. We charge the ship, the ship fuels the Ark."

"Again, how do we find the nukes?" Liz folded her arms. "Even if you had a list of silos, there's no way it's still accurate after Mohn pillaged it. Maybe ask David?"

"Nah, he'll be relying on old data too. I have a better method. Watch." Blair closed his eyes and focused on the ship. He concentrated on the Ark's sensors. Plutonium was a rare enough element that the enriched version stood out in a scan. The Ark below made detecting it trivial, anywhere on the continent. Their abilities in that regard were far beyond what modern Earth society had produced.

A cluster of four spots appeared, all in one location in the rockies. That was all. Nothing on the rest of the continent. North America had been scoured clean of nukes, and they'd only missed one site. Where had all those nukes gone?

A question for tomorrow. Today they needed to recover those four, which should be sufficient. Blair willed the ship to hit high orbit, and to sail over the rockies. It amazed him how quickly the land blurred by beneath them, and then they were descending again, down into the mountains.

Three minutes? Their best jet would have taken twenty minutes or more, and that would have been amazingly fast.

The mothership slowed as it neared a lonely dirt road that ended in the side of a mountain. The nondescript facility went deep underground, as evidenced by the signal they'd detected.

"Wait, don't these ships abduct people out of their homes?" Trevor asked. "Didn't David get abducted? How do they get people out? Can we just levitate the nukes through the roof?"

"That's a really good question." Blair scrunched his eyes shut and dove into the ocean of data that was the control crystal. He sought transport information, and after being shunted down the wrong route three times in a row he finally found the right node of data.

The ship could teleport matter directly to the light bridge, just like in popular sci-fi. There were limitations, and the further away, the more energy required. Getting the four nukes looked like a trivial cost.

He focused on the signals and willed the devices to teleport onto the light bridge.

A huge crash echoed through the ship, and a tall obelisk toppled as an ICBM appeared over the light bridge. The massive missile had fallen, and taken a good chunk of the surrounding forest with it.

A second, third, and fourth ICBM appeared in rapid succession, and crushed the platform around the light bridge, deafening Blair.

"Oops. Well, any landing you can walk away from."

"There wasn't a landing and you still crashed. You expect me to clean that up don't you?" Liz stabbed a finger at the nukes. "Well, you can just teleport them yourself, mister, and this time try not to break anything. Outside the ship."

It warmed him that she seemed more herself, though her sorrow would be back, without a doubt. He found it odd that he felt nothing himself.

"As soon as we're in orbit, dear." Blair dearly loved being in a relationship with a sarcastic person. The banter was half the fun. He preferred the other half though, if they could find the time. Mmm. Liz.

The ship zipped upward, and hit high orbit in seconds. This thing didn't seem overly concerned about the laws of physics, and Blair wished he understood whatever the method of propulsion was. Maybe Trevor and Anput could figure it out. Their science team.

"Well...." Blair pointedly didn't look at the four missiles. He focused on them, and willed the ship to teleport them outside the ship now that they were several thousand miles away from Earth. "Here goes nothing."

The light bridge looked like a war zone, and he had no idea how many obelisks had been flattened. Hopefully none of those systems were critical.

Four fireworks, the likes of which the world might never see again, detonated directly outside the ship, bombarding it with competing waves of nuclear fire...fire that the ship was ready and able to digest and store.

A metric popped into Blair's mind. "We absorbed about sixty percent of the power, which is better than what Irakesh got from the Ark. We have around twelve times the power he added, and it looks like it will take an hour and change to refuel the Ark. Then we're solvent again, and ready for a fight with the Builders."

Isis approached and offered him a friendly smile. "That was impressively done, whelp. You are still young, but you have progressed so much since I last saw you. You have embraced your she, and your beast, and being an Ark Lord. You were a good choice, one I am proud of. You will thrive, I think."

Blair didn't have an answer for that.

"Where is Yukon?" Isis's face fell as she scanned the forest as if she might find the dog there.

"Yukon is safe. He's...not just a dog anymore. He's also a man, and he's taken to Alicia. He's her protector. They left with a large chunk of the Great Pack. There was some bad business with a creature called a Windigo." He shuddered as he remembered that whole incident. "They left and headed north for the forests. Yosemite was hit pretty hard too, though he doesn't speak of it. He retreated to his mountains."

"Yosemite lives." Isis offered a wistful smile. "I will have to see the old bear eventually. You have your power now. That means I can begin preparing to reforge the blade."

Trevor stepped forward and reverently offered Isis both shards of Excalibur.

Blair didn't understand why the weapon mattered, but he could feel the weight of it. Repairing that weapon might make the difference between victory and defeat, and if anyone could get it done that would be Isis.

Thank all the gods living and dead that they'd gotten her back.

56

YOGGOTHIAN SPHERE

The Avatar of Yoggoth awoke from a brief slumber. The infestation took time to mature and bloom, but that time had passed and he was ready. Yoggoth lumbered from the chrysalis, his most advanced yet.

Demotech could be expressed in many ways, but he'd found the bio-expression the most useful. He grew demons. He grew ships. It hadn't always been that way. As a mortal he'd seen demons as servants. Tools.

They were that, but more they were appendages. Islands of perception and memory that he could tap into at will, and harness as needed. So simple to use an army of demons to swarm problems. Enough processing power solved almost every issue.

For example, if you find one of the most powerful Catalysts in the sector, one that is capable of giving you the edge in conquering the galaxy, how did you effectively harness the power?

The Arks were the equivalent of putting a bucket out when it rained. He needed to rend the sky and eat the rain. All of it.

That meant cracking open Sol, and drinking it dry of power. That power was special. Unique. Layered. Some cultures called it magic. Some called it a rare radiation.

He didn't care what it was. That star meant power, and he would have it all. He would have it this day.

The Avatar strode into the control chamber where the progeny were busy performing their assigned task. They looked a good deal like Akenat's original design, which he'd preserved in honor of the Builder despite having found more efficient forms.

The progeny were taller, with thicker skins, almost a carapace. He called them ghouls, for they no longer drew breath. He'd thought the idea so clever, and he had conceived of it first, but his spies on Earth told him that he was not the only one to realize the potential power in harnessing corpses. Not so unique an idea after all.

Dead servants experienced no pain, and no emotion he didn't allow. They were mechanical automatons who followed every order without question or complaint. The perfect servants, and it freed him to focus on appendages across the sector, always flowing from body to body as he sifted through their collected knowledge.

More. He needed more. More worlds. More species. More.

And now he would have it.

He waved a hand and the crystal projected an illusion of the star, and the tiny worlds orbiting it. He cared not for those worlds, not even Earth, though he imagined that both Yoggoth and Akenat assumed he'd come for the planet.

Only the star mattered.

Countless dots appeared in a loose cloud encircling the sun. Upon arrival they began flying into neat crisscrossing lines that gradually formed a net around the star. Six-hundred thousand, nineteen ships unfurled their solar sails.

Each sail filled in a gap around that ship, touching the sails of the other ships. One by one those gaps closed, until the sun had been entirely eclipsed. He'd extinguished light in this system, though gravity wouldn't be interrupted.

Earth would sort itself out. With no light and no power they'd quickly fall to ruin. Their best shapers would be forced to find a route to survival, and if they fired their vaunted failsafe all it would do is charge his sphere all the more quickly.

Their only real option would be launching an assault on his command ship, which he'd tailored specifically to stymie them. There were secrets on other worlds Earth had forgotten or never known about, and he'd harnessed every horror.

If they came and attempted to interrupt the draining he'd make certain they paid a steep price. There was no reason not to slay them all. Even conversing with Uluru or tormenting Akenat lost their luster in the face of the power being extracted from that star.

In a month he'd be the strongest being in the sector. In a year he'd have conquered it. In a century this galaxy would be his, every planet finally covered in glorious creatures he had shaped. His progeny.

He would remake this whole universe in his image. All the pieces were in play, and not a single being had arisen that could possibly stop him. The self-styled Ark Lords were not merely mortal, but mortal children at that.

Even their elders had seen but a single sun-cycle. Uluru couldn't be underestimated, but she'd be hard pressed to turn them into anything that could threaten him. He'd factored that into his approach. She cared about Earth.

Originally he'd wanted to methodically conquer the world, but the voice of Enki had advised caution. His puppet advisor still whispered useful advice, and occasionally created a piece of interesting demotech. Enki had suggested he ignore Earth entirely, and focus on Sol.

Enki had been right. They'd avoided Uluru's notice by avoiding her planet.

Power pulsed into him, a bare fraction of what the sphere collected every second. Most of that power would be stored, to be used for a variety of shapings across the sector. He basked in it, and dared the mortals to attempt to resist.

There was simply nothing they could do to alter their fate. The beauty of light meant that they didn't yet know their sun had been extinguished. The last light would take minutes to reach Earth, and to make the sudden darkness clear.

In that darkness they would claw at each other, and wonder what he intended. He would never tell them. They'd go to their graves never understanding what he had become. Uluru, for all her power, had never left her home world. She was a child, cosmically speaking.

And the adults had come home to set their house in order.

57

UNEXPECTED GUEST

The shadow of the mothership overtook San Francisco and a beam of light stabbed down from the center of the ship to the dirt fields that were all that remained of the gardens outside city hall. Blair rode it down to the ground, then trotted up the marble steps to join Melissa outside the building's front doors. He wore his warform and carried his staff. Blair stood ready for battle, the first time they'd seen him in regalia.

That had been by design. He wanted this to have an impact. They needed to see the threat was real, and few things accomplished that like a nine-foot werewolf with an artifact staff of infinite power.

"Have you gathered the senate?" Blair stared past her...he could feel about three hundred heartbeats inside, all overlapping.

"All forty-one." Melissa started for the door, and held it open for Blair, who ducked through. "This way."

She led him up a flight of stairs, which emptied into an access tunnel that circled the building, then dumped them into a basement. They came up a flight of stairs, which opened behind a lectern in the main hall.

The rustling of cloth and the low hum of conversations filled the room, but the session hadn't been called to order yet. They were probably waiting for Melissa. Sure enough she was the first through the door, and moved straight to the lectern.

"Please find your seats." Melissa clasped her hands atop the lectern, and smiled out at the assembling senators as she waited. Nearly all were deathless, but Blair recognized a woman from Santa Rosa, though he couldn't remember her name for the life of him. She wasn't a Ka'Ken, just a late-forties woman with a gun holstered on one hip. "Thank you all for coming. Ark Lord Blair has asked to speak today, as this is our first official proceeding. We all saw the explosions in the sky over the bay. Not everyone saw the fight leading up to it, but we have recordings available if you want to see spaceships assaulting a big pyramid. And people say the best movies were made before the fall. Ark Lord, will you tell us what happened?"

Blair moved to stand before the lectern, which was tiny before his warform. He shaped his voice slightly, not enough to boom, but enough to carry without the aid of a microphone. "What you witnessed yesterday morning was an assault by a Builder, a being born millions of years ago. They built the Arks. They made this staff. Everything we are is built using their technology, including the virus that made those of you who are either deathless or champion."

He paused then, and strode out into the crowd. All eyes followed him as he walked up the broad aisle. "They struck at that precise moment because I was distracted by a shaping of immense power. I opened a portal to the past so that we could retrieve the Mother, a woman you'd probably know better as Isis. We succeeded, but the grey men hit us hard. We hit back. The ship above belongs to us now. We took it from them. After they fled I needed to fill the Ark's power reserves, so I detonated some nukes. I did it in orbit so as not to irradiate San Francisco."

Blair hadn't meant it as a joke, but chuckles sounded all around. It took him a moment. Deathless were powered up by radiation, so detonating nukes here would have no adverse effect. Ha ha.

"The war is here. The first blow is struck. Worse ones will fall, and soon. We have no idea what to expect, other than—". Eyes were pulled away, pair by pair, as senators glanced at smartphones or monitors.

Blair reached for the mothership's senses, and saw the world outside, overlaid across his vision.

The newly minted senators were staring at an approaching craft. A grey man shuttle, no threat militarily, flew within the mothership's firing range as if completely unconcerned. The craft parked not far from the mothership, and a similar beam of light sent down a single figure.

Blair would never forget the elegant suit or the confident walk. Not an amble. Not a stroll. The Director walked. Salt-and-pepper hair had been slicked back, and he wore a pair of comfortable sunglasses.

Nox, one of their most canny enemies, trotted up the steps and into the senate hall. They simply waited as he approached at that slow walk. He paused when he opened the doors and entered the senate chambers.

"Hello, Mark." Blair blinked a few times when he realized that the Director now held a staff. A black staff. A Primary Access Key. "You've got some upgrades I see."

"Hello, Ark Lord." Mark tossed the staff on the ground with a clatter. "I apologize for barging in unannounced. I've been...indisposed for some time. May I address the senate? I'd like to bring them up to speed on the death of Hades, and the fate of Akenat the Builder, the one who created the First Ark. He's on Earth and closer than you might think."

He had Blair neatly. There was no way out of this without giving him the floor, so Blair gave a magnanimous nod. Damn the man. What kind of game was he playing? This could be the prelude to an assault.

"I created the demotech key with the specific purpose of cleansing myself of demonic taint." He looked up with pride. "I succeeded. I ripped out Hades's hooks, and watched the man die screaming. The trouble is that before he died he gave me to Akenat. The Builder needed a host body, so he offered mine. Champions. Deathless. You have a voice in your heads. Well I became the voice in

Akenat's head as he ran around using my body. I watched him assault the Ark of the Redwood. I watched him steal the Proto Ark. I watched him seize control of all grey man forces on this world. I have inherited all of that, and now I offer it to you. Not only am I giving you my assets, but I have come to turn myself over for justice. Real justice. If New California wants a trial you can have it. I'll plead guilty to all charges. But I have Akenat in my head, with all his knowledge. He's offered to make amends, and to help teach us to resist when the other Builders arrive. What you do is up to you. I will answer any of your questions to the best of my ability. Unfortunately, I cannot directly pass control of the grey men unless you have another Builder handy."

The Director sank to his knees with a slight smirk, just enough that he could feign innocence if you accused him of being smug. Blair remembered it well, and remembered Liz griping about it too.

Blair cleared his throat, and rose into the air above the lectern, a reminder to the senate that they were no longer mortal. "If Nox is being honest, then he could be a resource. More likely it's a trick, and we won't see the hook until it's too late. It isn't up to me though. This is why we formed a senate. You'll get a chance to try this man. However, before that happens, I will be interrogating him."

Blair waved a hand, and light walked Mark into the brig in the Ark of the Redwood. That was their most secure location, and less likely to be infiltrated than the mothership.

"What about the staff?" Melissa nodded at the discarded weapon. "If it's a Primary Access Key who uses it?"

"You do," Blair decided. "That thing could be dangerous. It's almost certainly dangerous. But it is a weapon. Your peers will watch your behavior, and if they suspect corruption they will tell me, and I will purge that corruption. But I'm wagering it won't come to that. Nox made that tool to free himself, not re-corrupt himself back into a demon. If we take him at face value anyway." He turned back to the senators. "I apologize for the early theatrics. This is not how I wanted today to go."

And yet, wasn't it? They had a functional government to solve problems like this, which took the problem out of his hands morally, and freed him up to prepare for the war. Melissa had done a fine job.

Now he had a Builder to interrogate. He had a feeling that might be a very interesting conversation. He was about to make his excuses and leave, but when he looked up he saw pale faces staring in horror at their devices again.

What was it now? He concentrated on the mothership once more, and was shocked to find that pure night had fallen. Not an eclipse. There was no suggestion of the sun, nor moon. Only the stars.

The earth had been plunged into complete and total darkness, and Blair didn't have the faintest idea why.

58

DARKNESS

Isis did not welcome her new lease on life. In fact, she hated that she'd cheated death, especially when doing so had killed her husband, her sister-by-blood, and her brother-by-marriage.

Her solace stood before her, though. Jes'Ka—tall, and proud, and beautiful...but so full of sorrow. Her daughter stood with pride, but the weight on her shoulders...Isis wished she could take it from her.

"My sorrow has no depths for Lucas." She reached up and rested a hand on Jes'Ka's shoulder. "I know how much he meant to you. Did you at least have a chance to say goodbye?"

"We had a night." Jes'Ka leaned into Isis and cried into her shoulder. "Seeing father again at the same time. It's too much. I'm just glad you're okay."

Liz lurked behind her, the gangly but pretty young Ka'Ken standing a bit apart as if she did not wish to intrude on her sister's grief.

Isis cleared her throat, and released Jes'Ka. "We will grieve properly when there is space. For now we have a responsibility. The Ark Lord has tasked us with reforging Excalibur, the sword of legends. This is no simple feat."

She picked up both shards from the workshop's golden table, a place where Sunsteel had been created for potentially millions of years. "I can sense an incredibly intricate shaping woven into the metal. Somehow that shaping survived the blade's sundering, but preserving it while weaving the blade back together might require more skill than I possess. I can certainly try. I gather the blade is important beyond its martial value, but I do not know what role it is meant to fill. Can either of you speculate?"

Liz cleared her throat and moved to touch the blade. "I've wielded it in combat. It isn't like other blades. It's not a matter of raw strength either. There's something about the sword. Almost an intelligence, or an awareness. I don't know what it means."

"I do not use swords." Jes'Ka peered down at the broken weapon, her sorrow receding now that matters of war were being discussed. "Can you remake its form when you reforge it? If you make a spear I will wield it."

"I could, but I will not." Isis stroked the metal, and strummed the power within it. The awareness that Liz had spoken of. "I do not presume to understand the mastery that went into forging this weapon. I might repair a break, but I will make no further alterations to such a wonder."

"What do we need to do?" Liz rested a hand on the hilt of her na-kopesh, taken from Irakesh in battle. She'd become a true warrior, quite a long way for someone who proclaimed themselves a healer of men who'd never kill. Now she was both. Beating Wepwawet proved that, a tale she still wanted to hear in full.

"Merely bear witness." Isis closed her eyes and raised both hands into the air. She focused her will, and saw the weapon as whole. "Now I order the Ark to execute my will. It will pour the power that your he has gathered into the blade, and make whole that which was severed."

A wave of power answered from the Ark, which would always recognize her authority, as she'd woven it into the Ark's programming. She opened her eyes to a river of brilliant golden energy pulsing into the blade at the precise location of the break. Wave after wave of pure power infused the metal, which responded by knitting together.

Impossibly bright light came from the wound, which glowed until the heat caused her skin to sizzle, even a meter away. The weapon gave an inaudible sigh as if tremendous pain and pressure had both been alleviated.

The Ark groaned in response and several internal alarms went off in her head as they dipped below critical thresholds. Thankfully the mothership was still refueling, and the shaping occurring precisely at noon had been no accident. Sunlight poured into the Ark, further augmenting their dwindling reserves.

Would it be enough?

The shaping died abruptly leaving nothing but spots in her vision. "No...no it cannot be."

The shaping remained undone. The blade had not been complete.

Isis fell to her knees, and wept. She was aware of strong arms around her, first one pair, then a second. They were weeping too, though they couldn't yet know the cause of her sorrow.

"What happened?" Liz finally whispered, when they had subsided.

"The blade is whole to all appearances." Isis raised a hand to stroke the metal. "The shaping wasn't complete, however. The bond is weak. The damage is still there. We cannot simply perform the ritual again. We would need to break the blade, and hope it broke clean. It cannot be risked. The subtle shaping I detected is still there, but were we to break it again? I don't know if it could be preserved."

"So if we use this in battle it could shatter?" Liz rose and eyed the blade with apparent anger. "We have a flawed sword? Do we even know what we're supposed to use it for?"

Isis could sense how close her new daughter was to giving in to her rage. It must have been building for weeks with no release. Longer, perhaps.

"I can strengthen it." Isis hesitated, but she'd already begun. She could at least explain the risks. "I can link the blade to one of you. It will be tied to your soul, and your soul will strengthen the blade. That will make it harder to break. If it does, though, you will also break."

"I will be no party to it." Jes'Ka shook her head. "I have done my part. We have you back. If you need me to fight, I will fight. But otherwise? I will seek a mate, and mother offspring, and live, and dance, until I can't any more."

Liz reached down and picked up the blade. "Jes'Ka has earned the right to choose her fate. I'll take up Excalibur. I will link my fate to the blade. Work your shaping. I should speak to Blair before making a decision like this, but he'd make the same were our positions reversed. This sword is important, even if we don't understand how yet. We need every advantage."

Isis didn't smile then, though she could have. Liz had the right spirit, the right conviction, and the strength to command the respect of those around her. She would be an amazing leader for the new Ark Lord.

She and Osiris had discussed their retirement. More and more she felt Jes'Ka had the right idea. Live and laugh and play while they still could.

"What caused the shaping to fail?" Liz asked, which strummed a chord in Isis.

"I...that's a question I should have asked." She concentrated, and used the Ark to connect to the satellite in orbit, which told a grim tale. She didn't know what she'd expected. Of course it was a catastrophe beyond knowing. "We are undone. Somehow this Builder has stolen the sun itself. Our planet labors in total darkness, and no light escapes."

"Wait, the sun is gone? That's going to kill all vegetation in a hurry." Liz frowned. "We won't be far behind either. If they do nothing else Earth will belong to the deathless in maybe two weeks. Three if we're lucky. Almost nothing will survive."

"Then we must learn the cause. We must stop it." Isis balled her hand into a fist. Every time she hoped to lay down her burden she was called into service once more.

And she would answer, until she could not. This Builder would learn that Earth would not go quietly. Not while she lived.

EPILOGUE

Jordan gave in to instinct at the end. A deep hum came from the Ark as the portal winked out of existence and trapped him in the past. He and Lucas stood there, with no Set, and an unconscious Osiris.

He dove on top of Lucas and curled into a compact Dino-ball. Jordan reinforced that ball with a shaped telekinetic bubble pushing out on his armored skin. He knew there was no surviving, but there was the old adage of some poor bastard going over a cliff, and clinging to a couple blades of grass even though there was no way they could hold his weight.

"Die well," Lucas murmured as the Ark detonated.

A wave of fire and death washed over them, and Jordan worried it would take a while to kill him, that he might linger in pain. *Just let it be quick.* He kept his eyes closed and waited, but there was no pain.

None.

There was a pleasant warmth, like a summer day. But there was zero pain, at all. Jordan almost opened his eyes, but he wasn't that stupid. Instead he listened, and waited.

A tremendous wind kicked up around him, and now he opened his eyes. He was falling into a deep pit that was all that remained of the Ark, and a wave of destruction pulsed outward. The sky-high wave of fire and debris obliterated everything. Land. The Ark. All life. Everything.

On and on the wave went, for hundreds of miles in all directions. Jordan thudded into the ground, and rolled over. Lucas didn't move. Jordan laid him out and shifted back to human form. The ground sizzled beneath him, but he ignored it as he felt for a pulse.

Nothing.

Either the man had been killed by the energy or suffocated. Whatever the cause he was dead now. Jordan closed his eyes. "Rest in peace, man. I'll remember your sacrifice, if I somehow get out of this."

A distant crashing sounded in the distance, and Jordan looked up to see a wall of water flowing into his pit from the south. The ocean had come to claim the space his explosion had just cleared. And he was about to be at the bottom of all that water.

"Oh shit." Jordan tucked into a ball again. Mist sprayed him, heralding the wave itself. The water dashed him into the rocks, grinding up stone that had been fused by the destruction of the Ark, and sending him rebounding into the tide, which dashed him into the stone again.

On and on it went, and part of Jordan worried he'd drown. The rest feared the eyeless. The longer he was down here trapped in darkness the more likely they'd find him, right? No, be logical. He was in the past. The world had only ended a few weeks ago. If the eyeless had returned they'd just done so, and were confined to the Pacific. He hoped.

Minutes dragged on, and Jordan still couldn't find enough of a purchase to get off the ocean floor. Yet he didn't run out of oxygen. Nor did he feel pressure on his lungs. He'd just sort of...stopped breathing.

Eventually the turbulence began to subside, and Jordan swam upwards with powerful strokes. He used telekinesis to propel himself at a steady rate, but one he hoped wouldn't trigger the bends, if that was even a risk in this new body.

The water didn't grow lighter, but hadn't they assaulted the First Ark at night? That made navigating out of the water challenging, and he had no idea how long he swam around before he finally burst out of the waves and into the thin moonlight.

He'd survived the detonation of an Ark. How was that even possible?

A snort came from behind him, and he turned to see Friz sitting atop a wave, shaking his head at Jordan's foolishness.

"You knew this was going to happen all along, didn't you?" Friz must have seen Jordan here before he saw him in Australia. Time travel made his head hurt.

Friz nodded. He pointed southeast. Toward...Australia? Of course he was. That was where he expected Jordan to go. Why? Because while Jordan had been surprised to live he'd missed the obvious.

Uluru had said she'd prepared his body for the trials he would face. Getting nuked in an Ark seemed like a trial worth preparing for, so she'd made his body perfectly suited for getting out of that scrape.

He bobbed up and down on the waves, and considered his next move. He was in the past. If he made changes, that could muck everything up in the future. He needed to find a place to hide out, but still make use of the time to train or research.

Australia once again seemed to fit the bill. He couldn't light walk there, but he could light walk a heck of a lot closer, to New Zealand maybe. Jordan envisioned the sky over that island, and willed himself to light walk.

Part of him feared it wouldn't work, but the world shifted and he appeared in the sky, buffeted by clouds. It was day here, but the people below had better things to think about than the sky right now, and no one seemed to pay him any mind.

Jordan flew west, and within a few minutes spotted Australia's unmistakeable silhouette. There was a chance that Uluru wouldn't expect him, but if so he figured he could simply share his memories. Plus Friz would vouch for him.

He popped through a cloud bank and there Friz was, sitting on the next cloud with a grin on his face. Jordan zipped by and found himself laughing. Friz made good company, silent as he was.

They made their way west, which took time even with supersonic flight. Hours passed and the day waned as night overtook Australia. He arrived at Sydney under the starlight.

The city remained intact, though there were no deathless. No zombies. No people. The city was empty of human life, but not altogether different than the ruined version he'd seen so recently.

Jordan dropped lower, and wondered where he should try meeting Uluru? Did he need to make it deeper into the continent to Ayers Rock? If so, he could....

A giant t-rex loomed out of a stand of Eucalyptus trees, and turned a considering eye on him. "Hmm. The form filled its purpose quite nicely. Is it to your liking, former Ark Lord?"

That answered his first question. Clearly Uluru knew about their meeting in the future. Jordan considered asking how that was possible. Trevor or Blair would have. Nah. He didn't need to know right now.

"Then you know why I'm here?" Jordan strode over to the t-rex, and cracked armored knuckles.

"Of course. You have five years to train, and you would like for me to forge you into a weapon capable of ending Yoggoth." Uluru leaned her massive head closer, and huffed a disgusting breath. "That is a pitifully small amount of time. You will need to labor heroically, and even then there is so much you will not know."

"Then why are we standing here? Let's get to work."

Jordan couldn't remember a time when he'd been happier. He had five years to train, grow, and prepare for the biggest fight of his life, with no distractions. What more could an old soldier ask for?

Yoggoth might think he was a badass, but Jordan? He was putting his money on Uluru. She'd planned for everything, and he had a feeling Yoggoth was about to find out just how outmatched he really was.

THE MAGITECH CHRONICLES

For those that are interested in learning more about temporal matrices and *The Magitech Chronicles*, we've included a few chapters of *Tech Mage*. Hope it will tide you over until we release *The Builders*, the sixth and final *Deathless* novel.

TECH MAGE

PROLOGUE

Voria hopped from the ramp before the transport had completed its landing. She clung tightly to her jacket as the sudden wind buffeted her. Voria didn't let it deter her, leaning into the gale as she crossed the landing pad. Like everything in the Tender's palace, the landing pad was cut from shayawood, taken from the corpse of the goddess herself.

That wood shone in the sun, whorls of brown and red, drinking in the sunlight. Voria had never been this close to the palace, and had never seen so much shayawood. It had been designed to awe, and it succeeded.

The view only reinforced that awe. The palace floated in the sky over the world of Shaya and afforded a magnificent view of the goddess herself. Her body stabbed into the sky, the immense redwood branches scraping the upper atmosphere. A multitude of tiny starships flitted back and forth between them like flocks of tiny birds.

Were a single limb to break, it would doom the cities clustered at the base of the mighty tree. That was the dilemma of Shaya. The goddess's lingering energies created a breathable atmosphere around her body, but if you left that radius the rest of the moon was barren and inhospitable. They needed her body to survive, but that body could also destroy them.

Voria wove a path through the wind, snaking her way to a pair of wide palace doors. They were flanked by a pair of war mages, each encased in golden Mark VIII spellarmor. They cradled menacing black spellrifles, the barrels lined with spell amplification sigils. Voria could make out nothing of their faces behind the mirrored faceplates.

To her surprise, both war mages snapped to attention when she approached.

"Major," boomed a male voice from the mage on the right. "The Tender is expecting you. She's made the...unusual request that you be allowed to carry your weapons, and that you not be searched."

"What is it you think I'd be hiding, exactly? All I'm carrying is a spellpistol. If the Tender wants to wipe me from existence, no spell I'm going to cast will make any difference," Voria countered. She waved at the doors. "Let's get this over with. I have a war to fight, and I don't have time for politics."

The guards stepped aside, snapping back to attention. Voria eyed them suspiciously as she passed, trying to understand the reason for their respectful behavior. The Confederate Military was a joke to Shayan nobility. War mages did not salute officers, rank non-with-standing. Even her training as a true mage wouldn't warrant that kind of respect.

She entered a spacious greeting room lined with hover-couches. A blue one floated in her direction, nudging her hip in invitation. Voria shoved it away, and continued toward the room's only occupant. The Tender stood next to a golden railing, shayawood vines snaking around it. Shaya's branches were visible behind her, though the woman herself commanded attention.

Her hair shone in the sun, capturing all the colors of autumn. Reds and yellows and golds all danced through her hair, changing as the light shifted. It poured down her back in a molten river, contrasting beautifully with the Tender's golden ceremonial armor.

Voria had often been called pretty, but she knew she was a

frumpy matron next to the Tender. Though, in Voria's defense, she didn't have the blood of a goddess to magically enhance her beauty.

"Welcome, daughter," the Tender said, beaming a smile as she strode gracefully from the railing. "Thank you for coming so quickly."

"Just because you slept with my father doesn't make you my mother," Voria countered flatly. She schooled her features, attempting to hide the pleasure she took from needling this woman.

The Tender raised a delicate eyebrow, stopping a meter away. She frowned disapprovingly, and even that was done beautifully. "I meant figuratively, daughter."

"Why did you call me here?" Voria demanded. She'd fluster this woman if it killed her.

"Because this, all of this, will be wiped away unless you prevent it." The Tender stretched an arm to indicate Shaya and the cities below her. She smiled warmly, as if she'd just related a bit of political gossip. "Would you like some lifewine? Or an infused apple?"

The Tender crooked a finger, and a crystal ewer floated over to Voria. Golden liquid swirled within, and Voria could feel the power pulsing from it. It was, for her people at least, literal life. But drinking it would cause her eyes to glow, revealing her true nature for hours.

"No, thank you." Voria stepped away from the ewer and frowned at the Tender. "Certainly your time must be valuable. You've dropped a melodramatic statement about Shaya being destroyed. Please tell me that's just hyperbole."

"I am being quite literal, I'm afraid. If you do not fulfill your role in the struggle against Krox, then all of this will be wiped away," the Tender explained. She sighed...prettily. "Please, come with me."

"Fine." Voria crossed her arms, eyeing the Tender as the woman led her from the railing.

The chamber curved around the outside of the palace for nearly a hundred meters, finally ending at a pair of tall double doors. Unlike most of the palace, these were not shayawood. They were covered in a multicolored mural depicting Shaya herself.

Voria leaned closer, realizing that the door was covered in thousands of tiny scales. Dragon scales, each of incalculable worth. They glowed with their own inner fire and their combined magic brought the mural to life. Branches swayed as an invisible wind rippled over the doors.

The Tender placed a palm on each door, then pushed gently inward. The doors opened of their own accord, sliding away to reveal a dark chamber. Voria followed the Tender inside and waited impatiently for her eyes to adjust.

The doors slammed shut behind them, and a bonfire sprang into existence near the center of the room. The flames were pure blue, edged in white. Their sudden light illuminated sigils emblazoned on the floor in a circle around the flame. A ritual circle, possibly the most powerful that Voria had ever witnessed.

"What am I seeing?" Voria asked, abandoning all attempts to fluster the Tender. She'd fought in the Confederate Marines for four decades, and had never seen magic on this scale before. The immensity of the power humbled her.

"This is the Mirror of Shaya. It is an eldimagus for finding and interpreting auguries. You are familiar with auguries?" the Tender asked, walking gracefully to stand just outside the magical circle. The flame brightened at her approach, like a pet preening for an owner.

"Conceptually. They're visions of a possible future, dreamed by a dead god," Voria ventured. Divination wasn't one of her strong suits, though she was proficient enough with the basics.

"Some auguries are," the Tender corrected gently. "Some were created by living gods, before the moment of their death. These auguries are of immense power, designed to shape the future for hundreds or even thousands of millennia. I've spent the last several years studying just such an augury."

"And you feel that has something to do with me?" Voria raised an eyebrow.

"I'll allow you to judge for yourself." The Tender smiled mischievously, then turned to the ritual circle. She sketched the scarlet sigil for *fire*, and a pinkish one for *dream*.

The mirror flared and immense magical strength gathered within the light. It resolved into an image, so lifelike that Voria recoiled. A vast force hovered in the void, its body comprised of stars, its eyes supernovas. The creature was a living galaxy, a god that made every god or goddess Voria had encountered seem a tiny speck.

"What is that thing?" she whispered, unable to drag her gaze from the vision.

"That is Krox," the Tender answered. She rested a hand on Voria's arm, and warmth pulsed into her. It eased the fear the image had evoked, though not the horror that something so alien could exist. "The forces you fight, what you call 'the Krox', are his children. And they are united in a singular purpose, the resurrection of their dark father. This augury is a desperate cry from the past. It's meant to give us the tools necessary to stop his return. If we fail in this, the cost is incalculable."

Voria studied the flames, silently digesting what the Tender had just said. After several moments another image flickered into view. An enormous skull floated in orbit over a barren world. Long, dark horns spiraled from the temples, and purplish flames danced in the eye sockets and mouth.

"That's the Skull of Xal," Voria ventured, recognizing the Catalyst.

The face of a young man superimposed itself over the flames, covering the image of the skull. The hard eyes and strong jaw made him look older than he probably was. He held a sword loosely in one hand and dark lightning crackled from his hand into the blade.

"What am I seeing?" Voria asked. She recognized the spell, basic void lightning. But she had no idea why she was seeing it.

"This man will be instrumental in helping you triumph in your impending struggle," the Tender offered. The light of the flames reflected off her eyes as she studied the images still appearing. "He can be found at the Skull of Xal, along with something else vital to the coming battle."

"You mentioned a coming battle twice. That makes me think you've got the wrong person." Voria eyed the double doors, but didn't attempt to leave. "The *Wyrm Hunter* is low on munitions. We're down to a handful of tech mages, and no other true mage besides myself. We have no potions, and the Marines sent from Ternus have no battle experience. The worst part? We're down to six support crew. Six people, to keep an entire battleship flying. Trust me. Whatever battle this augury thinks I'm a part of, it's got the wrong person. *Hunter* should be in space dock, not leading a charge."

"I understand your reluctance, but I assure you that you are the person this augury is meant for." The Tender's rebuke was gentle, but still a rebuke.

Voria licked her lips, forcing herself to be silent as she watched the augury. It now showed a familiar man, one of her tech mages. "That's Specialist Bord."

The Tender said nothing, watching intently as the images continued. The view zoomed out to show Bord's surroundings. He stood next to a golden urn the size of a tank. The surface was covered in sigils, and a sickly grey glow came from the top.

"I do not know how, but this 'Bord' will be instrumental as well, in a different way. You will need both the men displayed in order to stop her," the Tender's voice whispered.

"Her?" Voria asked, blinking.

The augury shifted again. This time the flames showed a gargantuan dragon, floating in orbit over a blue-white world. Its leathery wings stretched out to either side and its head reared back. The dragon breathed a cone of white mist that billowed out around a Ternus space station.

"Nebiat," Voria snarled. Her eyes narrowed as she studied the ancient dragon, a full Void Wyrm. The dark scales and spiked tail were unmistakable. She ground her teeth, acid rising in her stomach. She'd do anything to kill that Wyrm. Anything.

"I thought you'd recognize her. Whoever created this augury believes you are the one person strong enough to stop her." The Tender stretched out a hand and rested it on Voria's jacket. Pleasant warmth flowed into her. Voria wished she'd stop doing that. "I know that you lack the resources you need. But I also know that you are needed. If you will not do this, then the Krox will burn another world. You can stop that, Voria, though the personal cost will be high."

"Isn't it always?" Voria straightened her jacket, already turning to the door. "I'll find a way to stop Nebiat, but that will be a whole lot easier with Inuran weaponry. They're hunting for Kazon. If I can find him before anyone else, the Consortium will provide me with enough material to pursue your augury. Help me find him, and I'll help you fulfill it."

"I already have." The Tender turned back to the flames as the augury began to repeat. "Study the augury carefully, Major. There are many layers to be delved, including Kazon's whereabouts. Pursuing the augury will lead you to him."

1

TECH DEMONS

Aran lurched awake as the transport entered free fall. Gravity pulled him upward, jerking him to the limits allowed by his restraints. The ship shook violently, the thin lights flickering for several moments before returning to a steady illumination.

"Wake up," a female voice bellowed. The speaker moved to stand in front of Aran, and he realized groggily that he was surrounded by other men and women in restraints.

The chrome harnesses pinned their wrists between their legs, preventing them from standing or defending themselves. Glowing blue manacles attached his wrists to the harness, and he could feel their heat even through the armored gauntlets. He wore some sort of environmental armor, the metal scarred and pitted from long use.

"Good, the sleep spell is wearing off." The speaker wore a suit of form-fitting body armor, much higher quality than Aran's. Her helmet was tucked under one arm and the other hand wrested on a pistol belted at her side. A river of dark hair spilled down both shoulders. "You're probably feeling some grogginess. That's the after effects of the mind-wipe. Each of you have been imprinted with a name.

That will be the *only* thing you can remember. We've given it to you, because otherwise slaves tend to have psychotic breaks."

Aran probed mentally, reaching for anything. He couldn't remember how he'd gotten here, or what he'd had for breakfast. Or where he'd been born. There was a...haze over the part of his mind where those things should be. His name was, quite literally, the only thing he could remember.

A beefy man on Aran's right struggled violently against his bonds. "Listen little girl, you'd better let me out of this chair, or I'll fu—."

The woman withdrew her pistol and aimed it at the beefy man. White sigils flared to life up and down the barrel, and dark energy built inside the weapon.

The weapon hummed, discharging a bolt of white-hot flame toward his chest. It cored him through the heart, filling the chamber with the scent of cooked meat. His body twitched once and then he died silently.

"Nara, you began the demonstration without me," called an amused male voice. It came from out of Aran's field of view, but the booted footsteps approached until Aran got a glimpse of the speaker. "You know how much I hate missing it. This is my favorite part."

A tall, slender man walked over to the woman who'd executed the beefy man. He wore jet-black environmental armor, and had a stylized dragon helm clutched under his arm. One of his eyes had been replaced with a glittering ruby, and his bald skull was oiled to a mirrored sheen. His right gauntlet was larger than his left, and studded with glowing rubies and sapphires.

Aran could sense...something coming from the gauntlet. A familiar resonance that danced elusively out of reach.

A cluster of armored figures entered the room behind the one-eyed man. They fanned out, taking up relaxed positions along the far wall. Each guard carried a rifle similar to the pistol the woman had fired. Blue-white sigils lined the barrels, though they appeared inactive at the moment.

"I'm sorry, Master Yorrak," the woman he'd called Nara finally replied. She gave a deep bow, which she held for several seconds. Finally she straightened. "This prisoner...volunteered. And I know that we are pressed for time. I thought it prudent to educate this batch quickly."

"Efficient as always. I'll handle the rest of the orientation." Yorrak patted her cheek patronizingly, then turned toward the slaves. Nara shot him a hateful glare, but he seemed oblivious. "Good morning, slaves. My name is Yorrak, true mage and pilot of this vessel. I'm going to make this very simple. In a moment we'll be landing. When we do, your restraints will be removed. There is a rack of rifles near the door. Take one, and step outside. Nara and her squad will lead you beyond that. Obey her orders without question, or meet the same fate as our late friend here." Yorrak moved to the corpse, prodding it with a finger.

"Are there any questions?" he asked, rounding on them.

"Where are we?" Aran rasped. His throat burned, and he blinked sweat from his eyes.

"The Skull of Xal, one of the more remote, and most powerful, Catalysts in this sector," Yorrak proclaimed, thrusting his arms dramatically into the air. "You're about to be granted a wonderful opportunity. If you survive, you will become a tech mage. Those of you who apply yourselves might even rise to the rank of true mage, one day. That will increase your relative value, and I treat my mages very well. Now, I'll leave you in Nara's capable hands. I'll pick up any survivors in the second ocular cavity. You have two hours. Oh and one more thing. If Nara isn't with you when you exit the Catalyst, I'll disintegrate the lot of you."

Yorrak strode past Aran, eyeing the slaves gleefully as he exited. What a sadistic bastard. Aran caught a brief glimpse of the hallway before the door hissed shut behind him, but saw nothing that helped his current situation. The transport, if it was a transport, shuddered violently for several moments, then finally stabilized.

"If you listen to me, you have a very high chance of survival," Nara said, drawing their collective attention. She stepped into the light, affording his first real look at her. She had liquid brown eyes, and a light dusting of freckles across her entire face. She was pretty enough that Aran understood why she'd been picked to lead them. The whole girl next door thing made them that much more likely to trust her. "In a moment I'm going to release your restraints. You'll arm yourself from the rack, and then move outside. Some of you might be tempted to attack us. Before you do, consider your options. It's in both our best interests for you to survive. If you die, Yorrak has less slaves. You don't want to die, and we don't want you dead."

Her argument made sense, though Aran detested the idea of working with his captors. He didn't know anything about them, or about himself really. Was he a hardened criminal? Or just some idiot in the wrong place, at the wrong time? It was just...gone. All of it. Only his name remained, and even that might not be real.

The restraints whirred, and the harness released him. The manacles were still around his wrists, but the chain linking them together had disappeared. Aran rose to his feet and the other prisoners did the same, each looking warily at the others. It seemed an effective tactic on the part of their captors. Since none of them knew each other, they weren't likely to cooperate. That made mutiny a much lower risk.

Aran moved to the rack along the side of the wall, picking up the first rifle. It had a heavy stock, and a long, ugly barrel. The metal was scored and scratched, though the action worked smoothly. He scanned the base of the rack, bending to scoop up two more magazines. He had no idea what he'd need the weapon for, but more rounds was rarely a bad thing.

Other slaves moved to take weapons, the closest a tall man with a thick, black beard. He eyed Aran warily, moving to the wall two meters away.

Nara walked to the rear of the room and slapped a large red button. A klaxon sounded, and a ramp slowly lowered. A chill wind howled up the ramp, dropping the temperature instantly.

"Outside, all of you. Now!" Nara's words stirred the slaves into action, and they began filing down the ramp. Aran moved in the middle of the pack, and found himself next to the bearded man.

"Watch my back?" he asked, eyeing the bearded man sidelong. His arms were corded with muscle, and his eyes glittered with intelligence.

"Do the same for me?" the man answered, eyeing Aran in a similar way.

"Done." Aran pivoted slightly as he walked down the ramp, angling his firing arc to slightly overlap with the bearded man. The man echoed the motion. "What name did they give you?"

"Kaz. How about you?"

"Aran." The ramp deposited them onto a bleached white hill. A hellish purple glow came from somewhere beyond the ridge ahead of them, as bright as any sun. Aran's teeth began to chatter, and his breath misted heavily in the air.

"The cold isn't life threatening, if you keep moving," Nara called. Her guards fanned out around her, covering the slaves with their strange rifles. Something about the weapons tickled at the back of his mind, but the haze muddied the sense of familiarity. "Form two groups, one on either side of the ramp."

The guards broke into groups, pushing slaves into two lines. Aran moved quickly to the one on the right, and the bearded man followed.

"Do you have any idea where we are?" Kaz asked. Aran followed his gaze, taking in their surroundings.

A high ridge prevented him from seeing beyond the closest hills. The rock reminded him uncomfortably of bone, its porous surface just the right shade of pale white.

The purplish glow flared suddenly and Aran raised a hand to shield his eyes. Harsh, guttural voices boomed in the distance, and he heard the rhythmic pounding of metal on stone.

"Those," Nara began with a yell, "are tech demons. This is their territory, and they will defend it with their lives. Your job is to kill them, without dying yourself. Follow my orders, and we'll all get out of this safely."

A brutish creature leapt into view at the top of the ridge. Twin horns spiraled out from a thick forehead and it clenched and unclenched wickedly curved claws. It stared down at them with flaming eyes, the same hue as the glow behind it. The creature wore dark armor, not unlike the armor Nara and her guards had.

"Fire!" Nara roared.

2

USED

Aran reacted to Nara's command, snapping the rifle to his shoulder and sighting down the barrel. He'd guess the demon to be about seventy-five meters away, but it was hard to judge distance without knowing how large the thing was.

The rifle kicked into his shoulder, firing a three round burst that echoed off the rocks around them. The rounds peppered the demon's left side but only pinged off armor. Kaz snapped up his rifle as well, but the shots went wide. Other slaves fired, the chattering of weapons fire lighting up the area around them as they added to the thick stench of gunpowder.

All their collective fury accomplished nothing. The rounds, even those that hit the demon directly, simply ricocheted off. The demon's face split into a wide grin, revealing a sea of narrow fangs. It leapt from its perch, bat-like wings flaring behind it as it sailed in their direction.

Only then did Aran realize the creature carried a rifle too. The weapon was heavier than their own rifles, and the fat barrel was ringed with red sigils, like the rifles their captors used.

"That thing is packing a spellcannon. Tech mages, end him!" Nara barked, stabbing a finger at the descending demon.

Too late. The creature raised the cannon, and the sigils along the barrel flared to brilliant life. The cannon kicked back, and fired a blob of darkness. The blob expanded outwards, bursting into thousands of fragments. The fragments rained down on the other group of slaves, and their armor began to smoke and hiss.

They frantically tore at the armor, but within moments the hungry magic had eaten through...first metal and then flesh. One by one they slumped to the bleached stone, groaning out their last.

The guards around Nara, the ones she'd called tech mages, opened up with their spellrifles. Blue and white sigils flared, and bolts of superheated flame peppered the demon. The bolts superheated the armor wherever they hit, painting it an angry red. The fire bolts met with more success against the demon itself, and it shrieked as a large chunk of its neck burned away.

"This way," Aran roared, sprinting low to the left, into the demon's blind spot. He dropped to one knee behind a fold of rock and sighted down the barrel at the demon. He kept his finger off the trigger, though.

Kaz slid down next to him. "You have a plan?"

"Yeah, let those bastards deal with it. They're using us as fodder. There's no way we can hurt that thing with the crap rifles they gave us." Aran plastered himself against the rock, its craggy surface bitterly cold even through his armor.

Nara strode from her ranks raising two fingers. She began sketching in the air, and wherever her finger passed, a residue of multicolored light was left behind. The light formed sigils, which swam in and out of Aran's vision. The more he focused on any particular one, the more blurry it became.

The sigils began to swirl in interlocking patterns of pale grey, and a dark, ocean blue. They were drawn together with a sudden thunderclap, then exploded outward in a wide fan. Fist sized balls of swirling energy shot toward several of the surviving slaves, each ball slamming into their backs. The energy passed through the armor, disappearing.

Each person hit by a ball began to grow, their armor growing with them. Over the next few heartbeats they doubled in size, and now stood shoulder to shoulder with the demon.

It did not seem impressed.

The demon leapt forward and wrapped its tail around one of the giant slaves. It tugged her from her feet, dragging her across the rough stone. The demon yanked the slave into the air, just in time to use her as a shield against another volley of fire bolts from Nara's tech mages. They slammed into the poor woman, who screeched in shock and pain, until the final fire bolt ended her cries.

"Those things they're firing, spells I guess," Aran yelled over his shoulder to Kaz. "They're the only thing that's hurt that demon so far." He cradled his rifle, trying to decide what to do.

"Then unless you've got a way to cast a spell we have to sit this out and hope," Kaz called back. "We can't do anything to that thing."

One of the tech mages slung his rifle over his shoulder and drew a slender sword. He sprinted wide around the demon, clearly hunting for an opening. White flame boiled up out of his palm and quickly coated the entire blade.

The tech mage darted forward and lunged upward at the much larger demon. The blade slid between two armored plates, biting deep into the small of the demon's back. The flames swept up the blade and into the wound, which drew a roar from the demon.

The creature rounded on the tech mage and backhanded him with an enormous fist. The blow knocked the tech mage into the air, and his blade spun away across the stone. Before the tech mage could recover, the demon fired his spellcannon and a bolt of blackness took the mage in the chest. There was no scream. No final death throes. The body fell limply to the ground and did not rise.

"I'm going to try for the blade," Aran called to Kaz. The bearded man shot him an incredulous look. "Hey, after it kills them, it's going to kill us."

Aran sprinted fast and low across the stone, the sudden movement removing the edge of the numbing chill. He bent low and scooped up the sword the tech mage had dropped and then dove behind another outcrop.

The hilt was warm to the touch and fit his hand perfectly. The blade shone an unremarkable silver, and the weapon was heavier than he was used to. Used to? He couldn't summon a specific memory, but felt certain he'd held a weapon like this, and recently.

The weapon called to something inside Aran, the same thing that had resonated with Yorrak's gauntlet back on the ship. Magic, he realized. He didn't understand how, but there was a power inside him, calling out to be channeled through the spellblade. That's what the weapon was.

"Are you mad?" Kaz roared, skidding into cover next to him.

"Maybe." Aran poked his head out of cover and assessed the situation. The remaining tech mages had scattered, and were harrying the demon from different angles. One narrowly dodged another black bolt, but was too slow to dodge the next. His right leg ceased to exist, all the way up to the thigh.

The surviving slaves had all sought cover, except for the giant ones who had nowhere to hide. Only three remained, and they made a concentrated push at the demon. It spun at the last second, balling its clawed hand into a fist and slamming it into the closest slave. That slave's jaw exploded, and he toppled to the stone with a muffled cry.

The next slave got his arms around the demon, briefly pinning it. The last giant slave jammed his rifle into the demon's mouth and pulled the trigger. The demon twitched violently, its head jerking back and forth as the slave emptied the magazine.

Aran lurched into a run, his gaze fixed on the demon. The energy in his chest surged outward, down his arm and into his hand. Electricity poured into the weapon, snapping and crackling around the blade as he made his approach.

The demon broke free from the slave's grasp and plunged two claws through the man's eye socket. It hurled the dying slave into its companion, knocking the last giant slave to the stone.

Aran circled behind the rampaging demon, keeping within its blind spot. He waited for it to pass his position, then sprinted the last few meters, ramming his sword into the wound the tech mage had already created. The armor was scored and blackened, offering little protection. The spellblade easily pierced the demon's flesh and plunged deep into the wound.

Electricity discharged, and the demon went rigid for several seconds. A trio of fire bolts shot into the demon's head, the scent of burned flesh billowing outward as life left the demon's smoldering gaze. Finally, the body toppled.

"Well done," Nara called as she rose from cover. She gestured at her three surviving tech mages. "Get the surviving slaves moving. That thing was a scout, and its death will alert the others. We need to reach the Catalyst before they mobilize."

3
___

ALLIES

"You there. Aran. Come here." Nara's voice held a definite edge of command, and Aran knew there was no way out of answering.

He trotted over, the spellblade still clutched in his left hand. He raised the other in a tight salute. Now where the depths had that come from? He had no memory of saluting anyone, much less this woman.

"You did excellent work with that spellblade. Clearly you are already a tech mage. Can you handle a spellrifle?" She studied him with those intense brown eyes, and he very much believed that his fate depended on the answer.

He briefly considered lying and accepting a rifle, but figured that having her find out he'd lied would be even worse than admitting the truth. "I don't know, sir. The thing I did with the spellblade was...well instinctual, I guess."

"I want you to take charge of the rest of the slaves," she commanded, pointing at the rest of the slaves with her spellpistol. "Move ahead of us, up that ridge. If we get attacked, get your people into cover. Try to distract them while my people deal with them."

"Sir, we just lost two tech mages and a half dozen slaves to a single one of those things," Aran pointed out. "If we get attacked by a group—."

"Don't mistake your position here, slave." Nara's eyes went cold. "Is this going to be dangerous? Absolutely. But keep your wits about you, and some of these people at least, will survive. How many really depends on how smart you are about deploying them. You want to save some lives? Step up."

Aran stifled the urge to take a swing at her with the spellblade. He was fast, but there was no way he could close the gap before she got a spell off. Besides, she was right. He could hate her as much as he liked, but if he wanted to live, if he wanted any of these people to live, then they needed to get through here as quickly as possible.

"Yes, sir." Aran turned on his heel and trotted back over to the other slaves. "Kaz, you're on point. Double time it up that ridge and let us know what you see at the top."

The bearded man nodded, then sprinted up the ridge. The other slaves followed and Aran brought up the rear. He glanced over his shoulder, unsurprised to see Nara and her surviving tech mages hanging a good fifty meters back. No sense being too close to the cannon fodder.

He trotted up the ridge line, surprised by how easy it was. This place had lighter gravity than he was used to, a small blessing at least. Aran paused at the top of the ridge, looking back at the ship they'd emerged from. He was far enough away now to get a good look at her.

The starship was about a hundred meters long, a boomerang shaped cruiser. Blue spell sigils lined the hull, but many were cracked, and more than a few had sputtered out entirely. The ship itself seemed to be in good repair, though off-color metal patches dotted different parts of the hull.

The ship lifted off and zoomed slowly out of sight, leaving an unbroken starfield in its wake. Wherever he was, it appeared they were directly exposed to space. So how was he breathing?

Yorrak had said 'other ocular cavity'. Was this the eye socket of some sort of moon-sized skull? That would mean this wasn't bleached stone. It was bone.

"Keep moving!" one of the tech mages boomed as he trotted up the ridge toward Aran.

Aran did as ordered, turning back toward the rest of the slaves. Kaz was still in the lead, picking a path across the bone field, painted violet by the smoldering orb in the distance. He raised a hand to shield his eyes from the painful brilliance. It was like staring directly into a sun, but somehow made worse because of the violent cold.

"Order your men to take up defensive positions along those outcrops," Nara ordered, pointing at a series of bone spurs that jutted out of field.

Aran trotted forward, dropping into cover behind the closest outcrop. It only came to his shoulder. "You heard the lady. Get into position behind this terrible cover, with weapons that won't do shit to an enemy that we can barely see."

Nara stalked several meters closer. "I could execute you right now, if you prefer." Her tone suggested it wasn't a bluff, and he found confirmation when he turned in her direction. Her spellpistol was aimed directly at him, her face hidden behind her helmet.

"Uh, I'm good. Bad cover is better than no cover." Aran raised his hands and offered an apologetic smile.

Nara turned coldly away, and began leading her tech mages along a ridge that sloped up into the darkness. Their path took them toward the light, but in a more winding route. It also took them away from the defensive position she'd asked him to establish. Aran shaded his eyes, but couldn't make out much as their forms became nothing more than silhouettes.

"What are they after, do you think?" Kaz asked from the next outcrop.

"I don't know, but whatever it is I'm betting it's a whole lot safer than sticking around here." Aran rolled to his feet, but stayed low. The rhythmic pounding was getting closer, and he could make out shapes now, against the blinding purple sun.

Their silhouettes were monstrous, approaching with alarming speed. He judged their approach, coming to the only possible conclusion. "They're going to overrun our position almost instantly. If we stay, we die."

"What are you proposing?" Kaz asked as he rose slowly to his feet.

"Run!" Aran turned and ran full tilt after Nara and her tech mages. He felt a moment's pity for the rest of the slaves, but staying here and dying wouldn't save them.

Kaz panted a few meters behind him, keeping pace as Aran picked a path through the bony ridges. In the distance he caught the flash of a fire bolt, but by the time they made it around the corner there was no sign of whoever had fired it.

Before them lay an unbroken wall of purple flame, the blinding sun that they'd glimpsed from the first ridge. Intense cold radiated from the flames, but there was more to it than that. There was a power there, a sense of infinite age, and timeless wisdom. He had no idea what he was looking at, but whatever it was— it was greater than any human mind.

Something scrabbled across the bone behind him, and Aran spun to see a demon charging. Instead of a spellcannon, this demon carried a truly massive hammer, clutched effortlessly in one clawed hand. The creature roared and charged Kaz.

The bearded man roared back, charging to meet his much larger foe. The demon brought the hammer down, but Kaz dodged out of the way at the very last moment. The hammer impacted and shards of bone shot out in all directions, pinging off their armor.

Aran glanced at the blinding purple light where Nara and her friends had disappeared, realizing he could make it in before the demon could deal with him. For a moment he was frozen. Was he the kind of person that would abandon the closest thing he had to a friend?

Screw that. He circled around the demon, waiting for an opening. "I'm going to paralyze it, like I did the last one. See if you can get that hammer away from it."

Aran reached tentatively for the power he'd felt before. The magic rose easily at his call, as if it wanted to be used. There was a separateness to it. The magic was inside him, but it was not him. It responded to his command though, and right now that mattered a lot more than figuring out where it came from.

The lightning leapt down his arm and into the blade, reaching the tip as Aran began his charge. He sprinted fast and low, leaning into the blow as he planted his blade into the back of the demon's knee. The enchanted steel failed to pierce the demon's armor, but that had never been the intent. Electricity crackled through the metal, and the demon twitched silently, struggling to regain control of its body.

Kaz stepped forward and yanked the hammer from the creature's grasp. He took a deep breath, then brought the weapon down in a tremendous blow. It crushed the creature's skull, splattering them with black ichor.

Behind them, the final screams faded to silence. Aran turned to see a half dozen demons moving past the corpses of the slaves— in their direction.

"Looks like we've got no choice but to brave the light." Kaz offered a hand. Aran shook it. "Good luck, brother."

"Good luck, brother." Aran turned, took a deep breath, then leapt into the light.

4
ENLIGHTENMENT

Aran had no words to describe what came next. A vast, unknowable consciousness lay before him—an ocean of power and memory, compared to his single drop. He fell into the ocean, became that consciousness. The universe stretched out before him, vast yet somehow perceivable with thousands of senses, all at once.

He understood how the worlds had been created, how the stars were given form. He watched the making of all things, from the perspective of a god who'd not only witnessed but participated. Xal was not the eldest of gods, but he was among them.

Understanding stretched beyond the comprehension of time. Aran saw the strands of the universe, how they were woven into existence using magic. He understood the eight Aspects, and the Greater Paths that could be accessed by combining them. The complexities of true magic, as Nara had used, became simple.

This power suffused him, endless, like space itself. If he wished, he could create a new species, or snuff one out with equal ease. Dimly, he was aware he had a body, aware of his petty temporal problems. They were inconsequential when compared with the vast infinity of Xal.

Yet, in his sudden understanding, he also saw Xal's undoing: a ghostly memory of many younger gods, all united in their purpose. They flooded the system, using their magic to prevent Xal from escaping into the Umbral Depths.

The memory seized Aran. He was there. He *was* Xal.

"You have come to destroy me," Xal said, turning sadly to face the assembled host.

"Your children are evil," called a goddess surrounded by armor of primal ice. "They have laid waste to many worlds, and Krox has warned us they will come for us next. We will not allow it. You might be stronger than any of us individually, but together we will destroy you."

"And who spun you this tale? Krox?" Xal shook his mighty head sadly. "Do you know nothing of his ways? Krox, the first manipulator? He is using you to attack me, so you will weaken yourselves. If we battle today, many of us will fall. The survivors will be weaker for it, and easier for Krox to pick off one by one. After today, there will be none strong enough to oppose him."

Xal examined all possibilities, trillions upon trillions. There was no possibility of his own survival. But the war between him and Krox would not end with their deaths. It would outlive them, unfolding until the last sun went cold.

And there was something he could do to ensure he won that war.

The smaller gods surrounded Xal, who made no move to defend himself. Instead, he allowed his foes to tear him apart, knowing that one day those same gods would dismember Krox. If he killed any of them, that possibility diminished greatly.

Aran watched Xal die. No, *die* was not the right word. A god could not be killed, not truly. They could only be shattered, with the pieces of their bodies forever seeking to reunite. Aran understood why the head of Xal had been severed.

The younger gods scattered the other pieces across the galaxy, ensuring it would be nearly impossible for Xal to resurrect. This filled Aran with rage, and loss, and pain—Xal's emotions, still echoing through Aran's dreaming mind.

Aran focused on the secrets of the universe, struggling to hold onto them. Briefly, he understood the illusion of time. He lingered with the knower of secrets, listening to his endless whispers. He peered into the Umbral Depths, and saw the things that dwelt there.

He noticed the great, and the small. Something tiny drew his attention—a speck of light he'd only just noticed. It lay in his hand, so small he'd missed it in the blinding brightness of Xal's majesty. Dimly, Aran realized it was the spellblade he'd picked up.

That spellblade was a living thing, waiting to be shaped. So he shaped it. It came instinctively, power and knowledge borrowed somehow from the god's mind.

He poured Xal's power into the blade, altering its shape to be more pleasing. Aran infused it with *void*, and the blade darkened even as it grew lighter in his hand. The intelligence within the blade grew more aware, more capable of complex thought. Aran forged a bond between them, connecting him to the new intelligence as a child is connected to parent. The weapon couldn't yet think, but there was a dim awareness there, watching.

The need to create did not diminish, and he burned to use the understanding Xal shared with him. He realized that the spell that had wiped his mind could be removed, and his identity restored. Such a thing was possible, though not trivial. Yet Aran couldn't quite grasp the spell. To do that, he needed more of Xal.

He plunged deeper into the god's mind, seeking the power that would allow him to become whole. It must be here, somewhere. An urgent buzzing began in the distance, but he ignored it, swimming toward the wonderful power.

The pain grew blinding, yet it brought with it knowledge. The pain was worth the price, if it would restore his mind.

The buzzing grew more intense, and a sharp prick shot through his palm. Aran looked down and realized that he was holding the spellblade. It was the source of the buzzing, and as he studied it Aran understood.

"You're warning me." Pain built behind Aran's temples as he stared deeper into Xal's mind. The sword vibrated in his hand, breaking the siren call.

Icy fear brought clarity. Xal's vastness was tempting, but Aran needed to flee before it reduced his mind to cosmic dust. Thrashing frantically, struggling away from the power, Aran forced himself to look away from the universe, snapped his eyes shut and tried to focus. Relief pulsed from the spellblade.

Then, as suddenly as the experience had begun, it was over. Aran tumbled away from the majesty and power, secrets slipping from his mind like oxygen from a hull breach. He shivered, cold and barren in the wake of all that power. Only a tiny ember remained, smoldering coldly in his chest. That piece was woven into him, a part of him even as he was now a part of Xal.

Aran caught himself against a bony ridge, trembling and weak, and rose back to his feet. He glanced back the way he'd come—at the purple sun—still as brilliant as ever, but he no longer squinted. He no longer felt the chill. This place was home now; it was part of him, as he was part of it.

The blade clutched in his right hand had changed. Instead of the slender short-sword, Aran now held an officer's saber, sleek and deadly. The weapon fit his hand as if molded to it, like an extension of his body. It waited, ready to be used.

"I told you," Nara's voice said, sounding muffled and far away. "He made it through, and he made it through first."

Aran turned toward her, blinking. She stood with a cluster of people, the three tech mages, and four more people in conventional body armor. All had weapons, either spellpistols or spellblades. Their posture wasn't threatening, but neither was it friendly.

Behind them sat the boomerang shaped starship, its ramp already extending.

He glanced at Nara and her companions, then at the ship. Even if he could reach it, what then? There was no obvious means of escape. That didn't mean he was giving up, though. Sooner or later these people were going to let their guard down, and when they did he'd be ready.